LATTES
&
LACE

LATTES
& LACE

A NOVEL

Annora Green

green lane press

ISBN: 978-0-9991116-0-4

First published in the United States of America in June 2017.

Cover and book design: A.J.G.

Artwork designed by: visnezh / Freepik

Green Lane Press

Holland, Michigan

www.greenlanepress.com

For my family, who have always supported me.

To Alex, who encouraged me.

& for everyone who dreams of a happy ending.

FORBIDDEN

It was the height of the Christmas shopping season, but the holiday was the furthest thing from Sophia Black's mind.

She had debuted her spring collection only last month at a show, and the attention surrounding this particular collection - a spectacular one, if she did say so herself - was more than her work had ever received before.

Downstairs, she could hear the bell on the door chime over and over and the din of conversation and laughter. It was the last full weekend before Christmas, which fell on a Friday this year, much to the chagrin of most in retail. However, Sophia barely paid the buzz any notice, confident that her shop manager, Elle, would keep everything under control as she always did. Instead, Sophia lurked upstairs in her office, focused on writing notes to herself for her upcoming lines in one of the many little black leather notebooks that lined a shelf under her window. When she was done with that, Sophia went through photos that had been taken at a recent shoot, then clicked through the tabs in her spreadsheets that listed endless prices and margins for her clothing line in the months ahead, and glanced at a calendar showing the magazine writers and fashion bloggers who would be calling to talk with her about her collection and her successful online store in the upcoming two weeks.

There was a headache brewing in the area right around her temple, and she suspected that she had not had more than 8 hours of sleep in the past five days combined. She craved coffee, but her espresso machine, which she had imported from Italy only last summer, had broken earlier that week. She was grateful that it was Saturday. Her small team of designers and assistants normally worked in the upstairs studio near her office, chatting until all hours of the day (or night, depending on their deadlines), but she had tried to give her team a bit of time off on weekends this month so they could actually have something that resembled a normal work schedule around the holidays.

She glanced at her diamond-encrusted watch. She had 14 minutes remaining until her phone call with the journalist from *The Cut*, an important fashion industry magazine. It was supposed to be for a small write-up about the collection that she just debuted, but it was important, as Sophia had been hoping to catch the attention of the magazine for a while. They had significant influence in the industry.

Elle had brought up coffee earlier, something she picked up on her drive in to work, but it was from a mass chain of coffee shops and Sophia was less than impressed. Needless to say, she had no time to run out and grab a decent cup at her favorite place, which was at least 10 minutes' drive away (with no traffic).

Just then, she heard a hammering noise coming from outdoors, drifting up from the sidewalk. A low *thud, thud, thud.*

"What is that?" She asked no one in particular, tossing her sad cup of coffee into the trash and standing up, her black heels tapping across the polished dark wood floors.

She looked down at the sidewalk outside of the window of her second floor office.

Outside of the storefront next to her, a group of two men and one blonde woman was constructing what appeared to be a wooden platform. A patio of some sort.

Sophia let out an impatient sigh.

"Not now. Not when *The Cut* is calling in..." she was still talking to herself out loud, gritting her teeth as she checked her watch again "...11 minutes."

She grimaced as the banging grew louder, the sound seemingly reverberating directly in her temple. Voices trailed up from the sidewalk, accompanied by laughter. Who were these people, anyways? A "For Rent" sign had been outside of the brick storefront for at least three months after the last business had closed up shop. Someone new must have finally moved in.

Not only was the noise a disaster for her phone interview - she required the utmost silence for concentration, especially for such a high-visibility opportunity like *The Cut* - but it was also bad for her shop's business downstairs. She strove to provide her clientele a relaxed, calm, sophisticated environment in which to browse. The types of shoppers her store attracted enjoyed peace and quiet as they looked through her lace and silk pieces, calmly tried on satin robes and allowed themselves to be swept away by her soft, sexy collection of lingerie. If they needed assistance, the sweet, soft-spoken Elle would be there for them to make intelligent suggestions and direct them to the pieces they desired.

It was not supposed to be an experience marred by loud noise and racket that they could get while shopping at any average department store or chain retailer with obnoxious pop music and harsh lighting.

She began to pace, her phone in hand, the ear buds positioned in her ears, waiting for the call, hoping that the incessant hammering from outside would at least not be able to be heard over the phone.

One minute before the set meeting time, her phone rang.

"This is Sophia Black," she answered coolly on the second ring, settling into her designer cream-colored desk chair, crossing her legs under her dark, polished mahogany desk.

The hammering outside continued. Sophia grabbed an apple that she had put on her desk earlier in case she wanted a snack and gripped it like a stress ball.

On the phone was the one of the magazine's most well known writers.

"Ah, Christine. So wonderful to speak with you," Sophia cooed in a velvet, throaty voice, not betraying her frustration, stress, and the headache that had reared its ugly head.

Cool, calm, and collected, she began the interview.

··○··

Forty minutes later, Sophia hung up the phone. By now, her headache was a full-on nuisance that made her long to go home and close her eyes in her dark bedroom. The noise from outside seemed to keep pace with the throbbing in her temple. She walked over to the window and glanced down at the sidewalk again to check on her noisy new neighbor.

A remarkable amount of progress had been made in only an hour. At least they had managed to accomplish something. A patio had been built in front of the shop, and Sophia noticed that tables, chairs, strings of twinkly fairy lights and two of the most garish inflatable holiday snowmen were being erected as decoration.

It was a veritable winter wonderland.

"You have got to be kidding me," Sophia snarled, tossing her phone onto her desk and stomping over to the closet to take out her designer trench.

She marched downstairs, down a narrow, creaking wood staircase, through the back room of the store and pushed past a velvet curtain into her shop. She wondered what she would say to this new neighbor. The previous tenant, a cupcake shop, which had been a rather unsuccessful venture lasting barely 8 months, had at least been quiet and unremarkable. This new business must have just moved in over the past week and was certainly announcing its presence with a tremendous amount of commotion.

"Good afternoon, Ms. Black," Elle said a little too brightly.

"I wish it were a good afternoon," Sophia grumbled as she walked past, pushed the glass door open and emerged onto the sidewalk, the late-afternoon sun filtering through the tree branches.

She walked over to where all of the ruckus had been taking place and stood in front of the group of workers, hands on her hips.

"What is this?" she asked the group.

The two men and the woman stopped hammering. They put their strings of lights and sheets of wood down and looked over at her, clearly surprised at her tone. A woman and a small boy brushed past her to go into the shop, which was apparently open, despite the annoying amount of construction happening outside. Sophia glanced at the black and white sign hanging over the door.

The Little Cafe
Artisanal Coffee & Donuts

The sign, which was designed to look hand-painted and rustic, and the words all maddeningly scrawled in lower case, prompted Sophia to scowl.

"I'm Ari," the sole woman in the group stepped forward, a hammer in her left hand, offering Sophia her other hand to shake.

Sophia ignored the extended hand.

"Are you the owner of this... establishment?" she snapped.

Ari nodded.

"Yep. Just opened last week. We're scrambling to put up some holiday decorations to try to draw Christmas shoppers in for refreshments. Sorry for the noise," she said, grinning sheepishly.

"Apology not accepted. I'm the owner of the boutique next door and I cannot tolerate this kind of noise during one of the busiest shopping days of the season. Not to mention the fact that this *unique* choice of decoration doesn't blend well with the atmosphere that retailers find acceptable on this street."

Ari's smile disappeared and she crossed her arms. "Now wait a second, this is my place, what do you have against me adding a touch of holiday cheer to attract customers? Like you, I'm just trying to earn a living-"

"I assure you, Ms.- what is your name again?"

"Little. Ari Little."

"Ari Little?" Sophia paused, letting the cutesiness of the coffee shop name sink in, unimpressed. "Look, Ms. Little, you clearly didn't research the location before setting up shop. Let me fill you in. This is Palo Rosa, and our Retail Association has strict regulations about what can and can-not be placed in storefronts or outside on sidewalks. Number one, you cannot build an outdoor patio without permits and you may never put up garish Christmas decorations along the sidewalk. We have an image to maintain, an image that attracts a select sort of clientele. They prefer that we maintain an air of civility, order and exclusivity, since they select this area over strip malls and other banal places where one might find blow-up decorations."

Ari scowled, her hand on her hip. "I actually did research this area. It would have been pretty irresponsible for me not to when I want to invest my whole livelihood here, don't you think? How do you expect your precious Silicon Valley millionaires, millennial prodigies and their yuppie parents to shop until they drop without a cup of fair trade, single-origin micro-lot coffee, or a midday organic basil-blueberry donut or chia-apricot muffin break? Don't lecture me. I know what I'm doing."

Sophia took a small step back. She had not expected the woman to talk back. Normally, new people in town did the reverse and backed down when Sophia confronted them.

Of course, Ari's strong reaction only made Sophia want to give off more of an illusion of being calm and in control of the situation. Her face froze while she listened to the woman. She always preferred it if - and indeed, hoped - people would have a meltdown in front of her. It gave her great satisfaction when she, of all people, was the calm, reasonable, even-tempered one during an altercation.

Because it never failed to frustrate them.

As her mother had once told her, asserting power is all about breaking down the confidence and resolve of the other.

Sophia's mouth curved into a little smile. "Please explain how this winter scene you are constructing out here says 'fair trade organic coffee'? Which, by the way, that grotesque inflatable Santa over there infringes on my storefront space.

You can't have paraphernalia that close to my shop's entrance. Zoning laws, Ms. Little."

"So Palo Rosa also has laws against holiday cheer? I'll slide the Santa over. It's only going to be up for a week, 10 days at most. Christmas'll be over soon, and then it'll be gone, and you'll have your precious sidewalk back," Ari said, taking a deep breath, clearly willing herself to remain calm.

Sophia's sly little smile remained on her face, enjoying herself as the blonde woman grew more and more irritated. "Take it down, Ms. Little," she said firmly. "Trust me. You do not want to go up against me and the rest of the Retail Association on something this trivial."

Ari's mouth dropped open. "Are you serious? No. It's my cafe, my decorations. Deal with it for a week, and it'll be over."

The men who had been working with Ari and listening in on the conversation slowly started to resume their work, minus the hammering.

Ari stood, regarding Sophia, a hand on her hip and her long blonde hair blowing softly in the crisp afternoon air.

"We'll see about that," Sophia said finally, as Ari turned her attention back to several small white trees with neon lights that she had set up next to the entrance to the cafe.

Sophia turned around and started walking back toward her shop.

"Wait, what did you say?" Ari called after her.

"I said, 'we'll see about that,'" Sophia said, turning back around. "You might want to attend the Palo Rosa town meeting Monday night. 7pm. Until then."

"What do you mean?" Ari asked, a flash of worry crossing her face.

Sophia raised a perfectly manicured eyebrow. "I know some influential people in local politics."

"Local... you mean Palo Rosa?" Ari asked. "This is just a small suburb of San Francisco, how much politics could there be here?"

"Our town meetings are held the third Monday of every month. Come on Monday and we'll discuss your little display with the Palo Rosa Retail Association. Or remove it. Your choice. It all depends how much hassle you care to deal with."

"I'd see you there, then. I can't wait to check out what this Retail Association is all about," Ari replied somewhat facetiously. "Thanks for telling me all about it. Wait, what's your name?"

"Sophia. Sophia Black."

"Nice to meet you, Sophia," Ari said, a hint of bitterness in her tone.

"Until we discuss this matter again on Monday, Ms. Little, I'd advise you keep the noise levels down," she said sternly, glaring at one of Ari's workers who had just picked up his hammer again, and turned on her heels.

··o··

"Well, that was a hearty welcome to the neighborhood," Leonard, one of Ari's old aquaintances who had come to help her build the wood patio and set up the holiday decorations, grumbled after Sophia had walked away.

"No kidding," Ari said quietly, cursing under her breath.

After Sophia disappeared back into her store, Ari walked over to the door to read the name of Sophia's shop. She had not paid it much notice until now.

FORBIDDEN

"Forbidden..." Ari read the name, which was starkly printed in all capital letters on the glass.

She looked at the window display, which featured a large gold frame with a black velvet canvas. Pinned to the velvet were various pieces of clothing. Lingerie, to be precise. A camisole and matching shorts, made of what appeared to be a cream colored satin material and trimmed with delicate lace; a robe that was cut simply and in a feminine cream and black rose print, and a spectacular, but completely impractical, lacy black bra.

Her eyes widened slightly at the display.

"Was not expecting that," she said to herself, wondering how she could have missed such a sight the many times she had walked past. She must have been too focused on moving in and getting the coffee shop started. She had been scrambling the past couple of weeks to open, and besides, normally took the back entrance into her store, rather than the front, where she would have had more exposure to all of this.

Too bad. It was quite the display she had missed.

··o··

After Sophia returned to her office, she sent off a strongly-worded email to a few people who worked for the town council, and a few others who were in the Retail Association. Afterwards, the rest of the day passed in an unremarkable fashion. The hammering from outside had stopped. Sophia had no more calls to make, all that was left for the day was to look over a few spreadsheets with information about online orders and stock levels in her New York boutique, making sure that nothing was going to go too awry as a result of the Christmas-ordering frenzy.

Most of her sales came from her online store, but her boutique in Palo Rosa, California had been her first retail space and the one that was dearest to her heart. An upscale San Francisco suburb, Palo Rosa was her home, where she had lived for much of her life. Her boutique in New York was actually just a leased space nested within a larger department store; tiny, but popular enough to justify the added expense of maintaining a retail space there.

The funny thing about being a lingerie designer was that Sophia Black had never been that interested in being a fashion designer at all, and not to mention, had never been particularly enamored with lingerie.

She had studied business in school, and in her final year, she landed in an internship for a textile company that created and distributed some of the finest fabrics, silks, and laces. Not only did this company work with the highest quality of natural materials like silk, but also new, synthetic fabrics they had specifically designed through their own research and technology investments to be comfortable and beautiful. Some of their synthetic materials were as light as air but easy to wash, draped beautifully and came in virtually every color and never faded. It was exposure to these fabrics that made Sophia certain that she one day wanted to create something marvelous out of them.

Because of the internship, she applied for graduate school, during which she apprenticed for a fine lingerie designer. While she was absorbing all of the information she could during the apprenticeship, she filled many notebooks with her own original ideas and sketches for lingerie. She felt she could make better, more beautiful, more functional, and certainly sexier, pieces than the man she was reporting to, the lead designer at the company. Nevertheless, she was grateful for the experience and learned how to hone her eye for detail and enhanced her taste and natural abilities to create beautiful and romantic pieces that people could enjoy buying... and wearing. So, while her eye for detail and imagination propelled her designs, it was really her business acumen that allowed her to make her ideas into an actual, successful venture and survive in a competitive market.

Her hard work had entailed hours of toiling at all hours

of the day and night in endless classes, apprenticeships and internships during her grad school years, then in the months after graduation, taking a few random, short-lived jobs at a couple of fashion houses. Eventually, she finished a small collection of pieces made from some of her favorite textiles and sold them in an online shop. That was how FORBIDDEN was born: in the small living room of her first apartment after finishing graduate school. She spent long days designing and sewing and posting her pieces online from her home, then personally packaging and shipping them out the door.

Unlike many creatives whose dreams are short lived, at least Sophia's hard work paid off, because eventually she could quit all of her other jobs and work on her business full time, and as she applied herself towards her goal of growing it into something sustainable and successful, the years ticked by quickly. Eventually, she found she had little life outside of work.

After the FORBIDDEN line was featured on a few prominent style blogs, she started to see her orders increase. Finally, she could afford to expand her line, more frequently change the designs, hire employees to work with her on designing and sewing, purchase from better suppliers, and gradually increase the range of items in her line. And that was when she opened her first retail space, here at home, in the little pedestrian shopping district of Palo Rosa.

At 5pm, Sophia caught herself rubbing her eyes. Yes, all of the work she had put in over the past decade was finally paying off. Attention and print and online media coverage, boosted by a few high-profile clients who had raved about her products on their social media accounts, had actually grown her business into where she always hoped it might be. Popular and profitable.

She yawned.

Finally, a little after 5, she put her computer to sleep and clicked off all of the lights in her office and went back downstairs. At the moment, there was no one in the shop, but things tended to slow a bit around dinner time. They stayed open until 8:30 on Saturdays to try to catch shoppers - couples, ideally - who were in a good mood after dinner and drinks and were out for an evening stroll.

Elle was artfully arranging a display of black brasseries on a mirrored table. The shop was sleek and modern; the floors dark polished wood, the walls painted a deep, velvety grey, the lighting dim and relaxing, but with additional spotlights that were specifically pointed on her favorite designs, hanging strategically along the walls or displayed on tables. There were candles placed around the store: this year, copper was a popular accent metal, so candleholders glimmered throughout the space, and generous bouquets of white roses sat in massive mercury glass vases in the center of some of the tables, impregnating the air with their sweet perfume.

The interior of the shop was like a precious jewelry box: both sleek and soft, exactly the way Sophia had always imagined her store should look. It was her own little world, a space created in her imagination, come to life. She was proud of it

"I trust your interview with The Cut went well?" Elle asked, smiling kindly at Sophia. "I didn't have a chance to ask earlier."

Sophia forced a tired smile. "It did. And how were the customers today?"

"Not bad," Elle said. "Sales seem even better than last year."

"Percy hasn't been by yet, has he?" Sophia asked.

"Oh, yes, he has. But when he saw you weren't downstairs yet, he told me that he wanted to try out a donut from the place next door. He said he'd wait for you over there."

"Oh. At The Little Cafe?"

Elle nodded.

Sophia grimaced.

"What is it?" Elle asked.

"I didn't exactly have the most neighborly interaction with its owner earlier."

"Oh," Elle said, evading the topic, looking down at a stack of tissue paper and putting it away in a drawer.

She was used to Sophia's lack of people skills. After all, it was part of the reason Elle even had a job: Sophia needed her to be the positive customer facing ambassador of her business, a shining, bright, friendly, pretty face, while Sophia was firm and drove a hard line with the rest of the aspects of her work.

"Well, I suppose I should go pick him up," Sophia said, hoping that the cafe would be too busy for Ari to notice her stepping in.

She took out her phone and sent him a text, asking him to meet her outside.

As she waited for a response, she adjusted a negligée, which was hanging slightly off-kilter on its silk hanger. She then adjusted a few Christmas ornaments, simple spheres that had been hung artfully through the boutique, her only holiday decorations.

A customer came in, an older man in a pinstripe suit and holding a cane. Sophia glanced at him. She had seen him in here before.

"I have everything under control here," Elle told her gently, touching her on the arm to try to snap her out of her compulsive fussing, something Sophia was prone to doing when she was tired.

Elle then moved towards the gentleman to ask him if he needed any assistance.

Sophia nodded in agreement, too tired to argue, and left the shop.

Outside, her temper flared when she saw that Ari had not, in fact, removed the decorations. She had not even moved the garish Santa over. Instead, she had actually added to the grotesque display. She had since covered her windows in what appeared to be a sheet of twinkly lights, and the multi-colored white Christmas trees were now fully lit and created a miniature winter wonderland lining the entrance, cheerfully directing visitors inside.

Despite herself, she had to admit it looked festive. She might have even vaguely appreciated it if the place wasn't neighboring her precious, sleek, minimalist storefront, casting an unflattering, colorful glow on her windows and no doubt blinding pedestrians as they walked past.

She pushed open the door of the shop.

And when she stepped inside, it was not what she expected.

Judging from the flamboyant decorations outside, she had expected sticky chairs and tacky round tables, the smell of cheap coffee and overly glazed donuts. Or, she expected something like the former tenant of the space, Flourish Cupcake Co., whose owner, Carrie, had been as sickly-sweet in both disposition and taste as they came. The cupcake shop had not exactly been FORBIDDEN's ideal neighbor, either; the cutesy, twee pastel colors in that shop had clashed with the vibe that Sophia tried to cultivate for her own storefront. She had been relieved when Carrie decided to close up shop to pursue other interests. Or maybe she had gone out of business. Sophia was not sure.

The name "Flourish" had proven to be pure irony.

In contrast, The Little Cafe reminded her of the type of sophisticated cafe she might step into if she were in Paris or Vienna; it looked like a cafe one might stumble upon in a quant alley of a centuries-old city center, a hidden treasure, a cozy spot to pass an afternoon reading a newspaper or sketching or unwinding after a day of walking around the Louvre. Despite her outrage at Ari earlier, Sophia couldn't help but be slightly impressed by the elegant, yet comfortable, atmosphere.

The rustic wood floors, sleek benches punctuated by small round bistro tables, and the long counter where customers could be served on high barstools were all dark and sleek, but that was offset by all of the lighting around the room: there were many chandeliers hanging from the textured tin ceilings, casting a glowy light around the room. Tiny, twinkling lights were tastefully strung under the counter, and behind the bar, a giant copper-colored coffee machine glistened. Throughout the cafe, the walls had built-in bookshelves containing hundreds of books, photographs and paintings, adding an intellectual and well-worn feeling to the space. The whole environment seemed vaguely magical. It was certainly stylish. And, as she watched a patron snap a photo of a bookshelf on her phone while waiting for her coffee, it was a very social-media friendly space.

Not a bad advertising tactic, Sophia thought, impressed.

After gazing around for a moment or two, Sophia located her son sitting at the end of the counter, perched on a high bar stool.

"Here you are," she said quietly as she slid into a stool next to him. His hand was on a giant mug of what appeared to be hot chocolate - at least she hoped it was, even though Percy was now 13, she still discouraged him from consuming caffeine - and a plate with what appeared to be an enormous chocolate frosted donut on it.

"Hey mom."

"That looks good," she said, and put a hand on her stomach as she realized it was growling. She had only had a small salad for lunch, and that had been hours ago.

"It is," Percy said.

"Well. Didn't expect to see you in here," said a voice, and Sophia looked up to see Ari walking towards them from behind the counter.

Sophia clenched her jaw. "Ms. Little, this is my son, Percy."

Ari smiled at Percy and nodded. "We've already met. This guy's got great taste - chocolate-cinnamon donut and hot chocolate with a dash of nutmeg and cayenne powder. One of my favorite combos."

"It's great," Percy said.

"Thanks," Ari replied, beaming. "So, what can I get for your mom?"

"Nothing. We're going soon," Sophia answered.

"I insist. On the house. Anything you want. We have great pour-over coffee, cappuccino, cafe au lait, a massive collection of organic loose leaf teas... and of course, donuts."

"Do you make the donuts?" Percy asked.

Ari shook her head. "Nope, I'm in charge of coffee, but it's all I know, aside from my rapidly-increasing knowledge about keeping a business afloat. My employee and friend Rachel - the one over there - makes the donuts."

"I think I'll be quite all right," said Sophia, hoping neither of them could hear her stomach as it betrayed her by growling in the fragrant cafe.

"The kid's still got a ways to go on his snack. Let me at least make you a coffee? On the house. Neighbors always get coffee on the house," Ari explained.

Sophia studied Ari suspiciously. They'd stood on the sidewalk fighting hours ago, and now she was generously offering her a coffee?

She took off her black trench coat, resigned. "Cafe au lait, please."

Ari nodded. "Great choice. Never been to France, but had a French friend who taught me how to make them the right way."

Percy continued to munch on his donut hole and thumb through a comic book. Sophia gazed around the room, still impressed by the ambiance.

"I like what you have done with this place," Sophia said to Ari as she presented her with what appeared to be a perfect, milky cup of cafe au lait.

"Thanks," Ari said.

"It's better than the last place that was here. A cupcake shop, with whitewashed walls and crumbling antiques and pastels everywhere. You half-expected to see a unicorn wander in."

Ari's face fell. "Oh, well, that was my mother's shop."

Sophia bit her bottom lip and frowned. Great. Just when she was having a civil conversation with this woman - one that made her think she might be able to talk some reason into her about the display outdoors without making a scene on Monday night - she ended up insulting her mother.

Sophia nervously cleared her throat. "Your mother is Carrie?"

Ari nodded.

Ari was barely 30, if that, and she had always thought Carrie and her husband Dave were maybe mid-40s. A young-looking mid-40s. Barely a decade older than Sophia.

"My parents had me young," Ari added by way of quick explanation, reading her mind.

"I see," Sophia said. She knew a thing or two about that - Percy had been born when she was in her early 20s; she had not been ridiculously young, but younger than when she probably would have chosen to have kids otherwise. If she would have ever had kids at all, that is. She did not exactly have any romantic prospects at the moment, and she was rapidly approaching her 36th birthday.

Sophia decided to cover the awkward silence following that comment by taking a sip of the cafe au lait.

And it was divine.

Ari had wandered away to serve another customer who had just sat down at a small round table, so she missed the look of absolute bliss that crossed Sophia's face: her first truly happy expression all day.

The coffee was perfect. The beans were sweet, but deep and rich in flavor. The cafe au lait had been prepared to perfection, with whole milk, which was absolutely sinful, and likely the coffee had been poured into the warm milk and not the other way around, which was the authentic way to make a cafe au lait.

It was the best coffee she had had since the last time she was in Paris.

Sophia savored every moment as Percy munched on his donut and finished his hot cocoa. Sophia managed to steal a small bite of the donut. That was good, too, but a little too sweet for her liking.

Ari had disappeared; the cafe was getting busy again with the after-dinner crowd starting to wander in, and a few musicians with guitars and a violin were setting up on a small platform in the back.

She had to get Percy home, though. Mainly because she was exhausted. They left before the music began to play (and before Ari could make her way back over to talk again).

As they left, though, she made a mental note to send Elle over to The Little Cafe next time she was at work with her broken machine, and in dire need of a cup of coffee.

2

BATTLE WITH THE BARISTA

Sophia woke up on Sunday morning and she rolled over, her limbs feeling heavy under her crisp white Egyptian cotton sheets. She looked out her window: the day was cloudy.

She wanted to lay in bed forever.

But running a business meant there was always something to do, even on a cloudy morning in December. She dragged herself out of bed and put on her standard uniform, a red cashmere sweater that she had bought in London a few months ago and some black trousers. As she was waiting for a large pot of coffee to brew, she stood at her kitchen counter, her eyes glued to the screen of her laptop, page after page of sales reports that she didn't get a chance to review yesterday reflecting in her glasses.

Before she could dig her impeccably manicured nails deeper into the reports, however, the doorbell rang.

And thus began a day of unexpected visitors.

"Morning, sis!" A chipper voice greeted her from the front

porch.

Sophia's heart dropped at the sound of her sister's voice.

Her auburn-haired sister - who had a temperament that matched her flaming hair - pushed her way inside before Sophia could react.

"Sabrina," she said, uttering the greeting through gritted teeth.

"How's my dear nephew? Where is he?" her sister trilled, trotting into the foyer without waiting to be invited inside, peeling her leather gloves off of her hands and dropping them onto a chair near the door.

"He's a teenage boy and it's 9 am on a Sunday, so he's asleep. Coffee?" Sophia offered, moving over to her pot, which had just finished brewing.

"Oh, I don't drink coffee anymore. Would love some green tea, though. Loose leaf, organic if you have it," she said, handing Sophia her heavy wool cape and hat.

Her sister had a unique sense of style for a Saturday morning, thought Sophia, as she hung the cape and hat in a closet. Not that either one of them would ever be caught dead in jeans and a t-shirt, though, even on the weekend. Somehow their upbringing - with parents who were always dressed to the nines, even if it was a day when they were just staying home - prevented them from wearing jeans and a t-shirt.

Sophia silently walked into the kitchen after Sabrina, who was already making herself comfortable on a stool at the kitchen island, helping herself to one of the cranberry-apple turnovers Sophia had pulled out of the freezer and defrosted on a plate earlier that morning. They were something she had made from scratch last month on Thanksgiving weekend for Percy, and had frozen the extras for a rainy day.

Sophia filled a kettle for Sabrina's tea.

"I've been so busy," her sister sighed heavily.

Sophia rolled her eyes, her back to Sabrina while she turned on the stove and put the kettle on.

Sabrina had no job, children, or even hobbies to speak of, other than racking up bills on her credit card and paying them off with her piece of the family fortune. She lived to burn through piles of money each week, for little to no good purpose.

"How is the wedding planning going?" Sophia asked, making some attempt at civil conversation with her younger sister. She had no doubt their conversation would likely end in disaster, as it always did, but she could at least try.

"Oh, splendidly," Sabrina said, her bright eyes sparkling. "Everything about William is perfection... he is letting me make all of the plans. He's given me full control over the menu, the wine selection, the music we'll be dancing to... mummy hired the best wedding planner for the ceremony and reception, which is quite a lot to manage considering it's all going to be at home. I just hope mother and father can handle all of the excitement in the weeks leading up to it. And of course we booked the Japanese Garden for the bridal shower and engagement photos. Mother made a little call. Oh, and we decided: we're going to Barbados for the honeymoon! Two weeks of nothing but ocean, lush, tropical sun, dancing and drinks."

"Sounds like your perfect match," Sophia grumbled.

Poor, unfortunate soul who was about to be married to her lunatic of a sister, she thought to herself.

"He is a delight," Sabrina cooed, clasping her hands dramatically to her chest as Sophia set a steaming cup of green tea in front of her. "So handsome, so darling. I will treasure him forever and ever."

"He sounds more like a prize than a partner," Sophia pointed out.

She giggled. "Well, maybe he is. Nothing wrong with a little eye - and arm - candy, is there? So, sis. Enough about me. How's your love life these days?"

Sophia sat down next to her sister, frowning, and cradled her hot coffee in one hand while reaching for a turnover with the other.

"There's not much to speak of in way of my love life, but that's because I'm drowning in work," she said simply.

Sabrina shook her head as she delicately took another bite of the turnover. "So sad that you spend so much of your time on that silly little business. Haven't you made enough money to retire yet?"

Sophia sighed. "I'm 35. Not 64. And no, I'd rather not quit my career and drain my life savings in my 30s."

"Oh, but it's so much fun," Sabrina said, eyes wide, feigning concern. "I'm also worried you won't have a date to bring to my wedding. What a shame that would be, so many romantic couples swirling around to the live music, and you all alone, lingering off to the side... sad, really."

Sabrina's wedding was not even until the late spring. Sophia could scrounge up someone from her little black book by then, she thought. Couldn't she? Perhaps Walter... or Andre... or... wait, they were both married. No matter, she would figure it out.

"I have time," she grumbled. "I'll find someone. Don't worry, I won't embarrass you by showing up unchaperoned to your precious wedding."

"I'd hate to have to set you up with Cousin Phil," she said, her eyes flashing mischievously.

"That won't happen," Sophia said, unamused by the prospect.

"All right, if you say so. But let me know if you need any help in that department. I know lots of people, and so does William," she laughed to herself, clearly thinking of something.

Sophia chewed her turnover in silence.

"What about Percy? Will he bring a date?" Sabrina asked.

"Not unless you're talking about the wedding you'll have when he's 25," said Sophia, rolling her eyes.

..o..

Percy finally made his way downstairs just before 11, and Sophia sat with him while he ate his turnover and freshly squeezed orange-pineapple-ginger-kale juice - his favorite combination in her mandatory morning health juice repertoire. After breakfast, Percy left to hang out with some friends and visit a comic book store a few blocks from FORBIDDEN. After driving him into town, Sophia decided it was an opportune time to stop by her own store.

She normally tried to not make a habit of going into her shop on Sunday, but this was a busy season, after all, and her assistant manager, Seth, was going to be handling things in the shop today so Elle, who had worked 7 days in a row, could have a well-deserved day off. She had a few things she wanted to discuss with Seth about an upcoming New Year's event at the store.

But as she approached her shop from her parking spot a block away, she noticed a brand new spectacle outside of The Little Cafe and forgot all about her schedule.

Outside the cafe, there were now tables and chairs. A few of the inflatable decorations had been taken down and replaced with a live fiddle player, someone playing what appeared to be a ukulele, and a singer that was brooding moodily.

Sophia swore under her breath as she sized up the scene.

Then, she stormed into the cafe, her eyes adjusting slowly to the dark interior, searching for Ari. The smell of delicious, fresh, perfect coffee instantly called to her, but she forced herself to ignore it.

"Is Ari around?" She asked the barista behind the counter who made the homemade donuts - Rachel, was it? - who was setting a latte down at a table.

"Yeah, she is. Anything in particular you need?" Rachel asked, towering over her with a hand on a hip and narrowing her eyes that were coated with mascara and slick black eyeliner.

"I need to talk to her," Sophia said.

The woman raised her eyebrows, wiped her hand on the tiny black apron she wore over her sequined skirt and told her to hang on a minute.

Sophia went up to the bar and sat on one of the stools. Why did everything have to smell - and look - so good in here? She wanted to ignore the place altogether in hopes it would go out of business, but glancing around, it looked like today was even more crowded than yesterday had been. Every table was filled, and many of the stools at the shiny counter were occupied by patrons sipping and munching on fragrant treats, appearing to be content and well-caffeinated.

"Sophia. You're back," said Ari, stepping up to her behind the counter. "What can I get you today?"

"Ms. Little. Good morning. What I would like today is an explanation for why you decided to hold a ridiculous and noisy spectacle outside in the public space, destroying virtually every town ordinance concerning live performances."

Ari crossed her arms. "It's something for my customers to enjoy and is definitely not a spectacle. I put a few tables out there so my patrons could sit outside and enjoy coffee and music."

Sophia opened her mouth to speak.

"Wait. Let me finish, please," Ari said firmly. "I also want to let you know I spoke with Arnie of the Retail Association

- his name was listed on the website as the Association's contact person - and got all of the details on what I can and cannot do. I learned I was not supposed to have inflatable decorations because of some weird little bylaw, so thanks for your warning, you might've noticed they're gone now. However, I also learned that the other things I've got out there are totally acceptable. Plus, live music during certain hours of the day is also allowed with a permit, which I have," she said, producing a small piece of paper from her pocket. "I got it 100% approved by Arnie himself."

Sophia's jaw clenched as she studied the woman. "Why are you so insistent on attracting this kind of attention to your cafe, Ms. Little? Can't you understand that it is disrespecting all of the other quiet and sophisticated businesses on this street?"

"No, it's not," A woman said, overhearing their conversation, a to-go cup of coffee in her hand with the The Little Cafe logo printed on it.

Sophia looked over at her. She thought she recognized the woman from the gourmet salad restaurant across the street.

"We needed a coffee place around here. It attracts more customers to this part of town, they grab their coffee, shop more, get lunch at my restaurant afterwards. And this outdoor space looks real nice. Very festive," she said, nodding and smiling at Ari.

"It seems," Ari said, turning back to Sophia, "I'm not disrupting anything. Look, I'm just trying to get business. I'm also trying to follow the rules. My outdoor patio and festive Christmas display have both been approved by the right people. We're neighbors, so I want to be civil. You're welcome to ignore all of my decorations - which, by the way, will be gone after next weekend once New Year's has passed - and you can either ignore me, too, or take me up on my policy of free coffee for neighbors."

"I want nothing to do with your coffee," Sophia said. "I've got customers to serve. Talk to you later. Or not," Ari snapped, her expression dark, resuming her work.

"Goodbye, Ms. Little," Sophia replied, and without a backwards glance, left.

··◦··

Between the early morning visit from Sabrina and the bedlam that was having The Little Cafe next door, as she stepped into her shop, Sophia could only think about how she was suddenly regretting having given up smoking a year prior.

Behind the counter of her shop was Seth, politely answering questions from a woman who Sophia recognized as a regular customer.

Seth was an excellent manager, nearly as good as Elle. Organized, smart, impeccably dressed. The only drawback with him was that he was a bit unconventional, and at times glib, behind the scenes. He had a penchant for bringing up awkward topics with coworkers, everything from tales of his mother, to detailed descriptions about the type of women he liked to date, to the occasional, dreaded, thinly-veiled suggestions that he and Sophia should go out sometime.

Sophia ignored his passes, knowing that the same lack of reservation was what made him so good with customers on the floor (he didn't, mercifully, bring up awkward topics with her clients, and that, she decided, was what counted). On top of it, he was efficient and creative, and he'd offered many helpful suggestions, like exclusive sales events and exclusive evening soirees for her most loyal customers.

So she kept him around, as the benefits far outweighed the drawbacks, and gritted her teeth and dealt with it when, once again, that afternoon he brought up the topic of a new restaurant.

"It's Japanese fusion. Delicious, healthy, a well-known chef. It was reviewed in the newspaper and got top marks," he said.

"Did it?" Sophia asked vaguely, hoping her lack of interest carried through in her tone. She knew where this was going.

"Yes," Seth said, once again not picking up the hint.

He never got the hint.

"So, if you want to step out and want to try it at lunch sometime, perhaps next week..." he suggested as Sophia busily arranged a new display of bras in a back corner of the shop.

"I'll keep it in mind, Seth," she said noncommittally. "Now, would you mind going upstairs to fetch that box of silk robes for me, please?"

..o..

On Monday, Sophia arrived at work and found that the display in front of Ari's cafe has toned down ever so slightly. No live musicians, and the obnoxious inflatable decorations that she had removed were still gone, still not replaced with anything that could be upsetting. Just a wintery scene (or as wintery as California can get in December) of fairy lights and a few small potted trees, and the tables still outside.

Sophia had combed through her sales reports at home the afternoon prior. Earlier this morning Elle had texted her a link to a trendy fashion vlogger who had featured a few items from her winter line, which had subsequently made visits to her online shop soar. She was in a generally upbeat mood when she greeted Elle downstairs, who was folding crimson satin pajama sets on a table.

"How are you today?" Sophia asked her.

"Good! I got some Christmas shopping done yesterday, finally," Elle smiled.

"Anyone in particular you had to shop for?" Sophia asked.

To her knowledge, Elle was single, and she didn't have any children.

"Maybe a special someone," Elle said coyly. "How are you this morning?"

"Not too bad," Sophia said.

"Is Percy excited for Christmas?" Elle asked, sensing that Sophia was in a rare mood for small talk.

"He is. He emailed me a long wish list of video games a few weeks ago, so he'll likely find a few of those under the tree. I still have to bake our annual Christmas cookies with him."

"Molasses spice?"

"You have a good memory," Sophia smiled, as she moved towards the velvet curtain and went upstairs.

Her mood dampened slightly when she remembered that the coffee machine was still broken. Someone had pulled a tea kettle and French press out from some forgotten cupboard somewhere. Sophia studied the implements for a few moments and decided that a French press just wasn't worth exploring first thing on a Monday morning.

She said hello to two of her seamstresses who were in today. They were working on finishing up special orders from some of her more elite clientele who had the budget for bespoke work. A young man who handled shipments for her online store and managed her inventory, most of which was located in a warehouse some 20 minutes away, was also in the office this morning. He had stopped into the office to fill out some paperwork.

Finally at her desk, she opened up her laptop to discover that she had an email reply from the mayor of Palo Rosa, who invited her to present her grievances with The Little Cafe that evening at the monthly town meeting.

Sophia was tempted to reply and say she was dropping the issue until after the holidays. She really was busy. Ari's little spectacle had been a nuisance all weekend long, sure, but things seemed to have settled down this morning. She had more important things to do than to battle a blonde barista.

Before she could reply to the message, she was interrupted. First, by Elle, who had some things to go over with her about holiday schedules and a special post-Christmas, pre-New Year's event that Seth was coordinating. She was also brainstorming ways to drum up hype for Valentine's Day as soon as January was underway. Finally, she needed approvals on several custom orders that had come in over the weekend.

The second time Sophia thought about writing the email, she paused as she realized she had a headache coming on. This one was likely caused by the lack of a decent cup of coffee all morning. But as she tried to go downstairs to ask Elle if she would be willing to run over to The Little Cafe while Sophia kept an eye on the shop, she was bombarded with questions from her seamstresses about the custom orders and their work on new designs for upcoming collections.

The coffee was quickly forgotten.

By the time Sophia was finished, lunchtime had come and gone and it was only her growling stomach that reminded her it was time to go across the street to the salad restaurant for her usual Monday order of kale, pomegranate, quinoa and Meyer lemon detox salad.

She stepped outside, and out of habit, glanced towards Ari's cafe. Out front, as usual there were several people sitting at the bistro tables, but today, there was a new attraction added to the mix.

Rachel.

Rachel was standing outside in decidedly non-daytime attire and handing out samples of coffee and wedges of donuts, along with tiny slips of paper.

Sophia stood completely still, observing Rachel in the way

a hawk might eye its prey before swooping in for the attack.

It was not that Sophia took issue with Rachel's choice of attire. She was, after all, a designer of lingerie, and thus hardly a prude when it came to clothing. People could wear whatever they wanted to wear, for all Sophia cared. But the spectacle of it all, during the daytime on a Monday no less, felt so cheap; Rachel clearly positioning herself outside of the cafe to attract the attention of any and all pedestrians. She was, to put it simply, sending a less-than-desirable message and destroying the atmosphere of Palo Rosa.

And just when she had thought everything had settled down, no less.

Sophia forgot about the salad and growing hunger in her stomach and stormed past Rachel, pushing her way through the doors and entering the cafe.

And then it hit her.

She had had too little to eat so far that day, and finding herself surrounded by the luscious aromas of fresh coffee, donuts, and warm, yeasty cinnamon bread made her head spin.

Her stomach nearly caused her to surrender, turn around and just go get her damn salad, until she spotted the source of her annoyance innocently making a cappuccino.

She walked over.

"Do you have a permit for handing out food samples on the sidewalk?" Sophia demanded, not giving Ari the chance to get a word in first.

"A... what? Come on," Ari said distractedly, glancing up at her. "How and why would a permit be necessary to hand out free samples and coupons to pedestrians right in front of my cafe? Right where they're all already sitting and ordering food anyways?"

"I didn't make the rules," Sophia replied tartly.

"Look, Rach is practically inside, she's standing in the doorway. And it's only during lunchtime. Just trying to drum up business."

"I think Rachel is trying to drum up a little something else," Sophia said.

Ari rolled her eyes. "Didn't take you for a prude."

"A permit is needed to hand out food samples to the general public," Sophia said in a firm and authoritative tone.

Even as she said it, though, she knew she was exaggerating. Street vendors could not sell food without a permit. Handing out a free sample just outside one's entrance was hardly the same as being a street vendor. Sophia knew no one else would really bat an eye at Ari or her employees handing out free samples.

But these were not normal circumstances. This woman was starting to seriously irritate her. And Sophia wanted to make it very clear to Ari who had been first to set up shop in Palo Rosa, and who was entitled to enforce the rules and standards of practice around here.

"What is your problem? Seriously. Do you just really hate coffee, or what? What did I do to you?" Ari asked, starting to lose it, her cheeks turning slightly red over the steam of the machine.

"I love coffee. I don't like petulant coffee shop owners who march into town and think they can steamroll over our quiet mannerisms and way of doing business-"

"You're not really demonstrating 'quiet mannerisms,'" Ari interrupted her to point out.

Sophia ignored her and continued, "-and totally upset a retail environment where many small businesses have worked very hard to attract a very discerning clientele in a competitive market."

"Look around," Ari replied while pouring steamed milk

into a mug. "Does this shop look like some half-assed establishment that's taking away from the quality or prestige of your precious little shopping district?"

"I should hope it does not," said a familiar, velvety voice next to Sophia.

Sophia knew that voice. Her breath caught and she momentarily forgot why she was in the cafe. In fact, the sound of that voice instantly transported her to an earlier time in her life.

"Vera?" Sophia sucked in a breath and turned to look at the tall woman next to her, tall and platinum-haired, a ghost from a distant part of her past, completely anachronistic in the present setting.

Vera smiled vaguely at her in her deliciously tall, confident way. She was wearing a pinstripe suit and fedora, looking ever-so slightly like a modern iteration of Annie Hall.

"Veronica... you know Sophia?" Ari asked.

"We are acquainted," Veronica said, her icy blue eyes gazing down at Sophia.

Sophia's entire disposition changed in the woman's presence. She calmed down, softened her gaze, parted her lips in a smile.

"It's good to see you," she said nervously, tucking a strand of hair behind her ear.

Veronica did not reply, instead sitting down on a stool. Sophia was tempted to sit down next to her her, her little altercation with Ari quickly feeling very unimportant; certainly something she'd rather not continue in front of Veronica.

"How do you two know each other?" Sophia asked Ari curiously.

"Veronica's the one who helped me make sure this establishment didn't look half-assed," Ari said, working the espresso machine as she talked. "She's my interior designer.

The one I hired for this place."

Ari made Veronica a demitasse of espresso. She took it, nodding a thanks and raising it to her ruby lips.

"So, how do you two know each other?" Ari asked Sophia and Veronica.

"We're old friends," Veronica said before Sophia could answer, a small, knowing smile tugging at the corner of her lips.

"I didn't know you'd gone back to work," Sophia said to her.

"I've been doing a few projects here and there," Veronica said vaguely, taking another sip of the liquid.

Then she looked at Ari.

"Now why is it that you two girls are arguing? What kind of drama did I just step into?" Veronica asked.

"Sophia's not thrilled with some of my marketing tactics," Ari said.

"Right, because this is a cafe in Palo Rosa, not a car wash in a sketchy suburb where you can just send your leggiest employee out on the sidewalk to hand out coupons and wave people in," Sophia said lightly.

"I hadn't noticed," Ari muttered sarcastically.

"Sophia has a flair for drama," Veronica said in a bored tone. "Sophia, dear, it's a coffee shop. Not exactly threatening your domain. And most of your business is conducted online, anyways."

"It's the principle," Sophia protested. "What is so wrong with me wanting to maintain the integrity of this area? What my neighbor does impacts me."

"Have you ever considered that it's the same for me? And my neighbor trying to quell all of my creative ideas is going to be bad for my business," Ari replied.

"Well, Ari, perhaps you will want to show up at the town

meeting tonight," Sophia said.

"Why? What meeting?"

"We're going to discuss this cafe, your role and duties as a business owner in Palo Rosa, and the potential obstruction and damage your cafe has caused to the members of the Retail Association. We may even discuss the compatibility of your business here."

"Her role and duties are to make a damn delicious cup of coffee, and I'd say she does that splendidly," Veronica said calmly, sipping the last of her liquid from her demitasse and smiling condescendingly at Sophia. "What kind of nasty little chip is on your shoulder these days, dear, to set you off over a bit of coffee?"

"I don't have time for this," Sophia stated, standing up to leave.

Veronica and Ari watched her go, then Veronica turned to Ari.

"You should be careful, Ari. Sophia has some powerful connections. If you want to stay in business, you might want to find a way to get into her good graces. As difficult as she might seem, and as rude as she can be, she actually is a very intelligent woman and can be quite helpful and loyal towards her friends. Getting on her good side, as undesirable as it may seem to you now, is far better than dealing with her other side... trust me."

··○··

After perusing the overly detailed Palo Rosa website for any and all information about what Ari was beginning to discover was a shockingly regulated town for new retailers and restaurateurs, she left her part-time employee, Athena, in charge of closing up the cafe that evening so she could duck out of work early to scope out the Monday night town meeting.

Town meeting.

Attending a town meeting sounded like an activity from a 1950s movie about some middle America state. What kind of place had a town meeting these days?

As Ari walked, she realized she was craving French fries, and promised herself she would stop by a diner that she liked just off the highway after work on her way home. It was where Athena moonlighted on the weekends. Her family had owned the joint for generations, and they had the absolute best fries in the entire state, she was sure. Freshly cut from an actual potato, fried to a golden crisp, served piping hot. Athena's mom insisted she had learned the recipe from her father, who was from Belgium.

The Palo Rosa town council meeting took place in not a town hall but a small municipal office a few streets away from The Little Cafe. She arrived at 6:50, and a small crowd - though larger than she would have predicted, considering it was a Monday night close to Christmas - had already assembled.

Sophia was sitting at a small table at the head of the room along with two others. One was an older woman that looked kind of like an auburn-haired version of Ari. She had a stern, disapproving expression on her face and deep red lips. They were also sitting with a somewhat scruffy-looking guy in a plaid shirt and leather jacket.

Ari took a seat off to the side of the room, next to a table that was stacked high with file folders, pamphlets and brochures. An older man who was seated on her other side appeared to be half-asleep.

"Good evening, everyone," the man with a scruffy beard and a slight Scottish lilt said, stepping up to the lectern and dimming the room's lights so everyone could see the presentation that lit up a screen behind him. "If I could have your attention please, we'll get this meeting started and I'll explain our agenda..."

Ari stifled yawn after yawn while some sort of sidewalk maintenance funding proposal was discussed, the type of bio-fuel used in the buses was explained to two concerned environmentalists who had shown up that night, noise curfews were loudly debated by three middle-aged women who had various facial piercings, and letters were read from several constituents, most of which needed serious editing and had little to no relevance to anything that was being discussed.

As one hour turned into two, Ari wondered if Sophia had simply made empty threats. There was no indication of her coffee shop on the agenda that had been presented earlier, and she had been sitting there for over an hour without any verbal mention of it at all.

"Finally, as always, we will conclude with a word from our President of the Retail Association, who will also take questions and address any concerns from the public related to businesses in our town," the scruffy-bearded guy said. "Madam Black?"

Sophia stood up from the table, smiled politely, and took his place at the lectern.

Ari's stomach sank.

"Thank you, Mr. Hill," she said, smiling sweetly. "And thank you all for being here this evening-"

"She's the President of the Retail Association?" Ari whispered to the older man seated next to her.

He nodded, and replied in a thick accent of some sort.

"Yes. And that's her mother next to her. She is mayor."

"Are you serious?"

He nodded.

"She'll probably run for mayor soon when her mother's term is done. Her whole family's in local politics, see. They do politics for fun. Very influential people here. Very, very rich."

"A rich family in politics," Ari muttered to herself. "At least that explains the entitled attitude."

The man nodded. "Don't get in their way, they won't bother you. Get in their way, you will be out of business instantly."

"Right," Ari said, sighing, wondering if it was too late already.

Ari focused back on Sophia, who was confidently delivering a speech about community and organization and cooperation. Ari sat up straight, on high alert. Was Sophia going to take out her grief about The Little Cafe here, in front of everyone?

"We all understand the importance of maintaining order, beauty and harmony on our streets and sidewalks," she said, pausing as two people applauded. One of them was the older woman at the head of the table, who Ari now knew was her mother and the mayor. The other was the scruffy guy. Mr. Hill.

Someone in the audience coughed, and a phone rang.

"Therefore," Sophia continued, "I would like to propose new amendments to the downtown code that will gently enforce stricter requirements - and penalties - to retailers who infringe upon the public space of the sidewalks, or in any way negatively impact the beauty and serenity of our downtown streets and pedestrian shopping district."

The presentation on the screen behind her switched over to a new slide, where a list of about 20 points was displayed in small print. Ari squinted and tried to read them as quickly as she could. Around her, people shifted in their seats, impatient.

"Does anyone oppose any of these new guidelines? I'm sure

we can all agree that we want to keep our main shopping street as orderly as possible. I know we want to maintain Palo Rosa's reputation for a quality, curated selection of retail stores and restaurants."

Silence. Then another cough.

"Well then, I'm sure we are all eager to get home after a long day. I put it to the town council for a vote," she said, glancing back at the table with her mother and the scruffy guy.

Her mother, the mayor, nodded, urging her on.

"I object," Ari called out, jumping to her feet, not sure what the proper protocol was, but feeling she had been silent long enough.

Sophia - along with most of the others in the room - turned to look at her.

"Ah, hi, there" Ari said awkwardly, glancing around at everyone in the room. "Yeah, I think we should all read that slide over before anyone votes on it. I see some things I'm not so sure about, like-"

"Like what, Ms. Little?" Sophia asked, crossing her arms.

"Like the fact you can barely read anything on that screen. I think we all have a right to know what these new 'guidelines' are, uh, Ms. Black. Mrs. Black?"

"You may call me Madam Black," Sophia said in a grandiose manner.

Seriously? Ari thought, but she decided to play along.

"Right... Madam. So, I'm just saying everyone should have a chance to look that over. Especially the business owners who will be impacted by this."

Sophia pursed her lips. "Do you have any specific concerns that you would like to share with us here tonight?"

"Yeah, I have some concerns. But first I need to read this stuff over before I can tell you what all of them are. Can't you vote on this next month?"

"Ms. Little, I believe this is a simple matter. There's very little to debate, or understand here. It's merely to ensure that shoppers and business owners alike are protected and..."

"Can you at least hold off on voting, so we can just evaluate it ourselves?" Ari pressed.

"Ms. Little, please. That seems like a waste of time for us all," Sophia laughed nervously.

"You can wait one month, what's the problem with that?" The old man piped up from the seat next to her.

Sophia paused, pursing her lips. "I am sure that everyone here would agree that it would be best to push this through so we can all forget about this dull business and enjoy the holiday ahead..."

"I think you should let us read it, and we'll let you know if we have any problems with it at the next meeting," said a woman who Ari thought she recognized from the sushi restaurant down the street.

Sophia raised her eyebrows and shifted at the lectern, clearly growing more uncomfortable with the restless crowd. She glanced over at the table. The scruffy guy nodded at her.

"If you insist," she finally conceded to the crowd with a faux-smile.

"And now, I believe that concludes tonight's meeting," Sophia's mother, the mayor, said, and everyone instantly stood up.

The scruffy-beard man returned to the lectern as everyone was gathering their things. "Have a good holiday, and we'll revisit this at our next meeting in January," he said.

As Ari followed the small crowd out of the room, she felt Sophia's eyes on her. She didn't care if she'd hit a nerve with the woman. At least she bought some time to strategize on her next move, and she'd figure out what to do before the next month's meeting.

She had worked too hard opening up her coffee shop to go down because of one nasty, mean woman.

In fact, she was pleased with herself that she had stood up to Sophia, despite the fact that the woman was clearly irritated with her now and apparently everyone in the town was at least somewhat afraid of her.

Good, Ari thought to herself, smirking.

Let her be irritated. Sophia Black did not seem like the type who was used to being challenged very often. Let her fret that she might not get her way... clearly that did not happen to her very often. It was about time that it did.

··o··

Sophia put on her long black trench and gathered her things from a table in the corner of the room. She politely said goodbye as the town councilors and people who showed up for the meeting trickled out.

"Well, that was an interesting evening," said George Hill, who always officiated the meetings and had been sitting with her and her mother at the table in the front of the room all evening.

He scratched his scruffy chin and leaned up against the wall next to her, and Sophia scrunched her nose ever-so-slightly in distaste.

"It was," she replied, placing some documents in a folder.

"The new barista is an irritating one, isn't she?"

"She is. But I am always up for a healthy debate," Sophia said nonchalantly.

George studied her for a moment as she finished packing up her leather bag. He studied her red lips, then her eyes, heavily embellished with dark eyeshadow and eyeliner and either narrowed in concentration or frustration, he wasn't sure which. He had told her once that her eyes and skin were beautiful without makeup, and she didn't need all of the cosmetics she wore every day.

"I know I don't need it," she had said. "But what I need even less of is you telling me what I should or shouldn't do. I like wearing it, and that's that."

He backed off after that, but still quietly thought she wore too much makeup.

George pulled out a pack of cigarettes from his back pocket. "Want one?"

"No. You know I stopped for good months ago."

He raised his eyebrows. "What a bore you have become, Ms. Black."

"Remember to smoke those at least 9 feet away from any public building... town code."

"You liked her," he said, smiling slightly.

"I liked who?"

"The new barista in town. What's her name? Ari. Someone finally stood up to you, fought you. You enjoyed it."

Sophia glared at him. "That's ridiculous. She's a nuisance."

He raised his eyebrows again. "I know you like a challenge. You don't like things that are handed to you, Black. You prefer to fight for them."

Sophia laughed lightly. "Whatever you say, George."

He chuckled. "Care to grab a coffee on the way home?"

Sophia continued to arrange the folders and papers in her bag. "Sure. Just not with you."

She knew George was not asking for her to go get coffee.

How she had ever ended up hooking up with him last year, she will never understand... in his late 20s, the man was too young, aloof, and quite honestly, dull, for her.

Then again, he was also incredibly gorgeous.

He had been a little dalliance, nothing more. Every once in a while, since they had stopped their nighttime escapades months ago, he would drop a subtle hint that he was game for another round, but she had resolved that she was beyond that particularly unsavory time in her life.

At least he was a good sport about taking no for an answer and not holding a grudge or making things awkward at the town meetings.

"Fine. And I rest my case."

"What do you mean?" she sighed.

He shrugged, put on his jacket, jammed the unlit cigarette in his mouth, and walked out of the room.

With everyone else now gone, Sophia clicked off the lights and locked up the building.

"What did you mean?" she asked George again, as he walked out into the parking lot in back.

He took the cigarette out of his mouth and exhaled. "You know she's exactly your type."

"Ha."

"I'm serious. We both know you like women like that. Pretty girl, of course, with that wavy blonde hair and those legs," he said, letting out a low whistle.

Sophia rolled her eyes and walked towards her car. George caught up to her.

"But also, and more importantly, she's a sharp, driven one, isn't she? Makes a damn good cup of coffee. I stopped in the other day. And most importantly for you, she seems like she won't let you get away with everything. Something that us mere mortals haven't been able to manage," he said, taking another drag of his cigarette.

"Thank you very much for that assessment, George," Sophia said, growing impatient and getting into her car.

"Sophia Black finally met her match," George said. "Never thought I'd see the day. She's a rare one. Don't wait too long, or the barista will slip away."

Sophia made a low noise under her breath and started the engine of her black BMW.

"Good night, George," she said, and shut the door.

As she drove, she tried to put his words out of her mind. She had other concerns in her life. Percy would be waiting for her at home. She felt a pang of guilt as she realized she hadn't cooked dinner in a while, although for tonight she would have to stop at the store for take-out salads, soups and grilled chicken for dinner. Another non-homemade meal.

There were only so many hours in the day, she thought later, after picking up the food and pulling into the driveway. As she carried the bags into the house, she saw her phone screen light up with an incoming text. She looked to see if it was Percy.

"I'm home, I'm home," she muttered under her breath.

But when she glanced down at the message, she saw it was from Sabrina.

Nice seeing you this weekend, sis. Only 5 months 'til my wedding. Don't forget: go find some arm candy to be your date.

Sabrina had followed up the text with a saccharine photo of her and her fiancé kissing on a boat, taken during their trip to Fiji last summer.

Sophia tossed her phone into her bag and went inside.

3

COOLING OFF

In January, the weather turned cool - at least, as cool as California is ever likely to get in winter - and despite Ari's efforts to plead her case, the town passed Sophia's proposal to tighten restrictions on businesses and restaurants in the retail district. The Retail Association drafted a set of new rules with ridiculous stipulations like no live music outdoors without a special permit, or a maximum of two small bistro-size tables outside of a cafe or restaurant.

"What a bitch," Rachel commented the morning after the rules passed and were emailed to all local businesses, as she helped Ari put away the excessive tables that had been outside of The Little Cafe.

Ari just shrugged. "Sophia is a real piece of work, but I've wasted enough energy on her."

Ari decided it didn't matter much anyways. What's an extra table, or live music outdoors? Maybe if she gives Sophia this victory, the woman will finally leave her alone.

Aside from Sophia's harassment, so far business was good.

The location had turned out to be a blessing, as there certainly had been a need for a good coffee shop in the area, judging from the steady stream of traffic she always seemed to get, no matter the day or time. The quaint pedestrian district with its shops and restaurants seemed to attract couples escaping the city for a brunch or weekend shopping on the tree-lined streets. The Little Cafe was proving to be a favorite stop, offering a caffeine fix for those who needed a quick, mid-shopping spree pick-me-up. Anyone who craved an indulgent snack on a lazy Sunday afternoon was lured in by the promise of fresh-baked croissants or apricot tarts, or more savory treats like Rachel's mini-quiches or sundried tomato and fresh mozzarella baguettes.

Ari did not cross paths with Sophia again for a while after the infamous town meeting. She did, however, know that Sophia lurked in her shop or upstairs office for long hours, if the amount of time Percy spent doing homework, reading or playing his Gameboy and eating donuts or drinking hot chocolate in a corner booth at The Little Cafe was any indication. He regularly stopped in after school to buy a donut, pastry or hot chocolate and do homework or read his comic books before meeting his mom after she was done with work.

Ari always asked him what he was reading; she did not know a lot about comics, but she was mildly amused when he told her synopses of the stories' complex plots or the heroes' superpowers.

"Seems like our neighbor may have hit an after-Christmas lull," Rachel observed one day as she refilled a tray full of prosciutto, rosemary and marinated red pepper sandwiches on sourdough baguette. "No one is going in or out of her store anymore, although her son is here all the time waiting for her."

Ari shrugged, tucking a stray piece of her long blonde hair behind her ear as she focused on checking off tasks from her daily to-do list.

"Maybe she'll eventually go out of business," Rachel added.

"Not likely," Ari said. "Most of her business is from online sales, and her workroom or studio or whatever is upstairs. I guess she just keeps the storefront for fun."

"Have you been in there?"

Ari shook her head. "Nope. I like the look of lingerie better than the actual act of shopping for it. Or wearing it. Ugh, give me a tank top, sports bra and some leggings any day. It seems too fussy."

"I've been in. Her stuff is nice. Really. Very nice. And very expensive, not exactly something my budget can handle right now," Rachel laughed. "The store feels kind of cold, though. She's very into the shiny black and marble and metals and the whole minimalism thing. Not really a place I'd feel like browsing every day."

"Hm," Ari said, even less convinced to visit. "Maybe she'll eventually move her shop someplace else. Seems like the kind of store that should be downtown. Not out here in a tucked-away suburb.

Rachel shrugged. "I do my part to not make her feel welcome. I sometimes throw cigarette butts in the planters outside her store."

"Seriously?" Ari asked, not too impressed.

"Hey, she hasn't been nice to you. I don't exactly feel generous when it comes to disposing my cigarettes in an appropriate receptacle when her planters are a perfectly fine option."

Ari smirked. "As your employer, and a citizen concerned about litter, I should probably tell you not to do that. But I'll turn a blind eye to it this time around."

··◦··

The proverbial dust that Sophia's hectic schedule had kicked up before the holidays finally settled again in January. After claiming a small victory over the blonde barista next door, Sophia was content to go back to her real work, not those petty little details she had to focus on as head of the Retail Association. All was well: the sidewalk and storefront next door were virtually restored to its former peaceful self, just the way she liked it. Calm, serene, elegant, free of surprises, disruptions or flamboyant displays.

Sophia could get back into her routine: working with her designers, having video conferences with a freelance social media publicist in Los Angeles that she'd hired to drum up the online presence of her brand, meeting with buyers, driving into the city to cocktail parties where she could network with other industry professionals, fussing over her online shop and her brick-and-mortar boutique. And with the few hours she had remaining in the week, she attempted to engage Percy in conversation. These days, he was far more into his video games than chatting with her about school, although if his report cards were any indication, he was managing to hold on to straight As.

She could hardly ban him from playing video games when he was doing that well in school.

But just as she was settling into a comfortable daily routine in the new year, something rather uncomfortable happened.

She arrived at work one Tuesday about a half hour later than normal. She hated to be late, but she had had an early conference call with someone in New York and opted to finish the call at home before leaving. She had ignored a few calls so she could have time to drive out of her way to one of her favorite coffee shops before tackling a day that was booked with meetings, conference calls and an interview with a journalist. Her mind was jolted out of her schedule, however, when she pulled into a parking space across the street from her shop and saw Elle standing outside with two cops.

Sophia half-ran across the street.

"Oh, here's my boss now-" she heard Elle say to one of the policemen.

"What happened?" Sophia asked the two cops.

"There was a break-in early this morning, ma'am."

One of the cops stepped aside so she could see - a window was broken. The other cop was taping it up.

"How did this happen?"

"We don't know other than someone tried to break in. Your security company called us, and when we arrived on scene there was no one in sight. Do you have cameras?"

Sophia shook her head. "I don't."

"Well, I'm afraid it's unlikely we'll catch the culprit - this area's pretty sleepy early in the morning, but we'll ask around to see if anyone saw anything suspicious. Good thing your security system was in good shape, though. Elle said she didn't think much was missing - but let's go in and look around together, before we finalize the report?"

Sophia swallowed, barely hearing anything the cop was saying. Her throat felt dry, but she had left the coffee in her car when she saw the police standing outside, and it felt superficial now to go back to get it. She followed Elle and the cops inside to look around.

Later that morning, Sophia has just gotten off the phone with the insurance company about the window. She was still downstairs in the shop with Elle. There were very few customers that morning, thankfully, and Kate, who worked upstairs as one of Sophia's assistants for the online shop, was creative enough to find a sheet of plywood, paint it black, and position it over the broken window in such a way that was not too obvious it was covering up an unsightly broken window.

As she typed a memo to herself on her phone, Sophia noticed out of the corner of her eye that a man who she had seen in the boutique a couple of times before was coming in. He walked straight towards Elle, and she smiled, the first look of relief all day crossing her face as soon as she saw him.

"Everything all right now, Elle?" Sophia heard the man ask.

Elle nodded. "Sophia showed up only a few minutes after I did. I'm sorry I called you, I just panicked."

"It's no problem," the man said smoothly, resting his hand on her shoulder.

Elle tore her blue eyes away from the man to glance over at Sophia.

"Sophia?" she called out hesitantly. "If you have a moment, there's someone I'd like you to meet."

Sophia looked up from her phone and walked over. "Yes?"

"Sophia, this is Rupert - erm, Mr. Goldsmith. He's a good friend of mine," she said, smiling at him, her eyes sparkling.

Sophia gave Elle a brief, curious look, then a professional smile crossed her face and she shook hands with the man, who, for a Tuesday morning, seemed slightly over-dressed in his dark pinstriped suit.

"I believe I've seen you in the shop before," Sophia said.

"You probably have," the man said, his eyes steely.

He was quite a bit older than either Sophia or Elle. In his mid-fifties, likely. So. It seemed as though Elle had a bit of a May-December romance going on.

The man smiled coolly and made Sophia slightly nervous, though she didn't know why. It was rare for her to be intimidated by anyone, but this man was slightly imposing, despite his relatively short stature and calm demeanor.

He seemed to bring the polar opposite of the warm, friendly, youthful energy of Elle.

"I trust you've found what you are looking for here?" Sophia asked.

The man looked at Elle, and a small smile tugged at the corner of his mouth. "Oh, indeed I have."

Sophia glanced away. Well. She had walked right into that one.

"Good," she said, ignoring the subtext of the comment. "Pardon me, but I have to get back to work upstairs. I'm sure Elle will help you with anything you need today."

Mr. Goldsmith nodded. "I'm sure she will."

Sophia inwardly grimaced. Again with her poor choice of words.

Sophia didn't keep track of how long Mr. Goldsmith stayed at the shop, but it was a good while after she had gone upstairs. She was pacing around her office, trying to sort out how to reply to an email, when she caught a glimpse of Elle and the man on the sidewalk outside. Elle was giggling as Rupert said something to her. They shared a kiss that was just long enough to not be entirely innocent, and held hands briefly before Rupert wandered away down the sidewalk and Elle went back into the boutique.

A little while later, Sophia passed through the shop on her way out for lunch. Rupert had left, and there were no customers at the moment. She went up to Elle, who was typing on one of the shop's iPads.

"Everything all right so far?"

Elle nodded and smiled. "It is. And I don't think anyone's noticed the broken window. Oh, the person the insurance company arranged to inspect the window called and said they'll come tomorrow."

Sophia nodded. "Good. Although one other individual seemed to be aware of this morning's incident. Your... friend?

Mr. Goldsmith."

Elle flushed slightly. "Right. Sorry if that was awkward. He's a good friend. I called him, in a panic, right before you arrived this morning, after I saw the broken window and the cops."

"What a good friend to come to your workplace at the drop of a hat first thing in the morning." Sophia smirked slightly while Elle nervously played with a pen.

"I... well, yes. I think we are, at this point," Elle admitted. "I'm sorry he comes in so much while I'm working, he's a lawyer, but works a somewhat flexible schedule."

"Oh, I don't mind," Sophia said, waving it off. "Just as long as he isn't bothering you."

"No, not at all. And he does purchase things," she added quickly.

Sophia raised her eyebrows. "Does he? I wonder who for..." she said teasingly.

Elle, not one to divulge details of her personal life, pretended to suddenly be very interested in the message that popped up on the screen of the iPad in front of her.

Sophia studied Elle. There had been something about the girl lately. A certain lightness, cheerfulness. She never would have guessed that Mr. Goldsmith was the reason behind it.

"I'm going to lunch," Sophia announced, and she left the store, needing some fresh air after the morning.

..o..

Ari went to the post office to pick up a shipment of coffee beans around 12:30pm, and returned to find Rachel talking to Sophia.

What now, she thought to herself.

Ari wiped her hands on her pants and walked over to them. "Can I help you?" she asked Sophia.

Sophia turned to her, studying her briefly, her sharp dark

eyes raking her up and down, and Ari, for the briefest second, dropped her eyes. Ari felt suddenly, and ever-so-briefly, self-conscious in her jeans and plain white sweater next to the polished, professional woman.

Then she got over it, and crossed her arms and looked straight into the other woman's eyes.

Which, to her surprise, were full of worry.

"Someone broke the front window of my shop this morning. They apparently were not aware that I would have a security system, so they didn't do much damage beyond broken glass," Sophia announced. "Still, it's unnerving."

"It is. Sorry to hear about that," Ari said, dropping her arms, genuine concern in her voice.

"I was wondering if you know anything that might help track down the culprits? If you've seen anyone suspicious around lately, or have had any problems of your own with vandalism?" asked Sophia.

Ari shook her head. "No, I haven't seen anything out of the ordinary, and no problems over here. But I'll keep my eyes open."

Sophia's dark eyes lingered on Ari's for a few seconds too long.

Ari shifted uncomfortably.

"Is there anything else I can do for you?" she asked, crossing her arms again, hoping the tone conveyed that she was not exactly inviting the woman to linger any longer than necessary.

"No," Sophia said, pursing her lips, glancing up at the menu.

"Coffee to go?" Ari offered, following Sophia's gaze at the menu.

Sophia shook her head. "No. Thank you."

She turned to walk out... and nearly bumped into a tall

woman who was wearing a long black coat and sky-high heeled boots. Her long, wavy blonde hair was pinned up in a casual yet chic loose knot at the nape of her neck.

Today she looked like a femme fatale who had stepped straight out of a 1920s Hollywood flick.

"Vera," Sophia said, her voice cracking, looking up at the imposing woman.

"Hello, Sophia," the woman responded, gazing down at her.

"We're running into each other a lot," Sophia said, taking a step back and smiling nervously.

"So it seems," the woman said, appearing indifferent to this news, peeling off her gloves and glancing up at the menu.

"I was just going to have lunch somewhere nearby. Care to join me?" Sophia asked.

"I can't now," Veronica said.

"Another time? Tomorrow, perhaps?" Sophia pressed. "Lunch, or dinner?"

Veronica considered the invitation for a few seconds.

"I could do dinner tomorrow," she finally said.

"What time?"

"8:30?" Veronica suggested.

"That's late," Sophia said, more to herself than to Veronica.

"Oh?" Veronica said in a sassy tone, a wry smile crossing her face. "Have that many years really gone by? Do you need to eat at an early hour these days?"

Sophia smiled. There was the old Veronica she knew. Snarky. Sassy.

"You would know," she snapped back, smiling.

Veronica ignored the comment.

"8:30 would be fine," Sophia said quickly, before the woman could change her mind. "Meet me at The Grotto. It's a seafood restaurant a few doors down."

"See you then," Veronica said.

..o..

Sophia lost track of how many times she changed her clothes the next evening.

She made a quick dinner for Percy after work - leftover lasagna pulled out of the freezer and reheated, a salad, some fruit for dessert - and then sat with him in his room for a few minutes.

"Are you ok for a few hours?" she asked for the second time.

She always felt a pang of guilt when leaving him in the evenings after school, especially for a frivolous reason like having dinner with an old friend.

He nodded from his desk, glancing up at her. He was working on a paper for English class.

"Yeah, mom. It's fine."

"Finish the rest of your homework before watching any television or reading any comics, ok?"

"Yeah, got it. I got an A on my two tests I took last week. I know how to study," he grumbled slightly.

Sophia leaned down to kiss the top of his head and he sighed heavily.

"Okay, okay," she said. "I won't bother you any more."

She went to her room and sorted through things in her closet, debating what to wear. Pants, skirt, dress? Scarf, no scarf? Keep it simple and stick to her favorite color - black - or go with something bolder, like red? A deep red, or aubergine? She could not decide. And then, she felt ridiculous, sorting through her clothes, fretting like a high schooler going on a first date. This was *not* a date.

Not at all.

Just two friends catching up.

Two old friends catching up.

Two old... well, more than friends... catching up.

She hated how nervous Veronica made her.

In the end, she decided on a simple black shift dress, a stylish leather jacket that was cut just right for her, the lapels draped in a soft waterfall-style cut in the front.

"You look nice," Percy observed when Sophia went into his room to say goodbye just before leaving and to remind him that he had to go to bed by 11, no exceptions, although she would try to be back by then.

"I know, mom," Percy said gruffly.

It struck her tonight in particular how old Percy had gotten. One second he was a little kid who demanded her attention, and the next, he was independent, smart, accomplished. He had his own life and interests and schedule, and he did not really need her to remind him to go to bed.

Percy was an age where the transformation from a boy to a teenager had been almost overnight. It seemed like barely a year ago he had been playing on the playground, and now he was nearly as tall as she was and working on complex homework projects, telling her he's "got it." His dirty blonde hair had also grown out from a boyish bowl-style cut to a darker, messier, shorter style that also made him appear older.

Where had time gone? Sophia wondered as she returned downstairs and pulled on her black trench coat and favorite heeled leather boots.

Percy was quickly leaving his childhood behind. Sophia knew that the day when he would be leaving home, leaving her to go to college or travel or work, was probably drawing closer. There were only a few years left until she had to face that reality.

It was starting to dawn on her that this house would be so big and empty without him.

She shook her head to clear her mind, trying hard not

to think of that right now. The last thing she needed to do when going to a dinner (that she was already nervous enough about) was worry needlessly about Percy and things that were still several years away.

As she went out to her car and drove away, she shifted her thoughts from Percy to Veronica.

Vera.

She had met Veronica during her undergraduate program at college, in a course on Venetian art that she had taken as an elective.

She had been 21 at the time. Young. Foolish. Naive. Moody.

Veronica had been the young professor of the course.

Sophia had just come out of a terrible relationship. Only a couple of years prior, her mother, Callista, had forced her to break up with her high school sweetheart, Lucas. In a plot straight out of a fairy tale, her mother had said that the boy - who had truly been the kindest, sweetest man she had ever known, her best friend at the time - was not wealthy enough, not from a background worthy of being anything more than a high school crush for her. Callista had accused him of being only interested in her for her family's wealth and connections, which Sophia knew was not true. Lucas was genuine and kind.

Naturally, Callista's disapproval of their relationship initially galvanized it. Sophia grew distant from her mother and avoided family gatherings whenever she could. She hid in the comfort and safety of her little life with Lucas, in the tiny one-bedroom apartment they secretly rented together her second year of college. However, by her third year, Sophia began to be worn down by the tension between her family and her secret life with Lucas. At last, she allowed her mother to talk her out of the relationship.

After she broke up with him, Lucas, who was a year ahead

of her in school, graduated and was accepted into a MBA program on the East Coast. He moved to another time zone, disappointed and bitter after Sophia ended things.

He eventually got his degree, got a job at a prestigious consulting firm in Manhattan, and found his way into the arms of someone else, a woman with whom he would eventually marry and have three children. Sophia never forgot about him, nor did she forget the feelings of regret and even guilt at having allowed her mother to influence her feelings toward him. She was sure he had long ago forgotten about her.

Meanwhile, Sophia started her final semester of college, and her mother set her up with a young man named Scott. Even though she was still mourning the loss of Lucas, Sophia decided to give it a try. Scott was someone with a fancy Ivy League background, and a good pedigree as heir to a big chain of hotels that his grandfather had established decades ago and had since grown into an international empire. Scott was someone who, with his elegant family and upbringing, Callista felt was much more worthy of her daughter's time and affection.

Of course Sophia never loved him.

Deep down, Sophia knew her mother had, by and large, meant well, but she always was easily blinded by labels and appearances and had never really understood what would actually be in Sophia's best interest.

Scott was not in her best interest.

Scott was everything that a decent man - or human being - was not: arrogant, aloof, disrespectful of her thoughts, feelings, wants and needs. He felt he could throw endless gifts and money her way, take her out to extravagant parties and affairs, and believed that Sophia would be perfectly content with just that. To be fair, at first she liked it. He was different and worldlier than Lucas had been. But it did not take her long to see that he did not behave well. Although when they first dated he had always seemed interested in what she had to say, as time went on he preferred the company of his friends to her. When he did spend time with her - often only for his family's social events - she felt like the show pony she had once owned as a girl. Pretty and useful as a companion, but not something that was expected to have much substance or depth. She was a mere decoration for his arm.

His disrespect for her ran even deeper, to the point of resenting her for her intelligence and ambition. At one point, he tried to talk her out of applying for a graduate program, bluntly stating that it did not matter if she had the degree because she would never need to work. Why would she want a career when she could instead just take it easy and let him worry about the finances?

At the time, she was furious.

How can you possibly know what I want or how I feel about having a career? she remembered yelling at him one night over an expensive glass of red wine.

They had been eating filet mignon, seated next to a fireplace at the private club he was a member of.

Sophia, still desperate for her mother's approval at the time, felt obligated to give Scott a second, then third, then fourth chance. Perhaps he would eventually recognize her ambition - that she had an interest in working, an interest in learning and growing - and he would accept her for who she was. Maybe he would even learn to appreciate her. After all, he was still figuring out who he was, too, she had reasoned. And he was always under tremendous pressure from his father to perform well and eventually take on the family business. Perhaps that was why he did not have time to consider her feelings.

As a result of her optimistic and generous attitude towards

Scott, she gave him too much of her time. She went out with him the better part of her final year of college. But that summer, when he presented her with a three carat yellow diamond engagement ring a few weeks ahead of her 22nd birthday, she knew it was so wrong and everything about him made her miserable. She easily declined the offer and fled.

She was over relationships, she had decided. She had had enough. That summer she rented a studio apartment, alone, and she put on blinders and focused only on finishing the final two classes for her degree and applying to grad school, abandoning any more efforts at finding a relationship.

On the night of her 22nd birthday, she was still bitter. It was a Friday and a handful of her friends from school had insisted on taking her out to celebrate.

"You only turn 22 once!" one of her friends said, trying in vain to cheer up the freshly broken-up Sophia.

"We said that last year when we all turned 21," Sophia said, not impressed with the mantra.

But Sophia gave in and put on a tight dress and high heels, curled her long hair into loose waves, and agreed to let her friends take her out.

Not long after they arrived at the bar, she noticed one of her professors, a tall, formidable blonde who taught the Venetian art class, was also there.

Sophia quickly grew bored of drinking that evening (Scott used to drink a lot of fine spirits, and therefore alcohol, with the exception of wine and cider - the two things he never touched - had lost its appeal to her). She sipped on champagne for a little while, which was fun, but it made her head feel heavy and her body slightly lethargic, and so she slowed down as the night wore on.

Her friends did not slow down.

As they sipped on their drinks, they grew more and more

enamored with the men who kept dropping by their table to flirt and ask them to dance. Sophia was indifferent to the attention from strangers. At first, her friends encouraged her to get out on the dance floor, making sure to point out to the strange, leering men that she was the birthday girl. But as Sophia stubbornly remained at the table, as the night wore on, they turned their attention away from Sophia and back on themselves and their own needs.

Her friends gradually drifted away, getting on their feet to dance with the suitors. Sophia stayed at their table, growing impatient to get home where she could change into something comfortable and just sleep.

But as she lingered at the table, slowly sipping her champagne, her eyes kept drawing back to Veronica, a few tables away.

The other woman was also alone. Her long, blonde hair fell around her shoulders in a mass, covering her face from Sophia's view where she sat, but Sophia noted that the woman's shoulders were slumped over. She was also nursing a single drink.

Finally, when Sophia decided her friends had been absent from their table for long enough, Sophia picked up her half-full glass and went over to the woman.

"Professor Schaefer?"

The woman looked up at her, and Sophia's breath caught slightly.

Although she had often been distracted by the professor during lectures - she was tall, always smartly dressed, with full lips and long blonde hair that cascaded in waves over her shoulders - the woman was truly stunning in the low light of the room, her large blue eyes, full red lips, sharp cheekbones somehow more highlighted than usual despite the dim light.

Sophia mustered up her courage to speak again, shifting her weight to one side, hoping to look both casual and confident.

She took a deep breath.

"My friends left me for some guys they just met," Sophia explained matter-of-factly. "Mind if I join you?"

"Do I know you?"

Sophia cringed internally. Of course. She was in a class full of 50 or 60 other students... she stared at Professor Schaefer every day, but she doubted the Professor had ever given her a second glance.

"I'm in one of your classes. The Art and Politics of Renaissance Venice," she said, recovering quickly.

The woman took a sip from her glass and studied her for a moment with her darkly-lined eyes, then motioned for her to sit.

The night passed, and the two women did not talk much at first. They drank, slowly. They exchanged pleasantries, then brief, snide and snarky comments about the people surrounding them in the bar. Girls dancing in massive groups to subtly ward off the men swooping in on them like prey, people growing too tipsy to stand up straight or dancing in odd, trancelike ways, desperate single men trying harder and harder as the night wore on to catch the eye of women passing by.

The two of them observed and judged the social intercourse as couples at tables nearby flirted in the low light, then broke away from their groups of friends to disappear onto the dance floor or into a dark corner somewhere.

After a while, they both were talking, finding a renewed sense of energy with each other.

Later, they were both flirting.

When Sophia's "friends" never returned to their original table, having been swallowed up in the late-night chaos, she followed Veronica out of the club as if pulled by an invisible string, trailing her back to a large and elegant, but very dark and empty, apartment with a view overlooking the city skyline.

She did not question or overthink anything as the woman brought her a glass of wine, which Sophia promptly set down on the coffee table and left untouched.

The two women were in each other's arms almost immediately and spent the rest of the weekend together, neither one leaving Veronica's apartment until Monday morning.

··◦··

"So, I hear you have enjoyed quite a few achievements lately?" Veronica asked, taking a sip of sparkling water as she leaned back into the plush booth at the restaurant, observing Sophia as she mulled over her menu and tried to decide whether to order the mussels or the catch of the day.

"It's been a good year," Sophia said, smiling at her elegantly.

"It's good to see you are doing well," Veronica said.

Sophia kept smiling, her eyes soft, her shoulders relaxing somewhat. "Same for you."

"So. Sophia. What's next for you, my dear? Fame? Fortune? An empire built on lace and silk?" Veronica asked.

"Skipping the pleasantries and going straight to the point, as usual," Sophia said, setting down her menu.

Veronica smiled smugly.

"I want to be successful long-term," Sophia said after a moment of thought. "Not for fame, or fortune, but to prove to myself that I can make it. That I can take care of myself. I would be content to maintain a successful business, employing a few talented people and supporting their own careers and livelihoods along the way. That's all I want."

"Your mother isn't still pushing you into rotten relationships, is she?" Veronica asked. "I hope not... nothing will hold you back more than another Scott."

Sophia took a sip of her iced tea. She did not drink alcohol around Veronica.

"Not as much in recent years. I know better now. After Percy was born, it was easier for me to draw lines with her and find the strength to push back on her interferences in my love life."

"You learned to bite back."

"Precisely."

"What about your batty sister? Is she still enjoying hunting down beautiful prey to play with before devouring them?"

Sophia laughed. "You are as poetic as always. She's getting married this spring."

"What a terrible fate for her fiancé."

Sophia sighed. "I have to go to that wedding. Her third one. I also have to find someone to go with, otherwise my mother will jump on the opportunity to match me up with some miserable human being at the wedding."

"There isn't anyone in your little black book you could take?" Veronica asked, taking a delicate sip of her sparkling water.

Sophia shifted in her seat. She was hoping that Veronica would see their impromptu reunion at The Little Cafe as an omen, a sign that they should try things out again...

"I'm sure you will find someone," Veronica said. "And if not, I've never known you to be afraid to show up at a social event on your own."

"I'm not," Sophia said.

"What *are* you looking for these days? Outside of building an empire of pretty little nothings, that is."

Sophia paused.

"Nothing. I'm content with how things are," she said.

"So, Sophia Black is not after romance. It sounds like your

sole focus these days is Percy and your business. At least it seems things are going quite well for you on that front."

Sophia nodded. "Business is steady. I showed my collection at a show in New York at the end of last year. My next goal is to take my work to Paris, hopefully attract buyers to expand into European markets."

"You must have a lot of energy to keep up with the demands of your career and your son. Is he a teenager now?"

"He is. I always thought I could do it all, and in recent years, I have found I just about can. It helps that he's smart, and driven, and doesn't need a lot of parenting anymore."

"Sounds like he takes after his mother. But still, how do you manage it all?" Veronica asked.

Sophia shifted and took anther sip of her tea. "I just do."

"You're no longer the young, idealistic thing I used to know," Veronica said, somewhat wistfully.

Sophia laughed. "Young and idealistic? When you and I were the closest, I was cynical and burned out from a bad relationship. And naïve. I had a lot to learn still. You were my only real friend at that time in my life."

Veronica shook her head. "No. You were not in that bad of a place. A bright student, with her entire life ahead of her. I, on the other hand... I was a terrible person to be around back then."

Sophia took a deep breath.

"You were genuine and respected me. One of the few people in my life who was truthful and honest with me," Sophia said. "Your influence helped me grow up, pushed me to accomplish the things I needed to, in order to be where I am today.'

"How sweet, in retrospect. I am certain I was not that good for you. You were full of life," Veronica said nostalgically, her eyes unfocused, her mind conjuring up some memory deep within her. "That... brought me back to life."

"What do you mean?" Sophia asked softly.

Veronica looked into her eyes. "You know I wasn't doing well, back when we first met."

"Right," Sophia said.

Veronica leaned in. "After I left you, I sought help for my addiction. It took years before I felt normal again. Then I started my own business as an interior designer, finally doing what I truly love. I even managed to reach out and see my daughter again. She'd been living with her grandmother, but I started to see her more and more as I got better, and things are good with us now. Not perfect, but good. I don't know how I would have been motivated to get help if I hadn't been with you. I owe you my life, Sophia."

Sophia's heart beat faster and faster as what Veronica was saying sunk in. The tall woman, who had been in her younger self's eyes so intelligent, so full of mystery and intrigue and confidence, had been infallible. She had known Veronica had some issues with depression and with substance abuse back when she was with her. But Sophia also looked up to her, as someone who had accomplished so much by age 30, becoming a professor, with a great intellectual capacity and teeming with knowledge about the world.

At 22, Sophia had been too young and ignorant to realize the full extent of the demons that the woman had been battling.

"I'm glad you got help, but I'm not sure that was my doing." Sophia said quietly. "I was still too green back then to be of much help to you."

"No, you were. You had this... energy. You'd been through a bad relationship, I know, but you still had so much life and ambition. You spoke a lot about your goals and finishing school and your hopes for your career. I, in the meantime, had thought of... nothing, for a few years prior. I thought the rest of my life would be a black hole of university politics and research and waiting for tenure. That changed when I met you. I found new goals. I got a second wind. For that, I do owe you, Sophia."

"You owe me nothing," Sophia said quietly.

Their food arrived, and the women ate relatively quietly after that, saying little more than small talk about the food and the restaurant. Finally, as their meal settled and they sipped on coffee, Sophia felt brave again.

"I'm in a good place now," Sophia said. "I've learned a lot."

"I'm glad," Veronica replied. "And so have I."

"I'm happy you seem to be in a better place now, too," Sophia said.

"So am I," Veronica said.

Sophia leaned forward, gazed into Veronica's eyes and smiled warmly. "Come over to my house after dinner."

"For what?" Veronica asked, her lashes fluttering as she looked at Sophia, who was leaning so anxiously towards her.

"For... old time's sake," Sophia said, hoping her nerves weren't too evident in her voice.

Veronica carefully set down her coffee cup, it clinking slightly against the saucer, and a sad look crossed her face.

"Sophia," she began.

"We're both different," Sophia said quickly. "But in many ways, we're still the same. We're good for each other, Vera."

Veronica looked over at her with... with what? Sorrow? Pity?

Sophia felt herself grow agitated. From that look on her old lover's face, she knew what was coming.

"Sophia," she said softly.

Sophia gazed down at her empty coffee cup and played nervously with a napkin.

"I'm not the one for you," Veronica said simply.

"Why?" Sophia asked in a quiet voice, trying to remain calm, but her stomach sinking with disappointment and embarrassment.

Perhaps she had come across as too eager.

"I have a good balance in my life now, and I don't want that to change. And you deserve someone who actually is on the same page with you. Who wants someone else to come home to. Someone who you can be a true partner with, now, in your life and its present state. You're not a student any longer, Sophia. I know you, and you deserve someone who can give you more support. Everything you deserve. That person isn't me."

Sophia raised her eyebrows and looked down into her lap, slightly ashamed by the rejection.

"I'm sorry, dear," Veronica said softly, and from the way she said it, Sophia knew she was, although that did not take the sting away.

"I do have the most profound respect for you, Sophia. And it was truly nice to see you again."

The waiter came back and asked if they would be ordering dessert.

Veronica shook her head. "The bill, please."

"One or two?" He asked, glancing at them both, Veronica delicately averting her eyes as Sophia quickly brushed a solitary tear from the corner of one of hers.

"One," she said, and Sophia, still too wrapped up in the conversation they had just had, did not protest.

··o··

A deflated feeling filled Sophia after her dinner with Veronica. She was happy for Veronica, really. She was glad she seemed to be in a good place in life and had gotten better. And although she had left her academic career in the midst of her struggles, it seemed she now had a solid second career in a field she loved.

Happy endings for us both, Sophia thought morosely to herself.

Veronica's rejection still stung.

Sure, Sophia had moved on, too. It had been ages since they had ever been an item. Sometimes you just long to go back to a feeling from a period of time in your life that you had shared with a person, more than actually wanting the person themself back, she reasoned with herself. Maybe she did not really want Veronica. It was just that the ease and comfort that Veronica had brought to her during that time of life sometimes still seemed so very appealing.

As she always did when she was frustrated, in the days after that dinner, she threw herself into her work. When she was not agonizing over lace imported from Portugal and Belgium, inspecting bolts of sleek new microfiber fabrics from Asia or sorting through fine yards of satin from Turkey, she was attending her Retail Association and town council meetings, or scraping together what energy she had left after her long days to spend time with Percy. He assured her he was doing okay, despite his perpetually slumped-over shoulders and persistent desire to return to his homework or comic books rather than chat with her.

One Monday night after a town council meeting, Sophia was locking up. When she looked up, she noticed a man leaning against the wall of the building outside in the dark, smoking.

"No smoking within 9 feet of the entrance," she said matter of factly to the man in the shadows, stashing her keys back in her bag.

"Won't you make an exception for a friend?" the smoker asked in a Scottish accent.

Sophia sighed and walked towards the man.

"George. You should know better than to smoke here," she scolded, her eyes narrowed.

"And you should live a little," he countered, offering her a drag of his cigarette.

She took it.

"Everything fine at your shop? No more broken windows, I hope?"

"No." She exhaled, and then pressed her back against the wall, looking up at the night sky. "It's almost like someone is out to get me lately... broken window, we had a few issues with our website and some delayed shipments, and of course back around the holidays there was Ari and her endless string of headache-inducing concepts. It's been an endless parade of unnecessary stresses in my life."

"And how are things going with your neighbor? I haven't heard you complain about her lately," George said.

Sophia shook her head. "Nothing to complain about. She's fine. Haven't seen her in a little while."

"No more arguments over tables or decorations or who owns which part of the sidewalk?" He asked, his voice verging on laughter.

"It wasn't exactly like that," Sophia said defensively, rolling her eyes.

"It was a little like that," George countered, laughing.

"If you say so." she handed the cigarette back and turned to leave.

"Wait. Sophia."

"What?" she asked.

George flicked the cigarette into the gravel between the sidewalk and the road, underneath a short palm tree.

"Care to come back to my place?" He brushed a hand through his hair.

Sophia paused.

"Not particularly. I need to get home. I have meetings to-morrow-" Sophia said, but she did not move.

A moment passed. Then another.

Perhaps it was the stress, and her sheer desire to unwind. Perhaps it was the way that George looked at her. The way she sometimes wished more people would look at her these days. Or at least, if only a certain person she had dined with recently had looked at her that way.

She longed for that look.

She stepped towards him.

His eyes flicked down to her lips, seconds before she pressed her mouth to his.

They kissed for a few moments. But then she broke it.

Something did not feel right to her.

Sophia looked up into George's eyes and from the look on his face, she knew he felt it, too.

He raised his hand to his mouth nervously and looked away from her.

Their chemistry had all but disappeared. Veronica, and now even George, both were reduced to a distant memory.

She was not going to linger.

"Goodnight, George," Sophia said, clutching her hand around the handle of her purse and turning to walk to her car.

..o..

The next morning at work, Sophia watched out of the corner of her eye as Rupert brought Elle a coffee, delivering it with a kiss and a smile.

"You didn't have to," she overheard the girl coo gratefully.

"How could I resist a few extra minutes with my Elle?" the man answered in his low, gravelly voice.

Elle giggled.

Sickening, thought Sophia, rolling her eyes and scrolling through her emails on her phone as she walked towards the back.

Being in love makes one act like a child.

Later, in her office, one of her assistants had rolled in a rack of freshly-finished pieces that they had been working on for weeks. They were a part of her fall line, along with some ready-to-wear pieces, that would be shown to buyers at meetings in New York and Paris in upcoming weeks. Sophia inspected the final works carefully, looking at every detail, admiring the work that she had overseen from the conceptual phase, to the sewing room, and now this...

The black floral lace, deep, jewel-toned fabrics, soft, liquid satin. They looked like pieces from a mystical Queen's boudoir. Dark, sensual. Beautiful, elaborate, timeless, but still... wearable.

By the time she was done inspecting them stitch by stitch and determining, with a few of her assistants, which pieces would definitely be shown and in what order, it was a little past closing time at the shop. She took a few of the items downstairs to show Elle.

Elle's suitor was already back, waiting for her to finish up her day.

Sophia saw him, but ignored him, walking over to Elle.

"Look at these," she said, setting them on a table. "They're ready for the shows. Just finished. What do you think?"

Elle *oohed* as she delicately looked through them.

"Stunning. Absolutely beautiful work, Sophia. Your best designs yet," she said, gently holding up a translucent chemise that had a delicate floral pattern.

"Would you start to arrange some of these other pieces I brought down in a new display in the window tonight? I'll come down and help out in an hour or so," she said.

Elle nodded.

Sophia smiled, and went back upstairs to finish up her email for the evening.

Downstairs, Rupert walked over to Elle to take a look at the pieces.

"How ironic," Rupert said.

"What's ironic? Elle asked as she inspected a lace-and-satin corset complete with boning and trimmed with ribbons and hand-stitched beads.

"That a frigid woman who isolates herself in her office day in and day out, and according to what you said is not in - and has not for a long time been in - a romantic relationship, is ultimately a purveyor of some of the most sensuous garments I have ever seen. These are clearly the work of a mind that craves passion."

Elle looked up at Rupert.

"I'm not sure she's the type that would want anyone to feel sorry for her for being a lingerie designer who isn't actively in a relationship," Elle said.

"Oh, I don't feel sorry for the woman. I just find it interesting, is all." Rupert studied a chemise, his thoughts clearly elsewhere.

Elle smiled at him and gave him a tender kiss. "It looks like I'm going to be done a bit late tonight. Mind waiting for me next door while I finish up?"

He kissed her again, nodded and left.

4

INSIDE

Ari watched carefully as Jacques poured the fragrant, steaming coffee into the ivory-white hot milk.

"Don't use too much - watch and make sure the proportion is like this," Jacques instructed, lifting the press pot away from the cup and presenting the finished product to Ari with a flourish.

Ari nodded, then tried to make one of her own.

"Très bien, very nice Ari," Jacques said, nodding approvingly as she presented him the finished product.

"Not too shabby," their manager Nate chimed in, observing from the side. "You'll now be in good shape if the president of the company comes by."

"Is he French?" Ari asked.

The coffee stand where she worked was located in the front atrium of the headquarters of a software firm called Oscuro, the company where her mom worked as a corporate trainer in human resources, and her father worked in security. They had worked for the firm since Ari was a baby, working their way up in the organization, growing as the company grew. It was only fitting that Ari's first after school job would be at the place where her parents had spent their time all of these years.

Nate shook his head. "Nah, the president's not French, but he likes his coffee in that style. He was raised in South America, I think. Whatever it is, he likes his coffee in a more European way. Either a little shot of espresso, or made into a proper cafe au lait."

"I think I've got it under control," Ari said confidently.

She loved coffee, the smell of it, the taste of it... it was a perfect first job. And not only was she getting paid to be around something she enjoyed, she also got all the free coffee she could drink when break time rolled around.

Ari spent her days after school working the late afternoon/evening shift, observing all of the young, ambitious developers and marketing types, fresh out of college, grab their coffee in between meetings and type away on laptops as they worked late into the night. It was such a cool environment, she thought, observing tables of professionals only a few years older than herself brainstorming in the open, bright and airy atrium.

It was an ideal after school job, and Ari liked her coworkers, and after only six months she amassed a pretty respectable little savings in her bank account thanks to the job. The only thing she did not love about it was that her dorky dad sometimes dropped by to order a coffee, chatting far too enthusiastically with her coworkers, laughing and joking and generally being way too excited about his daughter working there.

"I'm busy, dad," she would groan when he stopped by to

bond with her and Nate or Jacques, whoever happened to be sharing her shift.

"It's a perk of my job that I get to see my daughter," he said, grinning widely. "Get it... perk?"

Ari rolled her eyes at the endless dad jokes, but she didn't fail to notice he also put a $10 in the tip jar before he left to go back to his cubicle upstairs.

Well, at least that was a perk, she thought to herself.

Only a few months later, however, the creative, upbeat buzz that had characterized the general environment at Oscuro that Ari enjoyed so much shifted overnight.

"What's up with people today?" Ari grumbled to Nate one afternoon when her fifth customer in a row had barked an order, complained about how something was wrong with it, and did not so much as leave a penny as a tip.

Nate glanced around, motioned for her to move closer to him and lowered his voice. "Rumor is this company's going to be bought out by a huge multinational. They're after some of the technology that's been invented here, but like a lot of other businesses they've bought in recent years, everyone knows they're probably just going to buy the company for its patents and trademarks and will maybe keep on a few people, but almost everyone else will be shown the door."

Ari's heart sank. Her parents... both of them worked here. That couldn't happen. She hoped it was just a rumor.

It was not just a rumor.

Oscuro was purchased a month later for a staggeringly large sum, and most of the employees were laid off shortly after, including her parents. Except, weirdly, for Ari and Nate and Jacques, who were offered positions in the food service program. Ari could remain a barista, working at one of several in-house coffee bars at the multinational company's headquarters (they called it a "campus") only a few miles away. She reluctantly took it, only so she could save up as much money as possible before she quit on her own terms.

She offered to give at least some of her paycheck to her parents, who in their late 30s were suddenly scrambling to find new jobs after nearly twenty years of stability, and trying to figure out if they could get her mom's lifelong dream of opening up a cupcake shop off the ground so they would have something to do other than collecting unemployment.

They refused to take money from their daughter.

Finally, after serving coffee to the very man who had ordered the layoffs of most employees at Oscuro for the eighth time in the same week - an old, quiet guy who was rumored to be dirt rich and yet absolutely talentless, but because of his power and wealth he was key in securing acquisitions of companies like Oscuro - Ari grew tired of being reminded of how unfair the world was.

She quit and spent the next couple of years driving around the West. She told her parents she was just figuring out what to do next. In reality, she was blowing off steam, knowing she was making mistakes by not having a plan for her future. Still, she prioritized escaping the cold, unfriendly, unfair and fake world that she left behind in Silicon Valley.

She vowed never to depend on anyone else for an income after the experience of watching her parents crash and burn after devoting their entire careers to a company that thanked them by kicking them to the curb in one fell swoop.

Once reality set in and her bank account was empty, however, Ari started to stay put for longer stretches of time and took up endless odd jobs to pay for food and gas during her nomadic life. Eventually, she earned enough to put herself through community college. Still, she never lost focus of the fact that she could not rely on anyone except for herself.

··o··

Present Day

Just when Ari had nearly forgotten about Sophia Black after not dealing with her for a few weeks, she glanced up one Wednesday morning to see Sophia next in line at the cafe, looking at her anxiously.

"Has my son been by here today? Have you see him?"

"I... um, no," Ari said, instinctively scanning the patrons in the cafe to confirm he really wasn't there. "I haven't seen him at all today. Why? What's going on?"

"I can't get a hold of him. His school just called, said he didn't come in today, which is completely out of character for him. I know he sometimes waits for me here after work, so this was the first place I wanted to check. If he's not here..." her voice trailed off, looking around the cafe.

"Is he at home?" Ari asked, motioning to Athena to come and help the next customer in line while she spoke with Sophia.

"He must be. I don't know. This day is the worst -" she said, touching her temple and scrunching up her eyes. "I have a meeting in an hour, I'd cancel it but it's the buyer for a huge department store, and I've been trying to get a meeting with him for months... I can't miss it. But I also need to know where my son is before I can focus on anything."

"Percy's not answering his phone? Texts? Nothing?"

Sophia shook her head.

"No. That's what's also strange. I don't understand what's going on," she said, looking down at her phone again.

"You should check at home. Maybe he's there," Ari suggested.

Sophia nodded. "I know, he probably just stayed home from school... he must have. I would check, but this meeting, I don't have enough time to get home and back by then."

"Can anyone else handle the meeting?"

Sophia shook her head. "No, I have to do it. Definitely."

"Tell you what. This afternoon's not that busy for me and Athena's here to keep an eye on things. You go to your meeting, keep your phone handy, and I'll go check at your house for him."

Sophia's shoulders relaxed slightly at the suggestion.

"Would you really? No... it's too much to ask."

"It's not," Ari assured her. "It's no problem at all if you tell me where to go and what to do."

"I'll give you my key," Sophia said, pulling her key pouch out of her pocket and handing it to her. "Just in case there's no answer, go in to check and make sure he's not there. If he's not there... I don't know what I'll-"

"I'm sure he's there. I'll find him. And actually, I've got experience with this sort of thing... tracking people down, that is." Ari said, trying to reassure her, taking the key.

"Okay. All right," Sophia said uncertainly, tucking her hair nervously behind her ear. "I'll have my phone the whole time; if he's not there, send me a message right away."

Sophia could barely concentrate on the meeting that afternoon. Luckily, she had meticulously prepared for it in advance. She had impeccable samples on hand to show the buyer, business plans and perfect drawings and every piece of information she could possibly collect that might be required to help him make his decision about buying her products easier. She was ready days ago.

Shortly before the meeting was wrapping up, Sophia quickly glanced down at the screen of her phone and saw that there was a new message from Ari.

Found him on the couch at your house. Sick with the flu, I think.

Relief flooded through Sophia. At least Ari found him, that was all that mattered. After that, she regained enough focus to wrap up the meeting, hopefully without the buyer from the store noticing that she had been a little off kilter.

The minute the meeting ended, she said goodnight to everyone and drove home as quickly as she could.

..o..

Earlier that afternoon, Ari calmly drove to Sophia's house. She drove along shady, suburban roads, winding up a hill.

"Is this it it?" she asked herself out loud, peering out of her windshield when the map app on her phone told her she had arrived.

It was a mansion.

Sophia must have only been, what, maybe five years at most older than her, and yet her house was large, elegant and sophisticated, located on a picturesque street on the side of a hill just within the border of Palo Rosa. It looked like royalty would live there. As stylish as Sophia was, the place was way out of synch with her image as a single mom, up-and-coming owner of an underwear (okay, sorry, *lingerie*) line, and part time small town Retail Association President.

Ari felt small as she unlocked the door and stepped into the foyer. In awe, she quietly walked through the pristine rooms and hallways, it crossing her mind that she should have maybe taken off her shoes to walk around on the spotless floor. The wood floors shone, the walls were a creamy white, the kitchen had beautiful marble countertops. She felt slightly like she was in a museum. The place needed a docent. She definitely felt like an intruder, but no alarms were going off (when Sophia had texted her the address, she had told her she turned off the house's alarm system remotely from an app).

After a second of looking around, she remembered her mission and began checking the rooms for Sophia's teenage son. Thankfully, that took all of 10 seconds, as she found Percy in plain sight on the couch in his mom's study, the television playing softly in the background. When she walked into the room lined with bookshelves and a fireplace as its massive focal point, he rolled over on the couch, squinted, and wondered aloud why she was there.

"Your mom sent me to try to find you. She didn't know where you were when she heard you weren't in school," Ari said.

Percy seemed satisfied with that answer, and closed his eyes.

It was clear Percy was under the weather, but with no children of her own - and having been an only child - Ari was slightly at a loss as to what to do for the kid when he was not ordering a donut or hot chocolate in her cafe.

She found Percy a blanket from a small linen closet under the stairs, brought him some water and herbal tea she found in the kitchen, and assured the kid his mom would be home in a while.

He thanked her for the water and tea and fell back to sleep on the couch.

Ari did not want to leave him home alone before Sophia arrived, so to kill time, Ari wandered through the house. She was trying to get a sense of the space, which was at once beautiful and elegant, but also lonely, as the house felt too big for just a single mother and her son.

The rooms, with their traditional, light and neutral colored decor had made quite a first impression when she first walked in, but the more time that passed, the more the house started to feel cold. Why did Sophia and Percy really need all that space, anyways?

Ari tentatively brushed her hand along the polished countertops, the velvet and leather furniture, the endless books in the cabinets. She inspected the two coffee machines, one an instant espresso maker imported from Europe, another, a complicated, more traditional style manual coffee machine. She was not daft enough to go upstairs, but she did shamelessly sneak a peek in the medicine cabinet in the downstairs powder room, where she discovered a small bottle of perfume. She gave it a light spritz and the air instantly smelled exactly of Sophia. Ari closed her eyes and sighed for a moment.

The woman was a real piece of work sometimes, but damn, she smelled good.

After that, Ari got bored of snooping and went back into the study and thumbed through a few coffee table books: one on horses, the other on a history of French fashion design.

About an hour later, a very concerned Sophia came home, heading straight over to the boy sprawled out on the sofa.

"What happened, Percy?" she asked, kneeling in front of him, feeling his forehead, talking to him softly as he stirred awake.

"My... ear..." he said.

"Does it hurt?" she asked.

The kid nodded.

"Let's get you to the doctor. Can you stand?"

Percy eased himself up, and Ari quietly followed them out the door, taking it as her cue that her help was no longer needed.

..o..

Ari returned to The Little Cafe, and to a quiet evening. The weather was unusually cold, and rainy, and no one in Palo Rosa seemed to be interested in heading out for a cup of coffee that night. Even her music booking for the evening had cancelled.

"Athena, go ahead and close up in a few. I'm just going to make something in the kitchen before I go," Ari said.

Athena nodded.

"Sure thing," she said as she started to close out the cash register and do a final pass at wiping off all the tables and the bar and counter space.

Ari wandered into the kitchen and started to prepare a little more food than she normally made for herself for dinner. She took a plastic container and threw together a salad: they usually had a gourmet salad every day around lunch time on the limited lunch menu, and today's had been cranberry-pecan spring greens with a vinaigrette, so she used the leftovers from that. She then found a few thick slices of bread, some thin slices of cheese, and dug out a wedge of butter from the back of the fridge, and put together some grilled cheeses. At the last minute, she added thin slices of pear and dijon mustard to the sandwiches, just to give them a bit more of a sophisticated flair. She wrapped them in foil wrap, and, on her way out, grabbed a few glass bottles of cold-pressed organic juices. And then, as an afterthought, two date-filled pinwheel cookies.

Without over-analyzing what she was doing (What was she doing? This woman had tried to make her first few critical weeks in business miserable...)

It was not at all rational, but Ari drove all the way back to Sophia's. When she arrived at the dark house, she took the food from her passenger seat, which she had packed in a canvas shopping bag, and walked it up to the front porch.

Just then, she noticed headlights behind her.

She cringed. She had thought she would be out of there before Sophia and Percy got back from the doctor.

She turned around, smiled, and waited awkwardly as Sophia parked and got out of the car.

She silently cursed herself for doing this. Would Sophia think it was weird?

Percy followed, dragging himself out of the passenger seat,

and Sophia put her arm around his shoulder, guiding him up the front step.

"Sorry, I didn't mean for you to see me again. I wanted to drop off some food on my way home - figured it'd been a long day," Ari said shyly, holding up the canvas bag of goodies.

"Come in," Sophia said, her voice tired and eyes a little unfocused, unlocking the door and helping Percy inside. He headed straight to the study to lay down on the couch, and Sophia motioned Ari to follow her toward the kitchen.

"What ended up being wrong with Percy?"

"Ear infection, apparently. He'll be fine. It gave him a high fever and made him a little disoriented today, which is why he didn't call me at first, and then his phone died and he fell asleep before it had charged. Anyways, we got his antibiotics... he'll be fine," she said, slumping over the counter, her energy clearly drained.

"I'm glad he's gonna be okay," Ari said.

"Parenting is...hard," Sophia said quietly, running her right hand through her silky, inky brown hair, the light reflecting off of a few slightly reddish highlights.

Ari shifted, not sure what to say. She was not a parent. She could not really commiserate.

Sophia blinked a few times, as though it had just sunk in that Ari was there.

"Thank you. For... everything today. I don't really..." she hesitated, as if trying to find the right words. "I just don't have anyone I can call for help with this sort of thing."

Ari shrugged. "Really no big deal. Glad to help out, you know. He's a good kid."

Sophia smiled, her shoulders relaxing. "He really is."

"Oh, and, I brought this," Ari said, remembering the bag she was carrying.

She unloaded the sandwiches, salads, cookies and juice,

spreading the items out on the kitchen island.

"I'm starving. You have no idea how welcome this is," Sophia said, taking a plate out of a cabinet and surrendering herself to the spread of food.

"What about Percy? Is he hungry?" Ari asked.

"He'll be okay. I think he wanted sleep more than anything. If he wakes up, I have some soup in the freezer that I could heat up for him."

Ari nodded. "Well, I guess I'll be out of your way, then."

Sophia looked at her, blinked, her eyelashes fluttering.

"No, stay. Please, Ms. Little."

"Ari."

"Ari. Eat some of this..." she motioned vaguely at the pile of food. "I can't get through it all on my own, and Percy's appetite seems to be gone."

Ari started to refuse again, but Sophia was already pushing a plate toward her, and so she gave in and sat down on a barstool at the kitchen island.

They ate in silence for a few moments.

"Any word on who broke your window?" Ari asked, trying to think of small talk.

Sophia shook her head. "No idea. Seems to be a lost cause."

"One of the guys I hire for odd jobs around the cafe, Leonard, might be able to help you with the repairs," Ari offered.

"That's appreciated, but I have someone. Besides, Leonard... is it?" Sophia cleared her throat. "I assume he's not my biggest fan because of the whole...well, being against festive holiday decorations thing?"

Ari laughed, despite herself. "Yeah, something like that."

Even Sophia cracked a smile, shaking her head. "Well then, I think I'll just go with the person I have in mind."

Ari shrugged. "No problem. But if you need anything else,

or if your person falls through, let me know. Us small business owners have got to stick together. Pool our resources. This kind of window smashing thing could've happened to me. It might've just been random, them choosing your window."

"Perhaps," Sophia said.

Ari studied her for a moment. She was unwrapping the grilled cheese from some foil.

"This is really good," Sophia said, staring down at her sandwich after she took a bite. "What do you call it?"

"Grilled cheese with pear and mustard," Ari shrugged.

"Nice combination. I wouldn't have thought of it."

"Well, I was just going to make a regular grilled cheese, but figured I'd fancy it up a bit. You don't really seem like the... you know, grilled cheese type."

"I suppose you're right. It's not something I'd typically gravitate toward. But I do appreciate this one. It has complex flavors."

"Usually I'm not that into complex things," Ari said. "The simpler, the better."

"Is that so?" Sophia said, raising her eyebrows.

Ari nodded.

"Well, I like complex things," said Sophia, munching thoughtfully.

After she finished her sandwich and salad, Ari offered her the cookies. Sophia seemed to be debating a moment, then took one.

"This is good, too. You're talented, you know. The food is good, the coffee is good."

Ari smiled. "I didn't make the cookies, Rachel did. But yeah, I love food. It's why I always wanted to open a cafe. I'm not a chef, I don't even really know how to bake or cook - that's why I hire people like Rachel to do the complicated stuff like pastries and donuts - but I guess I know good food when I see it. My parents were always out, busy, working when I was a kid, 'cause they had me so young. So I learned at a young age about how to, you know, put a grilled cheese together, or make something simple like tomato soup."

"Comfort food," Sophia commented, finishing the last of her cookie.

"Exactly," Ari said.

Sophia set her napkin next to her plate. "How much do I owe you for this?" She asked, taking Ari's plate and moving towards the sink.

Ari stood up.

"What? No, nothing. My treat."

"Nonsense. First I kept you from work by sending you here earlier to check on Percy, then you brought me all this food-"

"It was nothing. It's on me."

"Well, I must owe you something. Do you want to be able to put another table out in front of your cafe? Because I can turn a blind eye to it, if you do, and I'm sure..."

"Sophia," Ari said, lightly touching her shoulder.

Sophia looked down at her hand, clearly surprised, and Ari instantly withdrew it.

Ari cringed internally. Why had she touched her?

Ari tucked a strand of blonde hair behind her ear and continued. "The food's on me. Just helping out someone who needed it today. That's what neighbors are for, right?"

"I can't tell you the last time someone brought me dinner," Sophia sighed.

"It's late. I should go," Ari said, edging towards the entrance.

"Right," Sophia said, walking her out.

Ari noted how their footsteps echoed in the house as they walked.

"Goodnight. And thank you, again," Sophia said, walking

with her out to the porch.

Ari smiled. "Any time. Seriously. And tell Percy I hope he feels better soon."

Sophia nodded, crossing her arms against the night chill. "I will."

As Ari drove home and kept replaying the events of the day over and over in her mind - wondering if she had said or done the right things, wondering why she was even helping out her impossible and irritating neighbor to begin with - she also tried to make some sense of the woman, who seemed so unusually docile and tired tonight.

At least it seemed as though they were finally on better footing. Maybe they could, at a minimum, at last get along as neighbors.

As she drove, Ari was also relieved to know that she was returning home to her own tiny third-floor studio apartment situated above a little hardware store. Sophia's house was beautiful, but ridiculously big and empty. Ari liked things to be a little bit cozier. Her old, worn couch, warm wool rug and bed with the quilt on it that her mom had made sounded pretty good right now.

··○··

"Ms. Little, I apologize," Sophia's voice rang out above the din of conversation during the busy rush the next morning at The Little Cafe.

Sophia was ordering an Americano.

"For what?" Ari asked as she worked to fulfill coffee orders on one of the machines, trying to juggle three different requests for espressos and lattes at once.

"For bothering you. It was unprofessional of me to ask you for a favor when you were at work, and send you all the way to my house, no less."

Ari looked up from pouring creamy hot milk into the cups,

surprised. "Forget it. It was no big deal."

"It was a ridiculous thing for me to ask you."

"It wasn't."

"Yes, it was."

Ari used a rag to wipe some errant drips of milk off the counter. "Look," she said, studying Sophia. "I don't do anything I don't want to do. Well, except for pick up tables outside my shop that don't meet city code. But I wanted to help out. I didn't mind. It wasn't a problem."

Sophia pursed her lips.

"I won't ask for anything again," she said, taking the Americano and handing Ari a five dollar bill.

"It's on the house, remember? Neighbors, and free coffee, and all that."

"Just take it. You run a business, not a charity. You can't give away things left and right," Sophia said, practically scolding her.

"I don't," Ari said tersely, but took the money.

"Good day, Ms. Little."

Ari rolled her eyes as she watched Sophia march out of her store.

Ms. Little. After the informality of the previous evening.

And she had been silly enough to think that they had finally made progress.

What an impossible woman.

5
STRAWBERRY TURNOVERS

Percy was back on his feet within a few days, and Ari noticed him once again coming into the cafe regularly after school. He lingered in his usual booth in the corner, playing video games or reading comics, passing the time until his mom finished up work.

Percy still insisted on ordering cinnamon sugar donuts, coconut-caramel squares or any one of Rachel's daily dessert concoctions, but Ari, feeling a bit guilty about promoting so much sugar to the kid, began to push a few more grilled cheeses his way instead.

"Just for you, I'll give you any one of the grilled cheeses on our menu for the same price as a donut," she offered one day.

"I've never seen so many kinds of grilled cheese," Percy said, studying the choices listed on the chalkboard menu. "Um, how about the Nutella grilled cheese?"

"Good choice," Ari said, nodding seriously. "Sourdough bread, banana, cream cheese and Nutella. One of the best recipes Rachel's ever come up with."

Well, maybe it was not exactly a huge step up from a donut after all, Ari thought, but at least it was a little bit more substantial and that assuaged her guilt somewhat. Not that she was one to try to control her customers' eating habits - hell, she could not even control her own less-than-healthy eating habits - but she was definitely starting to get a sort of protective instinct when it came to Percy. At least the sandwich had a bit of fruit in it, right?

As for Percy's mother, to Ari's pleasant surprise, Sophia was following in her son's footsteps and becoming a more regular customer at The Little Cafe.

Now, nearly every day, Sophia came into the cafe in the mornings, ordered an Americano or cafe au lait (or sometimes both) before heading to work. Sophia was always cool and curt and insisted on paying, but Ari couldn't help but smugly take note of how indispensable her coffee seemed to have become in her morning routine.

Once or twice, Ari considered going to see what Sophia's store was all about. But as soon as she stopped in front of the big glass doors leading into the boutique, she always hesitated and jetted away. She had no reason at all to go into the place. She did not like frilly, fussy underthings... and somehow, even if she did need a new pair of underwear or a bra, it seemed way too awkward to get them from Sophia's store. Nope, she would rather just stick to ordering that kind of thing online or picking up something from a big-box discount store.

That was, until a phone call pressed the issue, and Ari decided it was time to suck it up and drop by Sophia's fancy boutique.

..o..

"I'm looking for something... um, still kind of casual, but you know, nice."

Sophia's ears picked up the sound of Ari's voice at the end of the day one Thursday. She had been shuffling through papers in the back room of the shop near the stairs, behind the velvet curtain.

"We just got these in, a brand new design for the spring." Sophia overheard Elle say.

"Fifty dollars for a pair of underwear?" Ari asked, sounding scandalized.

Sophia shook her head as she eavesdropped on the conversation. Go figure. Of course the woman who wore only jeans and t-shirts wouldn't have an appreciation for design, craftsmanship or quality in fashion.

"I understand the concern," She overheard Elle say in her usual easy, sweet way. "I mean, before I worked here, I was a girl who loved a good half-off sale, or 2 bras for $35, that kind of thing. But to add some context, Sophia's regular customers come here because of her exquisite designs, attention to detail, and especially because of the luxurious fabrics she selects. They are carefully chosen for both form and function. They drape beautifully, are silky and elegant, but also comfortable to wear and not too difficult to maintain.

"Yeah, but fifty dollars... seriously?" Ari asked, still hesitating.

"Here, I can suggest something else, over here, you might find these more reasonably priced..."

Sophia decided to emerge from behind the curtain. She was curious about why Ari would come in. To her knowledge, she had never been in the store before. And something about her presence made her nervous. Or suspicious.

"Is it for a special event?" Elle asked Ari.

"Yeah. I'm going out with a friend. Perhaps, well, you know. More than a friend? I don't know. It's complicated."

Well, well, well. Ari did not just live and breathe coffee and pas-

tries, then, Sophia thought to herself.

Ari had not yet noticed Sophia's presence in the shop. Sophia stepped behind the counter and pretended to be rummaging through a binder while she eavesdropped for another minute or two, listening as Elle struggled to get Ari on board with FORBIDDEN lingerie.

"I'm not sure this store is really for me," Ari said apologetically. "I didn't know. I just thought I'd check it out. I'm sorry if I bothered you."

"Not at all," Elle said.

Sophia decided it was time for her to rescue Elle from the impossible situation that was Ari. She walked over to the two women.

"Elle, it's nearly time to close. Feel free to finish up your things for the day," she said.

"Sure," Elle nodded, relieved, and slipped behind the counter and began working on the iPad.

Sophia then turned to Ari. "So, Ms. Little. What a surprise to see you here."

"It's Ari."

Sophia pursed her lips and tapped her toe impatiently.

"Welcome, Ari," she said.

"Nice store you have here. It's... modern. Sophisticated." Ari said, clearly struggling to articulate her thoughts on the store, which were obviously not to her taste.

"Can I help you find something?" Sophia asked politely.

Too politely.

Ari shook her head and took a step back. "I was just browsing. Maybe looking for something, but, um, this isn't really my usual thing to shop for."

"I can help," Sophia said smoothly, growing more confident as Ari tried to timidly back away. "In fact, why don't you come upstairs? It's far more interesting up there, it's where I keep most of my items, new designs, featured pieces on my website, and things that never even make it down here to the shop. We might be able to find something that suits your particular tastes."

Ari reluctantly followed Sophia upstairs, debating to herself whether the way Sophia had said "your particular tastes" was an insult.

"Welcome to the heart of my business," Sophia said, stepping into her workroom to give Ari a bit of a tour. She turned on the light. "It's a little late, my staff have all gone home, but normally we have a few people working here making patterns, sewing prototypes of my new designs or working on custom orders, inventorying fabrics and other bits and pieces, and helping me place orders from our suppliers."

"There's a lot more up here than I expected," Ari said, looking around at the machinery, the mannequins, the endless garments in various states of completion.

"It is a studio, workroom, brainstorming room, and corporate headquarters all in one place," Sophia explained. "But this isn't what I meant to show you, necessarily. I wanted you to see that I have many more pieces. Hopefully pieces that you would be more comfortable with," Sophia said, stepping toward a section of the room that was half-hidden behind heavy velvet floor-to-ceiling curtains.

"You don't need to take the time to do this," Ari said, feeling a bit like she was intruding.

"Nonsense. Actually, your lack of interest in what Elle was showing you downstairs was making me curious. I want to know what you like. For market research. If a woman - a potential client - isn't interested in what I'm selling, I want to know how I can do better."

"I highly doubt I'm your target market," Ari said.

"Perhaps not, but I am still curious, Ms. Little," Sophia said, stepping behind the curtain with rows and rows of clothing racks, pieces of undergarments, bras, camisoles, chemises, pajamas and robes hanging on nearly all of them.

"I only select a few items in my collection to put downstairs in the boutique. Most of my pieces are sold online," she explained.

Ari nodded, feeling supremely out of place. "Makes sense."

"Here," Sophia said, walking over to a small rack, and pulling a few pieces including a simple navy blue bra, a black silk robe, and, to Ari's surprise (and slight relief), a pair of navy blue, long-sleeved satin pajamas that was much closer to her kind of style.

"These are really nice," Ari said, instinctively reaching out to touch the pajama top, which was cool and smooth to her touch, almost like a liquid, she thought.

Sophia smiled proudly.

All around, Ari saw camisoles and brassieres, endless rows of every type and shape of undergarment. Some she understood, but others - like one nearby, with multiple strings that crossed and tied and crisscrossed again - she wouldn't have the least clue about how to put on. Or take off.

"You've got a lot up here," Ari said. "And to think I really only stopped in for a bra that would look decent under the blouse I want to wear tonight."

"Oh. If that's what you're looking for, then here..." Sophia waded into the racks of clothes and picked out a few bras in a variety of colors, covered in lace. Ari had to admit they were pretty, though a bit outside of her comfort zone.

"I'm used to things that are a little less fussy," she admitted.

"This one is our absolute best selling design. Everyone finds it is a flattering fit, and it looks lovely under any kind of clothing," Sophia said.

Ari glanced at the sizes and selected the plainest one.

"I could try this," she said reluctantly.

Sophia pointed her towards a screen that was off to the side of the room.

"Look around. Then you can try anything on behind there," she said. "There's a mirror back there, too."

Sophia left Ari alone with the racks of lingerie, letting her know she would be in her office. Alone in the vast space that still smelled faintly of Sophia's perfume, Ari felt slightly more relaxed as she searched through the endless rows for a few reasonable pieces to try on. In the room nearby, she could hear the muffled sound of Sophia talking on the phone, her shoes click-click-clicking across the floor as she paced.

Ari felt awkward in the space alone. It was strangely intimate, being in the heart of Sophia's world, a world that at once felt creative, a bit provocative, but also, perhaps paradoxically, quite serious.

Intimate was also the obvious way to describe a room full of lingerie. She decided to try on three of the bras she found. Hopefully one would be decent so she could pay for it and get out of there.

She had never afforded herself the luxury of picking out nice undergarments. It was not the worst, Ari thought to herself, trying the pieces on, looking at herself in the mirror.

"Did you find something?" Sophia asked a few minutes later when Ari stepped into Sophia's office with her choices.

She had chosen a bra, and had also held on to the blue satin pajamas.

"I don't think I've ever taken the time to pick out underwear and sleepwear like this," Ari said.

Sophia stood up and they went downstairs.

"Usually I just go to some big box store and grab whatever's on sale, then wear it for, like, 3 years," Ari explained as they walked downstairs.

When they were downstairs, Sophia took the pieces from her and began wrapping them in black tissue paper.

"I love these pajamas," Sophia commented as she wrapped. "I suppose most people assume I wear all of the elaborate, lacy things that I design to bed. But in reality, I wear these most nights."

Ari swallowed heavily.

"You said this is for a special occasion?" Sophia asked casually as she continued to delicately wrap up the pieces.

Ari vaguely noticed that Sophia even had tape with the FORBIDDEN logo printed on it in silver, which she used to close the tissue paper like a present.

Ari nodded. "An old flame asked me to be her date at a wedding this weekend."

Sophia didn't reply, placing the gently wrapped bra and pajamas in a crisp white paper shopping bag with the stark black FORBIDDEN logo printed on front.

"Well. It's a good idea to look your best when seeing old acquaintances," Sophia said matter-of-factly.

"Also a lot of pressure. I want to look better than ever." Ari smiled coyly.

Sophia handed the bag to her.

"I doubt you will have any problem with that," Sophia said, her eye catching Ari's for a flicker of a moment.

Ari sucked in a breath. "What do I owe you?"

"Nothing. It's on the house."

"What? No. You pay for coffee when you come into The Little Cafe.

Sophia shook her head. "You look out for my son. He goes into your cafe all of the time to wait for me."

"But he pays."

"I know. But it means something to me, for you to keep an eye on him. He tells me you do. I think you may have

even started to encourage him to eat more grilled cheeses
and fewer donuts, and for that I am grateful."

"It's nothing."

"It's not nothing. Have a good time on your date," Sophia
said, smiling and pushing the shopping back to her.

Ari sighed, resigned, and took the bag. "Thanks. But I'm
giving you free coffee for at least a week."

"It's a deal, Ms. Little," Sophia said, cracking a smile.

"It's Ari," Ari reminded her with a smile as she left the shop.

··o··

The next night, Sophia was looking out of her upstairs office window absentmindedly, tired after a long day of phone
calls and meetings, when she saw a car pull up and park along
the sidewalk outside The Little Cafe. A pretty dark-haired
woman got out and walked into the cafe. She was wearing
formalwear, which was unusual for the neighborhood, especially on a Friday when people were typically dressed in jeans
for a casual dinner or movie night.

Moments later, the dark haired woman emerged again, accompanied by a chipper and bouncy Ari, also dressed up.

Must be the big date, Sophia thought. They were going to
something formal. A Friday night wedding? Could be.

On Saturday morning, Percy was invited over to a friend's
house and Sophia decided to go into work. She went to The
Little Cafe to get her usual morning coffee. There no Ari in
sight, she noticed, just Rachel this morning.

She chatted with Rachel about the unusually rainy weather
they were having. Rachel was never the warmest or friend-
liest towards her, but she talked with her politely while
navigating the espresso machine, preparing her Americano.
Sophia got out her designer coin purse and paid.

As she turned to walk away with her coffee, she bumped
into a flushed Ari, wearing the same outfit Sophia had seen

her leave in the evening before.

"Oh, hey," Ari said to her. "Good morning."

"And good morning to you," Sophia said brusquely, quickly scanning Ari from head to toe, an eyebrow raised.

"Had to stop in this morning to grab something I left in my office," Ari said to Rachel, although it sounded to Sophia like she was trying to explain to her, too.

"Have a good day," Sophia said sharply and left.

"What's up with her being all judgey this morning?" Rachel asked Ari after Sophia walked out.

Ari shrugged as she ducked behind the bar and then into the back room.

"I know you two have been getting along better lately, but once a bitch, always a bitch," commented Rachel, wiping her hands on a tea towel and following Ari.

Ari didn't reply.

"But enough about her," Rachel said. "I take it you had a good night?"

Ari just smiled.

Rachel grinned, leaning against the doorway of Ari's office, a hand impatiently resting on her hip.

"Spill."

··o··

Sophia didn't go into The Little Cafe for coffee on Monday or Tuesday the next week. But by Wednesday, she had a lack-of-decent-coffee tension headache that was so bad, she gave up, grabbed her coin purse, and dashed down the stairs and into The Little Cafe.

The aroma of perfectly roasted beans, banana bread, chocolate muffins and a slight tinge of cinnamon hit her nose as soon as she walked in, instantly soothing her pounding head.

"Wondered how long you were going to stay away," Ari commented from behind the counter when she noticed

Sophia.

Sophia shrugged. "I've been busy this week."

"When you were busy a few weeks ago, you were in here more often for coffee, not less."

Sophia didn't reply.

"Was something wrong? Did I do something wrong?" Ari asked, narrowing her eyes.

Sophia looked surprised. "No. Why?"

"You haven't come in since Saturday."

"I said I've been busy."

"Last time you were here, Rachel didn't serve you a bad coffee, did she? Or a rancid blueberry muffin or anything?"

"No. Although, now that you mention it, I did try the strawberry turnover last week and it was subpar."

"Oh, so that's it. Subpar strawberry turnover," Ari said.

Sophia shook her head and crossed her arms. "There has been no such thing keeping me away. But since you brought it up, I should tell you that you don't do pastry crust well. It's not tender and flaky like it should be. It's far too rubbery and chewy."

"Rubbery and chewy?" Ari asked, indignant, but also somewhat playful. "Really? Are you some sort of expert, or...?"

Sophia shook her head. "I'm not an expert, but I know how to make a decent turnover. And yours is not a decent turnover."

"Okay, then. I'll give you free coffee for another week if you come in and show me how to make a tender, flaky turnover."

"Really?" Sophia asked.

Ari nodded. "I'm curious to know what a non-subpar strawberry turnover tastes like. Be my guest."

"Well then. I suppose I could come over tonight after work, if that suits you?"

..o..

Sophia was not sure what, exactly, had possessed her to suddenly be such a crusader for strawberry turnovers. But that evening, she wrapped things up at work around 7pm and headed over to The Little Cafe. The cafe was closed, but despite the CLOSED sign, Ari had left the door unlocked for her.

Sophia found Ari in her small back office, typing something on her laptop.

"I'm here for your strawberry turnover lessons, Ms. Little," she said.

"All right, I'm ready to learn," Sophia said, smiling gamely, although both women sensed that the meeting had been a bit of a silly concept, and now felt slightly awkward about the whole thing.

Ari, trying to diffuse some of the awkwardness, spoke up. "I should give you a bit of a behind-the-scenes tour while you're here. You've already seen my little office. Next are two exciting pantries, one for Rachel's baked goods and another that's basically just my coffee bean storage room."

"That smells delicious," Sophia said when Ari showed her the coffee-bean storage pantry, which was about the size of a small walk-in closet.

"It's my favorite smell in the world," Ari said proudly, her long blonde hair, which was tied up in a ponytail, swinging as she moved around, pointing things out to Sophia.

"Next up, this is where all of the magic happens. The kitchen," she said, and they walked into a small kitchen, Ari clicking on the lights as they entered.

"Welcome to my world. It's not bras and bustiers, but if you don't mind endless jars of coffee beans and mixers and kitchen implements, it's not a bad place to be. It's a bit of a cross between the messiest apartment kitchen you've ever been in, and a mad scientist's laboratory. Rachel's really into experimenting with her recipes, and I'm... well, I'm sorta messy."

"It's nice," Sophia said, gazing around at the small but cheerful room, which had white tile countertops, a clean white tile floor, and light blue walls.

On one of the walls there was a poster advertising the best cupcakes in Palo Rosa. Sophia wondered if it was from Ari's mother's shop.

"So," Ari said, handing Sophia an apron and then grabbing one for herself. "How did you become such a strawberry turnover expert?"

"It's a bit of a story," she said, tying on the apron over her white blouse and slim black trousers.

"By the way, help yourself to whatever you need. Flour and sugar are over there." Ari directed.

Sophia busied herself opening up drawers and cupboards, roaming around the small kitchen, gathering the things she needed. Then she explained her expertise on the subject at hand.

"Growing up, part of my parents' yard was filled with strawberries every spring and summer. And so every year my mother had to come up with a million ways to use them up. Or rather, she ordered the maid to come up with a million ways to use them up. It was my father who once suggested strawberry turnovers as an alternate to the endless string of strawberry pies and berry crisp, and together we figured out a good recipe. He has an innate sense for how to make a tender and flaky pastry dough. After several attempts, we perfected the right blend of ingredients for the filling, and ever since then we've made these great turnovers that were better than any pie or crisp recipe we'd ever tasted."

Sophia had begun pulling ingredients off of metal shelves around the room and the fridge. She arranged all of the ingredients on the counter and turned to Ari.

"What I will mainly focus on tonight is the pastry. The filling is easy enough. We'll do that second."

As they worked, they chatted.

"In general, do you think the food is good here?" Ari asked Sophia at one point.

"Sure," Sophia said. "What I've had so far I thought was good. Certainly above and beyond typical coffee shop fare."

"It doesn't sell all that well. Keeping all of the food and snack items in stock has kind of become a money drain," Ari admitted. "I just wondered if it was the selection we're offering, or a quality thing, or what."

"Running a business is a lot of trial and error I've found," Sophia said. "The important thing is to be really in tune with what customers want. If something isn't selling well, or if there seems to be a loss of interest or generally lackluster interest in anything, drop it, and try something different. Don't keep pushing stuff on customers and hoping they'll eventually fall in love with it. They have too many other choices out there and are unlikely to change their minds."

"How do you do it? I mean, keep track of everything involved in running a business. I knew it would be a lot of work before I got started, but really, I had no idea it would be like this," Ari asked.

Sophia nodded. "I remember thinking that. Keep a pulse on what your customers like, what seems to be going right, and focus on that - try to make the most money off of whatever's working - and stay flexible and willing to experiment with everything else."

Ari bit her bottom lip, deep in thought.

"It seems you're doing well for a new business," Sophia said, rolling out dough with a white rolling pin.

"It may seem like that," Ari said, watching Sophia's hands

as she worked, "But that's not totally the case."

Sophia gave her a smile and touched her lightly on the shoulder. "I assume you're being too hard on yourself. It's difficult, the first year or two of a business. It does get easier."

They continued working on the turnovers. Sophia walked Ari though each step, and Ari (with Sophia's blessing) wrote down notes throughout the process.

An hour later, Ari and Sophia were sitting at the counter on two wobbly wooden barstools, devouring the perfect, tender, flaky pastries. The kitchen smelled divine: warm, with the aroma of buttery pastry and the sweet smell of strawberries, comforting aromas that enveloped the space.

As they sat, chatting easily, any earlier tensions from conversations prior to that evening seemed to have dissipated.

And perhaps even more disarmingly, Sophia's mind kept lingering on some of the things that had happened while they were talking and baking.

Like the way Ari had watched her a beat too long from time to time throughout the evening: instead of writing down notes or watching carefully what was happening in the mixing bowl, she had caught Ari's eyes dwelling on her as she spoke.

At one point, noting that Ari was once again looking up at her instead of in the bowl, where she was showing her how to properly cut in butter for the crust, Sophia, slightly thrown off by the attention, had accidentally knocked a small bowl of salt off the counter.

"It's no big deal," Ari had assured her, bending down to pick up the bowl, laughing lightly as Sophia apologized.

"It's nothing. Keep going," Ari urged the woman.

So Sophia tucked a strand of hair behind her ear and continued.

As she worked throughout the evening, Sophia had the

distinct sense that Ari was frequently distracted.

However, Sophia was not entirely a victim in the situation, either. Once or twice, she had caught herself subconsciously allowing her hand to linger over Ari's, or brushing her shoulder as she reached past her for a spoon.

Each time they brushed shoulders or hands in a way that was a bit more intimate than either had consciously intended, there were quick blushes, hands that were pulled back quickly, and nervous glances away, as if by pretending that nothing was happening, that would make it so.

And somehow, despite their increasingly distracted moods, the turnovers were finally finished nearly two hours later.

"These are by far the best turnovers I've ever had," Ari stated as they sampled the final product in the kitchen.

"I'm glad you like them."

"I'll definitely be sharing this recipe with Rachel. Thank you so much for this."

"Did you get everything written down accurately?" Sophia asked, raising an eyebrow at the general direction of Ari's notepad with her chicken-scratch notes.

"I think so. But if not, you'll just have to come over sometime and bake them again," she said, smiling coyly and taking a second bite.

Sophia smiled, the first truly relaxed, open, kind smile Ari had seen from the woman. Her face was beautiful - completely radiant - when she smiled like that.

"Running a successful business, cooking perfect turnovers, being a single mom, being mayor, looking flawless all of the time even when cooking... is there anything you can't do right?" Ari asked, half-joking as she bit into a second turnover.

"There's a lot that I don't manage to be very good at," Sophia said quietly, dropping her eyes.

Ari laughed lightly. "I don't believe it."

"It's not... well, never mind, you wouldn't want to hear it," Sophia said hesitantly.

"What?" Ari asked. "You can't just say that and stop talking."

Sophia sighed.

"Well, in a nutshell, when I was younger, I thought I could do it all. Raise Percy - I had him when I was 23, right in the middle of grad school - and for a while, I did. I went to school, I raised him, I had internships or worked. I started my own business. But along the way, I let things go. I wasn't always perfect. And lately, as FORBIDDEN has grown, I've taken advantage of the fact that Percy is older and I leave him alone more. I'm not keeping up with everything like I used to. It's an impossible cause and effect situation. The more FORBIDDEN grows, the more the rest of my life suffers. Especially Percy."

"Oh," Ari said, her face growing serious. "Perhaps it's just temporary? Growing pains for the business?"

"Perhaps. But I don't think so. I'm choosing to do this all on my own, but sometimes I don't know if it's the right choice, especially when Percy is the victim," she confessed.

Ari stood up to refill her small coffee cup, and refilled Sophia's at the same time.

"So, maybe you should cut back?" Ari prompted.

Sophia looked at Ari with pursed lips, considering. "I don't know. But I know I can't be a good mother to Percy while I spend all of this time being devoted to work."

"You're not the first woman to have to try to balance parenthood with a flourishing career."

Sophia nodded, then cleared her throat.

"Anyways, enough about that. Thank you. Tonight was nice," Sophia said, splashing a bit of milk into the coffee. "It was fun getting a glimpse behind the scenes here."

"Likewise," Ari said.

"I miss having someone to talk to. You know, someone who is not an employee. You've reminded me of that tonight, Ms. Little."

Ari cringed at the continued formality. "It was fun. But considering we just spent a few hours baking up a storm, could you at least stop calling me Ms. Little?"

Sophia looked at her, their eyes meeting. Ari shifted slightly. Sophia blinked once, then nodded to herself.

"Ari," Sophia said softly, her name rolling off her tongue.

They were quiet for a moment. Ari wondered if that had been the right move, to ask Sophia to call her Ari. When she did, it felt as though there was a strange intimacy to it. It sounded odd to her, after so long of hearing Sophia call her "Ms. Little."

"Is Ari short for something?" Sophia asked, breaking the silence.

"Arianna. It's a weird name, I know," she added quickly. "My parents have always been into really romantic stories and romantic things, so they gave me a name that sounds like some kind of princess."

Sophia smiled, amused, imagining what it might have been like for the serious, straightforward, girl-next-door, no-frills woman before her to grow up with a mother who liked elaborate, girly names and aspired to run a cupcake shop.

"Arianna is a very pretty name," Sophia said.

When she said her full name, the word rolled off even more easily on her tongue.

"It is, but I've never thought it was me," Ari admitted. "My mom liked sweet, girly things. Arianna was the perfect name for her little girl, or so she thought. Unfortunately for her, though, I turned out to be a little more of a down to earth, tomboy, get my nails dirty kind of girl."

"I've never heard Ari used as a shortened form of Arianna," Sophia said.

"Growing up, my friends kind of condensed Arianna to Ari, and it stuck. Well, it stuck with everyone but my parents, who still call me Arianna."

"I also prefer 'Arianna,'" Sophia said. "There's something to be said for classic, elegant names. And it's not too girly. There's something strong and dignified about it."

"Thank you," Ari said, her blue eyes meeting Sophia's. "Although I still don't know if an elegant and dignified name is right for me."

"You are elegant, Ms. Little. *Arianna*," Sophia said.

It did sound like a strong name when Sophia said it aloud.

After she spoke, Sophia became acutely aware of the empty kitchen, and the empty cafe. The only sound was of the light music playing softly from a speaker that Ari had turned on in the kitchen while they had worked. That, and the ticking of the clock.

"I need to go soon," Sophia said quietly. "Back to Percy. But let me help you clean up."

Ari stood up and moved around the kitchen, putting a few things they'd used - a spatula, a small bowl - into the dishwasher.

Sophia helped load the dishwasher.

"So. I taught you how to make a decent turnover. I hope that by now perhaps I've atoned for some prior inconveniences that I may have caused to your young business," Sophia said.

"Hah. You were not the best neighbor I could've asked for at first, but I've gotta admit, this is starting to make up for it," Ari said, pleased to have finally reached a detente with this woman.

Sophia watched as Ari dipped her index finger into the remaining crumbs that were on her plate and quickly licked them off. Then, she put the plate in the dishwasher. She closed the machine and pressed the button to start it.

The dishes under control, Ari crossed her arms, leaned her back against the counter, and glanced at the clock. "I didn't realize how late it had gotten."

Sophia followed her eyes to the clock.

"No, me neither," she agreed quietly, her eyes flickering to her purse and coat.

Ari was about to offer to walk her out, but as she opened her mouth to speak, their eyes met again. This time, it felt to both women like an invisible thread was connecting them in that instant. Stranger yet, that thread carried a strong, profound vibration, almost like an electrical current.

The resulting heat Sophia felt when Ari's eyes met hers caused Sophia to hold her breath for a moment.

She impulsively shifted forward, moving a step closer to Ari.

Ari took a breath, and raised her hands, almost as if to welcome her in an embrace, but stopped mid-air.

Having closed that space, Sophia was now most definitely too close to Ari to mean anything other than what she wanted to do most in that moment.

Ari's eyes were still on hers, searching.

"I apologize for making your first weeks here so irritating, Arianna. Is there..." she whispered, her eyes flickering down to Ari's lips "...anything I can do to make up for it?"

Ari looked at her, her eyes growing wider, but she did not reply.

Sophia's eyes softened and darkened, and she leaned forward, hesitantly, but just enough to make her intentions clear. Just enough to allow Ari to pull away, to step back, for both of them to pretend nothing had happened, if that was the way Ari wanted things to be.

A few long seconds passed.

Ari did not move in the slightest. Instead, she took a breath, her eyes scanning Sophia's face, making sure she had read the situation correctly.

And when Ari swayed forward the tiniest millimeter instead of stepping back or turning away, Sophia made her decision in a fraction of an instant.

Every ounce of Sophia's body was suddenly a magnet, pulled into Ari, and without thinking or questioning any of it, the two were joined as one as their lips locked.

Sophia's senses were overwhelmed: by Ari's lips, soft, open, by the feel of her in her arms, her hair twining through her fingers, the faintest scent of lavender on her skin, her soft skin. Sophia wanted to press her against the wall, have her entirely at her mercy, but to her surprise, it was Ari who suddenly took over and drove their next movements, and so Sophia let her take control.

Lips still locked, Sophia surrendered as Ari steered her toward a wall, and moments later, she felt her back pressed up against it, her eyes still closed as Ari took a hold of her wrists and gently, so softly, but with confidence, pressed them at shoulder level against the wall. Sophia surrendered to the surprising - but welcome - gesture, shuddering slightly at the sensation of Ari's firm yet tender strength, and they kissed longer, time standing still. The clock stopped ticking. Nothing mattered except for the two of them, there, at that moment, simply existing.

When the two finally, reluctantly, pulled apart, Ari ran her hands down Sophia's side. Her fingertip began at her shoulder, tracing a line down her arm, side, and her hip, where she finally, reluctantly, lifted her fingers into the air and brought them back to her own side.

Sophia let out a soft breath right as Ari's touch lifted, and Ari smiled dreamily. Both fully opened their eyes, at last, the haze in the room that had enveloped them both gradually dissipating into the night.

Sophia's eyes were wide and brown, still slightly stunned by Ari's warm reception of her rash, impulsive decision. Her lips parted slightly and she brushed a strand of hair off of her face, holding eye contact with Ari the whole time. The way she moved, the way she melted her back against the wall, her expression dreamlike, it was clear that Sophia desired more.

Ari's expression, however, was surprisingly nonchalant, as though what had just happened was totally expected, her eyes relaxed and her mouth turned into a slight grin.

Finally, to break the silence that hung in the air after they both recovered, Ari spoke.

"That was..." she started softly.

"I have to go-" Sophia interrupted, her eyes returning to normal, as if she managed to pull herself out of the dream world that they had both accidentally wandered into minutes before.

She turned so that her back was to Ari and delicately wiped her mouth where her red lipstick had smeared slightly.

She walked out of the kitchen.

"I need to go home," she said firmly, and Ari followed her out into the cafe, where she watched as Sophia put on her coat.

"Okay," Ari said, standing in the middle of the cafe and watching helplessly as Sophia swung her purse over her shoulder.

Ari pushed her hands into her pockets.

"Goodnight," Sophia said, giving her a quick, almost silly looking, half-wave.

Sophia left the cafe, the bell on the door rattling slightly in her wake, signaling that the night was over.

6

FAMILY BUSINESS

Every time the door chimed the next morning, Ari looked up, expecting a woman in a sleek black pencil skirt, silk blouse, and mile-high heels to walk in. A few times, when she spotted a brunette out of the corner of her eye, her pulse raced a bit, and she would look up and notice it was, alas, not the brunette she wanted to see.

By 9:15, Ari realized that the one individual she hoped to see more than anyone else was not going to stop in. At least not that morning. Sophia usually came in for her morning coffee and beelined towards her work well before 9. Ari's stomach sank, disappointed.

Yet she was not surprised.

After all - as she had reasoned most of the night and early into the morning when she finally got up after a less-than-restful sleep - there could not be any way that the woman had been into what had happened last night. Their connection had been an impulse, a whim, a momentary thing, and it had probably already dissipated. Or, perhaps, there had not even been a connection at all. Maybe Ari had just imagined the spark.

It had been a weird, wonderful, awkward, amazing moment... that evaporated as quickly as it had materialized.

It was not like Ari could figure it out, anyways. The attraction. Well, okay, fine. She sort of understood it. She understood that she was attracted to the woman. Something about the way Sophia held herself. She was confident, smart, successful, stern, maddening... yeah, the whole package, basically. She had a few drawbacks - Rachel was right, she could be harsh and difficult - but she had other assets.

She *definitely* had other assets.

By the mid-morning lull, sometime around 10:30, well after Ari had given up any thought that she would be seeing Sophia that day, the front door opened and in she walked.

Sophia was wearing a simple grey sheath dress and a sophisticated black trench coat with conservative heels. No tight pencil skirt or killer heels today, but the way she was carrying herself - focused and serious and confident and, well, enchanting - Ari struggled not to stare.

"The usual?" Ari asked casually as Sophia reached the counter.

Ari desperately wanted the interaction to be normal. She wanted to give Sophia a chance to see that things could be fine between them. Relaxed. They never needed to acknowledge...anything. Not if she did not want to.

It was not like Ari was not experienced in this domain, after all. She had had plenty of little, frivolous flings in her day. Stolen kisses or heated touches that had seemed like a good idea at the moment but, later, were simply not meant to be.

"Yes, thank you," Sophia replied simply, not meeting Ari's eyes.

Ari got to work making her Americano. She watched

Sophia out of her peripheral vision as she worked. Sophia was, in typical Sophia fashion, glued to her phone as she waited.

Ari was paranoid that the woman would dash away again like a skittish cat in the night. Who knows when she would reappear if she did that. However, when she searched her mind for things to say, she could not think of anything that might be remotely charming or alluring. Mid-day in the cafe after a busy morning with a brain that had not had much sleep the night before was not exactly a prime moment for her to come up with clever conversation.

So, Ari tried as hard as she could to act normal. Just make the coffee, pour it into the paper cup, put a lid on it, a sleeve, and...

When she set it down on the counter, Sophia had the exact change ready and waiting.

"It's complimentary," Ari said.

Sophia pushed the money toward her. "I insist."

Ari shook her head in defeat, and took the money. "Have a good day Sophia."

"You too, Ms. Little."

So. They were back to that Ms. Little thing.

Ari dropped the cash Sophia had paid her into the tip jar for Rachel and Athena to split up at the end of the day. Then, she began zealously wiping down the counter around the espresso machine, where there were tons of tiny coffee grounds that had spilled that morning.

"That was weird," Rachel commented as she put a tray of raspberry-lemon muffins into the refrigerated case near the cash register, stocking up before the lunch crowds began.

"It was nothing," Ari grumbled.

"No banter? Quippy remarks? What's going on with you two? You act like..." Rachel stopped, studied Ari, who started to focus even harder on gathering up every last one of the pesky coffee grounds.

"No," she said quietly, her jaw dropping open. "Did... you two... did something happen?"

"Sssh," Ari hissed, scowling.

"It did," Rachel said in an incredulous whisper. "What... why?! And when?"

"Keep it down," Ari whispered, and then steered a half-surprised, half-laughing Rachel into the back.

"Seriously? With her?" Rachel asked, her eyes wide.

"I don't really want to talk about it. You're just gonna judge."

"Oh come on. I am not. The woman might be a royal pain in the ass, but look at her... well, ass. I can't really hold it against you. Plus, she designs lingerie. That's kinda hot, my friend."

Ari did not respond to that.

"So what happened?" Rachel prodded again.

Ari sighed, defeated. "She came in yesterday, complaining about the strawberry turnovers, and she offered to show me how she makes her family's vastly superior turnover recipe. Then she came back last night, after closing, and we baked and talked. It was nice. Friendly."

"You baked together," Rachel teased. "What a nice little domestic scene from a romantic comedy you two must have made."

Ari cringed. "Well, when you say it like that, it sounds really lame. But it was actually pretty interesting. She made a great batch of turnovers. And then, well..."

Rachel raised her eyebrows. "Wow. Wait, here? On the-"

Ari held up a hand. "No, not that. Nothing happened. Nothing... much. Not *that* much."

Rachel leaned against the counter and laughed. "Fine, but

how long until it does?"

"Not really any of your business, is it?" Ari muttered.

"It's not, but... you don't seem overly happy about it. Did she have second thoughts or something?" Rachel pressed.

Ari shook her head and crossed her arms, her eyes darting to the door where Sophia had left a few minutes ago. "I dunno. She seemed... eager to escape. And, well, she came in just now, which is good, but based on the way she just acted, she clearly wants to ignore that anything ever happened. I don't know what to do next. If anything."

Rachel nodded sympathetically. "Give it a day or two. Let it settle in, then go back to her and suggest you two go out somewhere, away from work, so you can talk."

Ari nodded, then glanced out towards the cafe.

"Speaking of work, we've gotta get back out there," Ari said, snapping back into boss mode. "The lunch crowd's going to start soon."

··o··

Ari was distracted the rest of the day. She screwed up three orders, which were three more than she normally got wrong. Luckily, Rachel was the world's best employee and picked up some of the slack while Ari plodded through the remainder of the day.

Sophia came in the next morning, and their interaction was similar. The following day would be Saturday, and Ari was not sure Sophia would be in again until Monday. Too antsy to wait a few more days, Ari decided to go over to FORBIDDEN and see if she could invite her out for a bite to eat on the weekend. Nothing too threatening - lunch, maybe, or even just a drink - and she would make it clear that they could go as friends. She just wanted to clear the air.

On Friday night, she asked Athena to close up so she could do something rare: leave early.

When Ari stepped into Sophia's shop, she saw that the merchandise had changed over, and the decor was fresh and pretty. There were little pots of grass and orchids set throughout the store. It looked brighter than usual.

"Good evening," a man wearing a suit and a narrow tie said as Ari stepped in. She had seen the man stop in The Little Cafe a few times. Seth, she thought his name was.

"Can I help you find anything?" he asked.

"Actually, I was just wondering if Sophia's still around?"

"She's upstairs, but her sister dropped by, so it might not be the best-"

As he spoke, Ari heard voices in the stairs. There was the sound of a shrill, almost sickly-sweet voice of a woman mixed with the familiar, lower, and much more even-toned sound of Sophia speaking.

"But you have to come this weekend, it's my bridal shower luncheon. And then after that I hope you're planning my bachelorette weekend. You do know my wedding is coming up, and you are my maid of honor-" the high-pitched woman giggled, "-and so you must plan something truly wicked for my last weekend as a single woman."

"I highly doubt it will be your last weekend ever as a single woman," Sophia grumbled.

The woman clutched her heart as they reached the bottom of the stairs, her mouth popping open dramatically. "How utterly unromantic and sad for you that you think that's how all marriages go, doomed for failure. Not all of our love lives follow your dismal patterns, sis."

"I'm not the one who is on my third marriage, Sabrina," Sophia said, a hand on her hip.

"Oh, those were just to test the waters. This one is for real," Sabrina said, waving the comment off.

Sophia rolled her eyes. "Right. Well, this is also bridal

shower luncheon number three, and bachelorette weekend number four..."

"Four?" Sabrina asked.

"Don't you remember? When you were going to run off and elope with... whatshisface... you made us throw you a bachelorette party before you left. And then you met the person who actually ended up as husband number one that night."

"Oh, yes," Sabrina said wistfully. "Those were simpler times..."

"I really don't have time to go to your bridal shower this weekend. Sabrina, I hardly see Percy as it is," Sophia said.

"And whose fault is that? You're the one working all of the time. I can't control the 52 weekends a year you do that. All I am asking for is one weekend."

"Working is productive. Sitting around with obscure relatives watching you get more gifts you don't need is not."

Sabrina scowled. "Come this weekend, or I'll get mother involved. And you and I both know you don't want to endure a painful call from our mother."

Ari, who was pretending to look through a row of short silk robes, cringed as she heard Sabrina speak to Sophia. Sabrina was clearly a real piece of work. She did not have siblings, but if she did... ugh. She did not think anyone deserved to have a sister who was so rude.

She guessed the brash, abrasive nature ran in the family. A few months ago, she could not have imagined someone more abrasive than Sophia. But this auburn-haired woman was a serious contender.

"Fine," Sophia conceded. "I'll do it. But under one condition: this is the last time. The last shower luncheon I'll attend, the last bachelorette party I'll plan, and the last wedding of yours I'll ever be at!"

"Honestly, sis, it's sad you're not more of a romantic. You won't need to attend any more, because this will be my last wedding. William and I will have beautiful children, with little green eyes like mine and blonde curls like his..."

"Spare me the details. Let's take it one step at a time," Sophia interrupted.

"Oh, and don't forget, you still need to find a date for my wedding. Time's running out, sis! Let me know if you want me to give cousin Phil a call," she laughed to herself as she was distracted by emerald green silk slips on a table. She delicately held one up.

"I quite like this, sis. Not bad," she said.

Sophia watched her warily.

"80 dollars," she said.

"This would be the perfect gift for you to give me for my bridal shower, then," Sabrina grinned.

"Maybe," Sophia said.

"Be a dear and wrap it up, won't you?" she carried it to the desk.

"I haven't decided if I'm going to give you that yet," Sophia said through gritted teeth.

"Oh, that's all right. Everyone knows you aren't good at making decisions, so I'll make one for you. You are giving me this, and I'll take it with me today. William should enjoy getting a preview of what the wedding night will be like..."

Ari cringed as she pretended to study the sleeve of a floral-patterned robe. What was up with this woman?

Sophia silently took the silk slip and wrapped it in black tissue and placed it in one of her crisp white paper shopping bags.

Sabrina giggled as Sophia handed it to her. "Lovely. Thank you ever so much. I'll see you this weekend at mummy's house."

The awful woman finally left the shop.

After she had gone, Sophia let out an audible sigh of relief.

"Dreadful woman," Seth muttered.

"Tell me about it," Sophia said, pulling a bottle of water out from underneath the counter and taking a sip.

"What was that she was saying about your cousin Phil?" Seth asked.

Sophia shook her head. "She likes to tease me about it. It's stupid. He's not really my - our - cousin. He might be a distant relative, tough to say. He's this man who is in his, I don't know, late 40s, lives at home, twice divorced, he's odd and we used to make fun of him when we were kids. She always threatens to make me go out with him. Finds it hilarious, for whatever reason."

"She's a real piece of work," Seth said, shaking his head.

Sophia cleared her throat, turning her attention to the blonde who had tried to make herself invisible in the far corner of the store while she was talking to her sister.

"Ms. Little. We're closing soon. Can I help you find something?" Sophia said, a bit of the usual edge missing in her voice.

Ari stopped looking through the robes. That damn "Ms. Little" thing again. Like nothing at all had happened between them.

She took a breath. "I just dropped in to..."

Her voice trailed off as she glanced towards Seth, who was looking at her and listening closely.

Sophia caught her drift.

"Seth, I just remembered there are a few parcels that I need to drop off at the post office on my way home. Would you mind running upstairs and getting them off my desk?" she asked him, smiling a little too widely.

He nodded. "Of course."

After they waited for Seth to disappear upstairs, Ari stepped closer to Sophia.

"I wanted to know if you'd have a little time this weekend to go somewhere and talk. For lunch, coffee, a drink, whatever. As friends."

"Well, as you heard, I have a social engagement this weekend. Between that, and work, and Percy, I don't know if I will have any spare time."

Ari nodded sympathetically. "Sure, but-"

Sophia interrupted her, continuing. "You can be certain, however, that I will have time to go out for a drink after my sister's dreadful shower/bridal lunch/whatever it is on Saturday. I like to go to a place called Alice's. It's on the coast. And should you also happen to be there, on Saturday, at around 5, for a drink... you'd be more than welcome to join me."

"That sounds like a plan," Ari said, surprised.

She had been prepared to have to convince Sophia a little more than that.

"Good. I'll text you an hour or so before I leave. Perhaps I will see you then, Ms. Little."

"Yeah, perhaps," Ari said.

..o..

On Saturday evening, Ari sat alone at Alice's, an unusual place that was at once quirky and classy. The bar was in a Victorian house with peculiar decorations and a sort of Alice in Wonderland theme. Unusual choice of decor aside, it was actually a pretty decent place. There was live folk music and a small menu of unique drinks, interesting yet not overly fussy. It was not, however, the type of hangout she would have guessed Sophia liked - she envisioned black and white, pianos, martinis, jazz and James Bond doppelgängers at the type of place Sophia might frequent - not this strange, fairy

tale-inspired, off-the-beaten-path hangout. At least the location was beautiful: Alice's was positioned at the end of a little
drive that overlooked a quiet, rocky beach.

Ari ordered a drink while she waited for Sophia, choosing
a Manhattan. It ended up being one of the best drinks she
had had in a long time.

She could not quite relax, though, questioning why she was
even bothering to meet Sophia like this. The events from
"the baking incident" - as she now referred to it in her mind -
continued to preoccupy her. They way they had laughed and
talked, got along so easily, haunted her. The way Sophia had
at one point spilled some flour on her sleeve, and then later
had dropped the salt on the floor, apologizing profusely. Ari
had been entranced by the strong, successful businesswoman
in her kitchen, taking baking so seriously, and it had been
endearing to her that her activities in the kitchen had not
been quite as sleek and polished as she usually carried herself
in the rest of her life. She was natural that night, normal. Ari
thought of the music they had been listening to, the amazing
way the kitchen smelled as they were baking the turnovers,
and later, after they ate, the way Sophia's eyes had locked on
hers as she leaned in...

Then, she thought of how Sophia had rushed out the door
and acted like nothing at all had happened the rest of the
week.

As Ari waited, she decided something. She was not going
to trail after this woman and put up with all of her erratic
behavior. No, Ari had had her fair share of dramatic relationships in the past, and was not going to get involved in
any more. She was at the cusp of tunring 30; she did not need
it anymore.

This conversation was going to tell her what she wanted
to know. Whether Sophia was genuinely interested in the

- whatever it was - that was going on, or if they should just pull the breaks and stop while they were still, more or less, ahead.

As Ari sipped her drink and mindlessly scrolled through her phone, she wondered what the odds were that the woman would actually show up. With every passing minute after 5pm, she figured her chances got lower and lower.

Until at last a leather purse was set gently in front of her, and she looked up from her phone to see a certain brunette sitting down at the table with her.

"Sorry I'm late," Sophia said, and as she ran a hand through her hair, Ari could see that the woman genuinely did look sorry. And tired.

"No worries," Ari said calmly, catching the eye of a waiter and passing her the off-white textured paper that the drinks menu was printed on. "Looks like you could use it."

Sophia smiled wearily, and glanced down at the choices.

A waiter came, wearing a purple shirt and a strange top hat. Sophia ordered a cider.

"The cider is very good here," Sophia explained. "It's from an orchard run by the family of the gentleman who owns this place."

Ari nodded, and held up her own glass, which was almost entirely ice at this point. "I believe it. This is a good drink. Or rather, was a good drink."

The waiter brought the cider.

"I like it here," Ari commented. "Quirky theme, but fun I guess."

"The service is also good here. As is the view," Sophia said, glancing out the window.

It was just getting dark.

"That it is," Ari agreed, not looking out the window at all, instead looking at the person across from her.

Sophia missed it.

Ari cleared her throat and sat up a little straighter. "How was your day?"

Sophia sighed. "It was... a day. My family is a real handful. But Sabrina had a good bridal shower luncheon, so that has been successfully accomplished, and we can all move on to the bachelorette party, which I have to plan as her Maid of Honor. It is not, in fact, an honor to do so."

"What are you going to do?" Ari asked, absently swirling the ice in her glass with the straw.

Sophia shrugged. "Have a party. Food, bartenders, hire a DJ. I'll have to get Percy out of the house, perhaps he can stay with a friend. I suppose I'll have to find something... scandalous. Like-"

Sophia cringed, "-exotic dancers."

"Ohhhkay," Ari said, sitting up straighter. "First of all, you've seen a lot of 90s movies if you think that's how a bachelorette party's supposed to go. Secondly, I highly doubt you want a bunch of your sister's drunk friends, DJs, bartenders and exotic dancers in your house. You'll be cleaning and repairing things from now until your sister's fourth and fifth weddings, and that's assuming your house'll even survive the ordeal in the first place."

Sophia took a sip of her cider and considered that information.

Ari continued. "Secondly, I take it your sister's a bit of a diva? Bridezilla type?"

"That's an understatement," Sophia confirmed.

"All right. Well, I'm assuming she's got some big expectations for her bachelorette. These things are destination events now, not wine and cheese parties at a home in the 'burbs. You've got to go someplace. It should be a whole weekend deal."

"My sister's entire adult life has been one giant party, blowing her money on vacations and restaurants and bars and clubs. An extravagant bachelorette party is not something she needs," Sophia protested.

Ari shrugged. "Ultimately it's your call. I'm just saying, I've seen some pretty crazy and elaborate bachelorette parties in my day."

"You've known a lot of bachelorettes?" Sophia asked.

"Not personally. Not really. It's just in my former line of work, I kind of had to deal with situations that included bachelorette parties."

"Right. Well then," Sophia said, sipping her cider and thinking. "You've given me a lot to consider."

"It's not like you don't have enough on your plate. I can imagine planning this is the last thing you want to do," Ari said, reading her mind.

"It is. I have some big meetings coming up in the next couple of weeks, and I might have to travel a bit. A bachelorette party - pardon me, a destination bachelorette party - is about the last thing I want to plan."

"You know, I could talk to Rachel. She's always talking about how she wants to start her own party planning business someday. I know she's thrown some killer bachelorette parties for friends, and this might be a good opportunity for her to cut her teeth on a professional level, so to speak. That is, if you'd be interested in someone else taking over and doing all the party planning."

"Yes," Sophia said, perking up at the idea. "Yes, I'm very interested. Tell Rachel I'll pay her literally anything if she would just take this off of my hands and mind."

Ari raised her eyebrows. "Anything? Okay, well, I'm sure she'd be really glad to do it, then."

Sophia ignored that comment, thinking. "My family also

has access to a private jet that we could use for the weekend. So the destination really isn't a problem, as long as the flight isn't too long. It's a shared jet, so I don't think we could get it for more than 3 or 4 days."

"Uh... okay. Well, that gives us even more options," said Ari.

Private jet? What kind of family was this? Ari wondered to herself.

"This is supposed to happen the weekend after next. Is that enough time for her to plan everything?" Sophia asked.

"That's really last minute. I'll check with Rachel, but if anyone could do it, it would be her."

"Good," Sophia said, all business, and taking another sip of her drink. "Then it's settled. Tell Rachel to name her price and give me a call as soon as she gets the chance and we'll get started."

"Consider it done," Ari said.

The waiter brought her a second Manhattan.

"So," Ari said slowly. "Moving on to another topic. I wanted to see you. Just, you know, to make sure things are ok between us."

Sophia shifted in her seat and licked her lips nervously. Her eyes darted towards the door.

"Everything's fine," she said, trying to act casual, taking a sip of cider.

"Really?" Ari asked, lowering her voice, "Because I don't really get the sense that things have been fine after, you know, the other night."

Sophia looked at her with eyes that were soft and brown and conflicted. She took a breath.

Ari braced herself for what was coming.

"Ari, I appreciate having you around. As a neighbor, as someone who makes excellent coffee, as a person who generously keeps an eye on my son every once in a while when I'm stuck in endless meetings or am late getting out of work. I don't want to jeopardize that. And getting to know me on a more intimate level... could jeopardize that."

"I see," Ari said, nodding, more than getting the hint.

Ari took a sip of the drink. It was stronger than the last one.

"Is there someone else?" she asked a few moments later.

Sophia shook her head. "No, of course not. I don't want to have anything with anyone, in fact. Not now. Not when I'm busy, and have Percy, and have my work, and I'm going to need to start traveling more soon. It's not right for my life right now."

Ari nodded solemnly, looking at her, cool and polished and professional in appearance.

And also rather cool when it came to relationships, too, it seemed.

"No one can do everything," Ari agreed politely.

Sophia looked at her, surprised.

Had Sophia expected Ari to pick a fight? Press the matter, argue the case?

Well, if she had, Ari thought, she'll be sorely disappointed.

Ari had been let down by people too often in the past to want to press an issue, especially when it was already a problem before anything had really even started.

I can accept this, she thought, leaning back in her chair. It was better than facing what would inevitably be more intense drama later on.

"I definitely can't do everything," Sophia said.

Ari took a sip of her drink.

Sophia changed the subject back to the party.

"I especially can't spend any more time than I already do stressing over my family and their extravagant tastes and requests. I hope Rachel is up for this bachelorette extravaganza. It may be quite a challenge for her first professional party planning endeavor."

"Oh, she's got lots of experience party planning. The business side of it, I can lend a hand with. I'll convince her to take you up on this offer," Ari said. "Leave it to me."

"Perhaps this time, I'll actually enjoy Sabrina's bachelorette party," Sophia said.

··◦··

Next Wednesday, Sophia came into The Little Cafe for her usual coffee but, not like usual, sat down at a small table and waited.

"Rachel's not working this morning, something came up with her family last minute, but she told me I could fill you in on her big plans for the party," said Ari as soon as she was free and had left Athena in charge, sitting down with Sophia and pulling up something on her phone.

"First thing's first, where are we going? I need to submit that information to the office that schedules the pilots and reserves the trips on my family's shared jet," Sophia said.

"Vegas," Ari replied.

"Las Vegas. How original," Sophia said, typing something into her phone.

Ari was not impressed by the sarcasm. "You wanna plan this thing, then?"

Sophia shook her head and looked up at her from the phone. "Absolutely not. Vegas it is."

"You're going to Vegas," Ari repeated, amused, "For good reason. Rachel's not just doing it because every bachelor and bachelorette party ever has been there, but we've both got some connections there that will make even the most discerning Bridezilla have an unforgettable experience."

"Who would you have 'connections' with in Vegas? Do

you know an Elvis impersonator, or a group of showgirls?" Sophia asked.

"Well, I worked there for a little while and kind of have a whole secret Nevada identity."

"Are you serious?" Sophia asked.

Ari knew she had finally impressed the woman.

"Yep," she said, sitting up straighter. "Over there, I'm Anna Summers. Nevada resident, complete with driver's license and voting record."

"Why would you..."

Ari waved her hand. "Long story, some other time. But it's convenient for getting a local discount on a ton of stuff in Vegas. Anyways, she'll have a memorable weekend. Or not memorable, depending on how much she decides to imbibe. There will be plentiful opportunities at her private party with a private bartender who, by the way, is making up a whole menu of cocktails specifically for your sister. Oh, you need to give me a list of Sabrina's favorite types of cocktails."

"That would simply be alcohol. And ice."

"Okay then," Ari said, typing something into her phone. "Duly noted."

"She has an affinity for the color green. Chartreuse liqueur, absinthe, emeralds, dollar bills."

"Oh, a color scheme. Rachel mentioned something about trying to get one. She'll be pleased," Ari said, typing another note into her phone.

"What else are we doing on this Vegas trip? Other than having a private bartender who will serve us custom green drinks?"

"Shows, dancing, more drinking, food to soak up all of that alcohol, entertainers, your usual Vegas fare with a lot of pre-arranged things that'll make your sister feel special and, ul-timately, secure you the distinction of Sister of the Year for planning such a personalized, extravagant and extraordinary bachelorette weekend. For the third time."

"Fourth, actually," Sophia grumbled.

"Right. Fourth. Anyways, fourth time's the... um, charm. Or something. It'll be a good time," said Ari.

Sophia shook her head. "It sounds tacky and ridiculous, all of it. Which I suppose is completely appropriate for a Vegas bachelorette party. So, thank you. Or thank Rachel for me, will you?"

She handed Ari an envelope. "The first payment for Rachel. It contains everything we agreed upon in the budget so she can start putting deposits down, as well as the first payment for her services."

Ari took it. "I'll get it to her. But I still have all kinds of details here for you to approve-"

Sophia stood up. "I don't have time. I trust her. If she really gets stuck on something, let me know, but it sounds like she knows more about how to throw a bachelorette weekend in Vegas than I'll ever know. Especially with all of your top-secret connections there."

Ari wondered if Sophia had just winked at her, or if she imagined it.

Winking seemed way too good natured for the woman.

"Are you sure?" Ari asked, standing up with her.

"Yes. Now, I have to get to work," Sophia said. "I have a conference call with a magazine editor in Paris this morning."

Ari nodded. "Just be sure you're ready next weekend for the tackiest and most ridiculous three days of your life. Oh, and what's your dress size?"

"Why?" Sophia asked suspiciously.

Ari gave her an innocent look. "No reason. Just for party planning reasons."

"I'll send you my measurements."

"I don't need measurements. Just a size."

"Sizes vary dramatically according to the label."

"Uh, this isn't for one of your fancy brands. An approximation should work. Small?"

Sophia rolled her eyes. "Yes, Small. 4, if it's a number. 8 UK. 36 European."

Ari typed it in. "Got it. Rachel'll let you know if she's stuck on anything. Otherwise, we'll see you at the airport this weekend."

··o··

It is a wonder, Sophia thought, that her sister has any friends. Such an intolerable person who has very little regard for any living soul other than herself.

Sophia was the first to arrive at the Executive Airport that weekend, just to make sure everything was in order for the plane to depart on time. It was a small jet, used more frequently years ago by her father before he went into semi-retirement, and now shared amongst a group of his friends, colleagues and other associates.

Soon after Sophia spoke with scheduling to make sure everything was all set and helped herself to a cup of espresso, Sabrina's friends began to trickle in. Not knowing any of them very well, Sophia had a few strained conversations with some of the first to arrive. As more came, they talked amongst themselves, mostly gossip about so-and-so; who had been married, or divorced, had a baby, had gotten cheated on, or had gotten Botox. The growing group of Sophia's friends allowed a relieved Sophia to shrink back off to the side.

Sophia was especially relieved to see Ari and Rachel arrive, both toting armfuls of shopping bags.

"Can I help you with any of this?" Sophia asked, following them as they made their second trip into the small terminal building from Ari's car parked outside.

"I'm good, but I think Rachel could use a hand with a few of her bags," Ari said.

Sophia took one of the brown paper shopping bags from the woman's overloaded arms.

"Thanks," Rachel said gratefully, teetering under the weight.

Sophia helped Rachel load all of the bags, boxes and a few suitcases onto luggage carts while the rest of the bachelorette party continued to arrive in the small lounge area in the terminal.

"Are we throwing a party for a whole army?" she joked.

"Your sister has some specific requests and very discerning taste," Rachel explained, setting a cooler down on a luggage cart.

"Don't I know it," said Sophia, motioning towards a porter who had been milling around the terminal building and started helping them unload.

"I'll be in shock if you're able to stay in budget," Sophia said. "I expected you to ask me sooner than this if you could go over."

Rachel smiled. "Hey, I am actually well under budget, believe it or not. I am nothing if not thrifty."

A high pitched squeal interrupted their chat, which was followed by excited conversation and laughter.

"Looks like the blushing bride has arrived," Sophia observed, watching her sister strut into the airport lounge like she was the star of a runway show. "With five suitcases. And people always assume I am the clotheshorse."

"Could I board now?" Rachel asked, watching as a porter started to carry some of the bags onto the plane. "I should get the champagne ready."

Sophia nodded. "I'll come with you."

They climbed the steps of the aircraft, their hair waving wildly as the pilot tested the engines.

"Rachel?" Sophia asked as soon as they were on board.

"Yeah?"

Sophia tucked a strand of hair behind her ear.

"I know we didn't get off to a great start a few months ago. I appreciate you doing this. It's a little outside of my comfort zone and I don't know where I'd be without your help. Probably just throwing Sabrina another lackluster party."

Rachel gave her a half-smile.

"And I really appreciate the check you wrote me and the huge budget. This is one hell of a way for me to kickstart my business," Rachel said. "And if I do a decent job, maybe you'll be a reference?"

"Sure. That is, assuming I survive the weekend," Sophia said darkly.

Rachel busied herself with the champagne glasses, and Sophia inspected the bottle of fine champagne in an ice bucket that was ready and waiting.

Then, Sophia neatly placed her carry-on bag on a seat towards the back of the plane.

"I'm going to try to get some work done on this flight," she announced to Rachel.

"Good luck with that," Rachel said, arranging several champagne flutes on a tray as Sabrina and her friends began to climb the steps to board the plane.

"It's you who needs the luck," Sophia said, settling into the seat and taking out her laptop.

"Everything ok in here?" Ari asked, boarding the plane, holding a box in one hand and two bags in the other.

Rachel nodded. "It's show time."

Sabrina's odd mishmash of friends began to settle in. Some of the women were minor celebrities, including a meteorologist who was mildly famous (at least for fans of 24-hour cable weather networks) for her work chasing tornadoes. There was also a well-known architect, Cassandra, who was one of the few women in Sabrina's squad that Sophia felt was reasonably level-headed when she talked to her earlier in the terminal.

In the less-than-reasonable group, there were two "actresses," a celebrity gossip reporter with a podcast, and a midwife who handed out crystals to everyone, which supposedly were to give them the power of clarity and relaxation (Sabrina had never been pregnant, at least not to Sophia's knowledge, so how her sister knew a midwife, she had no clue). Out of obligation, Sophia had invited their mother, but Callista had politely (and to Sophia's great relief,) declined. Along with it, however, Callista had offered to match Sophia's budget she'd set for the weekend, which was now, at Sophia's estimate, probably the largest bachelorette party budget a woman who had been married not once, but twice before, had ever been given.

Once the ladies - who had all boarded the plane in a cloud of perfume, laughter, and chatter - were seated and had been handed a glass of champagne, Rachel began to explain their first game, an icebreaker activity with a dirty twist. Sophia heard exactly three euphemisms for male genitalia before putting on her noise-cancelling headphones.

"Mind if I sit next to you?"

Sophia looked up to see Ari standing next to her.

"Ms. Little," Sophia said, pushing her headphones back off one of her ears.

In the chaos of the boarding process and Rachel starting the game, she had not realized Ari was still on board. "You'd better leave, the plane is taking off in a moment."

"Oh, I'm coming too. Didn't Rachel tell you?" Ari asked.

"No. Why would you want to come along on this trip?"

Ari shrugged. "I haven't been away from the café in weeks, for one, but mainly because Rachel said she could use a hand. I wanted to be supportive."

"What on earth would possess you to want to spend a free weekend away from work with my sister and her lunatic squad of friends?"

Ari shrugged again. "The more lunatics, the merrier."

And with that, Ari sank back into the leather seat and put her own headphones on. She smiled smugly.

Sophia raised her eyebrows, but quietly opened her laptop and began to type out some emails, and before she knew it, was engrossed with her work. She barely noticed as the plane took off.

7

What Happens in Vegas

An hour and a half later, they touched down in what Sophia had always considered the hottest, tackiest, and least pleasant city in the world. She wanted to get to her hotel room quickly, change, finish up another hour or two (or three) of work, and try to avoid as many of the activities Rachel had planned as possible. Maybe she would even be able to sneak in a visit to a spa for a manicure, or massage... but only if she wrapped up all of the tasks on her work calendar first.

"Where are we going, Rachel?" Sophia asked, trying to look out of the tinted windows of the SUV-limo-monstrosity they were being driven in from the airport.

Inside the limo, there were no fewer than two disco balls, numerous purple lights, and a stripper pole.

Horrendous.

Even worse, Sabrina's midwife friend was urging Sabrina to give the pole a try, claiming it would help clear out her sacral chakra. Mercifully, Sabrina politely refused, instead pouring more champagne for everyone and giggling loudly.

Rachel did not hear her the first time over the sound of laughter in the car as another woman tried out the pole. Sophia again asked where they were going.

"Hotel Panache," Rachel said.

"What hotel?" Sophia asked, thinking she had heard wrong.

The name was not familiar to her. She had not asked Rachel in advance what she was planning as far as accommodations were concerned, but she assumed they would be staying at one of the usual big name hotels on the strip, the ones with the thousands of rooms and entire cities contained within, where tacky restaurants were open at all hours of day and night, and endless slot machines scattered throughout the premises.

"It's called Panache," Rachel repeated.

"It's an elegant place," Ari chimed in, noting the look of concern on Sophia's face.

"I've never heard of it," Sophia said, glancing down at her phone, out of habit.

"And that's why you hired a Vegas pro to plan this weekend for you," Rachel said, grinning.

The limo SUV dropped them off outside the entrance to one of the main, monstrous hotels where Sophia had expected to stay.

"This isn't Panache," Sophia observed, taking her suitcase and pushing on her sunglasses.

"Nope, it's not," Ari said, helping the driver unload the rest of the suitcases.

Sabrina's friends had all but forgotten their whereabouts, much less their suitcases, focusing instead on laughing about some outrageous story that a tipsy Cassandra was telling.

"Put your phone down, sis, and stop being such a bore," Sabrina said, snatching the phone out of Sophia's hand and marching into the lobby.

"Hey!" Sophia said, rushing after her.

They walked through the massive lobby of the hotel, past endless shops, bars, restaurants and what appeared to be a river cutting through the entire lobby, and then, through an unmarked door. They followed a mostly-dark passageway for what felt like a mile, punctuated with backlit glass mosaic works of art, until they emerged in a surprisingly cool, quiet courtyard with small fountains, benches and ample lush greenery. They crossed the courtyard and found themselves walking through another door – and straight into what was a hushed, elegant, sophisticated boutique hotel lobby. Hardly anyone was in the space, and two bellhops and a receptionist greeted them immediately.

"This must be the bachelorette party," one of the bellhops said, rushing to take their bags.

"Reporting for duty," Rachel said, moving swiftly to the front desk to check in the group.

"What is this place?" Sophia asked, looking around.

"It's Panache," Ari said. "It's a hidden hotel."

"A hidden hotel?"

"You have to know someone who knows someone to even think about making reservations," Ari explained.

"It really does feel hidden," Sophia said, looking around the quiet, low-key lobby. "I'm impressed."

"All right, ladies, let's take the elevator on the right to the penthouse suite!" Rachel rounded up the animated group of women, including a distracted Sabrina, who was still holding her glass of champagne from the limo ride and haphazardly flirting with one of the bellhops.

Sophia stayed behind at the front desk.

"Waiting for something?" Ari asked as she also moved towards the elevator with the group.

"I want to check into my own room before going up," Sophia said.

"You'll be waiting a long time. We're all in the penthouse. But don't worry, it's huge."

"What? Are you serious? I am not staying with those women. No. I'm getting my own room." Sophia said firmly.

"Then you'll be waiting a while. This place is totally booked this weekend, next weekend, pretty much every weekend from now until... well, Sabrina's next wedding."

Sophia clenched her jaw.

"Then I'm going to another hotel. Like the enormous one we just walked through. Anything would be better than staying with this group of-" She waved absently at the group of women.

One of the actresses was laughing hysterically, already the victim of one too many glasses of champagne.

Ari touched her elbow, gently urging her towards the elevator with the rest of the group. "Maybe later. For now, join the party. You're technically the host, after all."

..o..

Upon arriving at the penthouse, Sophia had to admit it was massive and luxurious, even by her standards. It was a world unto itself that stretched over two floors, had a private rooftop pool, 24/7 dedicated butler service and unlimited drinks, several bedrooms and a massive grand living room overlooking the Strip.

As soon as they had all stumbled into the penthouse and their luggage was delivered by four smartly dressed bellhops, Rachel pulled her first trick out of her hat, which was a drinking game that somehow also involved answering dirty trivia questions and the losers - not the winners - received "prizes" that had to be worn out on the town later: t-shirts with sassy catchphrases about love and marriage, tiaras, Mardi Gras bead necklaces, and other outrageous junk that Sophia did not plan on touching, much less wearing. Needless to say, Sophia sat it out in a little impromptu office she made from a desk she found in a corner on the second floor of the suite.

"Here you are," Ari said soon after Sophia had settled into her tiny workspace. "Rachel was looking for you. You sure you don't want to win - or maybe lose is the better term for it - a light-up pin that says 'I'm with the Bridezilla' or a flashing tiara to wear out later tonight?"

"Light-up pin or tiara? Too last season for my tastes," Sophia deadpanned, pushing her glasses higher up on her nose and typing on her laptop.

Ari paused a moment, appreciating the view of the brunette in her dark brown-framed glasses. Sitting at the desk and studying her computer, as maddening as it was that this woman could not just chill out and take a break, Ari had to admit to herself that serious glasses-wearing Sophia was a sight to behold.

"At least pause for a snack. Our private butler for the weekend is putting out some food for lunch," urged Ari.

"I am fairly sure everyone is having a liquid lunch today," Sophia said, and as if on cue, the sound of laughter could be heard ringing from downstairs.

"They need to learn to pace themselves," Ari said. "We've got a lot more ahead of us. That's why it's time to fill them up with some food. Good, solid, greasy food. C'mon, sister of the bride, help me feed these ladies."

Sophia closed the lid of her laptop and reluctantly followed Ari down into the common area, towards a massive, open gourmet kitchen. "I prefer my lunches to consist of salads, or at least some fresh fruit and vegetables, if there are any?"

"Nope," Ari answered, then pointed to something on a tray. "Although there's garlic in those. Does garlic count as a vegetable?"

"Vaguely," Sophia grumbled, sitting on a stool at the counter next to the tray with the garlic-filled things, which happened to smell absolutely delicious. "What are they?"

"Garlic rolls," Ari said. "They're so good. We ordered lunch from one of my favorite places in Vegas."

"They do smell good," Sophia admitted.

"Have one," Ari urged.

Sophia shook her head, and took a sip of water from a bottle. "No. I happen to work in an industry that's not very kind to aging women with increasingly grim metabolism. I can't just down a bunch of garlic rolls for lunch."

"Aging?" Ari asked, pulling out another tray from the oven. "I doubt you really have to worry about that right now. What are you, 30?"

Sophia looked up at her suspiciously. "Nice try. Add a few years."

Ari presented her with yet another tray. "Big deal. Here, how about blooming onions with garlic-chili or honey mustard sauce?"

"Absolutely not," Sophia said, recoiling.

She actually really hated onions.

"Then take a roll. They're good, and they're not going to kill you, unlike these deep-fried onions."

Sophia reached for a plate and reluctantly took a garlic roll. She sunk her teeth into it, and... it was perfection. Pure, steamy, buttery, garlicky perfection.

"Well?" Ari asked. "How was it?"

"It's not the worst thing I've ever tasted," Sophia said coolly.

In fact, she observed as she chewed, it was butter and garlic heaven.

"Well, you have approximately 20 seconds to serve yourself before I tell the squad it's time to eat."

Sophia snatched another garlic roll, and a few minutes later, slipped back upstairs to her laptop.

··◦··

By mid-afternoon, Sophia caved. She put away her laptop and joined the group for a glass of white wine. Based on the inane conversation she was subject to, she made the decision to opt for a second glass 20 minutes later. When her sister started to dance, she determined it prudent to reach for a third glass of wine. This time, she switched to red.

Suddenly, she was more enthusiastic about going along with the group's bachelorette antics, and less concerned about her lack of personal space in the penthouse.

Late in the afternoon, Rachel had another surprise for them all: dance lessons with a Las Vegas choreographer. By the time they had all donned feathery skirts and headdresses and learned the moves from classic showgirl dances, Sophia had three glasses of wine in her system and was reasonably content to dance with the rest of the group.

"Nice feathers," Ari teased Sophia a little while later when she went into the kitchen for a glass of water - her first after the glasses of wine - and she looked down and realized that feathers from her showgirl costume had stuck to her designer black pants.

"You try dancing in a feather costume after three glasses of wine," Sophia said.

"No thanks, I'm good with staying in here," Ari said, pleased with herself.

When they went out for dinner around 7 at a loud, busy restaurant with live entertainment – against her best judgment, Sophia ordered ravioli and had a large helping of salad - her unsteady, muddled mind finally regained a bit of clarity thanks to the onslaught of carbs and cheese.

Unfortunately, her sobriety also meant that she had begun

to question her enthusiasm for the group's next plan: attending a show that Rachel gleefully teased would provide entertainment in more ways than one.

"That sounds ominous," Sophia muttered.

"Before we go," Rachel announced, standing up and waving to get the group's attention, "We have one more drink."

A waiter had materialized, carrying a tray full of green liquid in elegant crystal glasses.

"The poisoned apple," he announced proudly to the group, who cheered. "Guaranteed to get the bachelorette party night off to a tarty start."

"We heard you like green," Rachel said to Sabrina.

"I dooo, darling," Sabrina cooed approvingly, happily examining the drink that was placed in front of her.

The drinks were so green, they were practically glowing in their glasses.

"Looks aptly named," Sophia muttered to Ari, who sat next to her at dinner and was slowly sipping on a beer, the first drink Sophia had seen her have all day.

The waiter set a glass in front of Sophia, and she sniffed it disdainfully.

"You'd better drink that, sis!" Sabrina called from across the table. "Bride's orders, the Maid of Honor has to follow them! Bottom's up!"

"Ugh," Sophia replied.

"Come on, Sophia. When in Rome, do as the...well, Roman bachelorettes would do," an amused Ari said.

The group of women cheered, clinked their glasses and drank. Sophia reluctantly took a delicate sip from hers, closing her eyes as she did, then recoiled.

"Not to your taste?" Ari commented, amused by her expression.

"Absolutely not. I haven't had anything so horrendous

since my first year in college."

"It kinda looks like something that should come with a warning label," Ari admitted.

Sophia glanced over where Ari was casually leaning back in her seat and nursing her beer. "Wait, how did you get out of having one of these things?" she asked.

"I'm not an official guest. I don't really feel the need to partake in all of the activities," she shrugged.

"Oh, please," Sophia said, pushing the glass towards her. "Try it."

"No," Ari said, scrunching up her nose.

"You're at this table. When in Rome, do as the Roman bachelorettes would do," Sophia mocked.

"Touché." Ari reached for the glass, sniffed it, took a sip and promptly recoiled as much as Sophia had.

"Yeah, I definitely do not want to be in Rome right now," she said, giving the glass back to Sophia. Sophia pushed it towards the middle of the table, where it could hopefully disappear amongst the clutter of bread baskets and empty glasses.

"Not so fast. Maybe you should finish it," said Ari. "Might help with the next activity Rachel has planned."

"You mean this mystery show that we're all going to see?" Sophia asked.

Ari nodded, an amused grin forming.

"What do you know about it?" Sophia asked suspiciously.

"Two words. Thunder Mountain."

"What does that even mean?"

"It means you're seeing an adult-only vaudeville show with exclusively male performers called Thunder Mountain."

Sophia scrunched up her nose in disgust.

"Why the hell did I give Rachel free reign over this party planning? I knew I should have audited her work," Sophia said.

"What, in between your endless meetings and deadlines, you were going to go over plans with Rachel about what strip show she was going to take your sister and her eccentric group of friends to?"

Sophia groaned. "No, probably not. But is all of this really necessary?"

"You said your sister would want an over-the-top bachelorette party," Ari reminded her.

"I did," Sophia admitted as the waiter was directed towards her with the dinner bill.

"And it's pretty much the most classic part of a traditional bachelorette party to see a show or entertainment activity of some sort where men get really naked," Ari continued.

Sophia glanced at the bill, then passed her Black card to the man, who promptly swiped it.

"Lucky me," sighed Sophia.

After the group stumbled out of the restaurant, Rachel handed them all their tickets. The paper tickets were adorned with the photos of several shirtless men who looked like they had spent the better part of their life popping steroids.

"This shouldn't be legal," Sophia murmured, while the rest of the group squealed and laughed like a group of teenagers.

"Lighten up," Ari teased lightly. "Wouldn't have thought you'd be such a prude."

Sophia scowled.

"I'll see you later," Ari said to her as Rachel directed the fully re-energized group towards their next destination.

Sophia looked up. "You're not coming with us to this?"

Ari shook her head and laughed. "It's not really my kind of show."

"Right," Sophia said. "Nor is it mine."

"It's your sister," Ari urged. "Go be supportive, you've only got about 40 hours left of this weekend. You can do it."

"Come with us," Sophia pleaded. "You're the only sane one in this group that I can talk to. And the only sober one," she said, eyeing the group of women.

Ari laughed. "I actually do already have some plans with friends tonight, otherwise I might have taken pity on you and come along."

"Friends? Here?"

Ari nodded. "Yep. I used to work here, remember?

"Right. *Anna*," Sophia said.

"Well, my friends know my real name. But yeah, they're friends from a few years back. I promised I'd see them while I'm in town. You have fun at the show," she said, walking away quickly now, waving and disappearing into the throngs of people.

Sophia reluctantly followed the group to their next destination.

They were seated in a VIP area – who knew such a thing existed at what was essentially a glorified strip show – and served unlimited champagne, which Sophia wondered if her stomach could handle at this point after an afternoon and evening of drinking. Still, as soon as she saw the throngs of slightly tipsy women enter and seat themselves around her and she overheard her sister proclaim that she would go home with one of the performers in the show that weekend because, after all, what happens in Vegas... Sophia gladly accepted a glass of bubbly, if for no reason other than to focus on something other than her present surroundings.

She was not sure at what point she started to feel nauseous. It was perhaps the first few minutes into the opening act, which was a cringe-worthy homage to some nondescript Broadway show. Or maybe it was during the trapeze artist's performance, or, finally, the men in the cowboy uniforms doing the Can-Can. The room grew blurry around the edges, and she started to feel the Italian food churning in her stomach, the taste of garlic rising in her throat.

Sophia excused herself, pushing her way through the endless row of hollering and cheering women in their flashing pins, tiaras and bedazzled shoes, and had never felt so glad to burst into a quiet lobby.

"Bathroom?" she asked an usher standing near the doors.

The woman pointed off to the side, and despite every flashing neon sign making her headache worse, her temples throbbing and nausea still bubbling in her stomach, she made it to the ladies' room.

She stood in a bathroom stall for a few minutes, and as she listened to the hum of an air vent and felt the cool air circulating in the empty room, the nausea subsided. She found some peppermints in her purse, but she wished she had some water. That was all she wanted. Water, and maybe some saltines. She could not remember the last time she had drunk - or eaten - so much. Possibly never. And such strange mixtures, too. Not a piece of kale or detox juice in front of her all day. And so, so many carbs and so much butter. No wonder she felt horrendous.

When she was confident she was going to make it out without getting sick, she left the stall and washed her hands, then arms, and splashed some cool water on her face – though not too much, she didn't want to completely remove her makeup – took a deep breath, and went back out into the lobby.

She could step outside, she decided, but as soon as she did, she regretted it. She was still a little tipsy from all of the alcohol, and the heat of the night and the endless neon flashing lights threatened to trigger her nausea again.

She had no idea where she was. She could pull up a map up on her phone, she thought, but she wasn't sure she remembered the name of their hotel to navigate back to. Panache, wasn't it called? It was hidden within a larger hotel. She just had to find the big hotel. But where was the corridor? Past the bigger hotel's lobby? She only remembered the long hallway with the glass mosaics. Then, there was the issue of getting into the penthouse. She was not sure she even had her own key.

It would be no good trying to make her way back.

Instead, she decided she needed to think more clearly, and get something caffeinated, along with some water. Her throat was parched. She pulled up the maps on her phone and typed in "good coffee."

She expected some generic coffee chain to pop up, but to her surprise, a block away there was a place called "Second Wind Café + Bistro."

Perfect name, Sophia thought, skimming the first review that popped up, which promised that the place had the BEST coffee in Vegas.

She teetered along the crowded sidewalks and tried to look straight ahead so she wouldn't be subject to too many of the moving flashing lights, and walking directly toward the massive hotel in which the Second Wind Cafe was supposed to be located.

Five minutes later, she found the little café, tucked away in a small plaza. It was late at night, but all of the stores were open, and Second Wind was bustling.

The smell of coffee instantly perked her up, and before long, Sophia had ordered a large Americano and a glass bottle of imported carbonated water, which was served to her by a waiter in a crisp white shirt. She had never been so happy to see a clothed man in her life.

The Americano, chased with a generous dose of bubbly water, brought her back to life. The café had given her a small plate of little shortbread cookies, and she tentatively nibbled at one. Between that and the water, her stomach was finally settling.

"Sophia?"

Sophia looked up. For a brief moment, she was completely unsurprised to be sipping coffee and find Ari standing next to her table. But then she remembered where she was, and that Ari was with an unfamiliar dark-haired man about their age in a plaid shirt. There was also a pretty dark haired woman, who was dressed in a blue shirt and sequined skirt, walking towards them.

"Hey. What are you doing here?" Ari asked, concerned.

"I left the show," Sophia said, her voice cracking a bit. "I felt a little ill."

"That must have been some show," Ari said. "We're just heading out. Wanna join us?"

"Um, sure," Sophia said, not sure what else to say.

"Great," Ari said. "Sophia, these are two of my old friends, Nate – I met him a long time ago, at my first job back home in California – and Rose, also a former coworker, but we met when I worked here in Vegas."

They all shook hands, and as they made light small talk, Sophia hoped she didn't look as big of a mess as she felt.

"Hey, Ar, I'll go grab the car, you wait outside near the West entrance and I'll pick you up in a few minutes?" Nate suggested.

"Sure, thanks," Ari replied.

"And I'm taking off," Rose said. "Nice to meet you, Sophia, and enjoy the rest of your weekend here."

"I don't mean to impose on your night," Sophia said apologetically as she and Ari walked out. "I'm just not sure how to get back to our hotel, so perhaps you could point me in the right direction and I'll make my own way back?"

"It's no big deal. We're going back to Nate's place. He makes this great anti-hangover smoothie, perfect after a long night. It'll have you fixed up in no time."

"You're going to Nate's place?" Sophia asked, raising an eyebrow and slowing her pace. "Really, I don't want to impose at all."

Ari shook her head. "You're not, trust me. We're just old friends. And actually, it's not exactly Nate's place. I mean, he rents it. But it's my house."

"You own a house? Here?"

"It was an investment a bunch of years ago. I hate paying rent. So this house came along, and I lived in the living room in a sleeping bag for a few months and fixed it up and planned on flipping it for a profit, but then the housing market crashed and I just held onto it, rented it out to Nate," she said. "Nate's taken over most of the place, but I still keep a loft area on the second floor for myself, so I have a place to crash when I'm in town."

"Were you going to stay there instead of our penthouse party house?" Sophia asked.

Ari nodded. "You bet. I told Rachel she could crash there, too, but I guess she has her own friends in town, so she made other arrangements."

"You're making me feel left out for not having a whole second life here in Vegas. It would be so much more convenient for those times I don't want to spend the night with my sister at her bachelorette parties," Sophia commented.

"You don't really look like you're in much shape to go back to that hotel," Sophia said. "And I'm sorry to say it, but the night Rachel has planned for everyone doesn't exactly end with the Thunder Mountain show."

"You're kidding."

"Yeah, I'm not. Anyways, stay at my place if you want.

Recharge a bit so you can get back into supportive Maid of Honor mode tomorrow," Ari urged, walking towards a black SUV that had pulled up along the curb.

Sophia followed her. "I really don't mean to impose," she said again, not wanting to seem rude, or ruin Ari's night or plans in any way.

"Get in, m'lady," Ari ordered, smiling and holding open the backseat door for Sophia.

··○··

Ari's quiet suburban house was not a place Sophia pictured Ari living. It was a small, ranch style house. Relatively plain outside, it was open and light inside, with one great room and a little hall that led into what Sophia presumed were the bedrooms. There was a stairway that led upstairs to an open loft, and a high ceiling made most of the space feel airy.

The decor was what struck Sophia as being more like Ari. It was cozy and bohemian: there were musical instruments scattered around, artwork on the walls, blankets and rugs that seemed to have been lovingly collected over time.

"Sorry for the mess," Nate said, moving around the living room and picking up guitars and books that were scattered around.

Ari walked towards a vintage record player and put on what sounded like classic blues. It was easy to listen to and welcome after the onslaught of over-the-top entertainment and stimulation they had been subject to all day.

Nate went to the kitchen and got out a blender.

"No drinks for me, thank you," Sophia said.

He looked up. "This isn't an alcoholic drink. It's my hang-over cure. Or, in your case, pre-hangover cure. Don't worry, nothing weird. It's mostly ginger and honey and a couple of things that'll be easy on your stomach and make life more tolerable tomorrow morning."

Sophia raised her eyebrows skeptically.

"I'll give it a try," she said.

Ari disappeared up into the loft and Sophia perched at a barstool at the counter.

"Sophia, you'll stay up here," Ari called down a few minutes later. "I'll stay in Nate's spare bedroom."

"Good luck finding the bed," Nate called up. "I've been using that room as my computer room."

"You know I'm not picky about where I sleep," Ari called back down.

"That's an understatement," Nate joked.

"Hey!" Ari called. "That's the pot calling the kettle black."

Nate grinned and started the blender.

Ari returned downstairs and opened the freezer. "Do you have any pizza rolls, or those frozen cheese-stuffed pretzel things? I'm starving."

"It's all in the freezer," Nate said. "Help yourself."

"Pizza rolls, pretzels, and coffee," Ari said, dumping a bunch of brown-colored frozen food from boxes onto a tray and sticking it in the oven, then turning her attention to the coffee pot. "My kind of midnight snack."

"Healthy," Nate commented.

"She eats like my 13 year old son," Sophia chimed in.

"She's still got the taste buds of a kid," Nate said, smiling in Ari's direction.

"You wouldn't know it from her coffee shop, though. The Little Cafe has a good selection of sandwiches and salads, and even the baked goods are decent," Sophia said.

"Impressive," Nate said, watching Ari, who was pouring water into the coffee maker. "Wouldn't have guessed."

"What do you do, Nate?" Sophia asked.

"I'm a lighting technician for a show."

"Please tell me it's not a show called Thunder Mountain."

Nate chuckled. "Nope, Cirque."

"Oh, that's a good one. I would go see that."

"Here," Nate said, handing her a tall glass containing a pale liquid. "This should settle your stomach and mitigate the near-future consequences of your day of marathon drinking."

Sophia tentatively took a sip out of politeness, but was pleasantly surprised to discover that it was good. It tasted fresh, with a slightly bitter edge, but not altogether unpalatable. She took another sip.

Meanwhile, Nate and Ari chatted amicably and filled up the coffee table in the living room with various assorted junk food, hot from the oven, and poured big mugs of coffee. The three sat around the coffee table, chatting with the music still playing softly in the background.

"So, Nate, perhaps you can tell me about this mystery job Ari used to have in Vegas?" Sophia asked.

Nate shook his head. "I don't think it's my story to tell. All I can tell you is that the two of us worked together in a coffee shop on the campus of this big-ass company in Silicon Valley in high school-"

"What is with Ari and coffee?" Sophia asked, looking over at Ari, who was sitting cross-legged in an large chair and nursing her oversized mug of coffee as she munched on a soft pretzel.

"It's her thing. Though I'm pretty sure she just started a coffee shop so she could buy coffee beans in bulk at wholesale prices," Nate said.

"You've got it," Ari said.

"Clever woman," Sophia said, nodding. "Anyways, continue. How did you two end up out here?"

Nate glanced at Ari. "I think we both wanted to get out of the world we were surrounded by: we just saw all of these professionals in a rat race, running in circles, trying to keep up with everything – work, their boss' demands, pressure from peers, buying the latest trends – everything that Ari and I thought was meaningless. Ari left home first on a road-trip, I followed, and eventually we met up here."

"Vegas is an odd choice for two people who hate frivolous, shallow things," Sophia commented.

Ari nodded. "Yeah, we'd intended to go further East."

"But then we stopped here for a few days, met a few people, and kind of decided to settle in for a while. We both worked as bartenders to earn some cash at first," Nate said.

"I'm sure there are plenty of opportunities for that here," Sophia said.

"After a while we met these people at work, and learned there were ways to make more money, faster, which was pretty appealing in a city that's kind of expensive for a couple of 20 years olds to live in. They connected us to some guys who had a private investigation business, and we became private investigators," Ari said.

"That's not a career you hear about every day. Was it dangerous?" Sophia asked.

Nate shrugged, but Ari shook her head. "I never felt like I was really in danger when I was working for someone else. But as I became more experienced, I decided to start my own business doing it. Like an independent contractor, basically. That was a bit dicier."

"I didn't love that she started doing that," Nate commented. "I worried about her a lot, actually."

Ari shook her head. "It wasn't that bad. But after doing it for a few years, I grew tired of it, the constant stress of it, and yeah, I figured being in that career indefinitely really wasn't the greatest for my long term well-being and sanity. And my parents were always bugging me to move back home, and eventually I realized I really missed being around them. So I went back home, and took my savings and started The Little Cafe."

"You forgot your nine month stint in a hospital and physical therapy," Nate said.

"Yeah, there was that. Let's just say I got hurt on the job, busted up my back, and had to spend a lot of time in physical therapy. Decided to bow out of that profession before I could lose anything else," Ari admitted. "I threw myself into classes in community college during that time, so it worked out okay."

"Quite an adventure, all things considered," Sophia commented.

Ari nodded. "I always wanted adventure. You know, I saw my parents slave away at desk jobs my entire life and I knew that wasn't for me, especially when they were repaid for all their hard work by bastard execs at the company who laid them off."

"I can see why it didn't appeal to you, then. Although not all careers end so dismally," Sophia said.

"I guess Nate was a good wake-up call, though," Ari said. "He paid his way through technical college here in Vegas, which landed him this pretty good job in showbiz-"

"Managing the lighting for a show isn't exactly showbiz," Nate corrected.

"Well, it's a stable living, one in which you're probably not going to run across some lunatic who injures you and sends you to physical therapy for the better part of a year. Anyways, after finishing my college degree, I realized maybe I should go home, and lend my parents a hand with things, and after my mom's cupcake shop failed, it gave me the idea to start a coffee shop instead. I learned from her mistakes. I still wanted to own my own business, but offer more of a mainstay product - coffee never goes out of style - and it had lower overhead than baking a dozen different brand new flavors of cupcakes every day."

"It was a good business idea," Sophia said. "We didn't have any decent coffee in Palo Rosa before. You had to drive a couple of miles, in traffic, mind you, to get anything good. You rescued me from endless bad cups of coffee."

"See, Ari? Who said having a normal job couldn't make a difference in people's lives," Nate said.

"Very funny," Ari said, and then turned to Sophia. "This guy remembers everything. I said that to him, once. But I guess that's what friends are for... they remind you of how far you've come."

Sophia smiled. Ari and Nate's strong friendship was evident in the way they talked and interacted. Meeting someone who was a part of Ari's life outside of her work life made Sophia feel like she was getting a different perspective on the woman.

They sat in amicable silence for a few minutes, only commenting here and there about the food, the house, and the music. Sophia felt herself relax at last, sinking into the soft couch, even nibbling on a pretzel. It was not bad, and Nate's drink had definitely settled her stomach. She also concentrated on drinking the endless glasses of water that concerned Ari and Nate kept pouring for her.

As Ari and Nate chatted about music, Sophia felt herself drifting off, sleepy from the food, music and pleasant company.

"It's late," Ari commented finally, noticing Sophia yawning and sinking further down into the couch. "Here, let me show you upstairs."

Sophia followed Ari up the stairs to a loft. It was not the most private place, since it was open on one side to the entire main floor, but it was large and comfortable.

"It's nice," Sophia said sleepily, struggling to stay alert.

Ari shrugged, moving towards the bed and clicking on the bedside lamp. "It's nothing. I hope it's comfortable enough. It's not as, well, you know, fancy as your place."

"Oh," Sophia said, looking around at the art on the walls: there were paintings, masks, sculptures, and several dream-catchers scattered around. "I like it. The paintings are good."

"Thanks," Ari said. "I mean, I did them."

"You painted these?" a surprised Sophia said, looking closer at one that was hanging over the bed. It was semi-abstract, though it looked a bit like a desert landscape, filled with bright oranges, blues, yellows and reds.

"Yeah. I like to paint, though haven't had a lot of time for it recently. I used to work odd hours, when I was a PI, so it was a good hobby for random times of the day or night when I wasn't working."

"They are really well done," Sophia said, still studying the work.

"Thanks. So, the bathroom's right at the bottom of the stairs, there are fresh towels in that cupboard over there-" she pointed to the far side of the room, " and basically just help yourself to whatever you need. I've got aspirin in that drawer by the bed, all the water you can drink downstairs in the water bottle, and there are random shirts in that top drawer, t-shirts, flannel and plaid shirts, probably a sweat-shirt, whatever you might want to borrow."

"This is far superior to anything else I would have been experiencing tonight back at the party penthouse, so thank you," Sophia said, giving Ari a tired smile.

"Goodnight," Ari said, heading back down the stairs.

"Goodnight, Arianna," Sophia said.

Ari paused for a moment at hearing her name, smiled to herself, then continued down the stairs.

..○..

When Sophia woke up the next morning, she could not remember where she was.

She blinked a few times, the sun streaming in through windows on either side of the soft bed she was in. She was surrounded by painted dressers that looked vintage, low tables with art supplies, and various trinkets that looked like they had been collected over the course of many travels.

And paintings. Large, colorful paintings.

Paintings made by Ari.

Sophia sat up, the events of the previous day rushing back. She felt a little dizzy, and grabbed the glass of water on her nightstand.

She looked down at the bedding she was sleeping in. Soft, worn sheets, a blue quilt. The loft was homey and pleasant. The feathers from a dreamcatcher hanging on a nail in the wall nearby fluttered in the draft created by a ceiling fan.

She took a moment, while sipping on her water, to look at Ari's paintings some more. They were well done. Aesthetically pleasing, yes, but also bright, cheerful. Bold colors and lots of light. They were a little modern for her style, but she liked them nonetheless. They were not like any piece of art she owned.

She heard movement and chatting downstairs, and rolled out of bed, wrapping a throw blanket around herself as she shuffled over a chair where she had neatly folded last night's outfit. She was uninterested in putting it back on: her wrinkled dark blue blouse smelled vaguely of food from the Italian restaurant and seemed unappealing, although she could probably tolerate slipping into the black pants for another day.

She opened the top drawer where she had found the soft, oversized concert t-shirt she wore to bed last night and looked through it. Ari had said she could help herself to whatever she found in the drawer, and she located a clean, soft grey scoop-neck t-shirt that did not look entirely unwearable.

When she wandered downstairs a few minutes later, she was promptly offered a steaming mug of coffee and a bagel by Nate, who was managing the toaster.

"Sleep well?" Ari asked, looking up from the newspaper she was reading at the table.

"Yes, actually," Sophia said, settling down at the table next to her and taking a peek at the business section of the paper. "You have a very comfortable home."

"Glad to hear it," said Ari, as Nate joined them at the table, setting a plate with a bagel and cream cheese in front of both of them.

"Shame you're not at the hotel. They have a great breakfast buffet there," he said, grinning. "Lots of carbs and rubbery eggs. Perfect meal to kick off another day of nonstop drinking."

"Completely unnecessary, as I am never drinking ever again," grumbled Sophia.

"You'll probably want to spend the night here again, then, knowing what Rachel has planned for tonight," Ari said.

"What could she possibly do that would top the sophistication and understated elegance of last night?" asked Sophia.

"Pool party in the penthouse suite, private DJ until the wee hours, private entertainment if you know what I mean, and if you don't, well, it involves men dressed like police officers arriving at the door and, uh, 'arresting' your sister."

Sophia wrinkled her nose. "Please allow me to stay here."

"I've got to work a show tonight and promised some friends I'd leave to go camping with them early tomorrow, so I'll stay with a friend after work," Nate said. "You'll have the place to yourself tonight and tomorrow morning. Should I whip up some more of my hangover prevention juice and leave it in the fridge?"

"Maybe," Ari said, glancing warily at Sophia.

"I swear I'm not drinking again," Sophia said defensively.

"...just in case," Ari added to Nate.

Nate nodded. "Will do."

··o··

"The key to surviving bachelorette parties," Ari instructed as she drove them back to the hotel after breakfast, "Is to *pretend* you're drinking. Always have something in your hand, but everyone else should, in theory, be drinking too much to notice that your drink is the same one, hour after hour. Order something classic and inoffensive, like a gin and tonic, and spend most of your time holding it, taking the occasional sip here and there just to be convincing."

"Thank you, Ms. Little, for that enlightening insight."

"Hey, just trying to help out so you won't be as bad off today as you looked last night."

"Thanks," Sophia said.

Ari glanced at her quickly. "I mean, you looked ill. Nauseous. As far as your outward appearance, it's always good, even when you've turned slightly green and your eyes are unfocused."

"I don't know what to say to that. I think that was a compliment?"

Ari sipped iced coffee and did not answer. Even though they had had coffee with breakfast at Ari's, Ari insisted on stopping off the highway at one of her favorite coffee joints/diners.

"Best iced coffee ever," she promised, hopping out of the car to run inside and get her usual order. A few minutes later, she bought back a tall, milky iced coffee drink for Sophia that was a little sweeter than Sophia typically liked, but not altogether bad.

Ari glanced down at her phone, which had been tossed into the center console. "I think I see a text from Rachel. Will you check what she's up to?"

Sophia reached for it and stared at the screen. "It says the ladies are feeling like spa visits this afternoon before gearing up for the next phase of the party. I guess we're free until the extravaganza kicks off later this afternoon."

"Wish I'd known, I would have spent more time sleeping in and being lazy this morning," Ari grumbled.

"I should get some work done," Sophia said, focusing on her own phone and starting to scroll through her emails.

"What? No, stop that. Put that thing down," Ari instructed.

"I run a business. A busy, growing business. I don't get days off," Sophia insisted.

"So do I. But I also acknowledge that I'm not, like, a robot, and actually deserve a weekend away once in a blue moon," Ari said.

Sophia didn't say anything, but clicked off her phone just to placate Ari. She gazed out the window. It was bright today, and they were driving past endless houses.

"I never pictured Vegas as having suburbs," Sophia said.

Ari laughed. "There's got to be some place for all of the people who work at the hotels and shows and casinos to live."

Ari merged onto a highway.

"So, you want to hit up the spa with everyone else?" she asked Sophia.

Sophia shook her head. "Not particularly. I know I should, and I know that is one activity that my sister and I can probably both relate to enjoying, but I'm really not in the mood. Besides, it's hot today, and having a massage or sitting in a steam room or hot tub doesn't sound appealing."

"So what are we going to do to kill a few hours?"

Sophia glanced down at Ari's phone, where texts from Rachel were popping up on the screen. "Well, Rachel says she's going out and about, wants to do some shopping."

Ari groaned.

"Not a fan of shopping, Miss Little?"

"I'd rather visit the dentist," she said.

"I was eyeing a bag last night in a window of a store at the mall we were at. Let's meet her there," Sophia decided, texting Rachel back.

··○··

"I miss the days when you two didn't get along at all," Ari complained as she trailed after Sophia into the mall.

Sophia was making her way toward a French designer store with a flamboyant display of bags - from what little Ari knew of the designer, she figured one probably cost more than her car - and up ahead, they had spotted Rachel window shopping, already holding a glossy shopping bag in one hand.

"You're supposed to be at a spa getting mud masks," Rachel teased when she saw Sophia walking towards her.

"I get dragged through the mud enough from my sister as it is, I don't need to add masks to the equation," she replied.

"Well, who needs to waste their time with masks when you have this place to shop at. Everything in here is gorgeous," Rachel sighed wistfully as they walked in.

Rachel wandered over to a display of scarves, while Sophia headed towards a wall of leather purses. Ari hesitated, not sure what to do in the place. It was big, bright and a little bit crowded. Nothing in the store appealed to her. For lack of anything better to do, she walked over to a display of keychains and coin purses, touched one, and recoiled quickly when she noticed the price tag said $295.

"For a coin purse? I could buy a year's worth of clothes for that price. Who shops here?" she muttered to herself, gazing around, expecting to see movie stars among them.

She saw Sophia talking to a sales person about a red purse, and she slowly made her way over to her.

"...and is it Italian leather?" Sophia was asking the woman.

A cow's a cow. Who cares what country the leather was from? Ari wondered to herself.

"I would have to check, but we typically source our leathers from the United States or Argentina," the woman said.

"This isn't as finely crafted as the ones I saw in your shop in Nice last summer," Sophia observed.

The woman scowled. "I assure you this piece lives up to our exacting standards..."

"It looks like a red purse to me," Ari said cheerfully.

Both women looked blankly at her.

"But... don't take my word for it," she said, holding up two hands and backing away.

"Thank you for the information," Sophia said brusquely to the woman, handing the purse back to her.

The saleswoman gave them both sour looks, which Sophia haughtily ignored, and she motioned to Ari to follow her over to Rachel, who was now examining a rack of leather jackets.

"Why is this designer stuff any better than any other coat or purse that you could find someplace normal?" Ari asked her.

"It has to do with the craftsmanship," Sophia said. "I mean, that bag was not the best example – this brand has cheapened and become so commercial in recent years – but for the most part, luxury designers still manufacture their goods in countries where craftsmanship is taught from one genera-tion to the next, where the pieces can be hand made according to tradition, the materials are high quality and sourced wisely, and the processes in making them – from softening the leather, to ensuring the color is perfect – is simply much better than the mass-produced items that are sold at most retail stores."

Ari didn't have a response to that.

"Clothes, accessories, undergarments, these things aren't just frivolous and meaningless items," Sophia continued, watching Ari, who in turn was eyeing a buttery, caramel-colored leather jacket that Rachel was holding up to a mirror. "We wear them every day. We spend our entire lives in them. It's our first, most immediate way of communicating about ourselves when we step outside or meet someone new. Wearing things that are well made, and make you feel good, reflects who you are. Isn't that worth something?"

Sophia delicately touched the leather jacket that Rachel had held up moments earlier. "Here. Hold it up. Look at yourself in the mirror."

Ari held it up, looked, and quickly realized that the jacket would look awesome on her.

"It suits you," Sophia said.

"May I try it on?" Ari asked Sophia.

"Go for it."

Ari put it on.

"You look amazing," Rachel said as Ari admired how it looked in the mirror.

Ari shrugged, smiling shyly. She took the jacket off and put it back on the rack.

The women browsed a few more minutes, before moving towards the exit.

"Let's go before I spend the entire amount of money I'm earning off of this weekend gig, and then some. My plan was to invest my earnings back into my business, not just blow it on jackets and scarves," Rachel said.

"So why did you get into fashion?" Ari asked Sophia as they walked back out onto the plaza. "Is it because of what you said? About liking how clothes are how a person presents themselves to the world?

Sophia nodded. "Partially, yes. Clothes also made me feel better at times in my life when nothing else really seemed to."

"I can so relate. For years, every time I broke up with someone, I went out and maxed out my credit card. Terrible habit, but I have a killer wardrobe thanks to all of the asses who dumped me," Rachel chimed in.

"I guess the clothes help impress the next one who comes along," Ari said.

"Nah, I bought the clothes for myself." Rachel said.

"Exactly," Sophia said. "Clothes aren't necessarily to impress other people. They shouldn't be, at least. They're for how they make you feel. The experience you have wearing them. Your own personal enjoyment. If other people happen to notice and like them, too... well, then that's just a perk."

"I guess I can see where you're coming from," Ari said, as Rachel steered them toward the next store.

"But to finish answering your question," Sophia continued, "that's not really the reason I started Forbidden. I actually liked clothes, and I liked the science behind them. Especially lingerie. I liked the challenge of designing and selling a product that is both necessary and exciting for women. They are essential items that we all wear every day, but they can also be a fun and frivolous and a bit naughty. What else in a woman's wardrobe can do all of that?"

"I like the name 'Forbidden,'" Rachel said. "But how did you come up with it?"

"When I was trying to come up with names for a lingerie

line, I was thinking about mythology. Paradise."

"Forbidden fruit," Ari said.

Sophia smiled, nodding.

"Nice," Rachel said.

"Seems like your whole career was pretty meticulously planned out," Ari said. "Your education, work experience, your interests in textiles and business."

"My goal was always to have my own business. I never wanted to work for someone else. And I loved every step in the process, really. I liked building it, perfecting it, growing it. I like having a little empire of my own," Sophia said.

Ari nodded understandingly. "I never liked working for other people, either."

"Oooh, look at these dresses!" Rachel said, directing them towards a display in another store window. "Gorgeous. Let's go in."

Sophia and Rachel went into the shop, and Ari dragged behind, shoving her hands in her pockets and looking around her, once again feeling a bit like a fish out of water.

Sophia studied the leather dresses that Rachel had seen in the window. They were nice. She picked up a black one, a simple shape, short, sleeveless, slender-fitting, with blue-colored color blocked accents.

Rachel looked at a similar red one with leather accents and held it up to herself in the mirror.

"Everything about this is so me," Rachel said wistfully.

Sophia held up the dress she was looking at.

"That would really look good on you," Rachel said to her.

Sophia shook her head. "I have no place to wear it. Definitely not workplace friendly."

"You make lingerie, what exactly is the protocol for workplace-friendly attire in your world?" Ari asked, an eyebrow raised.

"It's not short leather dresses, I can tell you that."

"Come on, let's try them on," Rachel said.

"That looks damn good on you," Rachel commented a few minutes later as they both emerged from their dressing rooms, Sophia in the black dress with the blue.

Ari was sitting in a group of soft chairs outside the fitting rooms, waiting patiently. She looked up at both Rachel and Sophia.

"I have the wrong kind of shoes on," Sophia said, looking down at her plain heels.

"Here," Rachel said, sliding off her mile-high sparkly silver heels.

Sophia looked at the shoes disdainfully. She did not exactly make a habit of trying on other peoples' shoes; the thought was slightly off putting. But Ari and Rachel were looking at her expectantly, and she supposed she was in the middle of some sort of bonding moment that was going shockingly well. She could not remember the last time she bonded with someone outside of work (or a fling). Not wanting to ruin the moment, she didn't say anything, took the shoes, slid them on, and...

"Much better," Rachel said approvingly as Sophia studied her reflection in the mirror. "You've got to get that dress."

Sophia turned in front of the mirror, inspecting it from different angles. The dress was really good.

She glanced over at Ari, and the places where Ari's eyes were lingering said everything she needed to know.

She decided to get the dress.

The three of them emerged from the store thirty minutes later, Rachel asking Ari if she was sure she did not want to buy anything before they had to go back.

"I'm good with my jeans," Ari promised her.

Rachel had also decided to leave the store with a new,

slim-fitting, short dress, although she ended up going with one that was red and trimmed in lace.

"Now to find the right occasion for this dress," Sophia said.

"Tonight," Rachel answered. "It'll be the perfect night for wearing sinful dresses. And speaking of sin, it's time to go back to the hotel so we can meet up with the bachelorette group when they return. Their spa break is almost over so they'll no doubt be all refreshed and ready to dive headfirst into some more debauchery."

"Couldn't they just have spent the rest of the day at the spa?" asked Sophia, scrunching up her nose.

"Sophia had a little too much to drink last night," Ari explained to Rachel.

"Well, what did you expect, we're in Vegas," Rachel teased as they got into the car.

"Vegas is clearly for people who don't have a 8am meeting on Monday with suppliers in Japan, followed by a 10am meeting about social media marketing with an agency in New York," muttered Sophia.

"That's two whole days away. Can't you just let work go this weekend?" asked Ari, pulling out of the parking garage.

"At least your workaholicism is paying off. Your stuff is really good, Sophia. I've stopped in your store a few times after work," Rachel said.

"Thank you," Sophia said, genuinely pleased by Rachel's compliment.

"You know... my cousin is a professional stylist in New York and has a good social media following. He does tv shows, photoshoots, styling for magazines, that sort of thing. He gets lots of clothes sent to him all of the time by designers who want to have him feature their stuff. If you wanted to send him a few of your things, I'd let him know to look out for them. He'd be more likely to take a look if I give him a heads up," Rachel offered.

Sophia tucked a piece of hair behind her ear. "That would be fantastic. Sure. I'll arrange to send him a few pieces next week."

"I'll text you his mailing info," Rachel said, "And I'll let him know to watch for something from Forbidden."

"All right, enough shop talk. We've got to go back to the hotel and get this Saturday night party under way," Ari said, interrupting them.

"Wonderful," muttered Sophia, the high of the shopping trip and the slightly unnerving, but pleasant, experience of shopping with friends (were they her friends?) starting to wear off at the prospect of rejoining her sister for more bachelorette shenanigans.

"My goal tonight is to give your sister the Saturday night party of her dreams," Rachel said. "Maybe it'll be so good her marriage will stick this time."

"My goal tonight is to not need Nate's hangover cure," Sophia grumbled.

Ari glanced at her and smiled. "He texted me to say there's plenty in the fridge back home if you need it."

"Back home?" Rachel asked. "So that's where you two were last night. At Ari's."

Sophia and Ari didn't reply. Sophia glanced at Rachel in the backseat and noticed she was grinning.

"Back to the grind," Rachel announced a few minutes later as they pulled into the valet parking for Panache. "Shopping and partying. I love this job."

··◦··

Sophia woke up. She kept her eyes closed for a few minutes. The bright sun was shining through a nearby window and she did not quite feel like opening her eyes to face the day yet.

She tucked the soft sheet closer under her chin, and rolled onto her back, sighing to herself.

And then, she felt something she had not felt in a while.

Someone moved next to her in the bed.

She paused, immobile, afraid to wiggle an inch, but popped her eyes open.

Where was she?

The light filtered through her eyelashes as she blinked, and the first thing she noticed was a vividly colored painting on the wall of the room she was in.

She was back in Ari's room.

There were more small movements next to her. She barely breathed, as though any motion on her part would cause whatever reality awaited her to crash in. In her half-awake state, she struggled to recall the events of last night.

She slowly turned her head to look over at the other half of the bed, and noticed a long sweep of wavy blonde hair splayed out across the pillow. Somewhere underneath the covers, her companion was stirring.

And then memories of the night before came flooding back to her.

8

...Stays in Vegas

"You aren't drunk, Sophia, are you?" Ari asked, her eyes glimmering and her mouth half-curled into an amused smile, clutching her phone in one hand.

Sophia held up her half-empty glass and raised her voice so she could be heard over the music. "Not tonight. Not from half a glass of a gin and tonic that I've been pretending to sip for the past three hours."

"Now you're getting the hang of it."

"It would appear I am," Sophia said, raising her voice again as the music crescendoed, the beat reverberating through the penthouse. All around them, Sabrina's friends were dancing, drinking, and laughing.

"Having fun, sis?" her sister asked, gliding past her, a full glass of red wine in hand. "At least you don't look boring, for once."

Sophia decided she would accept that as one of the few

compliments her sister had ever given her.

She watched as her sister was shuffled towards two men, dancers hired to add some liveliness (and gender diversity) to the party, giving Sabrina's mishmash group of friends something to focus on other than the continuous flow of booze.

Earlier that night, Sophia had to admit that while watching her sister get lots of attention from two greased-up male strippers dressed as policemen might have been a scene that was straight out of a million really horrible, D-list movies, it was still entertaining... and best of all, a delightful source of blackmail material. She took several pictures, just in case they might ever come in handy.

Although having said pictures would be contingent on ever getting her phone back. Sabrina had caught Sophia out on the rooftop terrace checking emails on it. Her sister reacted by grabbing it out of her hands and throwing it into a large container with a palm tree.

"No more of this," Sabrina had called out over the music, slurring her words slightly. "You're never going to get a bachelorette party of your own unless you give up this damn phone. Come with me."

Sabrina and one of her friends - Sophia seemed to recall her name was Cassandra - pulled her into the dizzying fray of music, giddy friends and the hired dancers. Sophia reluctantly found herself amongst a lot of bodies, hands, and swaying hips.

Sophia humored her sister for a while by dancing, only cringing once or twice when someone smelling too strongly of booze brushed up against her (or worse, when it was one of the hired dancers, who all smelled way too strongly of cologne), but when Sabrina inevitably became distracted by one of the dancers - a tall, dark, handsome man with teeth that were almost too white and perfect - Sophia found the opportunity to edge out of the fray of people. As she did, she spotted Ari off to the side, scrolling through her phone.

Sophia hadn't seen Ari do anything all night other than sip a drink or two and chat on the sidelines.

Sophia paused and studied her for a moment from a distance. Ari's blonde hair tumbled in soft waves over her shoulders. She stood tall in her high leather boots, which had a bit of a heel to them, and her eyes seemed soft as she looked down at the screen of her phone. She looked pretty like that.

Shame that such a beautiful, charming woman would spend the whole evening as a wallflower, Sophia thought to herself.

Sophia took a breath then waltzed up to Ari, delicately took the phone out of her hands, her eyes shining gleefully, and gently tossed it into a nearby pot of flowers.

"Not tonight, Ms. Little," she said firmly, speaking loud enough to be heard over the music, and, taking her hand, pulled Ari with her into the mix of people dancing.

At first, they danced carefree and friendly, Ari laughing as soon as she got over the shock of being whisked away from the sidelines, shaking her head in pretend annoyance, but ultimately playing along and swaying with the rest of the group. After a while, in one of those moments that felt like it should have happened in slow motion, one of Sabrina's shirtless dancers accidentally bumped Sophia from behind and Sophia was nudged closer to Ari. Out of instinct, Ari reached out and caught her as she was pushed close.

There was a moment, then, when both of their eyes met, Ari gripping Sophia's forearms. As soon as Sophia found her balance again, Ari let her go.

Then, in a split second decision, Sophia reached out and pulled Ari back towards her, so they could continue to dance. This time in much closer proximity.

Ari seemed caught off guard for a moment by the gesture. She looked nervously at Sophia, but the determination in Sophia's eyes told her all she needed to know. For a moment, Sophia rested a hand on each of Ari's shoulders. One of her hands dropped, finding Ari's hand and squeezing it reassuringly.

Ari relaxed.

They stayed that way until the music shifted again a minute or two later. The all-too brief spell was broken. Ari excused herself, and before Sophia could follow, the blonde disappeared somewhere into the crowd.

Sophia went back outside for a breath of fresh air.

··o··

MIDNIGHT

Eventually, the party entered that state where everyone had lost track of time and all sense of decorum had long since flown out the window. The music, the laughter, the booze, their dizzying view over the Strip, the antics of the hired dancers who would occasionally put on a bit of a performance of their own - a solo dance in the middle of the floor, a not-so-serious but delightfully over-the-top declaration of love to one of the guests - just to keep things interesting, everything providing nonstop distractions and endless entertainment. Some of the dancers had paired up with the guests to dance during slower songs. At one point, Sophia even thought she saw Rachel dancing with one of Sabrina's friends, Cassandra.

Who knew? She mused to herself, watching the two of them for a few seconds as one song that the DJ was playing transitioned to the next.

Everyone around her had became a little bleary-eyed from the hours of drinking, dancing and operating in a low-light atmosphere, punctuated only by the flashes from colorful dance lights that had been strategically placed around the space.

She thought she spotted her sister sitting out on the roof-top garden at one point, her head resting against one hand, her fiery mane of auburn hair tumbling out of the elegant updo that it had been in earlier that evening. She seemed quiet for once.

Sophia still had not had much to drink. She saw Ari once again after Ari had wandered off after their dance, but she felt too tongue-tied to approach her. She noticed when Ari spoke with Rachel at one point, then Cassandra, then laughed at some joke that the three shared. Ari then grabbed a few tortilla chips from the array of snacks set up in the kitchen before wandering into another room, disappearing again before Sophia could make her way over.

Sophia nervously brushed her hand through her hair. She cursed her eyes for constantly being drawn to the woman. It was irritating. Yet, she found those lingering glances some-what impossible to control.

It was not a feeling she was accustomed to. At least not in recent years. It reminded her of a time when she was young-er, back in her school days, when her draw towards certain people had been more natural. Back when her romances were less about the instant gratification of a conquer, but rather, more about chemistry and gentle attraction to anoth-er human being. Discovering them as a person.

In recent years, she had enjoyed the cat and mouse game so much that she almost forgot what it was like not to be in hot pursuit of whomever she found herself attracted to. She relished the chase. The challenge of cornering her prey. The exquisite satisfaction when she finally did. The act of forget-ting about it entirely afterwards.

But with Ari, once again, it seemed different. Sure, some

primal part of Sophia still instinctually wanted to play cat and mouse with her. Ari herself seemed to realize that about Sophia. She was game for it, even, judging from her knowing attitude around Sophia.

Ari was not sitting prey. She was the kind of prey who bit back.

Sophia appreciated that Ari was her own person and was not, by any means, weak or naïve.

In fact, bottom line, Sophia was not sure if Ari was interested at all. Perhaps she was amused by her, even. Flattered by the attention, perhaps, but not *into* it.

Either way, Sophia felt Ari had made it very clear to her that she would be just fine one way or another, with or without Sophia's attention.

Ari could take her or leave her.

And so for Sophia, this time, the game was different.

Because of that, as much as she was drawn to Ari, Sophia was also quite uneasy around her.

Sophia took a sip of water.

There was also the way that Ari did so much for her, despite everything. Took a genuine interest in her as a friend. Sophia was not used to having friends outside of work, and was not sure how to manage it. She was not even sure why she deserved Ari's time. She was not used to that kind of attention - attention that did not seem to come with any strings attached - and she did not think she liked the unknown aspect of it. This was foreign ground to Sophia.

Trying to forget about Ari for a moment, Sophia turned her focus elsewhere and noticed Sabrina had moved back inside, and having clearly found her second wind, was starting to get a little too flirty with the bartender. Sophia rolled her eyes and decided she simply did not want to find out where *that* was going, and so she walked around the pool, further away from anyone.

After a night of dancing and hours of socializing involving endless conversations and drinking games with Sabrina's inane friends, it must now be after midnight. Sophia determined that her sister and friends were content. Once again, Rachel's evening soiree could be declared yet another success, and thus it seemed her own maid of honor duties had officially been fulfilled for the night.

A waiter passed next to her with a tray of glasses of champagne, and Sophia took one.

Cheers, she thought to herself.

She was off duty for the night.

As she leaned against the railing, sipping her champagne and looking out across the sparkling, light-filled view beyond of flashing signs and neon lights and massive, larger-than-life hotels, she heard footsteps behind her.

"Still faking the drinking?" Ari asked her.

Sophia stood up straight and turned around.

"No. I believe my duties are done for the day, so I am capping off the night with something real."

"Cheers," Ari said.

Ari raised her own glass of wine, and they clinked their glasses.

"Tonight, I think I actually enjoyed myself. Almost," Sophia said.

Sophia hoped Ari couldn't detect the slight waver in her voice. Ari suddenly made her nervous.

"Almost?" Ari leaned against the railing and looked out at the view.

They were on the far end of the terrace, separated from the party by the pool. The blue water was sparkling in the dark, the lights underneath the surface of the water casting a soft, luminescent glow around them.

"I haven't had as terrible of a time as I thought I would," Sophia said slowly. "And I haven't thought - or even worried - about work for hours."

"That is an accomplishment," Ari said, raising her glass again. "Glad you finally found a distraction."

You have no idea, thought Sophia.

She took a sip of champagne, then spoke. "Ms. Little?"

"Yeah?"

"Why... all of this?" Sophia asked.

"Why all of what?"

Sophia took a deep breath, and dropped her voice.

"Your idea that I have Rachel plan the party. Your help every step of the way, even coming along with us. Your general support, when I am fairly certain you could have chosen a million more appealing things to do with a weekend off than this."

Ari shrugged. "It's nothing."

Sophia looked her in the eyes and pursed her lips.

Ari stilled under Sophia's gaze.

"It's not nothing," Sophia whispered.

Ari did not reply. She looked back out over the view, a light breeze making her soft hair flutter slightly.

Slowly, steadily, Sophia reached out to Ari. Her hand found hers. It was soft, yet strong.

And as they laced their fingers, standing in the cool night air, an indescribable current of energy running between them, they both knew it wasn't nothing.

"I've never really had a lot of friends," Ari said quietly. "I wanted to help out because I consider you a friend. And I've noticed a funny thing with us... things tend to turn out better when the two of us collaborate on them. On pastries. Or parties. Whatever it is."

"Oh. I see. You were just being friendly. A good neighbor,"

Sophia said softly, a teasing smile playing across her lips as the breeze lifted her own hair around her shoulders.

Ari dropped Sophia's hand.

"Stop," Ari breathed, moving back just a bit, her blue eyes searching Sophia's deep brown eyes. "It's not like that. I really don't have ulterior motives."

"Oh, I know. I can tell you're being genuine, Ms. Little. And I really do appreciate everything you do."

She paused.

"But I also feel - over these past few weeks - you flatter me with your attention," she said, closing some of the space between them. "And I don't need flattery. It makes me nervous."

"Sorry," Ari said, staring at Sophia, wondering what was coming next.

"I don't like someone catering to me all of the time. I don't want to be the needy neighbor, the needy friend, the needy single mom next door that has to have help all the time," Sophia said, her eyes narrowed and voice low, her head tilted slightly.

"I don't think any of that," Ari said.

Sophia ignored her. "I like to help. Contribute. When someone does things for me, too many things for me, I feel like I am indebted to them. That need to repay them. And I don't like that feeling."

"That's not how things work. That's not how I see it. Or how I see you."

Sophia did not answer right away. She studied Ari for a moment, and Ari held her breath.

"You make me nervous, Ms. Little," Sophia admitted in a low voice. "And I don't know what to do about it. You have left me utterly at a loss."

Sophia walked away before Ari could collect her thoughts and reply, her heels tap-tap-tapping their way around the pool. She went back inside, leaving Ari alone.

••○••

1:30 AM

"What was that all about?" Rachel asked Ari a few minutes later, restocking a table in the kitchen area with clean glasses, pitchers of water and various snacks: chips, guacamole, salsa.

The party had slowed, but not ended. The music continued, albeit somewhat looser and lower key than it had been an hour before. The dramatic, low, slow beats seemed to echo Ari's shift in mood.

"I don't know," Ari said honestly, her heart still racing.

"Is Sophia... is she flirting with you?" Rachel asked, a hand on her hip, her eyes narrowed.

"I really don't know," Ari repeated, shoving the hand that Sophia had held moments before into her pocket.

"It sure looked like she was," Rachel said. "So what are you waiting for? Go after her."

"After her? Where did she go?" Ari asked.

Rachel motioned towards the entryway to the suite. "I saw her leave. I don't know. But it was just a few minutes ago, she couldn't have gotten far."

••○••

Ari got into the private elevator. It appeared to have just returned to the penthouse from the lobby. Where was Sophia going? It would be impossible to find her in the vast hotel-within-a-hotel complex they were surrounded by if she had already left the lobby of Panache.

Ari felt like she was in the elevator forever, descending, wondering where she would go next to find Sophia.

And wondering what she would do when she found Sophia.

Finally, Ari reached the ground floor and stepped out. She glanced around. The lobby was relatively quiet at the late (or was it early?) hour, hardly anyone around.

She thought she saw movement beyond a glass door leading to a courtyard. She went outside, into the dimly lit courtyard. There was a small, illuminated fountain out there. The motion of the water and the light reflecting on it cast sparkling flecks of light onto the surrounding walls. Above the fountain, wisteria grew upwards from large pots, the branches creating a leafy roof over their heads. Strings of fairy lights illuminated their twisting branches, making for a heavenly picture above them.

Ari scanned the courtyard. It was empty except for Sophia, who was standing by the fountain, staring into the water.

Ari walked over to Sophia. Sophia looked up, but did not say anything. Her eyes were soft, wide.

Ari took one more step toward the brunette, and kissed her firmly.

··o··

Sophia stumbled a bit in surprise, but recovered quickly. Ari continued to press herself toward her, maintaining the kiss for a moment, but then pulling back for just a split second, giving Sophia a moment. Sophia took the opportunity to take charge and pressed her lips into the other woman's, and it was Ari's turn to close her eyes and lose herself in it, allow herself to be pulled into their own little world, the one where only a fountain, sparkly lights, wisteria branches and Sophia existed. She allowed herself to simply surrender.

Finally, Ari pulled away.

"What is it?" Sophia whispered, gazing into the woman's blue eyes.

"Are you sure?" Ari breathed, her eyes searching, desperately trying to read Sophia's expression.

Sophia nodded slowly.

"You really didn't have too much to drink, or anything?" Ari asked, worried.

Sophia laughed lightly. "No, I have not. I know what I'm doing. What about you?"

Ari smiled.

"The same," she said, and she leaned in and they continued to kiss.

··○··

They stayed that way for a long while, in the quiet, secret courtyard. It was their own world, and they were lost in the night and the unfamiliar, but cozy, surroundings.

"We're going to eventually have to leave," Sophia reluctantly noted after they had been there for what could have been hours. Or maybe it had only been minutes. They had found their way to a nearby bench, and were now seated, listening to the soft trickling sound of the water.

"I don't think I can go back upstairs," admitted Ari.

"Me neither," Sophia agreed.

"So... we're here," Ari said.

They stayed that way for a little while longer, thigh touching thigh, shoulder touching shoulder, hands interlaced on Sophia's lap, afraid to move, afraid to break the magic.

But finally, they were forced to re-enter reality when a group of three women stumbled into their private, quiet little courtyard, talking loudly and waving their phones around, laughing.

"We're in Vegas," Sophia whispered, touching her own forehead tenderly to Ari's, as the intrusion forced them awake from their reverie. "It's probably only about two in the morning. There's still plenty of time left in the night."

Their faces still flushed and eyes glimmering with anticipation of what could be next, they stood up and ventured into the night.

··o··

2:25 AM

They spent some time walking. They spoke very little, but the invisible electricity in the air between them spoke louder than any conversation topic could. Both felt it: the energy, the connection, that completely unexplainable draw they had to each other, despite their best judgment on the matter. Both knew that what had just happened was not something that could be easily ignored this time.

They were desperate to find out what would happen next. Neither wanted the night to be over. They were on a high, enjoying a brief respite from reality, and enjoying their unfamiliar surroundings together.

"I don't want to be boring," Sophia declared after they walked a while.

They stood on a sidewalk somewhere... she had lost track of where they had gone. They were surrounded by neon, by flashing lights, by people walking, shouting. By noise and music.

"You are not boring," Ari assured her.

Sophia did not respond. She put a hand on her hip, surveying her surroundings. There were signs for casinos, gambling. But that was not her thing.

Then another sign caught her eye.

"Tattoos?" Ari asked, following her gaze. "Trust me, you do not want to do that."

"Why not?" Sophia asked, "It would be a unique way to remember a very unusual weekend. I'd always have something to prove that I can just let it all go."

"Yeah, but do you really permanently want that on your skin?"

Sophia sighed. "What's a little one? To prove that I am not a complete bore?"

"You don't need to do something like that to prove it," Ari said, her hand resting gently on her arm.

Sophia glanced down at it, and saw a small tattoo of a heart peeking out on Ari's wrist.

"Says the woman with a tattoo," Sophia said.

"Yeah, but I thought about this one, planned it for a while..." Ari protested. "Look, it's up to you if you get a tattoo, but first, I really need food."

"What do you suggest?" Sophia asked.

"There's a good burger joint nearby. Do you accept burgers and fries in your life once in a while? You know, the food that most people consider a viable alternative to salads?"

"I know what a burger is, and yes, I do eat them on rare occasion," Sophia said.

"See? More proof you're not a bore," Ari teased.

"I'm adjusting to this Vegas thing. A night that included my sister being 'arrested' by a stripper, engaging in public displays of affection, seriously considering a tattoo and now burgers. I'm ready to do anything at this point," she said, smiling.

"Anything?" Ari asked mischievously. "I might just keep that in mind for later."

Sophia tried to laugh at that, but Ari noted that there was a certain nervousness in her reaction.

They grabbed burgers to go from Ari's burger joint and sat outside near some fountains, watching the groups of people walk by in the night, mulling around, taking pictures even in the late hour. In fact, there were people around doing everything conceivable in the night: two men were jogging, and a group of early 20-somethings was walking, zombie-like, towards the burger joint while debating where they would go after.

"These are delicious," Sophia confessed, stealing a few fries from the pile that Ari had bought as a side to share.

Ari grinned. "They're my favorite in Vegas. Among my favorite in the country."

"Everyone's big idea of rebelling and going wild is getting drunk and watching naked people strut across a stage, but true rebellion to me is eating a cheeseburger and fries at three in the morning," Sophia sighed after she finished the last of the greasy burger, slouched back on the bench, and admired the view around her - the people, the fountains, the lights, Ari - enjoying the utter bliss of detachment from her usual world.

Ari studied Sophia. She looked so pretty in the soft, low light at night, her hair slightly disheveled from the evening, her dress hugging her body tightly, some of her harsh make-up from earlier in the evening now worn off, so she now looked less severe. It was the first time Ari had ever seen her truly relaxed.

"We have to move from this bench eventually," Ari said, tearing her eyes away from Sophia to watch another loud group of men stumble down the sidewalk, a group of laughing and chatting women not far behind.

"I suppose I should be a good sport and go back," Sophia said.

"Or, they'll all be too trashed to even notice you're not there at this point," Ari pointed out.

Sophia sensed it again: that electricity in the air between them. With their food eaten and their minds settled back on the night at hand, it had come back.

"Remember what we talked about this morning? You can sleep at my place again tonight if you want." Ari said, trying to sound casual, but her voice catching slightly in her throat as she spoke.

Sophia pursed her lips, thinking.

Objectively speaking, the offer to go back to Ari's instead of the party penthouse had seemed like the obvious choice that morning. Now, considering the events of the evening, it felt far more complicated than it had last night. They had just spent the last little while in a blissful haze, and she was not sure either one of them was ready for the temptation that might come next if they went back to the house together.

Ari sensed her hesitation. "I am merely offering it as a quiet alternative to the penthouse."

Sophia nodded, making up her mind. Somehow managing to convince herself that it could still be innocent, ignoring that surge of electricity that was sparkling in the air between them, and ignoring her mind that was screaming at her that she was surely complicating things, she agreed.

"Let's go, then."

She and Ari got up and left.

··◦··

3:55 AM

"So, you know your way around now," Ari said quietly, stating the obvious, turning on a small lamp as they stepped into Ari's house.

It was nearly 4, and the night was at its darkest. It would be dawn soon, Sophia thought vaguely.

Ari slowly walked into the house, dropping her keys onto a table. Sophia set her purse on a chair near the door. It was nearly morning, but neither of them felt tired after their middle-of-the-night adventures.

"Something to drink?" Ari offered vaguely, heading towards the kitchen.

Sophia did not reply, just followed her. When they reached

the kitchen, Ari did not turn on any lights, but she opened the fridge, casting a strip of light briefly onto the floor while she removed a pitcher of Nate's special tonic.

"You don't seem to be nearly as intoxicated as you were last night, but hey, the stuff tastes decent and better safe than sorry, right?" Ari was saying quietly.

Sophia detected the nerves in Ari's voice.

Sophia focused on the way Ari moved, studied her as she took out two glasses from the shelf and set them next to each other, then poured the drink into each one. Sophia smiled subtly to herself at the way Ari's hair draped around her shoulders, the way her eyes sparkled as she talked, her graceful movements. She wanted to memorize everything about her.

"Ari?" Sophia asked finally, touching her on the shoulder as she poured the two glasses.

"Yes?" Ari asked, setting down the pitcher and turning to her.

"The only thing I'm intoxicated with is..."

And she finished that thought with a kiss.

Urgently this time, she pressed toward her more intimately than they had dared be with each other in the courtyard, her whole body seemingly trying to merge with the other woman.

Ari responded for the briefest second by freezing, but settled into the kiss quickly. She let Sophia take control here, enjoying her enthusiasm.

Both knew, with quite a bit of certainty now, what came next.

Sophia heard Ari groan softly as she felt the woman's tongue dance along her own. The intimacy felt comfortable, natural, and both settled into it easily.

Sophia pressed Ari against the kitchen cabinets and counter... her mind was racing as Ari sensed her distraction and took back control, gently urging Sophia towards the living room. Ari slowly navigated the two of them to the couch, where she urged Sophia to lay down on her back. Sophia complied, and from there, in that position of both passion and vulnerability, underneath the other woman... it was clear, very clear, extremely clear, that there was no going back.

Sophia moaned slightly as Ari moved her lips down to her jaw, her collar, and then, urging Sophia to sit up slightly, wrapped her hands around her back in search of the zipper for the dress.

"Are you... is this... okay?" Ari whispered.

Sophia nodded, her eyes closed, already lost to the moment and to the sensations. "Yes. Very much so, Arianna."

"I want you," the blonde woman said, longingly, and from that moment on, their words were few and far between, as the dress came off, and Ari's blouse and jeans were also eventual victims of their wandering hands, kisses, trailing lips and explorations on the sofa. Eventually, Ari shifted lower, and lower, until the sounds of Sophia's sighs and heavy breathing were all that she needed to guide her through the rest of the night.

..o..

9:30 AM

As Sophia slowly looked over at the other half of the bed and noticed a long sweep of wavy blonde hair splayed out across the pillow, she felt Ari stirring.

As memories of the previous night - or, technically, it all had happened earlier that morning - flooded back to Sophia's mind, she recalled flashes and snapshots of the time they had spent in that darkest hour of the night. They had been awake, exploring, smiling, laughing, lost in their reverie all the way until the sun was well above the horizon and the birds were singing. At some point, both women had finally, at last, become completely sated and not to mention slightly delirious from not having slept at all that night.

They had not, technically speaking, even been to bed by that point.

Most of their activities had been everywhere but the bed.

They finally stumbled up to the bedroom loft and fell asleep, and a few hours later, Sophia woke up.

She lay still as the memories of the night before returned to her. The sounds of the woman breathing next to her were soothing. She was basking in the fact that she felt more relaxed than she had in months. She was still for a while, not wanting it to ever dissipate.

But eventually, she grew restless.

She gingerly got out of bed. Ari stirred, but did not seem to wake up. Sophia tiptoed over to the dresser to find something to put on, just in case someone came back - Nate, or whomever - and then went in search of her phone.

After looking through her purse, she remembered that it had been tossed into a planter back at the penthouse the night before.

It bothered her, suddenly, to be cut off from her phone. What if Percy had sent her a message? How could she be so irresponsible as to not have checked it already that morning?

She went downstairs and did a quick survey of the room. There was an old MacBook on an end table near the couch. She figured it was probably poor form to be in someone's house and use their computer, but she really was desperate to at least check her email.

"Trying to find out my deepest, darkest secrets?" Ari called down sleepily from the loft a few minutes later.

Sophia looked up at her sheepishly. The computer was still turning on.

"I'm sorry. It's just that I don't have my phone. It was tossed under a palm tree at the hotel last night by my lovely sister. I want to check my email and make sure Percy hasn't sent me anything."

"You've managed pretty well without that thing for, what, 11 hours?" Ari observed. "I'm impressed."

Ari walked downstairs.

"What ever did you do to distract yourself for all those hours?" Ari smirked, heading to the couch, where she crawled up next to Sophia and kissed her.

It was a quick, sweet peck, her blonde hair brushing Sophia's cheeks.

Sophia paused at that, looking up from the computer, and grabbed a piece of Ari's shirt, gently pulling her back towards her.

She gave her a deeper kiss.

"Mmm," Ari said a few moments later, her eyes closed. "The computer's got a password on it. You're gonna need me to unlock it."

Sophia smiled, but pulled Ari back towards her, kissing her yet again, this time even more deeply.

Ari settled into it for a few moments, then broke it off, laughing. "I need to make breakfast, otherwise we're going to be late."

"Password first?" Sophia asked, passing the computer to her, and Ari typed something in.

"There. I think you earned that. I'll go make coffee."

"Thank you," Sophia said, feeling relieved as she logged into her email.

Ari turned on some music and started to make coffee, while Sophia settled into the couch in the sun-filled room, scrolling through her inbox.

There was an email from Percy, but it was just a photo of a hike he'd taken yesterday with his cousins, who he was staying with for the weekend. She smiled, writing him back, promising she'd see him that night.

She then scrolled through some of her work emails. It was too tempting: her email inbox had nearly a hundred new emails since Friday, not including the spam, junk and advertisements. She was clicking through a few, and then she read one in particular that caused her to make a surprised sound out loud.

"What is it?" Ari turned, hearing Sophia.

"I have to go to Paris," Sophia said, re-reading the email to be sure that was right.

"Whoa. When?"

"It's to meet with a buyer - a huge department store - I've been trying to get their attention for months. They want to meet with me this coming week. I have to book a flight now."

"Now? Are you serious?"

"I am," Sophia said, clicking over to an airfare search website as soon as she understood exactly when they wanted to meet with her.

"Wow. Well, I guess we're all going home today, so the timing's good at least."

At the sound of disappointment in Ari's voice, Sophia paused her search, stood up, and wandered over to the woman.

"Last night," she said quietly to Ari and reaching out to rest her hands on the other woman's waist, "was one of the best I've had in a long time. And I mean that in more ways than one."

She looked into Ari's eyes.

"Thank you, Arianna," she said, pausing after she said the

woman's first name, savoring how it sounded as it escaped her lips, "For getting my mind out of my world and into yours. I needed this. And I didn't even know I needed this."

Ari gave her a smile. "Any time."

"And Arianna?"

"Hm?"

"Thanks for talking me out of getting a tattoo last night."

Ari laughed.

Smiling, Sophia kissed her again, and returned to the laptop.

"I should take you to Paris," Sophia said as Ari brought her a mug of coffee, typing her credit card into an airline website.

Ari looked up. "What would I do there?"

"You could stay with me, see the sights during the day while I'm at meetings. Let me show you some of the perks of my world."

"I don't have a passport," Ari confessed.

"Oh." Sophia paused. "You should really get one, for the future. Just in case."

"Okay," Ari said, somewhat uncertainly.

"I'll be back in a week," Sophia assured her, confirming a flight that departed from San Francisco that night.

Ari nodded. "I'm happy for you. That sounds like a great opportunity. But let me remind you that, for the next hour, you're still here, so let's have some coffee and something to eat before you jet set away."

"It's a deal," Sophia said, shutting the laptop and turning her focus back to the beautiful blonde who had plopped down onto the sofa next to her.

"Do you think we have time to..." Ari started to ask, burrowing into the cushions next to Sophia.

"There's only one way to find out," Sophia said, smiling as she drew the woman closer to her.

9

DREAMS

Sophia returned back to California that afternoon with everyone else on the jet. She was happy to pick up Percy, who had been staying with her parents, but then faced the task of apologetically breaking the news to him on their drive home that she would be leaving for a work trip that night and he would be going back to her parents' house.

"You're going to be gone again?" he asked, his mouth dropping open at the news.

Sophia let out her breath and closed her eyes for a second. She felt a pang of guilt at the hurt in his voice. "I'm sorry, Percy. I have some important meetings set up for this week. I really need to go."

"Can I go with you?"

"I don't think so. You need to go to school."

He scowled at that. "I wish you weren't always leaving! You're always at work, or traveling, or doing something away from here!"

He stormed upstairs as soon as they got home.

"Please be packed by four o'clock!" she called after him.

Her moping son now shut away in his room, Sophia decided it was a good time to drive by her office to pick up a few things she needed for the week. She filled the better part of one of her two suitcases with many, many samples from her workshop. She also gave Elle, who was working that afternoon, instructions to mail Rachel's cousin a few pieces from the shop in the hopes that he might feature something from her collection on his social media accounts; if he was as influential as Rachel said, it would not hurt to try.

She dropped her moping son off back at her parents' house and then drove to the airport to catch her flight to Paris that evening. As the plane gradually climbed in altitude and the sun set into the ocean behind her, she informed the flight attendant passing out dinner menus that she did not want to be disturbed until they served breakfast. As she pulled a silk sleeping mask over her eyes, she felt the magic that had surrounded their weekend dripping away behind her. She could not believe that early that very morning she had been cozied up with Ari on the couch, sipping coffee. 12 hours later, it seemed like an eternity - and world - ago.

··◦··

At The Little Cafe, Ari was also feeling the magical sparks of the past weekend disappear into thin air.

Even her connection with Sophia seemed to fade as soon as they parted ways at the executive airport. Everyone had deplaned and was saying goodbye. Not wanting to make a fuss in front of everyone, Sophia had discreetly squeezed Ari's hand seconds before Sophia left to go home and take care of Percy and catch her flight that night, and Ari drove back to her quiet studio apartment.

A few days later, their communication had devolved into quick texts.

Monday, 6 PM Central European Time

I arrived. I'll miss your coffee this week. S.

Monday, Noon Pacific

Knock their French socks off, Sophia.

Tuesday, 1 PM Central European Time

On my way to afternoon meeting. Hope your week is going well.

Now that was a little impersonal, Ari thought to herself when she saw the latest text one morning, scowling slightly, before sending what she hoped was a warmer reply.

But it was better than what came the day after. The next day she did not receive any texts at all from Sophia.

Later that day, however, Ari happened to see Percy when he dropped by the cafe after school.

"I missed the grilled cheese," he explained, sitting down at the counter.

"Hey," Ari said, glad to see him, and a few minutes later she brought him a plate of grilled cheese with a small side of potato chips and tossed salad. "On the house."

"Thanks," Percy said, putting down his video game to inhale the plate of food.

"Who are you staying with while your mom's away?" Ari asked.

"My grandparents. They live kind of far away, but it's just a train ride from school," he replied.

Ari knew she should not fish for details about Sophia from Percy... something about it did not feel right. But the minimal texts, the abrupt departure, and the fact that her mind generally could not get off of the woman, she just could not resist.

She tried to sound casual as she asked, "Have you heard anything from your mom?"

Percy shook his head. "Not much. I think she's in a lot of meetings."

"I'll bet." Ari said, disappointed, though unsurprised, at the lack of news.

"Let me know if you need anything," she said to him and she went back to work.

··○··

"You're staying late a lot this week," Rachel commented later that night after the shop had closed and Ari had put away a few dishes, wiped up tables, and refilled canisters with coffee beans.

"Yeah, I've got some stuff to catch up on after the weekend," Ari said as she typed on her laptop in her office.

In all fairness, she really did have to catch up on some things. She was attempting to look over some spreadsheets of her finances. It was a task that she had been dreading, but had vowed to herself to deal with after the weekend.

"Like emailing a certain brunette?" Rachel asked.

Ari thought about the emails she had received that day: invoices, ads, junk. Nothing very exciting.

"Not many of those to reply to," Ari grumbled.

Rachel paused. "It's not like you to just mope around. What'd she do, give you the cold shoulder in Vegas?"

"Not exactly," Ari said, studying the spreadsheet.

"Far be it for me to stick my nose into any of your business, but something happened. You're not really good at keeping a secret. And then she left," Rachel observed. "So, I'm guessing whatever passed between you two wasn't stellar."

Ari sighed and leaned back in her chair, still looking at the laptop. "I don't really want to get into it."

"All right, then," Rachel shrugged and turned away.

"Wait," Ari said, changing her mind and tearing her eyes away from the computer screen.

She pressed her thumb and forefinger to the bridge of her nose, thinking.

"Something did happen in Vegas. But it's not like that. It wasn't bad," she said slowly.

"Oh?" Rachel said, leaning in the doorframe.

"That last night in Vegas, we... well..." Ari could not help but look up and give her a half-smile.

Rachel perked up at this. A knowing grin spread across her face. "I knew it. Something did happen."

Ari took a deep breath. "Yeah. We were both in this place, well, literally we were in Vegas, but we were in this place where things seemed different. Stuff back at home felt so far away. Problems. Reservations. Whatever our friendship, whatever this is, it didn't seem so complicated, suddenly, when we were there."

"You're not exactly the only one who's ever had that experience. What happens in Vegas and all that," Rachel said.

"Yeah, I know, how original of us, right? But seriously, for that brief time when we were together after the party Saturday night, I forgot - or, I let myself forget - that a while back, after we first kissed weeks ago, we'd had this talk. She told me she didn't want anything romantic. With me, or with anyone. And at the time she told me that, I thought that was fine. I mean, I was glad she was clear with me, you know? I thought I could accept it."

"Okay," Rachel said, waiting for more.

"I thought I'd accepted it. I saw her in here almost every day, I helped you plan this thing for her sister. But when we were there, together, it was just like... it all fell back in place, and I forgot about what we had said or agreed on in the past. We left the party, kissed, laughed, had a midnight burger, a great time really. She seemed less inhibited that night, and I forgot that I had decided to respect her wishes, to be honest. Well, not that I forgot, it's just she sent me mixed signals. And those mixed signals ultimately led us back to my place. And then she sent me some very *non*-mixed signals."

Ari paused.

"And then after the afterglow wore off, your magical weekend was over," Rachel finished for her.

"Basically. The next morning we had breakfast at my place - we were both so comfortable and relaxed that morning - but I was reminded who she really is when she read an email and found out she had to leave for Paris right away on business."

"It's just a business trip," Rachel said. "She'll be back. Unless something else happened?"

"No, nothing happened. Actually, she asked me if I wanted to go with her. I had to admit to her I don't even own a passport."

"She wanted you to go with her to Paris? That's quick. And extravagant," Rachel commented.

"Yeah, but it must've just been a passing thought. Ever since she left on Sunday night, she's backed off. Way off. I've only had a few brief messages from her."

"She's probably busy. And jet lag, and all of that," Rachel said.

Ari nodded. "Probably. It's just weird. She's so hot and cold. On and off."

"She's been that way from the beginning," Rachel reminded her. "Don't forget her terrible temper about the most mundane things like Christmas decorations or coupons being handed out on the sidewalk."

"She's exhausting," Ari agreed, closing the lid of her laptop. "What is this, high school? Am I going to be sitting at home by the phone, waiting for her to ask me to the prom, only to hear from my best friend that she's going with someone else?"

"Um, no, because actually you're almost 30, Ari, and above all of this," Rachel said. "You can do one of two things. Wait around for her to come around, or just go out and live your life and let whatever happens, happen."

"I don't know what 'going out and living my life' would be right now," Ari confessed. "The last few months have been all about keeping this place up and running, figuring out money and suppliers and customers and interior design, and the exercise in patience that is my next door neighbor. Who has led to a whole other series of problems in my life."

"You can hang out with me," Rachel offered.

Ari sighed. "I probably shouldn't. I don't know. What are you doing?'

"Seeing a friend," Rachel replied vaguely, smiling.

"A friend?"

Rachel flushed slightly. "Okay, don't laugh. But it's actually one of Sabrina's friends. And we're kind of more than just friends now."

"What? Since when? Who is this?" Ari asked, forgetting all about Sophia for a second.

"Cassandra," Rachel said. "The architect. And it's new, just since the weekend."

"Wow," Ari said.

"Hey, you're not the only one who had stuff happen in Vegas, but in my case it didn't stay in Vegas," Rachel replied, grinning. "We've made plans every night since we got back. And you're welcome to join us tonight. I think we are meeting up for drinks, and a few of her friends might be there. It'll be casual."

"Okay," Ari said, standing up from her desk, deciding that a break from thinking about Sophia could be exactly what she needed. "I'm in. Let's close up and get out of here."

··◦··

9 AM Friday, Central European Time

Ari, where are you? I didn't see a text last night. Hope all is well.
Sophia

6 PM Friday, Central European time

What are you up to, Arianna? Miss hearing from you. S.

7 PM Friday, Pacific time

Went out w Rach and some friends last night.

Hope your meetings were good.

What time are you getting back home?

7 AM Sunday, Central European time

I need to talk to you about that.

··◦··

"Sophia's staying away for another two weeks?" Rachel asked, incredulous.

"She arranged more meetings than expected while she was over there and needs to stay a while longer," Ari said.

They were between shifts. Athena was on her way out, Rachel on her way in, and they were standing behind the counter, a conversation about schedules for the weekend having devolved into gossip.

"She didn't ask you to meet her there again, did she?" Rachel asked.

"Not this time."

"She wanted Ari to go to Europe with her?" Athena asked, raising her eyebrows.

"It's kind of romantic, you have to admit. Wanting to whisk you off to Paris," Rachel added.

"Yeah, but is this chick serious about you, or does she just see you as some sort of accessory?" Athena asked, scowling. "Because right now, she sounds indecisive about everything except for her occasional desire for a quick f-"

"Hey, there are customers," Ari cut her off loudly, looking around nervously.

There weren't many customers at the moment, though. It was a low time of day.

"Wow, well, aren't we the cynical one?" Rachel teased Athena lightly.

"You used to be way more cynical - and fun - before your whole Cassandra fling," Athena grumbled.

"She has a point. Love has softened me," Rachel admitted, batting her eyelashes.

"It's only been a week," Athena pointed out.

"I feel your pain," Ari said to Rachel, taking a sip of coffee.

"Look at it this way, Ari," Athena said, resting her elbows on the counter. "She isn't prioritizing you at all. She sounds like a cold, heartless b-"

"Customers!" Ari warned again in a low voice.

"-lady who doesn't have any concern for how anyone feels except for herself. She even left her son home, right? The kid doesn't have his mom around for three weeks. Staying with some relative. Forget about her and go live your life. She's not worth it," Athena said, shaking her head in disgust.

Ari could only nod, thinking maybe Athena had a point.

··o··

Ari started unbuttoning Sophia's blouse before their hotel room door had even fully clicked shut, and the two quickly found themselves in a tangled mess on the bed.

Some time later, Sophia was perched a wrought iron chair outside on the small terrace, wearing a loose, long, button-down white shirtdress. Sophia was relaxed, her feet were bare, propped up on the seat of the other little bistro chair. She had a glass of red wine next to her, an assortment of foods - bread, cheese, grapes, strawberries, slices of meats - laid out on a platter, a laptop in front of her.

She was also smoking, inhaling softly, exhaling the smoke up towards the clear, ultramarine evening sky.

Ari sat up from the bed where she had been napping. She grabbed her t-shirt from earlier that had been tossed haphazardly onto a nearby chair. She gathered her jeans, and put those on, and moved out onto the terrace to join Sophia.

"I didn't know you smoked," Ari said, her voice still full of sleep. She popped a strawberry into her mouth.

Sophia looked up at her, smiled dreamily, and snuffed out the cigarette in a small glass ashtray, setting it aside. "I do on occasion. More people smoke here than back home, and it makes me miss it. It's an old, bad habit from my college days."

She paused and noted Ari's look of concern.

"If it bothers you, I can stop," she offered.

"I don't mind, I guess."

Sophia moved her feet and Ari sat down next to her.

"I can arrange a tour for you," Sophia said. "I have meetings all day tomorrow, but I know someone who does a wonderful private city tour."

"I think I might just wander," Ari said. "I should work on some art while I'm here."

"Good place for that," Sophia noted.

"Are you still working?" Ari asked, scowling at the laptop.

Sophia shook her head. "It's an email my sister sent. I need to let her know who I'm bringing to the wedding.

"Oh," Ari said. "Anyone in mind?"

Sophia looked at her and smiled. "Well?"

Ari gave her a half-smile. "Am I really who your family wants to see you bring as your date?"

"I don't care what they think. And besides, they'll be too busy thinking about themselves to care about me."

"There are a couple of reasons they'll care when they see me with you," Ari said in a serious tone, reaching for a piece of bread.

"My family knows I've seen women in the past," Sophia said.

"So that's not an issue?"

Sophia shook her head. "No. That ship sailed a long time ago. They've grown accustomed to it, although they also don't take it very seriously."

Ari stopped chewing.

"I take you seriously," Sophia quickly assured her.

Ari swallowed. "Do you?"

Sophia nodded.

"I don't believe you," Ari said after a beat, her face darkening. "You told me once you didn't want anything. I don't think you want me here. And you know what? I don't want to be here, either."

Ari stood up and, in her bare feet and t-shirt, left the room, the door clicking behind her on the way out.

Sophia stayed on the terrace, frozen in place. She could only lean over to look at the street several floors below her, and a few moments later, she saw Ari walk out of the hotel, go down the street, and disappear into the night.

··○··

Sophia woke up with a start.

She rolled over in bed, her hand reaching out, trying to find a pillow, something to grab on to and ground herself.

As she slowly pulled herself up to shake off the sleep, she gazed out of the window and onto the terrace beyond. It must be early morning; she could just barely make out in the grey light that the terrace was empty, save the wrought iron table and chairs that had appeared in her dream. They were bare. No wine, no food, no cigarettes (though it was true that she had been smoking since she arrived back in Paris. Bad habit. After that dream, she vowed not to do it in front of Ari. Not that she ever smoked back home, anyways, and she would certainly never do so around Percy.)

Ari was thousands upon thousands of miles - and an ocean - away. She was not sure how she felt about that fact: relief that that conversation had not happened in real life, or disappointment that the woman had not, in fact, been here with her.

She sat up, remembering something about how she had mentioned Ari should come to Paris. She had blurted it out that morning, the morning after, while curled up on Ari's soft couch in Las Vegas, searching for airline tickets. She had been on an unusually giddy high that morning. For a little while, anything had felt possible. But then Ari had told her, in a strained voice, that she didn't have a passport, and Sophia realized how silly it had been for her to suggest the woman do something so frivolous. What would Ari even have done in Paris, anyways? Sit around at the hotel all day? Be a pretty accessory for Sophia to show off at business dinners and cocktail parties? Ari was a busy human being, with a job and a life, not something Sophia could drag around Paris.

Ari had her own life. And Sophia had to stop interfering in it, being a mental drain on the woman, taking up her time.

This is exactly why she did not do relationships, or love, or anything of the sort. She was, quite simply, bad at it.

Part of her craved the days before Ari, when it had been

so simple to be with others. Flirting, games. Perhaps a conversation or two about their pasts, but never really going into detail. Followed by the pure, simple bliss of a few nights together. And then she would usually never see that person again. Or not see them many more times.

Ari had, no doubt, ruined that type of experience for Sophia.

After experiencing Ari, she could not fathom ever being satisfied with anyone else.

She wished she did not like spending time with Ari so much. She could have been over it by now, both of them moved on with their lives.

Sophia was both puzzled and resentful of the fact that she could not get Ari off her mind.

Now, she longed for that feeling she had that one morning in Vegas; comfortable on Ari's couch, the sun streaming through the window, Ari making her coffee while she scrolled through her emails and booked a flight. She wished she were doing that now, instead of being in a small European hotel room, so far from Ari's strong presence, soft touch and calming demeanor.

She picked up her phone from the end table and looked at it. If she sent a text now, it would be the late evening in California. Ari might still be up.

She typed a few things:

Hope you're well.

She erased it.

How's the coffee? Have a cup ready for me when I return?

Sophia cringed at her attempts at flirty messages and promptly erased them both. The first sounded like the start of a business email. The other seemed too cutesy and desperate. She was clearly terrible at communicating what she really felt.

Hi, I have conflicting feelings about you. I don't want to bother you, or get involved in anything serious for a very long time, if not forever. It will probably take so long for me to come around that you will move on. But in the meantime, let's sleep together and the morning after have breakfast and be next to each other because that was one of the best things I've ever experienced.

She definitely would not send that one.

She wondered how to flirt over text. She had come of age just before texting had become a key element in a relationship, and did not think that her mid-thirties was the most promising time to experiment awkwardly with flirting via text for the first time. She would hate to make Ari into a guinea pig for that.

If only relationships were as easy as business.

For lack of a decent idea about what to write, she wrote nothing and put her phone back down on the end table.

··◦··

2 WEEKS LATER

Percy came into Ari's cafe again after school one day. When she saw him, she wondered if she could once again get away with fishing for more information, or if doing so was going to make the kid suspicious.

"Long time no see," Ari said. "Haven't seen you since that grilled cheese a few weeks ago."

"Yeah, sorry about that. I'm waiting for my mom to get out of work today," Percy said.

"What do you mean? She's back?" Ari asked, surprised

The last text she had received from Sophia had been a few nights ago, over the weekend. It had been brief, a cursory hello, hope she was doing well kind of thing. Sophia had not mentioned anything about a return date.

"Yup, two days ago," Percy said.

"You must be glad to have her back. No more train rides," Ari said, her mind wrapping around the news.

Percy nodded.

Rachel brought Percy a hot chocolate, and as Percy turned his focus back to a video game, Ari told him she would find him something to snack on.

That settles that, Ari thought stubbornly. *It's back to square one with Sophia. Very little communication, cordial at best when we do communicate. She didn't even let me know she was coming home.*

Maybe she should follow Athena's advice.

At home that night, Ari struggled to not think about what to do about Sophia. She flipped through television channels, picked up a book and then promptly put it back down again. As she fixed a little snack of crackers, cheese and nuts in her kitchen, she heard a text come in.

Not many people other than Sophia texted her, so she had a feeling it might be her. Still, trying not to get her hopes up, she picked up her phone and discovered that it was indeed from the very woman she was trying to forget.

I'm back and I have a business proposition for you, Ms. Little. Would you be free to meet me at my office tomorrow?

..o..

Ari agreed to meet Sophia partially out of curiosity at this "business proposition" and partly because she wanted to clear the air, and assure Sophia - if the topic came up - that what happened in Vegas could indeed stay there. Ari wanted things back to normal so Sophia could at least drop by and have her morning coffee at The Little Cafe again. She preferred to just try to get through this like normal adults.

They met in the middle of the afternoon, around 2. Sophia had chosen the time that was best for Ari: she knew it was a slow time at the cafe, after lunch but before mid-afternoon coffee breaks. Unfortunately, it was a peak time at FORBIDDEN: downstairs the boutique was busy with shoppers who seemed to have come from out of town, but Elle was doing a good job as always with the rush. There were many people working upstairs as well. Seth was upstairs today, as were some of Sophia's staff who helped get together online orders and ship out merchandise.

Ari walked past a man carrying a stack of boxes and knocked on Sophia's heavy wooden office door, which was closed.

'Come in," Sophia said, and Ari entered.

"Go ahead and shut the door," Sophia directed.

"Welcome back," Ari said in a cool voice, letting the door click shut.

"Thank you," Sophia said, standing up from her desk and taking off her glasses.

"You can come by for coffee, you know," Ari said.

"What?"

"Coffee, at the cafe. You haven't stopped in since you got back from Paris. You're welcome any time, like always."

"Oh, thank you," Sophia said distractedly. "We did fix our coffee machine here finally, but yours is better. Now, please, sit down."

She gestured toward the chair in front of her desk.

"What can I do for you?" Ari asked, not sure what topic was going to come up during this meeting.

"I'm working on a marketing campaign. I was inspired while I was in Paris," she said. "I had an idea, last night, when looking over one of my many sketches. I've started to be drawn to works of art that... well, that were similar to the ones you painted. The ones I saw at your house in Las Vegas."

"Really?" Ari asked.

Sophia put on her glasses back on, and Ari could not help but think Sophia needed to stop wearing those glasses if she was going to be okay with *just* being friends or business acquaintances or whatever it was she was with Sophia.

"I am wondering if you would consider selling me some of your works of art. Either the ones you had hanging in your home, or new ones that would be painted in a similar style. And by selling them, would you also sell me the rights to use them in a marketing campaign? I want to use them as a backdrop in photos of my lingerie."

"Wow, sure. I never thought I could sell a painting, much less actually have it be used in a real... thing," Ari said, struggling to find words.

"Well, now is your chance for your work to be in a 'thing,'" Sophia said, businesslike.

Ari nodded. "So do you want me to make one special for you, like a commission, or would you prefer to buy one of the ones you saw? That I already did?"

Sophia thought for a moment. "If you'd be willing to take on a commission, perhaps that would be best. I have some colors that I might prefer for you to incorporate, to compliment my pieces. If you don't mind."

Ari nodded. "That could be arranged."

"Now, let's talk pricing," Sophia began, looking down at a notepad on her desk.

"I'll be honest, I don't know what my work is worth," Ari said.

"And to be honest, I don't have the highest budget. I may have a modestly successful business on my hands, but margins are thin right now, and my marketing budget isn't amazing."

"That's okay," Ari said. "I just like the idea of my artwork being out there."

"You are a terrible negotiator," Sophia said with a slight smile tugging at the corner of her mouth, writing a number down on a sticky note and passing it across the desk to Ari. "I can give you this for each piece, which includes the rights to use them in the one upcoming marketing campaign. I think I would want three or four paintings. It's not much money, I know, but I truly don't have a lot of wiggle room as far as marketing goes. I still have to hire photographers, graphic designers, copywriters, the works."

"Sold," Ari said.

Sophia smiled smugly. "Like I said, terrible negotiator."

"...with one caveat," Ari added quickly.

"What?" Sophia asked.

Ari lowered her voice. "Have dinner with me."

Sophia sucked in a cheek and shifted impatiently. "I'm busy the next couple of weeks."

Ari let out a low hiss of frustration.

"What is going on, Sophia?" she asked quietly. "Last time we parted, we'd just slept together and you were telling me I should get a passport so I could travel with you, and now we're back to the same place we were weeks ago? Just acquaintances?"

Sophia glanced at her and then back down at her hands, which were folded on the desk in front of her.

"I told you I was bad at this kind of thing," she said softly.

"You did." Ari said quietly. "But Sophia, we did-"

"-a thing adults sometimes do when they're swept up in a moment," Sophia finished, looking up at her with a stoic expression on her face.

"Right," Ari said, leaning back, partially hurt, partially just mad. Her jaw clenching, she averted her gaze, focusing instead on the side of the room where several silky, floral-print chemises and lacy underwear daintily hung from silk hangers.

"I apologize, Ms. Little, for what I did. It wasn't fair to you," Sophia said this time, clearly trying to sound firm, but Ari sensed a slight quiver in her voice. "It was just a... whim."

Ari looked at her, studied her for a moment.

"It wasn't." Ari said finally.

"What?" Sophia asked, her eyes flashing.

"It wasn't some throwaway night," Ari said firmly. "It was something more. I can tell when you're lying. You're lying now."

Sophia really was lying, Ari thought. The way the veins in her forehead became more pronounced, the way she pursed her lips in a way that made the skin around them tighten, her expression was souring... Ari could tell.

Sophia scowled briefly at Ari's observation, then her face softened.

"You're right," Sophia admitted, her voice softer now, letting out a deep breath she had been holding. "It was more than nothing."

"What do you want, Sophia?" Ari asked. "I'll respect your decision, either way. But all you've been giving me so far are mixed messages."

Sophia looked into her eyes, and Ari's breath stopped, her world seemed to stand still for a second.

"I'm a coffee shop owner. I live in tiny loft. I'm a pretty modest person. But I also know what I want. And it's likely I'll wait around for a little while, but maybe not forever, you know?" Ari said gently. "And I get it. Really. You're building a fashion empire and still somehow manage to raise a really great kid. You're busy."

"I am," Sophia confirmed.

"You're also incredibly frustrating, you know," Ari said a moment later, looking into Sophia's eyes and leaning forward on the desk. "Because you're wearing these glorious glasses and are sitting in this office surrounded by delicate, lacy underthings. And I think you know what I wish I could have this very second."

Ari thought she heard Sophia suck in a little breath.

Sophia leaned back in her chair, listening, at a loss for her own words.

"You're also stubborn." Ari grinned.

Sophia rolled her eyes.

Ari laughed a bit at that.

"Sophia Black, if you can ever admit out loud what you want, either way, you'll know where to find me," Ari said. "That is, if it's not like five decades from now and The Little Cafe no longer exists, and I'm not 80 years old and haven't moved on already with, oh, I dunno, give or take a dozen other people. Probably take. Who am I kidding."

Ari tried to keep the tone light, but in reality, she was starting to feel almost foolish having this conversation. Again.

Sophia's silence made her feel like she was talking too much.

Oh, how she wished things had gone differently. How she wished they were back in that easy, comfortable place they had been in Vegas, before Sophia went away. Maybe she could have done a better job reassuring Sophia somehow, tried to make her less skittish, before they had left that little bubble.

She just wanted to go back to work now. Put some distance between herself and the frustrating brunette.

Sophia remained silent and the only noise was a tap-tap-tap of her pen against a pad of paper. She took a sip of water out of a crystal glass that had been resting on a marble coaster. Ari could not read her expression.

At last, Ari remembered why she was there that afternoon.

Her voice turned businesslike. "So, when do you need the paintings by?"

Sophia cleared her throat. "Two weeks, if you can. But if you need more time, just let me know."

Ari nodded. "Done."

Sophia stood up. "I'll walk you out."

They went downstairs. Ari was starting to feel disappointed in herself that she had ever let the woman sweep her up in the moment.

Ari had been screwed over by enough people in her life that she should have known better than to trust anyone, especially someone as seemingly independent and dangerous as Ms. "I don't do relationships" Black.

A woman who owned a business called FORBIDDEN, of all things. Why had she not taken that as a warning sign?

Ari crossed the floor of the store and was saying a quick goodbye to Elle when she heard a familiar trill.

"Ari! Oh, darling, how good to see you again!"

It was Sabrina. Otherwise known as the last person, after Sophia, Ari had any interest in seeing at the moment.

"You and Rachel planned one of the best weekends of my life," she said, stopping Ari and giving her an air kiss.

Ari nearly choked on the cloud of perfume that seemed to surround Sabrina, then smiled. "Glad to hear it. It was mostly Rachel's doing, I was just there to lend a helping hand."

"And so I hear you did," Sabrina said mischievously, glancing over at Sophia.

Sophia's icy disposition faltered at that. For a split second, Ari nervously glanced over at Sophia, and Sophia nervously tucked a piece of her hair behind her ear.

She recovered a moment later.

"I was just saying goodbye to Ari," Sophia said, smiling coolly.

"So soon?" Sabrina asked, disappointment crossing her face. "You know, the three of us should really get together sometime. And Rachel, too. We need to catch up. Ari, maybe you can tell me what other great Vegas activities I've been missing out on all of these years, things I should do the next time I go back."

"We'll keep that in mind. We really shouldn't keep Ms. Little from her work," Sophia urged.

"Oh, but one thing before you go. I need your address, Ari, to send you an invitation to my wedding."

"Oh... it's okay," Ari said, shaking her head.

"I wouldn't dream of having my wedding without my fabulous party planners there," she said. "Please do come!"

"I don't know," Ari said slowly, glancing over at Sophia again, whose expression was unreadable. "I guess I could text you my address."

"You have to. And let me know if you will be bringing a plus one."

"Sure," Ari said. "Is Rachel going?"

"Oh, of course she is. I would have sent her her own invitation, but it seems she's already acquainted with my dear friend Cassandra, and will be going with her. So that means I need to send you an invitation; unless, of course, you met anyone else in Vegas who will be attending my wedding and care to accompany them instead," she said, smiling pointedly at Sophia.

Okay, based on that look, she'd definitely heard something, Ari thought.

Sophia crossed her arms angrily, pouting.

"We really don't need to bother Ari with your wedding," Sophia said. "She's very busy with work."

Ari thought Sophia was just trying to get her out of having to go to the insane extravaganza that was sure to be Sabrina's wedding, but a part of her was disappointed that Sophia was so insistent on excluding her.

"Oh, stop it, sis," chided Sabrina. "I want you to be there, Ari. Please do come."

"Sure," Ari said quickly, to placate Sabrina and get beyond this awkward situation as quickly as possible. "Thanks. I'll be there."

"Remember to send me your address and I'll get an invitation out to you straight away," Sabrina said as Ari edged toward the door. "I'm so pleased Sophia will have someone to socialize with at my wedding other than dreadful Cousin Phil!"

10

WINE COUNTY

Sophia was seething. She knew exactly what her sister was doing. Trying to meddle in her affairs yet again. She would never understand why her sister and mother lived for these petty games. They did not understand her at all. Or her life. Or how she had far more important things to think about and therefore had very little tolerance for this kind of behavior.

Sophia returned upstairs after Ari left, leaving Sabrina in the shop to look around and be her usual nuisance of a self out of her sight. Elle could deal with her. At least, Sophia hoped she could.

Elle was due for a raise soon... she might owe it to her after today.

Sophia sat down at her desk and was greeted with an extraordinarily long list of emails that had arrived in her inbox over the past hour or so.

Her eyes glazed over as she mechanically scrolled through

the messages. She did not need any of this from her family right now. She was completely irritated, completely miserable, and she hated that her emotions about the situation were getting in the way of her attention to her work.

After a few minutes, she decided that she needed a little kick-start for her focus, so she went in search of coffee. When she reached the newly-fixed coffee machine outside of her office, she found one of her assistant designers was refilling its water reservoir. With one glance at her, the designer immediately jetted away.

Moments later, Sophia was even more irritated to discover that they were completely out of coffee pods.

"Seth!" she called.

"Yes?" the man promptly trotted over from his desk.

"Make sure that more coffee capsules are ordered immediately. We're out."

He nodded and muttered something about doing so right away.

She stormed downstairs, her heels tapping angrily on the floor as she crossed the boutique and went outside.

Moments later, she pushed open the door to The Little Cafe, the bell chiming a little too merrily for her liking.

Rachel gave her a warm smile from behind the counter.

"You look like you could use some caffeine," she said, clearly unfazed by Sophia's sour face.

"I could," Sophia said, deciding to forego the quips and depositing herself on a barstool while Rachel set to work making her usual order.

"Hey," Ari said, carrying some empty mugs from a table. "When I said you were invited here for coffee any time, I didn't realize you were this desperate. Would've reminded you to come by sooner."

"We're out of coffee," Sophia said.

"Gotcha," Ari said. "Rachel took your order?"

Sophia nodded. "But since I'm here, I want to apologize for my sister's behavior. She loves to overstep boundaries and generally acts inappropriate at the most inopportune times. It's her thing."

"Actually, Sophia, I think she was just being nice by inviting me," Ari said.

"You don't have to go to her wedding. It will be a ridiculously tacky, over-blown affair. I'd hate to subject you to that," Sophia said. "Or to my nosy family in general. It won't be a pleasant day."

"Thanks for telling me how I'd feel about going," Ari said lightly.

Sophia scowled as Rachel handed her coffee. Rachel was not quite as chipper as she had been a few minutes ago, having overheard the harsh tone Sophia used with Ari. She drifted away to serve other customers, but not before giving Sophia a brief warning glance.

Sophia took a sip of the coffee. Perfect, as always. Who needed a coffee machine when working next door to this place?

"I'm sorry," Sophia said a few minutes later, the coffee revitalizing her as she watched Ari organize things behind the counter. "I don't mean to be so... indecisive with you. I didn't know what to say to you while I was gone, and I don't want to lead you on when my work life is a poor match for a love life."

"Look, Sophia," Ari said, moving closer to Sophia and sounding a touch impatient. "First of all, I'm a big kid. I have been around the block. Stop pretending you're somehow protecting me by not communicating with me."

"Okay." Sophia scowled.

Ari gathered up some empty glasses from behind the counter. Sophia watched her as she worked.

"I don't understand, Ari. Why are you as patient with me as you have been? Why do you still even bother with me?" Sophia asked.

Ari sighed and put down the glass she was holding.

"Look, I might be crazy for still tolerating you after all of the times you've gone back and forth with me. There are times when I think I should just shrug this off and walk away. But... I also get where you're coming from. I get not wanting to let people down, and being busy with stuff and having family obligations, not wanting to stretch yourself too thin, all of that," Ari said. "I really do believe that's what you're struggling with most. And I'm patient because I understand where you're coming from."

Sophia let out a breath. Most people she had known would have just drifted away by now.

"What I don't know is why you keep saying you're bad at relationships and bad at being with people, although I'm sure you have your reasons," Ari continued slowly, her voice less impatient than before. "And if you'd ever stopped to ask me how I felt about relationships, I would've told you not to worry about it, because we'll figure it out, and that our lives aren't a public social media status and we don't have to define what we're doing in any way, to any one. We could just be ourselves for a while and see where it leads."

Sophia suddenly felt ridiculous. She had been so focused on herself and her own conflicted feelings, that she had been neglecting how Ari must feel through all of her indecisiveness and lack of responsiveness.

Ari was right. She was not protecting her from anything with this behavior.

"Do you really want to go to my sister's wedding?" Sophia asked curiously.

"To be honest, I kind of do. I like spending time with you, Sophia. I don't think that's any secret. And yeah, I'm even a little fascinated by your family, and your wacky sister. Sure I'll go."

"The food should be very good," Sophia said, at a loss for what else to say to Ari.

"In that case, I'll definitely RSVP," Ari said. "Meanwhile, I've got to get back to work."

Sophia stood up. "I do as well. I placed an order for the coffee capsule refills for our machine, although they're really for my employees. I, on the other hand, will be back here. Your coffee is far superior."

"And if you ever wanna make good on that dinner that was a part of our negotiation earlier, you know where to find me," Ari said, grinning. "But if you don't, I'll still do the paintings anyways."

Sophia laughed lightly. "I appreciate it."

··o··

Sophia drove about an hour or so outside of town, heading deep into wine country, early in the morning on the day before Sabrina's wedding day. Percy was half-asleep, his head pressed against the passenger window, headphones over his ears and his eyes shut.

With every twist and turn in the drive, she felt herself growing more and more nervous. It would be a whole weekend with her family. They were all wild cards. Her father was fine, but he was quiet and often lost in his own world. He would drift off to chat and drink and smoke cigars with his business partners, and her mother would complain that he wasn't fulfilling all of his social obligations to the rest of their "friends." He would just passively shrug her off.

Speaking of her mother, Callista, she might be perfectly tolerable, and Sabrina may be fine as well, but then when everyone least expects it, her sister could very well say something ridiculous and cringe worthy or not even go through with the wedding at all. What a headache *that* would be to deal with while managing all of the family members and guests who were there for the occasion. Her mother would be useless, consumed by horror about what to do in the face of such a breach of social protocol. Her mother might take out all of her stress on Sophia, like she sometimes did, channeling her nerves into bitterness, her sharp tongue lashing out at Sophia.

It was too bad Percy was dozing. Sophia knew her thoughts were spiraling out of control, but without any distractions, she had nothing to combat them with.

Callista had very high expectations for Sophia. Sophia braced herself for comments about how she had done her hair, or makeup, or what she wore, and how it all could have been done better, differently. Or worse, her mother might start saying these sorts of things to someone else - commenting about a guest, a cousin, another family member - causing a small altercation that Sophia would then have to sort out, all while shielding her sister from the drama. Not because her sister needed protecting, but because, despite all of the weddings her sister had already been through, Sophia hated to think of their mother dampening her sister's spirit on a wedding day.

When Sophia finally arrived at the spa and resort where she and Percy were staying, which was a few miles from her parents' country home, Percy kept his headphones on as he unloaded his suitcase and trailed after her to their suite.

After getting settled, they went downstairs some time later to have lunch at the resort's restaurant.

While they were eating, an old friend of her father's, Hank, walked in with his daughter and was seated at a nearby table.

Sophia said hello as soon as she noticed them.

"Why, Sophia! So nice to see you," he said, greeting her before he sat down. "And is this Percy?"

Hank shook Percy's hand.

"This is my daughter, Isabella," he said, introducing a pretty girl with a mass of curly brown hair who smiled and politely greeted them both.

Sophia thought she noticed a faint flush cross Percy's face as he said hello to Isabella.

As they ate, Sophia had a polite conversation with Hank. They discussed travel, how his business was going, and news of a few other old family friends. Percy was quiet, but Isabella seemed friendly and slowly wedged Percy out of his shell, and soon the two of them were deep in their own conversation about music.

"I suppose we'll see you at my sister's wedding tomorrow?" Sophia asked as they all finished up their lunches.

"We'll be there. I've been to all of her other ones, it would be a shame to not make it to this one," Hank smiled, and Sophia laughed.

They all stood up and gathered their things. As they did, Isabella spoke up.

"Percy, there are some hiking trails around here. I was going to go on one after lunch. Do you want to come with me?"

Percy looked over at Sophia. "May I?" he asked.

Sophia hesitated for a second, but then nodded. "Just be back by five. We have a rehearsal dinner to attend tonight."

··○··

"It's raining on my wedding day," a tearful Sabrina announced the next morning, as soon as Sophia walked into her old childhood bedroom. She was pouting next to the window, where long, grey stripes of water cascaded down the glass.

Sophia hesitated, observing the pitiful of sight of her red-headed sister next to the window watching the dreary day outside.

Sabrina was in a long, white silk robe, the extravagant wedding dress she was about to put on hanging next to a mirror to the side of the room. Her hair and makeup had been done... and, Sophia had to admit, her sister looked more gorgeous than ever.

Sophia hung up her royal blue Maid of Honor dress and began laying out her makeup bag.

"Everything is indoors. We'll manage," Sophia said, trying to keep her tone even and patient.

"It's never rained on my wedding day before," Sabrina said, still pouting.

"Well, maybe it's a sign of good luck," Sophia offered, coaxing her away from the window and calling over the hair stylist and makeup artist that had been hired for the day.

The photographer came over as well, eager to snap a shot of every moment of the pre-wedding bridal pampering.

The wedding was to take place that evening. Like the resort where Sophia was staying, the Black family Napa Valley home was perched high on a green hill, surrounded by a lush, rolling landscape covered in endless vineyards. It was a picture-perfect setting. Truly everything about it was enchanted. The property had even been featured in one of the top architectural magazines.

For the wedding, every square inch of the home had been impeccably decorated, staged and lit cheerfully by some of the top interior designers and wedding planners, ready to welcome the 200 or so guests who were to attend. A team of servers was waiting to pour endless glasses of wine and champagne that had been sourced from one of the most exclusive small producers in the region. The Peruvian-

Japanese-French fusion cuisine was being prepared by a famous chef, flown in from Lima just for the event.

The guest list included a veritable who's-who of Silicon Valley. The influential friends of Sabrina's husband-to-be might have been torn from the pages of a society magazine. William, as it turned out, was more than just a pretty face. He was in fact quite successful in his own right as an an engineer, entrepreneur and investor in a up-and-coming electric car manufacturing company.

Sophia spent the day focused on keeping Sabrina happy, making sure Percy did not wander off for too long so she could direct him to all of the wedding-related events (including the ceremony, photos and reception) on time. She also mitigated the damage caused by her mother, who, as predicted, made it her personal mission to critique every last detail of the day, causing everyone from the photographer to the makeup artist to the wait staff serving champagne and tapas to turn red in shame or fear, scurrying to keep up with her last minute whims and demands, or having mini-breakdowns in the pantry.

Sophia could barely find a moment to catch her breath all day long. She was in perpetual motion getting Sabrina into her dress, through an admittedly beautiful ceremony during which the rain managed to pause for a little while, then during a post-ceremony cocktail and, finally, dinner, during which she was occupied by chatting with the enormous stream of guests. Finally, when the dinner had finally wound down and the music got louder, as guests began to stand up and shake off their massive multi-course dinner of ceviche and sautéed beef and coconut-white-chocolate-guava cake and mingle and dance, Sophia could at last sit down at her assigned table and reach for her first glass of wine of the evening (she had not had a chance to enjoy one earlier, though she had certainly tried). Just as she took her first sip, a familiar silhouette caught her eye.

Sophia had tried to forget that her sister had invited Ari to the wedding.

Tried being the key word.

Things had been all right with Ari in the few weeks since Sabrina had invited her to the wedding. Most of Sophia's days had started with a fresh cup of coffee at The Little Cafe, and if Ari was not busy, they talked about normal, comfortable things, friendly things. Since she had been busy this weekend, she had tried to suppress any thought of Ari, or what to do about her, if anything, being at the wedding reception.

She looked down at the plate of barely-touched food in front of her.

She glanced back at Ari, who was already heading over to her.

Sophia sat up straighter and stabbed a potato with her fork.

"Hey," Ari said, sitting down in the empty seat next to hers, which had been assigned to none other than Phil. A diabolical joke on Sabrina's part, she was certain. Thankfully the tiresome man had wandered off a while ago to discuss some sort of trading card game with a relative of William's.

"Mind if I join you?" Ari asked. "I'm getting a little tired of being hit on by some guy named Carleton who claims to be an 'old acquaintance' of your mother's, whatever that means."

"I wouldn't ask," Sophia said. "About Carleton, that is. Yes, you are always welcome to join me. I hope you don't mind I'm still eating, I haven't had many chances to have food today."

"No worries. Sabrina had been keeping you on your toes?"

Sophia nodded. "But soon this wedding will be over, and I will be free of Sabrina's weddings for at least a year, maybe two if I'm lucky."

"At least you've gotten a lot of practice with managing her weddings," Ari offered. "You certainly looked like a pro today."

Sophia smiled.

They fell into an easy sort of conversation then, Sophia finishing her food (she had not realized until that very moment how incredibly hungry she was), while Ari chatted with her. A waiter brought them both a dessert wine, which they enjoyed with slices of the cake

"You look very nice, by the way," Sophia said when she finally finished eating, and leaned back comfortably in her chair as a waiter served them espresso.

Ari looked down at her outfit, a long, dark blue skirt and a matching sleeveless top that was slightly cropped and showed a little peek of skin. "Thanks. Totally Rachel's cousin's work, though. We texted him for wedding outfit ideas and he sent this to me two days later."

"I was complimenting you, Ari. Not the outfit. Although that is lovely as well."

"Oh," Ari said, flushing slightly. "Thank you."

"Although now that you mention it, I don't think I've ever seen you in a skirt,' Sophia said.

"You probably haven't. This might be the first one I've worn in years," Ari said. "By the way, you're looking pretty great yourself. And that color blue suits you. How'd you talk Sabrina into letting you wear blue instead of green?"

"Years of experience. Sabrina knows I hate green, and she finally gave in and let me choose the color. And the dress."

"Well, it was a good choice," Ari said, her eyes raking Sophia's figure.

Sophia suddenly felt her cheeks grow a little warm. She took a deep breath.

"Would you like to dance, Arianna?" she asked.

Ari started a little at the unexpected use of her first name.

"Sure," she said softly, eyes wide, and allowed Sophia to guide her onto the dance floor.

As they danced, a few of the usual curious glances were cast their way, but not too many. Sophia felt her heart beating rapidly, blood pounding in her ears. She was nervous. Not just because she was surrounded by family and friends, and that made her nervous for any number of reasons, but because she was surrounded by family and friends *with* Ari.

It had been ages since she had indicated any romantic interest in anyone with family around.

There were a few surprised glances - like from Aunt Constance over there, who could not stop staring and then whispered, scandalized, to her table-mate - but for the most part, her family was used to the fact that she had kept her romances to herself and had never been married, yet had a child. To them, she was aloof or disinterested in relationships, a complete contrast to her sister, who always openly and vigorously threw herself into one relationship after another.

As they swayed to the music, Sophia was aware of the fact that the great scandal of her dancing with Ari was not that she never brought anyone to family events and at last had someone to dance with, nor was it that that person was another woman. No... most likely, the real scandal was that Ari was totally unknown. Certainly, she could not be anyone noteworthy, at least in the circles that her family and family's friends traveled in. Ari did not have a recognizable face or name. No one knew anything about her. She was a mystery. It had to be scandalous to them... and maybe even a little intriguing.

Of course, Ari's relative obscurity, materializing at the wedding out of thin air, was something that Sophia rather enjoyed. She liked that Ari was unknown. To her, Ari was a breath of fresh air because of it.

"You're thinking too much right now," Ari said quietly.

"What do you mean?" Sophia asked, snapping out of her thoughts. "I am not."

"You are. You're all tense," Ari observed, using her hand, resting at the small of Sophia's back, to hold her slightly closer. "C'mon, relax."

"I'm trying," Sophia whispered.

"I don't blame you though," Ari whispered a few minutes later. "I sorta feel like we're being watched."

"That's because we are," Sophia said. "My family likes to keep tabs on things. One of the many reasons I avoid them as much as possible."

"What is on my tab, do you think?" Ari asked, her eyes scanning the crowd, curious.

Sophia smiled gently. "Hmm. Pretty. Good height, nice blonde hair, decent clothes, good bone structure, decent posture. You probably pass the test."

"You make me sound like a commodity. Or a... what do they call it? When socialites parade around their daughters who are eligible for marriage."

Sophia laughed. "Debutante. More of an East Coast thing. Although who knows, perhaps some of them are wondering if you had been one."

"Sorry, but no. Hate to disappoint."

"You don't disappoint me," Sophia said, and almost out of defiance, moved closer to Ari, resting her chin on her shoulder.

They stayed that way for a few more minutes, until Sophia noticed a familiar silhouette on the dance floor. She craned her neck to get a better look, and Ari felt her tense up.

"What is it?" Ari asked, following Sophia's gaze.

There, on the dance floor, was Percy. Dancing with Isabella.

"Oh, wow, so Percy's got a girlfriend?" Ari asked, amused.

"He most certainly does not have a girlfriend," Sophia countered.

"They look pretty friendly," Ari observed.

"They'd better not be," Sophia growled.

"Oh, come on, Sophia. He's a teenager. This kind of stuff happens."

Sophia frowned, considering that. "I don't know. I could've waited a few more years before dealing with this."

Ari gave her a look that asked, *Are you serious?* but Ari refrained from saying anything out loud.

"I think we should take a break," Sophia said, gently backing away from her. She and Ari walked back to the table.

..o..

"Photo time, Sophia," Callista said later, coming up to their table, casting a slightly judgmental look toward Ari, who was nursing a bottle of beer.

"Thank you, mother," Sophia said primly, uncrossing her legs and standing up.

"Are you ok here for a bit?" Sophia asked Ari.

Ari nodded. "Go. I'm fine."

A few minutes later, Ari decided she'd had enough of the loud music and dancing, so she wandered outside onto a deck overlooking the lawn where a photographer had arranged Sophia's family under a stunning, bright canopy of fairy lights and candlelit lanterns.

"That's great," the photographer was saying, an assistant running around and adjusting Sabrina's dress, positioning everyone for the photos.

A few other guests were outside near Ari, milling about and watching the scene, sitting on the benches in the cool night air, drinking, chatting quietly, laughing. Ari relaxed, leaning up against the balcony railing as she observed Sophia's family. Callista, despite her reputation of being bitter and petty according to Sophia, was quite elegant. She was petite, auburn-haired, with pursed lips that did look a little sour, and sharp brown eyes that watched over everyone, at all times.

Sabrina looked nice, if not over the top, in her jewel-encrusted, long white gown, wearing a stunning emerald necklace. William was handsome if not somewhat lanky, wearing a tux, and there were a few other men standing around him.

"Come on, dad!" Sabrina motioned to a man who had just been shuffled over to them. He was a small man, short, white-haired, but had an air of dignity to him that hinted of a lifetime of power and privilege. Ari watched as he was arranged next to Callista in the pose.

"Looking good!" the photographer called, snapping photos.

Ari's eyes remained on Sophia and Sabrina's father. He looked oddly familiar. She could not quite place him immediately, though. She was pretty sure he had never been at any of the town hall meetings. So where was he from?

She took another sip of her beer. She was certain she had seen him before. If only she could remember where... she almost felt like she had seen him in back in her Vegas years? Or maybe on television?

She watched as the photographer started taking pictures, continuing to call out instructions to the subjects on where to look, how to stand or pose, while the photographer's assistant shuffled around them and adjusted skirts or hands or hair, assuring them they were doing great.

Ari took another sip of beer. It was late, and she was starting to feel sleepy. She should have gotten another coffee instead.

Coffee.

Coffee.

That was where she remembered the man from. Her first job, when she was in high school. Ten years ago he had been the stern, unfriendly man who had come to the coffee kiosk in the atrium at the company her parents worked for, Oscuro. She could even remember that he had snapped at her once for not making his order just right.

And a year or two later, he laid off her parents.

He was the man who owned Oscuro, the company her parents had worked for. He was the reason they had been screwed out of jobs after two decades of devoted service to his business.

Ari's heart sank. How had this never come up in conversation with Sophia before?

Sophia had not really talked about her family a lot. She avoided the topic, actually, and Ari never really brought it up otherwise. She knew Sabrina, and Sabrina's friends, and had gotten the general idea that their mother was not Sophia's favorite person to spend time with. After seeing Sophia's stern mother at the town hall meetings, she was not overly keen on meeting her parents face to face. Aside from knowing that Sophia's family had enough money for multiple houses, business investments and sharing a private plane, she had not had a chance to ask for much more detail.

Ari tried to make sense of it. Sophia's wealthy family... of course, her father was a successful business owner. And she clearly inherited his obsession with work. Ari remembered hearing how the man who owned the company would make impulsive decisions and not give much thought about who was impacted by them. She also remembered her parents talking about office rumors that his wife, who sat on the board, was really the one running the show behind the scenes.

That must have been Callista. Ari could see that. The town meetings must seem really minor to her nowadays.

Ari glanced at the rest of the family, still posing for photos. Callista continued to purse her lips and watch over her husband and daughters' movements like a hawk.

Ari looked at Sophia's father again. This guy, and his company, were the reasons her parents had been laid off and had struggled all of the years since. He was the reason that she had been turned off of the idea of having a "traditional" job in the first place.

Oscuro... she'd always thought it was a strange name for a company, but remembered someone told her once that it was a Spanish word for dark, or shade.

Dark. Black. Sophia *Black*.

The Black family.

It was almost poetic, thought Ari.

But she felt too disappointed in this revelation to appreciate it.

She suddenly did not feel like watching the family take any more pictures. She went back inside.

··o··

"I was looking for you," Sophia said when she found Ari a half hour later, sitting alone in a dimly-lit room filled with shelves of books.

It was a study, a room off of a grand living room, where many of the wedding guests had congregated now that the evening had grown late. "We're finally done with the last of the pictures."

Ari did not answer.

"You okay?" Sophia asked.

Ari smiled sadly. "I'm okay. It's just... Sophia? What company does your father own?"

"I told you, it's a software company."

"Oscuro," Ari said.

Sophia adjusted her dress and sat down. "How did you know that?"

"Why was it a big secret?" Ari asked, hurt in her voice.

"It wasn't a secret. I suppose it just never came up in any of our conversations," Sophia said, sitting down in a chair nearby.

"It's a pretty big company. He's a public figure," Ari said.

Sophia looked at her, concern on her face. "That's true. Although I didn't realize you were so familiar with tech companies."

"I recognize him because I used to serve him coffee. I worked at the coffee bar in Oscuro's headquarters - it was a kiosk in the atrium - when I was in high school."

"Small world," Sophia said.

"Yeah, and his company - your family's, I guess - laid off my parents."

"Ari," Sophia said gently.

"I mean..." Ari said, holding up her hands. "I know it has nothing to do with you. Really. It's fine. It's business. It just surprised me, that's all. To see him here, and to realize who your family is."

"I'm sorry my dad never came up in conversation," Sophia said. "Truly. I had no idea it would be so relevant to you. Do you want me to introduce you two tonight?"

"No, it's okay," Ari said.

"Really? Maybe he'll recognize you," Sophia said.

Ari shook her head. "No, really. It was a pretty long time ago, and besides, I think the few times I did serve him coffee, he got impatient with me for being too slow or getting the order wrong or something. No need to remind him of all of that."

"He's a different man at home. Work is work."

"Yeah… work is work," Ari said, unconvinced.

"Come on," Sophia urged, smiling kindly. "There's still music, and I enjoyed dancing with you earlier."

"Maybe in a bit," Ari said. "I'm going to find a bathroom first - I'll meet you near your table."

"I hope you will. I'm not a great dancer. I'm better when you're with me," Sophia said, and it was not lost on Ari how she fluttered her eyelashes a bit at that.

Ari gave her a half-smile. "I'll be back," she said.

··◦··

Sophia returned to her table, which was empty, though the candles were still flickering merrily in their frosted glass holders. Sophia had just gotten a fresh glass of wine, and was taking her first sip when she heard her sister call out her name.

"I saw you dancing with Ari earlier!" Sabrina said, her eyes sparkling as she moved toward Sophia. "I'm so proud of you."

"Why?" Sophia asked.

"Because you looked happy, and I feel like I never see you looking that happy. I know you make fun of me for all of my weddings, but being in love makes me happy. Maybe you're not so different after all."

"Hold on, I'm not in love," Sophia corrected her.

"Well, you're in lust then, I can see it in you. You're positively radiant tonight, my dear sister."

Sophia put her hands on her hips. "It's nothing. You know me. I can't get into anything serious. I'm too busy, and Percy-"

"Percy seems to have gotten his own life, in case you haven't noticed yet," Sabrina cut her off, then motioned towards the dance floor where Percy was, once again, dancing with Isabella. This time, the song was fast-paced, and both were laughing and seemed to be having fun.

Sophia frowned, watching him, wondering what to think.

"You can't use him as an excuse for not having a life for much longer," Sabrina added.

Sophia wanted to snap back at her, but stopped herself.

"I know," she admitted a moment later.

Sabrina's eyes widened in glee. "See! There we go. You admitted it. Ari is quite a catch, sis. A beautiful girl, a booming business of her own. If you don't snap her up, someone else will. Just a word from the wise."

And with that, Sabrina dashed away, back to the dance floor, where William was waiting for her.

Ari did not go back to the table and find Sophia right away after they talked in the study. Eventually, Sophia was pulled away from her table by more relatives wishing to talk, to say hello, or to say goodbye. Once or twice Sophia thought of finding Ari herself, but her family swallowed her up, as always, to talk about work, or business opportunities, foreign travel, to ask her if she was seeing anyone, whether she would eventually get married. The usual.

At one point, the groom rescued Sophia from a particularly awkward conversation with an aunt about the horrors of children who grow up without fathers. He asked her for a friendly dance, and as they danced, Sophia decided that he was significantly better than the rest of the men Sabrina had married. She secretly hoped that it would work out between the two of them.

After William, she danced with a man named Roger, who was the husband of one of her good friends from college, Bree. Bree and Roger had both ended up working for her father's company after college and had become family friends, and were now bursting with the good news that they were expecting a child. A heavily pregnant Bree sat at her table, too tired to dance, but she sweetly waved at the two of them on the dance floor as they talked.

"Times really have changed," Sophia said to him.

"Indeed they have," Roger beamed. "For the better, I hope."

"I hope so, too," Sophia said, wishing she could dance with Ari next.

After that, she was released from her social obligations - for a short while at least - and she could finally make her way around the room to find Ari. She finally found her chatting with Cassandra and Rachel, who were standing with a large group of Sabrina's friends, clustered not too far from the open bar. All of them were holding an array of colorful drinks.

Sophia lightly tapped Ari on the shoulder. "Come outside for a bit of fresh air with me?"

Ari excused herself and followed Sophia outside.

They stepped onto a massive deck off of the study that overlooked a dark valley, lit only by the nearly-full moon. Sophia had a quick flashback to the outdoor rooftop garden terrace at their penthouse suite in the hotel in Vegas.

"It's nice here," Ari said. "It must have been pretty neat to grow up here."

Sophia nodded. "It was lovely. Are you enjoying your stay?"

"Yeah. I've actually never been here, believe it or not, even though the city's really not that far away."

"I'm glad you could see it, then. When are you going home, Ari?"

"Tomorrow morning," Ari replied. "I found a little hotel not far from here for the night. Or what's left of it, at least."

"I'm staying at a resort nearby. Join me for breakfast. I want to show you something afterwards."

"What's the name of the resort?"

"The Black Valley Spa and Resort," said Sophia.

"Black, as in...?"

Sophia nodded. "One of my family's many business ventures."

"Wow. Do you guys, like, own the entire state?"

Sophia laughed. "I don't think that would be the best investment. I assure you, we just own the land and house here and the spa and resort I'm saying at. And my parents have a property in Palo Rosa. And I own my house in Palo Rosa."

"So, not very much at all," Ari joked, thinking of her studio apartment. "Okay. I'll meet you for breakfast before I head back home."

Ari started to move away, but Sophia reached out and took Ari's hand, gently stopping her.

"You agreed to one more dance, remember?" she asked, smiling coyly.

Ari gave her a friendly smile. She hesitated for a moment, squeezed Sophia's hand briefly then pulled away.

"I have to go. It's late. I'll see you at breakfast."

··o··

She wanted to dance with Sophia.

Truly.

She just did not know where a dance might have led that night. When it came to Sophia, close contact late at night was not safe. Nothing was simple with Sophia. A dance was not a dance, a kiss was not a kiss. There was always that underlying force that she felt when she was near the beautiful, maddening brunette... a force that told her to either run far, far away, or plunge in and never look back.

She was playing it cautious until she knew where Sophia stood. Whether she was still doing her "let's just be friends" thing, the back and forth thing, or whatever.

Breakfast, however, deep in wine country, early in the morning, with the bright sun shining outside, before she headed back home... that seemed relatively safe.

Ari wound her car through the twisting lanes. For some reason her phone's GPS kept cutting out so she was following some confusing instructions that she saved from an online map. This resort and spa was set back in a very secluded area. She turned down a small, narrow road and was just second guessing whether she was going the right way when she saw a small sign for the resort, thankfully pointing in the direction she was driving. She continued, winding through the woods, crossing over hills and peaks overlooking the fertile green valleys. It really was beautiful out here.

She was also looking forward to breakfast. Not just because she would see Sophia, but because she really needed something to soak up all of the colorful, liquor-filled concoctions Rachel and Cassandra had pushed on her the previous night. Her stomach was feeling a little unsettled.

She drove at least three more miles down the quiet, winding road, and just when she was about to second guess the directions again, she saw what looked like a large house ahead. No, château would be a better word, because it was like a manor, complete with turrets, made of ivy-covered stone, a slightly forgotten look to it. A sign indicated she had indeed arrived at the Black Valley Resort and Spa.

As soon as Ari parked and walked into the lobby, she knew she was in a different kind of place than the rustic, almost rugged, exterior suggested. The lobby was filled with massive tiled fireplaces and wood paneling and chandeliers. It looked like a French country castle.

"May I help you, madam?" a man asked.

Ari nodded. "I'm supposed to meet someone for brunch?"

She glanced down at her jeans and the simple sweater she had tossed on, wondering if there was a dress code.

"Of course, right through here you'll find our dining room," he said, walking her over.

Ari expected a typical restaurant, but after crossing through two parlors and an arched doorway, instead she found herself in what looked like a formal dining room out of a historical movie set.

There was a big wraparound porch outside with more tables, and outside at one of the tables is where she found Sophia.

"Hi," Ari said, and as she approached the table, Sophia looked up at her then stood up to greet her.

How the woman looked like a million bucks first thing in the morning after a late night filled with wine and champagne, Ari would never understand.

"Thanks for coming, Ari. Please, sit."

Ari sat down. From the outdoor patio, they were overlooking a small valley, the hillsides around covered in vineyards. At the bottom of the valley there appeared to be a small, still lake. Complete with the turreted manor they were at, the location seemed a little surreal.

"A drink?" Sophia offered.

"Hair of the dog?" Ari asked, eyeing the champagne glasses warily.

Sophia smiled. "You could say that. Don't worry, they're not strong. These are a specialty here, actually, made with an elderflower liqueur, local champagne, and fresh citrus juice."

"I'm more of a coffee girl with breakfast, as you probably know, but I'll try it," Ari said, taking the delicate champagne flute that she was offered, which was filled with a bubbly light liquid and a curl of lemon peel as garnish.

They both looked at their menus, printed in gold lettering on a small piece of thick, textured paper. There were only three choices. Ari decided to go with whatever a yeasted waffle was, and Sophia ordered an egg white omelette.

"I trust you had a good time at the wedding last night?"

Ari nodded. "No regrets. At least until the end, when Rachel and Cassandra insisted on doing a third round of shots."

Sophia smiled, but she seemed nervous.

"I wanted to ask you here this morning for two reasons," she said in a measured tone. "One, I wanted to show you something. But two, I also want to say that what you said a while back really made me think. I realize that I do tend to over think things."

Ari looked up from her menu, watching the woman, who was carefully concentrating on the words she was speaking.

"I over-thought that I over-think," she said, rolling her eyes. "Let me start again. You said we don't need to make a relationship fit some label, and I confess that that is exactly what I was trying to do. And that is partially what was terrifying me. I have a hard time knowing what to do with someone who has come into my life like you. Actually, I have never had someone quite like you come into my life."

She paused, took a delicate sip of her drink, then continued.

"I decided that I would like to try out whatever it is that we began trying out. If you would like to, too," Sophia stated. "If it's not... too late."

Ari hesitated.

"Unless, of course, you've already grown tired of it all," Sophia said quickly, nervous. "I know my intentions have not exactly been clear. My hesitation has not been fair to you."

Ari smiled tentatively.

"I just need to take everything slowly," Sophia said.

"That goes without saying," Ari said, nodding.

They ate breakfast after that, the tension in the air having diminished somewhat. They spoke like they were friends... but made eyes at each other like they were more than just friends.

Neither was 100% sure where this was going, but they felt more at ease than they had the night before.

They were taking baby steps, Ari thought.

After breakfast, Sophia told the waiter to put the meals on her tab - even after Ari insisted she could pay her portion - and Sophia took her on a small "behind the scenes" tour of the Resort.

"It's like a small castle. My mom would love this place," Ari commented as they wandered through the kitchens and then out onto another deck overlooking the scenery. "She loves all things that are old fashioned and romantic like this."

"Wait until you see where I'm taking you," Sophia said, motioning for her to follow her past a closed door, then down two flights of stone stairs.

"You're not going to murder me in the basement or something, are you?" Ari said, joking as they descended deeper underground.

"Not likely," Sophia replied.

They emerged in a wine cellar, a beautiful, cool space. It had a dark cement floor and dark walls, with strips of low lights artfully placed along the walls to allow for some light, but not too much, to be cast on the racks upon racks of wine bottles.

"Many of these are from the winery owned by my parents," Sophia explained. "They have a winery here in California, as well as one in my father's home country, in Argentina."

Ari admired all of the bottles.

"Is this what you were going to show me?" she asked, impressed.

Sophia shook her head. "Not exactly, although it is interesting in here, isn't it? No, I'm taking you to see one of my father's private art collections."

"Seriously?" Ari asked.

Sophia nodded. "I think you'll like it."

They approached a door, and Sophia tapped out some numbers on a key pad.

Sophia opened the door, and a few low lights switched on as they entered the small room.

"Your dad just keeps art down here?"

"The temperature is just right, as is the humidity, there's no natural light, so it ends up being a good environment for him to store some of the pieces he has invested in," explained Sophia, stepping back and allowing Ari to move into the room. "He rotates the pieces, putting some in my parents' home or in his study, while keeping others down here for safekeeping and preservation."

"These are amazing," Ari said, gazing around the room.

She did not really know much about the history of art. She had never studied art formally, but she appreciated seeing the works, which were similar in style to hers: semi-abstract, playing with color, light. Ari paused in front of a painting that looked almost like a cityscape, and then another with several figures dancing in a circle.

"Most of these were collected by my father and his associates during their travels over the past few decades," Sophia explained.

"Here, look at this one," she said, directing Ari over to a small painting in the corner, secured in what appeared to be a clear glass or acrylic box.

"Is that...?" Ari asked for a moment. "That's not a Pollock, is it?"

Sophia nodded. "It is."

"Whoa," Ari said.

"He's never been my favorite," Sophia said. "Here, I like this one-"

She pointed out a colorful semi-abstract painting, full of

movement.

"This is my favorite. It was purchased from an artist on the street corner in South America. He was completely broke at the time we bought this piece, but he was quite well known back in his heyday. I keep asking my father if I can have this painting, but he keeps forgetting to have it wrapped up and sent to me. Whether it's genuine forgetfulness or if he's still too attached to it, I'm not sure."

When Ari had looked at all of the paintings, they left the little room, the heavy door clicking shut behind them.

"Your life is filled with magical little secrets, Sophia. Rooms full of paintings, resorts and spas owned by your family in Napa. It's all so, I don't know, magical I guess. If it were me, I'd be tempted to kick back and relax and enjoy the view. And yet you still work to build a whole empire of your own."

Sophia laughed as they walked slowly back through the underground wine cellar. "I'm not exactly as successful as my father. No empire yet."

"Yeah, but you must have inherited something from him. You're driven."

"It's my mother, really, who motivates him daily. I think he would have kicked back and relaxed and enjoyed a glass of wine decades ago if it weren't for her giving him new ideas, planting new ambitions in his mind, telling him to do more, to continue to work and stay busy, even in his retirement."

"Well, then you're like your mother."

Sophia looked slightly nervous at that comment.

"I'm afraid I'm too much like her. I don't want to be. She was obsessed with appearances and also put my father's ambition and success ahead of paying attention to me, or to Sabrina, when we were children. She was always scheming and plotting every move, from business decisions to arranging our social engagements with key acquaintances and friends. She even dictated to Sabrina and me the careers we should have, the things we should study. My dad was like my sister and me: at the mercy of her dreams and schemes."

"He was successful, though. Look at all of this," Ari pointed out.

"Perhaps. But does my family really need all of this?" Sophia asked. "At some point, it became frivolous."

Ari looked at Sophia curiously. This was more than she had ever heard about Sabrina's family before, and it went a long ways in explaining Sophia's particular personality and attitudes.

"I think you're like them all," Ari said. "You're driven and tough like your mom, focused like your dad, and still... I don't know, warm in a way. Like your sister. She's warm toward the people she cares about, like you, and her friends. You're a little bit like all of them... but also, you're very much your own person."

Sophia considered that. "Perhaps."

"You know, last night when I found out who your dad was, that he'd been the one responsible for laying off my parents, I was really put off. I mean, that whole experience changed me. It made me reluctant to ever want to work at a big company. I learned to rely on myself and work for myself. It gave me an entrepreneurial spirit. And so I thought it was this bad thing in my life, that my parents were unemployed and eventually I had to move back home to help them, but in reality, I guess it also taught me that I needed to be self-reliant, and it forced me to do a lot of things differently than I might have otherwise. Ultimately, it's why I started The Little Cafe. I guess in a weird, roundabout way, I owe him for that experience and insight."

Sophia looked at her. "That is an interesting way of looking at things."

Ari shrugged. "I guess what I'm saying is, there's a silver lining to everything."

Sophia stopped walking. They were still underground, walking past rows and rows of wines.

Ari stopped next to her, her back to a shelf filled with wines.

"You've brought something to my life these past couple of months, Ari. Something I never had. Your friendship, your patience, and your astute observations have helped me think about things, especially the way I see the other people in my life. People I'd really taken for granted for so long."

Sophia reached over and gently, lightly, touched Ari's cheek, combed a few strands of her long, silky blonde hair behind her ears, allowed her hand to rest on the other woman's shoulder.

"I feel better with you around, Arianna. You bring a certain lightness into my life, happiness. It scared me at first, but now I invite it in, because you make my life better."

Ari smiled shyly.

"I hope I can somehow make yours better, too," Sophia said quietly.

Ari reached up, took Sophia's hand, and kissed it.

Sophia was studying Ari's lips.

Ari looked at her.

"Sophia," she said in a warning tone.

Sophia did not respond. Instead, she sighed heavily and closed her eyes. Her back was to a shelf filled with wine, and her face was half in the shadows.

Ari reached out and touched Sophia this time, moving a hand to her waist, stepping closer, though still maintaining some distance. She could not help but steal a lingering glance at the woman with her eyes half closed, looking so pretty, almost looking as though she was surrendering to her there, in the cool, dark cellar.

Sophia fluttered open her eyelashes a few seconds later and caught Ari staring longingly at her, not knowing what to do next.

"Just kiss me," Sophia instructed quietly, her eyes wide, quickly biting her lip.

Ari knew she should resist, but ignored her inner warnings not to succumb.

"You are such a-" Ari started to say, obediently leaning closer to Sophia.

But just then, they heard footsteps on the stairs.

Sophia heard them first, gave a bit of a gasp, and straightened herself up. Ari took a big step backwards, following Sophia's eyes to the stairs.

"We should go," Sophia said a moment later, breathing a little more heavily than normal.

They watched as a man, possibly just a waiter from the restaurant, searched through the shelves nearby, not yet aware of their presence.

Sophia smoothed out her skirt and led the way to the stairway, her stride long and purposeful. The man glanced over at them, surprised, but Sophia nodded to him solemnly.

"Good morning," she said.

"Good morning," he replied.

When they were back upstairs, Sophia turned to Ari, gently touching her upper arm, and lowered her voice to almost a whisper.

"I would invite you to my room, but Percy is due back shortly. It doesn't seem like a good idea."

"Probably not," agreed Ari.

For more reasons than one, she added to herself.

Her eyes, which were still wide and bright, betrayed the ideas that were currently floating through her mind.

"I'll tell you what," Sophia said in a low voice, taking Ari's hand in her own, her heart still racing a little. "I remember I owe you a dinner. Come over next week and I'll make good on that deal."

Ari laughed.

"You don't have to do that. Besides, you made up for it with breakfast this morning."

"Well, you don't have to come over if you don't want to, of course. It's just there are some matters we could... tend to," Sophia said, her voice thick with implication.

Ari smiled, her eyes soft.

"On second thought, dinner sounds great," Ari agreed through a wide smile.

Ari looked into Sophia's eyes as Sophia raised Ari's hand to her lips and kissed it gently.

"See you next week, then."

11

DINNERS

Sophia opened her door a few days later to find Ari standing on her porch, holding a bottle of wine, dripping wet from the rain.

"Don't you have an umbrella?" Sophia asked, eyeing Ari's wet blonde hair, which hung limply around her shoulders.

Sophia ushered her inside.

"I don't mind a little rain."

"I'll send you home with one," Sophia said, and gratefully accepted the bottle of wine that Ari handed her.

Although she noted the variety of wine did not exactly go with the pasta and fish she was serving, her eyes lingered on the label. Ari had chosen a more exclusive wine than your run-of-the-mill grocery store or liquor store bottle. She must have gone out of her way to get it. Sophia found it endearing that Ari had tried so hard to pick out a special wine just for the evening.

"This wine looks delicious," Sophia said, then led her towards the kitchen, where they were enveloped in the warm, rich aroma of a fresh tomato pasta sauce bubbling on the stove.

"I don't know a lot about wine, I hope it goes with what you're fixing," Ari said sheepishly, then added, "Which, by the way, smells great."

"Thank you. This wine will be perfect to sip on while we wait for dinner to finish," Sophia suggested, getting two glasses out of the cupboard.

"Is Percy around?" Ari asked, glancing around expectantly.

Sophia shook her head. "No, he's at a friend's house tonight. It's just the two of us."

"Oh," Ari said, taking the glass of wine Sophia offered her.

"Can I help with anything?" she asked.

Sophia shook her head. "It's all under control."

"Turnovers, pasta... is there anything you can't make perfectly?" Ari asked a half hour later after Sophia had poached some fish in her fresh, homemade tomato and rosemary sauce, then served it all over thick homemade tagliatelle.

Sophia was the image of a gourmet chef. The meal had clearly been made to perfection, and it looked and smelled good enough to be featured on the cover of a gourmet magazine.

"Lots of things," Sophia said, smiling. "I know my limits, and I only make tried and true recipes when I have guests over. Guests who I actually want to stay a while and not scare away, that is."

"Hmm, you want me to stay," Ari commented, her eyes glimmering mischievously as she took a sip of the wine.

Ari sighed a few minutes later as she took the first bite of the pasta, relishing in the fresh, herby tomato sauce, the homemade pasta, and the delicate fish, which complimented the dish perfectly.

"This is definitely never going to scare anyone off," Ari

commented.

Sophia elegantly took a bite of her pasta and followed it with a sip of wine, beaming.

"Is this pasta homemade?" Ari asked.

"It is. Although I have the help of a machine. I can't exactly sacrifice an afternoon to making pasta these days. Then I freeze large batches of it, in case someone comes over."

Ari smiled. "A stash of pasta in case a suitor comes calling."

"Precisely," Sophia said, still smiling a bit saucily.

Their conversation continued to flow effortlessly. Sophia and Ari had a rhythm where they could talk about many things, easing from one topic to the next. As they spoke, it dawned on Sophia how - after the past few days - she had settled into a surprising level of comfort with Ari. Something that she really had not experienced in a long while. Not with her sister, or colleagues, or any friends. Certainly not with any recent romantic partners.

Her life before Ari had opened The Little Cafe now seemed so distant. She could not imagine days without the witty and ever-surprising blonde nearby during her long days at work.

Dinner stretched on. Neither woman wanted to rise from the table and risk cutting the evening short. They continued sipping wine, their cheeks growing rosy and their laughter ringing a little freer. The music that had been playing in the background throughout dinner added to the pleasant ambiance.

From time to time, Ari would watch Sophia biting her lip just so. Or Sophia would observe Ari's little movements, her lean body twisting gracefully to pick up a napkin that had dropped on the floor. Their eyes would then meet. They smiled, they laughed. They flirted.

Finally, with the salad, pasta and garlic bread consumed and both women knowing they could no longer dwell at the table, Sophia suggested they move into her library and have a nip of her favorite apple liqueur.

They continued chatting over their drinks, Ari crisscrossing her legs on the midnight grey Italian leather couch, cradling her glass in her lap. She was taking small, careful sips, aware of how strong Sophia's nightcaps were.

At first Sophia sat in a separate armchair, perched regally as she delicately sipped on her drink and chatted with Ari, but after she stood up to refill both of their glasses, she sat back down not in the armchair but on the sofa next to Ari.

At one point, Sophia reached over and placed her hand on top of Ari's. They were in the middle of a conversation about work, Ari talking about sourcing organic coffee beans and Sophia was chiming in about how the cumbersome process was not all that different than trying to source a rare type of silk she often used in her work. When she felt Sophia's hand on hers, Ari paused, looked down, and then continued talking without missing a beat. She just acted casual. But she slipped her hand away a moment later.

Sophia cleared her throat nervously after that, and decided to change the topic.

"How are the paintings coming along?" Sophia asked.

"I'll show you the paintings soon," Ari said, suddenly looking a little nervous. "I would have shown you sooner, but work's been a little demanding. So many little details, employees, paperwork and other stuff to deal with. My days fly by. Which, I guess you can understand."

"I'm sorry. I didn't meant to bring up a stressful topic. I was just trying to make conversation."

"Oh, it's all right," Ari said, sighing and sinking back into the sofa, closing her eyes part way. "They're nearly complete, actually. Just not quite finished-finished. If work will stop getting in the way, I'll have them to you soon."

"Anything in particular stressing you at work?" Sophia asked.

Ari hesitated, then shrugged. "Not really. I am just trying to get a handle on some money things. You know, the usual. Tough stuff to deal with sometimes."

"I do know," Sophia said.

Seeing as how the subject was dragging Ari down, she did not want to bring up the topic of work again during an evening that still held so much promise.

Instead, Sophia quietly studied Ari, reclining on the sofa, her drink in her hands, her eyelashes fluttering shut as she sank deeper and deeper into the sofa, relaxing in the dim lighting of Sophia's study and the sound of the fire crackling in the fireplace.

"I missed this, Ari," Sophia said softly. "Ever since that morning in Vegas..."

Ari fluttered open her eyes and sat up a bit. She knew what "this" meant. The familiarity, the comfort and intimacy of the two of them when they were together.

"Sophia," Ari said in a warning tone.

"Arianna," Sophia echoed.

"This can't be a game any more, right?"

Sophia looked down at her lap and took a breath. "Right."

"I've been trying not to miss this. To not miss you," Ari admitted and dropped her voice, "But it's hard. I just don't know what's going to happen, whether our lives can ever really get in synch."

Sophia touched Ari's cheek gently and swallowed.

"I want them to," she whispered.

Ari took her hand, clasped it, but moved it away from her cheek.

"Sophia," she whispered in a warning tone. "You know what happens when you do this."

Sophia ignored her, slowly leaned in and gave her a gentle, sweet kiss on the lips. She lingered delicately for a few moments, reveling in the taste of Ari, her scent, her warmth.

But then Sophia pulled back, never deepening the kiss.

"You're right," Sophia whispered. "I don't want to poison this. There's something about being around you... but we already agreed. One step at a time."

Even as she said it, Sophia realized that her familiar nerves - the ones that used to flare up every time she was around Ari - had diminished slightly. She was finally feeling confident tonight. All night, she had felt great. But those nerves were now replaced with concern, concern that she had already alienated Ari. That it was too late. That she had already caused too much damage before she could do right by the woman before her.

Tonight, it was Ari's turn to feel uncertain about the situation.

Sophia recognized that.

"I should go," Ari said, her face clouded with concern.

Sophia stood up, walking towards the fire, which had burned down low in the fireplace. She stared into it for a few seconds, taking a deep breath, trying to quell her disappointment, then nodded, and gave Ari a sad smile.

Sophia walked Ari out of the study and towards the door. Sophia handed her an umbrella from an elegant iron stand near the front door.

"It's still raining," she said, glancing out the window next to the door and noting the drops still clinging to the outside of the glass.

"Thanks. Although my car isn't that far away," Ari said, accepting the umbrella. "And thanks for dinner. Really, one of the best meals I've ever had."

Sophia smiled. "Any time."

Ari opened the door and was about to step into the inky-dark night.

"Arianna? One more thing," Sophia said.

"Yeah?" Ari turned back, her blue eyes meeting Sophia's.

The formidable Sophia Black took a breath, feeling suddenly small and insecure in front of the woman whom she'd come to adore.

"Percy will be out of the house again the night after next. Would you like to have dinner with me again?"

··○··

Sophia made wild Atlantic Canadian salmon two nights later, served on a bed of homemade pasta with a garlic, white wine, and butter sauce and a side of tender, steamed asparagus. It was incredible.

And Ari had thought that nothing would top the previous meal. It was so good, in fact, that Ari could not help but mourn the fact that now she understood what a really, truly good meal was, and therefore all future dinners in her life would no doubt pale in comparison.

"I don't know why I own a cafe when you're the one who cooks so well. I'm also not sure why you don't have a line of suitors wrapped around the block every night for this," Ari said at dinner.

"Maybe that could be my next business," mused Sophia. "Although I don't have a life as it is, so I have a hard time imagining being able to handle a restaurant on top of everything."

"Plus your side job in the Palo Rosa Retail Association - which, by the way, sorry I haven't gone to any other town meetings since the winter."

"I noticed that," Sophia said.

"They got kind of boring, to be honest, when you stopped ripping into me for breaking town codes or whatever."

"I could find a town code that The Little Cafe is no doubt breaking and bring that up at the next meeting if you would like."

"It's okay," Ari said. "I have enough challenges keeping the place afloat as it is."

"Oh?" Sophia asked, concern flickering across her face as she set down her glass of wine. "Those finance issues you mentioned the other night?"

"Yeah. I mean, nothing special. Just the typical boring challenges of running your own business. Balancing the books, staying on top of payments to suppliers, rent, the usual."

"I experienced all of those problems at one point," Sophia said.

"At least you've been successful at dealing with them," Ari continued, reaching for another piece of bread. "I mean, look at all of this. A beautiful home, a son, a great business, even your involvement in the Retail Association."

"My term is up soon," Sophia replied. "In the Retail Association."

Ari laughed. "Okay, fine. You really do have everything else, though. You're an example of hard work really paying off."

"I have almost everything," Sophia corrected. "I've been missing something."

"What?" Ari asked.

Sophia shifted slightly and took a deep breath. "Ari, you know what I'm missing."

Ari stopped chewing and her eyes met Sophia's.

Sophia continued, waving her hand around to emphasize a point: "Someone to share it with. My sister reminded me that Percy is growing up. You saw it at the wedding, dancing with Isabella, being his own self."

"He's not exactly on the verge of moving out and getting

married," Ari pointed out lightly.

"I know. Of course he's not, and he'll be at home for a few more years. But it made me realize I won't always have our little family. He'll grow up and move on and I will still be here in this big, empty house. Alone," said Sophia.

"I didn't know that being alone bothered you," Ari said.

Sophia seemed to relish being on her own. Ari figured it was one of the main reasons she had been so quick to run every time they started to get close.

"It does," Sophia said. "I'm used to it, I know nothing other than it, it's the easiest thing in the world for me because it's my life. But at the same time, I'm restless when I'm alone. I know there's something better. That's what makes it also so unbearable."

Ari thought that sounded a little dramatic, but Sophia really did seem agitated. Her forehead was scrunched, her hands clasped tensely on the table, resting on either side of her plate.

Ari just kept listening.

Sophia took a deep breath, then slowly looked up at Ari as she spoke. "I know that having someone to share everything with is better."

Ari smiled gently, and to diffuse Sophia's tension, raised her glass. "To not being alone. Not at this very moment, at least."

Sophia smiled tentatively and nodded, following suit and raising her glass.

"I have a surprise for you after we're done with dinner," Ari said when they had sipped the last of their wine.

"A good surprise, I hope?" Sophia asked, sitting back in her chair, relaxed again.

"I'd only bring a good surprise for you," Ari said, smiling as she tucked a piece of blonde hair behind her ear.

"Well then, how about I clean up and you prepare the surprise?" Sophia asked.

Ari nodded. "Seems fair. Also, you don't want me to clean up, I'm terrible at doing dishes."

"Sure you are," Sophia said, laughing lightly. "But the surprise is a good incentive for me to do them, so it's a deal."

"Can I set it up in the study?" Ari asked.

"Of course," Sophia said. "Assuming it's not going to leave any sort of mess, is it?"

"Probably not," Ari laughed.

Sophia worked quickly to clean up the dishes and put things away, listening as Ari made a few trips out to her car and back.

"It's ready whenever you are," Ari called to Sophia after a while.

Sophia wiped her hands on a dishtowel, clicked off some of the lights in the kitchen, and went into the study.

"Surprise," Ari said, and she stepped aside so Sophia could see four paintings, completed.

Sophia looked at the paintings. Two were up on the mantel over the fireplace and the other two were propped up in the leather chairs. They were exactly what she had commissioned Ari to make.

The colors were beautiful, melding perfectly with the swatches Sophia had supplied her from her notes and inspiration boards for her lingerie collection. The paintings were exactly what she was looking for. Ari's work - the swirls of color and semi-abstract images - were real, beautiful, elegant, filled with artistry. A wonderful compliment to the marketing campaign she had in mind.

"Well? Are they okay? I can change anything if they're not right," Ari asked nervously, and Sophia realized she had not yet said anything.

"They're perfect, Arianna," Sophia said, genuinely pleased. "These are exactly as I imagined. They're going to work beautifully."

"Good," Ari beamed.

"I can't wait to use them," Sophia said.

Ari smiled. "I'm glad you're happy."

Sophia looked at her, a little startled by that. "I suppose I am happy. I can't wait to get started on this. Thank you for all of your help, Ari."

"Well, thanks for asking me to help," Ari said.

"How did you have time to finish them? We were only talking about them the night before last and you said they weren't yet complete," Sophia asked.

Ari shrugged. "Haven't been able to sleep much lately, and painting has always been my favorite thing to do to relax. They offered me a distraction."

"I appreciate all of your work on these. I'll send you the rest of the payment," Sophia said.

Ari did not say anything. She did not really want to get back into talking about business. Not tonight.

"Do you want any dessert?" Sophia offered brightly. "A little something to celebrate? I bought a carton of that organic gelato from the farmer's market... or perhaps something with a little bit more edge? A nightcap, perhaps?"

"I don't know if I should stay much later," Ari said, hesitating. "I just wanted to be sure to show these to you tonight."

"Stay," Sophia said softly, taking a step closer to Ari. "Please."

"Sophia," Ari said in a semi-warning tone.

They were doing so well. She hated to ruin this rhythm they had gotten into. She did not want Sophia to do anything she might regret the next day, to fall back into her old habits before they had even given this different - slower - approach a chance.

Sophia took a breath, her eyes soft. She took another step towards Ari. Her posture tonight was strong, confident, almost feline, but her expression was relaxed, calm and inviting.

Ari bit her lip, watching her.

She knew it might be a bad idea, but it was also thoroughly alluring.

"I told you, I am ready for this," Sophia said softly, then glanced at Ari's mouth and placed a hand on her shoulder. "And I think we both know by now that the two of us can't just be friends."

Ari nodded slowly. It was true. She could never just be with this woman, sit with her, converse with her, and then... just walk out the door at the end.

"Agreed," she whispered.

Sophia took a deep breath and rested a hand softly on Ari's cheek, her touch as light as a feather.

"You told me, a while back, that I was frustrating and infuriating," she began. "But so are you. You call me out. You see things in me that no one bothered to see before. You force me to challenge assumptions about myself."

Ari did not respond.

Sophia continued, "And your patience with me in of itself has been almost infuriating these past few months, because I don't know how anyone can stand it. I know you don't like games, and until recently that was all I really knew how to do with my romantic life."

Sophia paused, pursing her own lips while looking at Ari's, the urge to kiss them written all over her face, but holding back.

"The games I've played in the past usually result in me losing. I don't want to lose any more," Sophia whispered.

Ari looked into her eyes, searching, making sure Sophia was speaking the truth.

She was.

"You're trembling," Ari reached up to touch Sophia's hand, and then smiled warmly, trying to calm the woman down, to get her to breathe. She eased her back, urging her to sit on the sofa.

Sophia looked slightly flustered. "Sorry."

"Relax," Ari urged her softly. "If I'm going to stay, I'm going to do something. Like pour a drink. Maybe that really awesome cider we had a few nights ago?"

"I'll get the glasses," Sophia offered.

"No, sit. You made dinner and cleaned up, you've done enough," Ari insisted. "I'm pretty sure I know where you keep your crystal, and I definitely saw where you kept the liquor. Let me get it."

Sophia nodded. "Well, all right then."

"You're not the only one who can be bossy," Ari said, smiling playfully. "Stay here."

Sophia hated sitting still, especially when she felt so nervous, excited, agitated about having just bared so much - too much - to the woman. While Ari went out in search for the drinks, Sophia stood up and got a self-starting fire log and a few pieces of wood she kept stacked neatly near her fireplace. She put them in the fireplace, arranged a bit of wood around the log to make sure the fire would last for at least a little while, and lit the flame. The night was damp and rainy again, so there had been a bit of a chill in the air. The fire provided a comforting ambiance.

Ari returned to the study after taking a while, holding more than just the glasses in her arms.

"Problems finding the glasses?" Sophia asked.

Ari shook her head. "No. Found them. Then I got distracted. I found some art supplies in the kitchen."

"Oh, Percy left them there the other day. He was using them for an art assignment at school."

"It gave me an idea," Ari said. "Let me draw you."

"What do you mean? Draw me? Like..."

"'Like one of your French girls,' yeah," Ari said, laughing.

"I hope you don't intend on drawing me au naturel," Sophia said, crossing her legs primly, but grateful for the change in topic.

"I was, in fact, hoping that I could," Ari teased, then quickly added, "But I didn't realistically think it would be your cup of tea."

"You thought correctly. I'd hate to have anything like that around; it could come back to haunt me. I'm a mother, involved in the local community, a business owner... it doesn't seem wise," Sophia explained.

"None of those things mean you can't have any fun, but I get your point. Sit down. Relax. Sip this," Ari instructed, handing Sophia her glass of cider.

After Ari gave her a few brief directions on the best angle to sit relative to the light, she encouraged Sophia to relax and she set to work. They chatted a bit, but mostly sipped their drinks while Ari worked on her sketch from where she was perched in an armchair, a location with a beautiful view of where Sophia sat. Sophia's face was soft, her eyes lowered, looking down at her hands in her lap, occasionally stealing glances at Ari as she worked. Half of her face was in shadow, and the other half illuminated by the light of the fire.

As Ari fell deeper and deeper into her drawing, she propped her feet up on the coffee table, and Sophia bit her tongue and chose not to comment on the assault to her antique table. Instead, they both sipped their drinks and relaxed to the sounds of the fire crackling and popping, a comforting sound on a night where they could also hear the rain hitting the window outside.

As her pencil traced across the paper, Ari's hand sketching Sophia's graceful curves, her defined face and brows, her soft face, she realized that Sophia looked more peaceful and content tonight than she had ever seen her. The tension from their talk earlier had melted from her shoulders and arms, her hands were resting gently on her lap.

Ari's sketching seemed to generate a new atmosphere between them, both sensing a heightened conscientiousness in the air and space between them, as well as that peculiar intimacy that accompanies the act of observing - or being the one observed - so closely.

It was over an hour before Ari finished. Sophia stood up, stretched, and went over to Ari, still sitting down, so she could see the work.

"It's still a sketch. But I can fill it in, make it a proper portrait later," Ari explained.

It was good. And Sophia loved that Ari had done it with such care, admiring the detail of the shadows of her face, the fine lines of her hair.

"Thank you," she said, standing up, wrapping her arms around Ari, and gently giving the top of her head a kiss.

A few moments later, Ari turned her face up, closed her eyes, and invited Sophia into a proper kiss.

Sophia broke away from the tender kiss a few seconds later, gazed into Ari's beautiful, soft blue eyes, and smiled seductively.

And suddenly, everything felt right for both of them.

"I suppose we are both artists," Sophia said in a low voice, emphasizing each word, and reaching to slowly unzip the light grey sheath dress she was wearing.

She turned her head to the side, facing the fire, the light

of the flames dancing off of her face and her body. Sophia shrugged her shoulders slightly, allowing the fabric to melt onto the floor. She then expertly stepped out of the dress as it pooled at her feet.

Underneath the demure, conservative, unassuming dress was an elaborate satin slip, made of lace and soft fabric that - when Ari instinctively reached out to lightly touch it - felt smooth and silky, almost like water under her fingertips. It was short, barely hitting mid-thigh, and the top around her breasts was delicate lace, leaving nothing to the imagination.

Ari's breath caught in her throat.

"This is my art," Sophia whispered, standing before Ari in just the slip and her heels.

Ari slowly rose to her feet, and Sophia leaned in to kiss her, then after a moment, used a hand to gently press her back into a seated position on the sofa. Ari allowed her to direct her into place.

Sophia leaned in and continued to kiss her.

The kiss was not demure and sweet like it had been the other night. This time, it was filed with urgency. In the heat of the kiss, their lips parted, and both were suddenly lost, swimming deep in a sea of abandon.

Sophia, however, did not lose her bearings, and was the first to resurface. She encouraged Ari to lay down this time, and Ari, through half-closed eyes, watched as Sophia was the one to pepper her shoulders with kisses, starting gently at first but then scattering a few light nips for good measure. Ari's heart was racing, beating wildly as the woman worked her way down her stomach, then stopped. Sophia lifted her head slightly.

"Let's go upstairs."

Ari's breath caught, wondering if she could even move, but nodded.

Moments later, Ari stepped foot for her first time in Sophia's bedroom. She did not exactly pause for a tour. They were drawn to each other like magnets as soon as they were in the room, Sophia directing them slowly over to her large bed as they kissed.

Ari paused her for a moment when they were next to the bed.

"I like your work," she whispered, barely maintaining her breath as she raked her fingertips up and down Sophia's side, "but I'm afraid that lingerie, as nice as it is, is lost on me. I much prefer what is underneath."

And in one fluid movement, she finished undressing Sophia, the beautiful, delicate slip falling lightly to the floor like a leaf from a tree, Sophia stepping willingly out of her heels.

Sophia bit her lip and made a deep, throaty sound at that, betraying her impatience once she found herself completely bared in front of the other woman, who was still dressed. She then took back control and walked Ari backwards, gently urging her onto her back on the bed, which welcomed the other woman into it like a soft, fluffy cloud. The sea of pillows felt silky next to Ari's cheek, and her head sank deeply into one of them.

Ari, while still fully dressed, was utterly at the mercy of the other woman, who positioned herself on top and took Ari's wrists, gently pressing them above her head, amidst the endless pillows, and resumed kissing the woman deeply.

Ari made a deep noise in her throat, and Sophia continued to kiss the woman's mouth, her neck, the tender spot just under her ear, all while relishing the odd sort of control she had over the situation. Ari lowered her hands and made an attempt to remove her own shirt, but Sophia stopped her, gently taking a hold of her wrists and repositioning them back above her head.

"No," she instructed gently, but determinedly. "Remember what we said about taking things slow? I want to savor every second of you here on my bed, but *slowly*. And I want you to enjoy every second of being here, on my bed, as I-"

She kissed her neck, just below her ear.

"-pleasure-"

She edged her hand up Ari's shirt, skimmed over her bra, and kissed her collarbone while caressing her side gently with her other hand.

"-every-"

She moved her hands to Ari's waistband, and unbuttoned her jeans, and kissed just above her hip.

"-square inch..."

She lifted her head again and looked directly into Ari's eyes as Ari whimpered slightly.

"...of your body."

Ari gave another little whimper as Sophia hovered over her for another kiss, but allowed the woman to remain in control and guide her through the rest of the night.

And for that night, Sophia successfully managed to ignore the nagging voice in her head that had told her for months that any romantic pursuit of Ari was wrong and would end in heartbreak.

The wandering, exploring hands, the heated kisses, the firm instructions to breathe, and then, to let go... her feelings of uncertainty was far away as the night wore on.

The night was one wonderful, lively, spirited catharsis after the next, and when they were too tired for more, they stopped, and rested, laying next to each other for a while, until hands began to wake up and wander again, to feel, to embrace, searching until they both felt they had thoroughly enjoyed everything that was humanly possible to experience that night.

The whole night was decadent and wonderful.

And at last, they had exhausted themselves.

··○··

The next morning, when Sophia woke up to a view of golden blonde hair splayed out on her pillow, she was filled with warmth, and admired how the strands caught the early morning light that filtered through her window. It looked shiny and ethereal, like straw spun to gold. Everything about Ari seemed light and magical.

Ari was so beautiful, she thought to herself as the woman slept, and so she grimaced when, at long last, she could no longer put off getting up. She needed to get to work, and she knew Ari did, too.

They both went their separate ways, neither having enough time that morning to linger in the golden morning light that streamed through Sophia's window, no time to process the previous night (or repeat any of the activities of the previous night, even though both women yearned to). They drove to their respective workplaces separately, since Ari had taken her car to Sophia's the night before, and they knew it would be best to not leave it there, lest there be too many questions to field from Percy later when he came home. But as soon as they got to work and parked, Sophia went into The Little Cafe, and like any other day, began the morning with her favorite cup of coffee.

And that is how things continued for the next little while. By day, they remained two professional women who worked near each other, Sophia stopping by for coffee breaks, friendly banter being the hallmark of their daytime interactions.

But by night, Ari might visit for dinners that, when Percy was not around, involved late nights of long talks, jokes, playful quarreling and conversations interspersed with caresses and kisses and gentle touches of soft fingertips on fiery skin.

One week, when too many days had gone by without privacy at Sophia's house, Sophia snuck Ari upstairs into her office after hours. They wandered into the dark room and indulged each other amongst scraps of silk and lace that peppered her table and shelves.

As they had agreed, they did not stop to try to label what they were doing, or discuss it in detail. Instead, they had fallen into a comfortable, perfectly natural rhythm: just the two of them, together.

And it was lovely.

12

EXCHANGES

"**W**hy didn't you tell me that The Little Cafe was struggling?" Sophia had come over to the cafe after she finished work to pick up Ari for dinner. It was Ari's turn to select the restaurant, and pizza was the plan for the evening.

("Let's have it in the park, overlooking the water," Ari had suggested over the phone earlier that day, and Sophia had to admit, despite the casual choice of food, all things considered, it was a pretty romantic date plan.)

But when Sophia arrived at The Little Cafe, she found Ari, usually so upbeat, was in a sour mood. After she walked behind the counter, she overheard Ari complaining to Rachel that the cafe was once again dangerously close to being in the red that month.

"It's not struggling," Ari grumbled as Sophia made her appearance, interrupting the conversation she was having with Rachel. "Just not sure how to reconcile some things in the books. I feel like business is decent, but at the end of the month, we're not making a lot of money. Not as much as I need, and definitely not as much as I want to be making."

"What does your accountant suggest?" Sophia asked as Rachel slipped back out into the cafe to wait on customers.

"Nothing. He just takes care of tax stuff."

"Okay. Well, what about suppliers? Are you getting the best prices for the volume of materials you are purchasing? Or leftover inventory? How many things do you have to toss at the end of the week? What expenses do you have that you can trim?"

"I... I don't know, really, I'd have to start keeping better track," Ari admitted.

"You might want to," Sophia said. "Tiny details and expenses here and there might not seem like a big deal on their own, but everything adds up."

"Would you mind taking a look at my books?" Ari asked. "You have tons of experience, and I'm still new at this whole running your own business thing. And, clearly, I'm really new to this whole staying out of the red thing."

Sophia hesitated.

"Never mind," Ari said quickly. "You're busy. I don't want to bother you."

"No, that's not it. I just don't want to get in an uncomfortable situation where I'm giving you advice on your business. I don't know everything. A lot of what I do know was learned simply through trial and error, and probably a dose of luck. I don't want to steer you in the wrong direction," Sophia said.

"Right now, I have no one to give me *any* direction. My parents try to help, but let's face it, their cupcake shop failed. I'm doing better than that so far. I'll take any advice I can get, because otherwise I'm on my own," Ari said.

Sophia smiled. "All right. It's not a problem, I'll take a look. I'll let you know what I think, if there's anything I see that might help you out. But right now I suggest trimming any costs you can in the short term."

"Like... what?" Ari asked warily.

"Well, what about striking some of the pastries and the little snacks that don't sell as quickly off the menu. Or reduce the choices of different filtered coffees you brew every day, so you don't have to buy so many different types of beans. Little things like that."

Ari considered. "I know I should've been trimming more things like that, but I hate to do it. I like offering customers a larger selection. I think it makes my place seem special, worth going out of the way to visit, you know? Compared to the average coffee chain."

"It's hard to edit when it involves the things you love. Trust me, I know. But you can always do it for a little while, until business picks up. Then you can slowly experiment with re-introducing more things."

"You're probably right," Ari admitted.

"And I'll look at the rest of your paperwork this weekend," Sophia said, taking the folder that Ari offered her, which was stuffed with papers.

As they walked to the pizzeria, they chatted lightly, dropping the work topics for the rest of the evening. They relaxed, enjoying their food as they sat overlooking the water at a park just a stone's throw from the pizzeria, enjoying the warm evening weather.

"I haven't met your parents yet," Sophia pointed out as they were eating. "You've met my family - unfortunately - but I have yet to meet yours."

"Strange you haven't run into them. They come by the cafe once or twice a week, although they usually come over in the middle of the day, when you're at work," Ari said. "We could all have dinner sometime if you want. My mom would love

Percy. She adores children and I think she always wished she'd had more."

"You don't have any other siblings, do you?"

Ari shook her head. "No."

"Your parents really worked for my father's company?" Sophia asked, hesitantly bringing up the topic for the first time since the wedding.

Ari nodded. "Yes."

"What did your father do?"

"Software programmer," Ari said.

"And your mom?"

"She was in human resources."

"My father retired a long time ago, but he's still on the board and involved in some things around the company. I came across the company's job postings recently, and there are some positions open that might be a match for your parents," Sophia said, trying to sound casual.

"Really? I don't know..." Ari hesitated. "I don't know how they'd feel about being hired back at the same place."

Sophia shrugged. "There's been a lot of turnover in the years since they were laid off, I doubt it would be too difficult to transition back in, especially if they left on good terms. I could see what I could do."

"We're talking business again," Ari warned.

"It's more about your parents," Sophia defended herself, smiling.

"Yeah, you volunteering to pull some strings for me. Seems a little shady."

"How do you think most of corporate America runs? You scratch my back, I scratch yours." Sophia said, then grimaced. "That's truly a disgusting expression, isn't it?"

Ari laughed. "I feel weird asking that kind of favor of you. As you just pointed out, you haven't even met my parents."

"It's not a favor, I offered. And I'm not guaranteeing any-thing. It's just a thought. You've done a lot for me, Ari. I'm happy to do something for you."

Ari gave her a serious look. "Things don't have to be ex-actly equal all the time, you know."

Sophia swallowed. "I know. But I just feel like doing some-thing helpful if I can. Think about it. Maybe mention it to your parents sometime."

"Why don't you mention it yourself? Maybe I will plan something, and you can finally meet them."

··○··

Meeting the parents was a rare event for Sophia.

She had scarcely gotten far enough in a relationship - at least in the past decade - to do the whole meet the family thing. But that is exactly where she found herself, in that "meet the parents" stage, with Ari.

The summer was drawing to a close, and although they lived in a temperate coastal climate, there was a heat wave in August and everyone flocked outdoors to bask in the sum-mer weather. Ari called her on a warm, sunny Sunday after-noon and said that her parents were grilling and wanted to know whether Sophia and Percy would like to join them for dinner.

Sophia arrived a few hours later, toting a bored-looking Percy with his eyes glued to the screen of his phone. Percy was suddenly inseparable from his phone these days, mainly thanks to a new friend.

Sophia knew he was texting with Isabella.

"Oooh, apple pie," Ari said as she greeted Sophia at the door of a small but cozy bungalow that was actually only a few blocks away from The Little Cafe, tucked away on a steeply-sloped residential street.

"I didn't have anything else in the house other than apples,"

Sophia explained as a woman with chin-length dark brown hair and a heart-shaped face like Ari's greeted her at the door.

She was followed by a tall blonde man with a charming smile.

"Welcome! Oh my goodness, that pie looks delicious," the woman said, a grin spreading across her face.

"Sophia, this is my mom, Carrie, and dad, James. Mom, dad, meet Sophia, and her son Percy."

"So lovely to meet you both," said Carrie, reaching out and giving Sophia warm hug, then Percy, and ushering them both inside.

"Glad you could join us," said James, who was wearing a red apron and holding a spatula, and promptly excused himself so he could return to the backyard where he was grilling.

"Don't want the burgers to burn!" He explained.

"Come outside and have some lemonade," Carrie offered, leading them all out back to a small deck overlooking a cheerful yard filled with trellises laden with flowers and shady trees. Birds were chirping and splashing in a small mosaic birdbath in the far corner of the yard.

"It's so charming back here," Sophia said, looking around at all of the flowers, tidily planted in patches around the yard, and a few kitschy decorations like flamingoes and gnomes interspersed amongst them. "I also enjoy gardening."

"Oh, do you? I just love being outside, taking care of my yard," said Carrie, pouring them all tall glasses of pink lemonade. "We're so lucky it's been such a nice and warm summer."

"My parents don't drink," Ari whispered quickly in Sophia's ear as Sophia took the glass of lemonade.

Sophia nodded slightly as she listened politely to Carrie talk about her future plans for the garden.

Before long, James announced that the burgers were ready, and Sophia followed the rest of the group indoors and helped

Ari and her mother finish up with the coleslaw, beans and various other side salads.

"You have made so much food," Sophia said, picking up the bowl of coleslaw to carry outside. "It looks delicious."

"I love to cook," Carrie said. "And I especially wanted to invite you over. I'm so sorry, we would have invited you sooner, but Ari was a little secretive about you... we only recently found out."

"No apologies necessary," Sophia said as they settled down around the outdoor table, watching as James plated up the hamburgers and brought them to the table. "It's just nice to be here and meet you at last."

Percy politely put away his phone when they started to eat (Sophia had at least taught him that much, although not by example... most nights she herself had issues putting down her phone at dinner), and they all chimed into the conversation, talking about outdoor activities and travels to the beach.

Although things were going smoothly, Sophia felt a little strange. She could not remember the last time she ate outside, and she was distracted by how odd her own family must have come across to Ari. Sophia's harsh, stubborn mother and eccentric sister were so different compared to Ari's incredibly soft-spoken, polite and, well, normal, parents. From her mother's nitpicking to her sister's over-the-top parties and wedding, Sophia's family was such a contrast to Ari's completely pleasant and lovely parents, who were practically an image off of a 1950s greeting card.

Sophia wondered what it must have been like to grow up with parents who were kind, did not drink, smoke, or swear. They stuck to completely appropriate conversation topics, asking Percy about school or Sophia about her work. It was a delightful, pleasant experience, and the setting was downright idyllic in their sunny, flower-filled backyard. As the afternoon wore on, Sophia began to wonder how Ari could grow up in such an environment and yet still accept Sophia's family's eccentricities. Carrie and James may have been somewhat vanilla, and rather ordinary, but they really seemed to be everything anyone could want from their parents.

Sophia was also very conscientious of the fact that her father's company had been the reason these lovely people had been having a difficult time for the past couple of years. She assumed by now that Ari's parents knew who her family was. And although she was not directly responsible for their predicament, she could not help but feel a little bit guilty about it all.

Which was why, perhaps, over apple pie and vanilla ice cream (Carrie had offered the ice cream on the side, and it seemed perfect in the warm, slightly humid afternoon), Sophia cringed when James asked about her parents.

"Oh, they keep busy. My mother does some work for the Palo Rosa municipal government, sits on the boards of charities, and plans fundraisers. She always finds something to do," Sophia explained. "And my father still does a few business projects here and there. He's retired, but he is on the board of his company and finds things to keep himself occupied with."

"We visited one of their properties," Ari said. "When I went to Sophia's sister's wedding, I visited a hotel and spa owned by Sophia's family in Napa. It's really nice there. Secluded and relaxing. Sophia's family has great taste."

"Oh my goodness, I would love to go there someday," Carrie said, clasping her hands.

"You are welcome there any time," Sophia said. "My treat. Just let us know when."

"Oh, I couldn't possibly," Carrie shook her head politely, backing off.

"You should at least visit for lunch sometime. You'd like it," Ari said.

As the sun crawled across the sky and edged closer to the treeline, Sophia began to wonder if there was anything at all imperfect about Ari's parents. But then, at one point just as the sun was sinking behind the trees, Sophia reached out to Ari's hand as Ari joked about something or other. She rested her hand on top of Ari's on the table and squeezed it lightly. As she flashed Ari a quick, adoring smile, she noticed out of the corner of her eye Carrie's eyes linger on their joined hands. Carrie stiffened at the sight, and for a moment, a shadow crossed her face.

Sophia delicately lifted her hand and took a sip of lemonade.

So, she thought. Maybe Ari's parents were not so perfectly supportive about everything after all.

Sophia had obsessed so much over what Ari might think of her own family that she had neglected to wonder whether there were any issues regarding what Ari's family might think of *her*. She had not wondered whether it had been at all difficult for Ari to tell her parents about the two of them. Ari seemed so at ease with herself all of the time, the thought had not crossed Sophia's mind.

She could not help but wonder exactly how many women Ari had brought home to her mom and dad before. From Carrie's reaction, it did not seem like it had been a regular occurrence. She filed the question away in her mind to ask Ari later.

··◦··

"Have you taken many other women home to meet your parents?" Sophia brought up the question gently that night.

Ari was laying on her bed next to her, the sheets wrapped

tightly around her body.

Sophia and Percy had gone home first, and after Sophia had made sure Percy was settled in for the night, Ari turned up a half hour later. Sophia quietly let her in.

Now, basking in the lazy, sated feeling of an afterglow, Sophia's thoughts slowly turned back to the afternoon.

Ari cringed a little. "You noticed."

"Your parents were nice. But they both seemed a little uncomfortable at times, as hard as they tried to hide it, especially when I took your hand. I didn't think I was doing anything - well, I mean, I'm sorry for doing so - it was just an impulse," Sophia said.

"You don't need to apologize," Ari said quietly, stroking her hand along Sophia's arm, which was propping up her head. "And to answer your question, no. Not really. I mean, my parents know that I exclusively see women. And except for when I first told them years and years ago - that was a bit touch and go back then - they are generally supportive and okay with it. Otherwise I would not have brought you to meet them at all. But, you know. I think it's never going to be completely, 100%, totally cool with them. They try, and I value my relationship with them and I just want to get along, so... it is what it is."

Sophia nodded. "They were very nice. I didn't mean to contribute in any way to making them uncomfortable."

Ari smiled sweetly. "You did not. Quite the opposite, both seemed to like you very much. And Percy, too. You have nothing to worry about."

Ari's hand snaked under the covers and found Sophia's waist. She pulled it closer, urging Sophia to move in closer to her own body.

"You were - and are - perfect," Ari said softly, then kissed her lightly.

"I'm not perfect," Sophia countered, before threading her hand through Ari's hair and kissing her deeper.

..o..

Everything about Sophia's life suddenly felt a little more in focus, a little more manageable, even a bit more balanced.

She had always thought the opposite would be true. She used to think that if she got into a relationship, it would consume her fully, and that something - work, Percy, or the relationship itself - would simply implode because she would never be able to handle being spread so thinly across so many different responsibilities, so many people who depended on her.

Instead, Ari's presence in her life eased her mind in a way that she had not known was possible. She found herself scheduling her days at work better, more thoughtfully, knowing that at the end of the day, she could spend time with Ari, or spend some time with Percy, or sometimes both. Often she would meet Percy at The Little Cafe, and Ari would sit down with them, and the three of them would have a light dinner made from things left over from the day. A few extra salads, Ari's gourmet grilled cheese, the leftover soup from lunch (which had recently been added to the menu to try to attract a lunchtime crowd) or - if they felt it was time for a special treat - some of the leftover pastries. If there even were any. Those tended to sell out quickly.

One day, Sophia brought over the photos from her marketing photoshoot that had incorporated Ari's artwork. She spread them all out on a larger rectangular table in the cafe around closing time, and then she, Ari and Percy walked around the table, studying them one by one.

"I can't believe I'm seeing this. I'm like a real artist," Ari said, sounding a little in awe.

Sophia laughed. "Not 'like.' You are one."

"It's pretty cool, Ari," Percy said.

"Have you ever considered putting some of your paintings up on the walls in here? Perhaps you would even sell some. At the very least, they'd be a more personalized decoration than the black and white photographs you have hanging up currently," Sophia said.

"I never thought of that, no."

"Mom's right. The walls would be more interesting with them up," Percy chimed in.

"If you don't want it all to be your own work, you could maybe display or sell other artists' work on consignment," Sophia added. "The artwork itself wouldn't make a huge difference in revenue flow for you, but it could be a way to draw extra people in, and maybe even garner a little more buzz if you make this space into an art gallery of sorts. It could be a niche for you."

"Not a bad idea," Ari said, clearly thinking about it, staring at the bland photographs on the walls. "I could use something more original in here. If displaying art was successful in drawing more people in... well, sure beats having Rachel stand outside and hand out coupons."

"And it's not against town code," Sophia said playfully. "Win-win."

Other nights, Sophia lent a hand to Ari with sorting out a few of her spreadsheets. They were finally becoming less scattered and more accurate than they had been before, and Ari was starting to realize the financial benefits of having a more organized financial record keeping and tracking system.

After Sophia thoroughly reviewed Ari's files - spreadsheets where she kept track of her expenses, payroll documents, lists of the items that she purchased each week, even her insurance documents and lease - Sophia had found some major issues that needed attention right away. Over coffee one evening, seated at the counter as Rachel was closing up, she pointed them out to Ari.

"Could you look over my expenses, too?" Rachel asked, overhearing them talk as she refilled Ari's coffee mug. "I desperately need an expert opinion on how to even get business in the first place."

"I thought party planning was going well?" Sophia asked.

"It was okay at first. I keep busy with enough jobs here and there, mostly for birthday parties or bridal showers or little things. But it's not exactly a full-on business yet," Rachel sighed.

"Which is good for me," Ari said. "Because I get to keep you here longer. But it's also bad, 'cause I want you to be successful."

"Slow at first is normal. There's no reason it won't pick up in the future. Just keep promoting whenever and wherever you can," Sophia suggested.

"I'm trying," Rachel said. "I've advertised everywhere I can think around town, I promote on every social media platform I can think of, all of my friends are well aware of my business, but it's still not enough."

"Word of mouth - referrals after you've done a few successful parties - can go a long way," Sophia suggested. "Speaking of which, I'm hosting a cocktail party in about two weeks for some of my VIP customers. I could use someone to make the arrangements. I was going to have my associate Seth deal with it, but it's actually too important of an event to simply hand over to him. Would you be interested?"

"I'd be happy to," Rachel said, brightening up at the suggestion.

Sophia laughed. "Let's discuss it tomorrow. For now, though, I've got to focus on Ari."

"I thought it would be really liberating to own my own business, but these past few weeks I've longed for the perks of working for someone else. Perks like direct deposit," Ari admitted later on, as their session over the spreadsheets wore on and Rachel had long since gone home. "It's hard to be responsible for every little detail, every day."

"I love being in control of it all," Sophia confessed. "Although it does consume your life. I sometimes think I would have been a better mother if I had just had a normal job, one that allowed me the luxury to go home and get away from my phone and email in the evening. Percy has been all the worse for it, I'm afraid."

Ari gave her a look. "Don't say that. Percy has turned into a bright young kid, so you're doing something right."

"I sometimes wish I felt as competent being a mother as I am running a business," Sophia sighed.

"Couldn't you delegate more at work? Get someone else to manage it, or part of it? Even sell it... you're not exactly void of options here," Ari said.

Sophia nodded. "I know. But I love getting up and doing what I do every day. There's no chance I'll leave it behind."

··◦··

Sophia second-guessed her decision to hire Rachel for a formal work event a few days later when she considered the fact that she was only familiar with Rachel's portfolio of bachelorette parties. Luckily, her doubts were unfounded, as Rachel ended up managing the evening event like a true pro. She arranged a caterer who made fresh sushi, hired an amazing bartender who made artisanal cocktails and served fine beers and delicious local wine, and insisted on bringing in an edgy live musician who ended up setting the tone perfectly for the evening. Rachel created an event that Sophia felt was on-brand with her business, yet she would have never managed to dream, or coordinate, it on her own.

"You're a visionary, Rachel," Sophia said to her halfway through the evening. "From bachelorette parties to elegant corporate affairs, you can do it all."

Rachel beamed with pride. "I'm glad you liked it. But I can't chat now, we're running low on maki."

Sophia waved her off. "Go. Don't let me distract you."

Although the cocktail party was intended for her most loyal customers and featured special purchase discounts and gift baskets for all of the guests, Sophia also used the party as an excuse to invite members of the media.

After Rachel's cousin had given FORBIDDEN a shout out to his social media followers a few months ago, some of her pieces had gotten more attention from a younger crowd than they had before. She was not sure if Rachel's cousin's shout-out was why more media showed up to the event than ever before, but Sophia was pleasantly surprised when she saw that an assistant editor from *Corset* - a trendy, edgy fashion publication - had accepted her invite and was at the party.

"This was quite a change from planning a Vegas bachelorette," Sophia said to Rachel after the evening was over. "Did you enjoy it?"

"I loved every second of it," Rachel said. "Although I have got to get some nicer shoes. I just got these at the mall on sale. Does everyone in the fashion world own $1000 French designer heels?"

"Just the types that came to this party," Sophia said. "But I can give you a pair."

"Wait... give me a pair of the shoes? Are you serious?"

"I have an extra pair that I never wore. They didn't fit me well, nor were they really my style, but I think they'll suit a party - or should I say, *event* - planner who has impeccable taste."

"Thank you," Rachel said, "But it's too generous. I can't."

"Don't worry about it. I'll send them to you. Consider them my investment into your future."

Later that night, after everything had been cleaned up and Rachel left, Sophia went back upstairs to pack up a few things before heading home for the night.

"Don't let me scare you," a voice said from inside her dark office before Sophia had a chance to turn on the light.

"Arianna?" Sophia asked, recognizing the voice, her eyes not yet adjusted to the dark.

She peered inside. A single, small candle was flickering on a bookshelf, and her favorite blonde in the world was sitting at her desk.

"I snuck in earlier, but the party wasn't quite over. I didn't want to disturb anything, so I came up here to wait for you."

"You must have waited a long time," Sophia said, stepping inside, and clicking the door shut behind her, even though nobody else was left in the store other than the two of them. She left the lights off.

"For you, I'd wait even longer," Ari said, standing up and walking towards Sophia.

Sophia made a sound in the back of her throat. She kicked off her shoes and stepped out of them, dropping in height by about four inches. Ari noticed Sophia's eyeshadow - usually so dark - was a bit smudged, and her sleek hair was frizzing just slightly. She was no longer the picture of perfectly polished as she must have been hours before.

"I like you like this," Ari found herself saying, gently raising a thumb to brush Sophia's cheek, helping remove the smudge.

"Like this...?" Sophia questioned, her eyes fixed on Ari.

"Like yourself. After a long day, when you've put in your hours and everyone you had to please or put on a little act for is gone. When you are ready to go home, and just be you," Ari tried to explain.

"Arianna," Sophia sighed, reaching out, wrapping her arms around the blonde, burying her face in her feathery-soft sheet of hair as she pulled the woman closer.

I did not want to fall in love with you, Sophia thought to herself. *But I did anyway.*

She could not bring herself to say the words out loud, but in her heart, she knew them to be true.

"I'm glad you're here," Sophia said sleepily, feeling heavy and drowsy after a long day, but the scent and touch of the woman bringing her slowly back to life.

"You are probably ready to go home," Ari said hesitantly.

"Yes. And no," Sophia admitted, taking one of Ari's hands. "Since you're here, I think I could stay a bit longer."

Ari kissed her. "We don't have to. It's been a long day."

"We never have to," Sophia said, kissing her back. "But I always want to."

She steered her onto a large, armless, plush chair, the one sitting in the corner of her office, and they stayed until much later.

••◦••

The next day, Corset magazine's blog and social media accounts featured a mention of the event and even talked about Sophia's latest lingerie collection. Sophia was pleased by the additional exposure that the cocktail party had brought her work.

Sophia also received two emails from attendees asking who had planned the event, and would her event planner be interested in working on any upcoming projects with them? Sophia gladly passed along Rachel's information.

Things were going very well. *Too* well. As the season changed to fall and the days became crisper and the apples ripened on the trees, Sophia was starting to wonder why she had ever doubted her ability to make things work with Ari in the first place, when the past few weeks had been so fulfilling professionally, and personally.

And then she received a call.

13

FRANCE

"Is this Sophia Black?"

"Yes," Sophia said, half-distracted that morning. Her coffee was almost gone; she supposed she would have to run over to The Little Cafe soon for a refill. She would go as soon as she got off this call.

"Sophia, this is Christophe, with the Gaulle-Boisvert Group," said a heavily French-accented voice on the other end.

"Hello," Sophia said, perking up.

She recognized the name. She had met a few people from that company in Paris months ago about the possibility of her line being carried in their retail stores throughout Europe.

"Ms. Black, our Executive Vice President would like to speak with you concerning FORBIDDEN. Would you be available for a conference call tomorrow or Wednesday?"

"Of course," she said, scrambling to open up her calendar.

Sophia booked the appointment, and immediately focused all of her attention and energy on preparing for the call. She knew that they would want to see her collection, especially the newest pieces she had made, and possibly hear the story of her label, her sales forecasts for the future, that sort of thing.

They might be interested in carrying her line in their stores.

She kept repeating that, over and over, in her mind. She could barely believe it. If her lingerie was carried in their stores - they were one of the most extensive networks of retailers in Europe - it would be a huge boost for her business. The Gaulle-Boisvert group owned department stores and boutiques under a few different names in countries throughout Europe. She had shopped in their large, beautiful old flagship department store many years ago when she was studying in Paris.

That prospect alone was enough to make her crave all of the coffee in The Little Cafe and left her on edge with nerves and anticipation.

The next few days flew by and before she knew it, it was Wednesday and time for her call. She sat alone in her office, in front of her large computer screen, wearing one of her sharpest blazers and an elegant silk blouse, a table full of men in smart suits and ties on the other side of the camera.

Now the executives at the retail company that she had admired so much a decade ago were speaking with her, listening intently to her as she gave a brief history of FORBIDDEN, explained the concept behind it, then she gave a roadmap for its future. They asked about the line's target market, its performance in the past few months and how she managed to grow a viable, loyal base of customers despite a volatile industry.

She did what she was best at: giving a good, strong story about her business. She stayed positive, talking about everything that was going well, focusing on all of the merits of her work and how the lingerie was unique from anything else of its kind.

She told them a story. It was the fantasy she had crafted through her work. Her pieces, after all, were more than just lingerie: it was a story of love, she told them. Her labor of love, but the love that a woman felt when she touched a delicate piece of lace, or satin, that rush when she found the perfect piece to wear for a special evening, an anniversary, a holiday. The boost of confidence it gave her, the connection a woman felt to the meticulously crafted fabric and lace as the piece wove itself into a little piece of the wearer's life.

The executives loved it.

In return, they gave her a presentation about themselves. About their company, its illustrious and storied history. Its continued success. Their large network of retail stores, their hopes for growth and expansion while continuing to improve their reputation and the range of products they offered their customers.

As she sat and listened to them, she felt more and more confident that this meeting had been a success. She half-expected them to immediately offer her a contract, discuss selling FORBIDDEN in their stores. She was eager to see her work in front of a more international audience, and in the back of her mind, she wondered how many additional employees she might have to hire now, to keep up with what would undoubtedly be increased demand.

She waited for the offer to come at the end of the meeting. But it did not.

Instead, they proposed something entirely different.

··◦··

"They want to acquire FORBIDDEN?" Elle asked, her eyes wide.

In her haze following the end of the call, Sophia had gone downstairs and found Elle. There were no customers in the shop at the time, and so she had taken her aside to share the news.

Which had not been a good call on her part.

As soon as she explained the outcome of the meeting, she realized she would be worrying Elle, her loyal, long-time employee.

"They want to purchase the rights to the entire line, but as a part of the negotiations, I would keep this boutique and run it separately," Sophia quickly assured her. "I already said as much to them and they seemed to not have a problem with that. I don't mean to scare you. I have no intention of allowing this boutique to close."

"What else did they say?" Elle said, although she still looked concerned.

"I went into the call thinking they were going to negotiate a contract to carry my pieces in their stores in Europe. Instead, the Gaulle-Boisvert Group extended an offer to buy the entire company. The online store. The rights to the name and the line. The designs. All of my work. They would manage its creation, the manufacturing of the pieces, oversee collections, manage it, market it, sell it. Everything."

"What about you?"

"It would appear I am a part of the deal. They went on and on, and I took notes, but I think they wanted me to work for them. They told me they would like to keep me on as a consultant for at least two years - perhaps permanently - as a part of the acquisition, so I could oversee the direction of the line and work in even greater capacities within their organization. I think they intend to offer me a fairly good title. And salary."

"That is wonderful," Elle said, and she smiled sincerely, although still seemed nervous.

"I am concerned about everyone here," Sophia said, going back to the topic that had seemed to cause unease on Elle's part. "That's why I asked if this shop could be left out of the acquisition, if I could still run it separately, and at least have the right to carry the line here. They agreed. I didn't want anyone who has worked here to be negatively impacted."

Elle smiled a sad smile. "I appreciate that. I'd hate to leave. I love this store."

Sophia smiled. "I do, too."

"But can you picture yourself working for them? It would be quite a promotion, wouldn't it?" Elle asked.

Sophia took a breath. "I suppose that working for a company as well-known in the industry as the Gaulle-Boisvert Groupe was something I saw myself doing at one point. You could even say it was a dream job, back when I was a student, or struggling to get this line started. The road to reach this point has been long. As much as I've loved growing and building FORBIDDEN, it could be nice to no longer shoulder the burden of running all of this, and finally reap the rewards of my work."

Elle studied her. "It sounds like it might be the right opportunity for you."

Sophia nodded. "Maybe. Elle, would you keep this between us, for now? I don't mean to announce it to anyone else until I decide what to do."

"Of course," Elle said.

Sophia thought about going next door to get coffee, but decided she did not want to go into The Little Cafe right now. She quietly went back upstairs and for a little while and just sat, alone in her office, tapping a pencil softly on the blank notepad in front of her, contemplating what had just happened.

..o..

"Someone upset your apple cart?" Seth asked as she eventually ventured out of the wood-paneled cocoon of her office to get a coffee refill, this time from the office's machine
which was, by some small miracle, working today.

"You could say that," Sophia said quietly.

With Seth standing next to her, suddenly it hit her that she
needed to find out more about what this deal entailed. She
was responsible not just for herself and her company, but an
office full of people who depended on her for work. Sure,
during the call she had casually asked whether she could keep
this store, but what about everyone who worked here on
making her pieces? Or, what if they wanted to open up other
FORBIDDEN shops in other cities... would she have any say
whatsoever about those stores? How they looked, what they
sold? She could not quite imagine putting her beloved empire in the hands of strangers. Suddenly, the thought of re-
linquishing control over everything she had built made her
nauseous and anxious.

"Anything I can help with?" Seth asked.

"Not now," she said quietly, and returned to her office and
closed her door.

The first thing she did was call her lawyers. She had not
needed to draw upon their services very often, thankfully.
They were not exactly budget-friendly. She explained the
situation to them, requesting that someone read over the
contract that the Group had emailed her, then arranged a
meeting for them to discuss it with her.

Once that task was underway, her thoughts turned elsewhere. There was Ari to think about.

Sophia was not going to see Ari that evening. Ari had said
earlier she was working late because there would be live
music at The Little Cafe that night and she expected larger

crowds than usual. Sophia had also invited Isabella and her father over to have dinner (she had promised Percy a while back that she would. The timing turned out to be very good: she welcomed the distraction).

Their schedules continued to be in conflict with each other through the weekend and she did not end up seeing Ari at all for several days. At the last minute, Ari said she needed to work all day Saturday and had to cancel their plans for dinner. Sophia, who was going over the designs for an upcoming New York fashion show, spent the time working. Or at least, pretending she was working. In reality, she delegated most of the work to some of her employees who had come in to help her finish up the pieces, and so she could mull over things on her own in her office.

Finally, on Sunday, she and Ari scheduled a lunch date for Monday.

"Everything okay?" Ari asked as they picked up sandwiches from a kitschy, retro-style delicatessen and planned to drive to a park outside of Palo Rosa to eat.

Ari suspected something was up. Sophia could tell she was suspicious.

"I know we've both been busy, but I feel like you've been avoiding me," Ari said.

"It's fine. Just distracted about some work things," Sophia said, hoping Ari would accept that answer.

Sophia needed more time.

She knew she should not keep the news from Ari for long. She knew that as time wore on, it was not going to get easier to tell her. At the same time, she had to sort out what she was going to do. She had to decide it on her own. She knew that much... it was her decision.

Other than that, she did not really know how to proceed.

As they ate their sandwiches, overlooking a little pond that seemed home to various types of ducks and seagulls, they made small talk. Ari updated Sophia on her progress managing The Little Cafe's finances, which seemed to be going smoother ever since Sophia had lent her a hand.

They were both calm and relaxed, the sun bright, high in a blue sky, a light breeze causing Ari's golden locks to stir around her shoulders.

"How do you think we're doing, Sophia?" Ari asked, looking at her with her pretty, soft blue eyes, taking the last bite of her sandwich and licking something off of her thumb.

Sophia smiled regally at her, trying to come off as calm and relaxed, but she was sure Ari had the faintest hint that something was off.

"I have no complaints," Sophia said carefully, giving Ari what she hoped was a relaxed smile. "Why do you ask?"

Ari leaned back and sighed, staring at a duck that was a little smaller than the rest in the pond, floating off to the side on his own.

"Relationships I've been in are usually messy after a while. It's difficult to get two people to figure out how to... coordinate their lives enough to ever really come together as a unit, you know? It's hard. And yet, the past few months, minus a few weekends like the last one when we were both pretty busy with work, have been pretty easy."

Sophia felt a pang of guilt. Should she tell her? She glanced at her watch. They both had to be at work in a half hour. Now was not the time.

"We had a messy beginning, Arianna. Perhaps we paid our dues early on and are getting to enjoy an easier time now."

Ari laughed. "Remember how you didn't use my first name for so long."

"Arianna is such a lovely name. It's a shame I called you 'Ms. Little' for so long," Sophia said, biting her lower lip and taking Ari's hand into her own.

Ari smiled easily and leaned back on the bench. Sophia leaned in and kissed her sweetly as the ducks continued to swim and the breeze continued to blow.

··◦··

On Monday, Sophia heard back from her law firm.

To her surprise, she found out that the lawyer the office had scheduled a video conference with her to review the contract was someone who had been a frequent visitor to her shop.

It was Rupert.

Elle's boyfriend. (If such a term could even apply to him? The man, well into his fifth decade and possibly older, was not exactly a *boy*.)

They exchanged pleasantries, then Sophia jumped straight into business.

"How is the offer? Sophia asked.

"I can only answer from a legal standpoint," he said. "But it's a solid offer. There are only a few redlines I'd recommend you go back to them with."

"Is it too good to pass up?" Sophia asked.

"That is for you to decide," Rupert said, maintaining a professional, distant tone. "But the main caveat I saw - and I am sure you did as well - is that you would need to move to Paris for two years in order to work in the consulting position they are offering you."

"Paris?" Sophia repeated, floored by this piece of news.

Rupert nodded.

"Paris," he said.

"I had not seen that. I was so surprised after the call that I could barely do more than skim the contract," she admitted.

He pointed out a few other things she should take a look at before signing, but for the most part, he said, he didn't see any reason why she should hold back if she felt she was in fact ready to hand over FORBIDDEN.

"It's a solid deal," he concluded, after going over everything with her, from intellectual property to the amount she'd receive from the deal.

All she could do was nod.

"Any other questions?" he asked.

She shook her head, glancing at her watch. She was sure she was being billed for all of this, so she should wrap up the meeting.

"No, thank you."

"Have a good morning. And I'll see you soon. I believe I am coming by later," he said.

"For pleasure, not business, of course," he added, grinning in a way that made Sophia feel a little unsettled.

..o..

Sophia agonized over the decision for another day, but she started to receive daily phone calls from Christophe, a Vice President at the Gaulle-Boisvert Group who seemed to have been tasked with following up with her and schmoozing - that was really the best term for the all-too-polite and upbeat calls she was receiving from Christophe - as the company seemed anxious for her to make a decision. They also seemed to be on a somewhat short timeline. This was not going to be a long, drawn-out offer; they wanted a decision from her, and soon.

It was a good offer and Sophia knew it. In an industry where so many businesses went bankrupt, thrived one year only to close the next, to have such a generous offer with both financial value, and value to her career, was outstanding. It would secure her - and Percy's - financial future, allow her to live comfortably off of a small fortune that was her own making. Not just a hand-me-down legacy from her father. And that had, ultimately, at the heart of it all, been the driving force behind everything she had ever accomplished, the reason why she had not settled for the same lifestyle as her mother and sister. She had always pushed herself for more.

Sophia had made it. She had done it. She had created an empire, and was about to reap the rewards.

On top of the financial benefits, she would not be out of her career. Quite the reverse: this would be a big leap. She would go from being a relatively small business owner to someone who was a part of a legendary fashion name. Plus, their acquisition of FORBIDDEN would ensure that her vision lived on longer than perhaps it would have if she were indefinitely at its helm. It would give FORBIDDEN the broader audience that she felt it deserved and lend it more prestige, taking it from a niche line to a real label associated with luxurious Paris department stores and a well-regarded parent company.

The job they were offering her posed new opportunities as well. The consulting position reflected her level of experience and expertise, gave her the type of cushy position and prestigious title at a prestigious firm that she had always envisioned herself having one day. Career-wise, it felt like a step up. No more day to day petty management of a fledgling business, worried about coffee machines and shipping orders on time. She would have time freed up to think, reflect, and strategize about the larger picture. It sounded like an almost indulgent career move.

There was also Percy to consider. Although she could imagine he would be reluctant to move overseas, ultimately, she felt like he would get a lot out of the experience. He would be off to college in a few years, anyways. Working more regular hours during the week would mean that she could come home at night, cook dinner, spend time with him. Enjoy those precious few years they had left before he set out on his own path in the world.

There were, quite honestly, no drawbacks that she could see.

Except for one major one.

Sophia gazed out the window of her office, the very window that she had first seen Ari through nearly a year ago in December. Ari and her friends had been building a patio for her outdoor seating, and putting up those garish Christmas decorations. She recalled how the racket on the usually quiet street had given her a headache.

Funny, she thought, as she remembered that during the conference call with the Gaulle-Boisvert Group, someone had actually mentioned that press write-up, the one she had been interviewed for that day. Strange how things worked out.

She did feel sad at the prospect of leaving town. But more than that, she felt a strange sort of pain, almost a longing even though she had not yet left, when she thought about living in Paris. Ari would be so far away from her; her friendly, warm presence no longer comforting her in the middle of the day when she needed a break or late at night, when she needed to abandon the world for a little while.

Sophia sucked in a breath. This was not who she was. She was not the sentimental type. She always made a decision based on what was right, what made sense, what she felt was supposed to come next.

And if she took Ari out of the equation, she knew that signing the offer was the right thing for her.

It was, after all, everything she had been working towards professionally for so long. And on top of it all, it would benefit Percy. She could finally spend more time being his mother.

··◦··

She read the contract, reviewed the redlines her lawyer had given her, and at long last, emailed it back to the Gaulle Boisvert Group. She explained to them she was attached to the store in Palo Rosa that she had lovingly designed and worked so many long hours in, and did not want to see it close. She was relieved when they agreed to put a clause into the contract that allowed her to keep the shop and run it as her own, as well as gave the store the right to continue to carry the line of FORBIDDEN lingerie there.

The rest of the label would be absorbed into their portfolio.

Shortly after, they sent the final version of the contract back to her to sign.

··◦··

Sophia barely slept the nights following the receipt of that final contract. She sat wide awake in front of her computer screen, researching schools for Percy in Paris. She figured out the cost of living in the city, agonizing over and over again about the details on where they could live, what was safe but centrally located, close to transportation but also close to parks or open spaces where they could get out and get fresh air.

The only issue - the one provision she could not write into her contract - was Ari.

Of course it had crossed her mind to ask Ari if she would move to Paris with her. But Ari, she knew, would stay behind. For all she knew, Ari still had not even gotten a passport. Of course, the woman would not leave her parents behind, and more than that, she could not - and should not - leave behind The Little Cafe, which was really starting to take off and was finally on solid footing.

Finally, one Friday morning, Sophia made her decision, and she knew she could no longer keep this decision from the world. Except for the brief conversation she had had with Elle that day after the initial call, she had spoken about it to no one.

She knew she needed to tell Ari first.

That morning, she was slightly late for work. She walked into the shop a little after opening time to see a very upbeat Elle with a small group of FORBIDDEN employees - Seth, a seamstress that had come in for the morning, and the man in charge of mailing online orders - gathered around Elle, admiring something on her hand.

Elle looked up as Sophia walked in and gave her a wide smile and waved her over.

"What is this all about?" Sophia asked, walking over.

The small group parted so she could see Elle's hand.

Elle held it up. "Rupert proposed to me last night over dinner."

Sophia pasted a smile on her face. "Congratulations. Such thrilling news for you."

She was happy for Elle, but she also inexplicably felt a little pang of sadness in her heart.

It briefly crossed her mind that she could very well never be one half of a happy couple again after today.

"Thank you," Elle said. "Sophia, mind if I chat with you a moment?"

"Of course," Sophia said. "Come up to my office when you are ready."

Elle nodded.

Sophia went up to her office, leaving her staff chatting excitedly with Elle downstairs. She fixed herself a coffee in the still-working coffee machine and went into her office to look at her emails. She had barely sat down when she heard a knock at the door.

"Come in," Sophia said.

"Hi," Elle said, taking a deep breath and nervously smoothing out her skirt as she stepped inside.

"Please, sit down," Sophia said, motioning towards the chair in front of her desk.

"Sophia, I just wanted you to know... I'm pregnant," Elle said, still standing up.

"Goodness. Well, another congratulations is in order then," Sophia said.

Elle smiled nervously. "Thank you. I had to tell you - I'm already four months along."

"You have quite a few changes coming up in the next little while then, don't you?" Sophia asked.

Elle nodded. "I wanted to let you know, because, well, I'm not going to come back to work after the baby is born."

"I see."

"And I wanted to give you plenty of notice. I'd be happy to train whomever takes my place, do whatever you need me to do."

"I appreciate that," Sophia said.

Sophia observed the young, flushed, excited woman standing before her. The woman had certainly chosen an interesting man to tie her future to, she thought, but opposites do attract.

"I'm afraid there are quite a few changes coming here as well," Sophia said after a moment. "Please, sit down."

"Oh?" Elle asked, finally sitting down in the chair in front of her desk. "I suppose that means you made a decision?"

"I was planning on announcing it tomorrow, but I might as well tell you now. Yes. I'm taking the offer. FORBIDDEN will be sold, although this boutique will remain open, I negotiated it as an exception in the acquisition of the line. In addition, I'm taking an offer by the company purchasing it to become a consultant for them. I'll be moving to Europe to do that job. To Paris."

"Oh," Elle said, clearly surprised the news. "Paris. Now it's my turn to congratulate you on your big news."

"Thank you. I'm pleased about it," Sophia said, and as she said so, she realized she really was.

Elle nodded. "Well, my offer still stands, I'd be glad to do anything to help before I leave the store."

Sophia nodded. "I respect your decision, but are you sure you don't want to stay on, even part time? I would feel better leaving knowing that the boutique is in good hands while I'm overseas."

Elle took a breath, clearly considering that. "I will think about it. But I don't believe I'll want to work in any significant capacity. Maybe very part time."

Sophia nodded. "I hope we can work something out. At the very least, I would like you to supervise the transition for the first few months I'm away."

Elle nodded. "I would be glad to. We should discuss this... but maybe not now. I should get back downstairs to work. I left Joe from shipping in charge of the store."

"Of course. And like I said... I'll let everyone else know tomorrow," Sophia said.

"Is there anything else?" she asked Sophia, standing up.

Sophia took a deep breath and forced a smile. "No. No, that's all."

Elle nodded.

"Congratulations again, Sophia," she said, walking out of the office.

"You too," Sophia said quietly as she walked out, a wistful smile crossing her lips.

As Elle clicked the door shut behind her, Sophia was embarrassed to discover that tears were brimming in her eyes. She quickly wiped them away.

··o··

Despite her unexpectedly emotional response during her meeting with Elle, the decision about whether or not she wanted to pursue this opportunity was, in the end, still clear to Sophia. Her real challenge was still telling Ari, breaking the news to the woman that the beautiful, safe little world they had managed to make together in recent months would soon be something of the past.

She texted Ari, asking her to dinner that night, and Ari enthusiastically accepted.

··o··

"You...want to go," Ari said slowly, realization dawning on her face.

They were at dinner.

Sophia had taken her to one of their favorite places to tell her. It was a beachfront restaurant, about a thirty minute or so drive out of town, along the coast, located in a sleepy, coastal town.

The restaurant was not busy, although there was live music - a type of jazz - and tonight there was a special on one of Ari's favorite foods, an appetizer called beachy keen cheese poppers, little puffs of cheesy, garlicky goodness that were shaped like sand dollars.

But the cheese poppers had been largely ignored once Sophia started telling Ari her news.

And as Ari sat across from her, her blue eyes studying Sophia, reading her, oscillating from happy and excited and congratulatory to heartbroken and torn and sad - all of the emotions hitting her at once as Sophia explained the conditions of the offer - Sophia felt the pang of sadness and guilt and hurt hit her, too. The very reason she had never wanted to get into a relationship - those conflicting feelings she had felt in her early days with Ari, having drinks with her and stating that they could never be more than friends - all of her reasons for not wanting to get into a relationship suddenly felt perfectly justified again, because here she was, sitting with Ari and feeling absolutely ashamed that she was making another human being feel so poorly.

She was feeling quite poorly herself.

"You got the offer, and you want to take it," Ari repeated, knowing the end of the story before Sophia had finished.

Sophia looked at her nervously. "I really do."

Ari nodded, her eyes narrowed and forehead crinkled in concentration.

"Any reason you didn't tell me sooner?" There it was, that edge, that bitterness that Sophia so dreaded hearing coming from her, as deserved as it was.

"I only got the offer mid-week last week. I had to take a few days to think about it, plan things out, and decide. I didn't want to leave you in the dark for too long," Sophia said, looking at her hands in her lap, nervously playing with her bracelet. "I knew I had to tell you by today."

Ari nodded, relaxing slightly, though her brow was still furrowed in concentration.

"Well, you should take it."

Sophia looked up at her, slightly startled by her sudden and straightforward assessment of the situation.

Ari smiled, slightly sad, but yet a smile that was filled with genuine warmth.

"You've clearly worked hard, built a wonderful career. Now it's time to go where you are meant to go after all of this hard work."

"I never wanted it to end like this. To do this to you,"

Sophia said. "I tried not to fall for you. Because I knew in the end, it would be..."

Ari reached across the table and took both of her hands in her own.

"I know. And you warned me not to get involved with you, and I went against your warning anyway," Ari said, smiling. "You said to me that this was an impossible game. But I chose to play anyways."

"And I'm glad you ignored me," Sophia said, half-laughing, half-teary eyed. "I really am. These months have been some of my happiest."

"But ultimately, life is more than just the two of us," Ari continued. "You should do what's best for every aspect of your life. This is for Percy, too. It sounds like this will give you a more normal job, more time to spend with him."

Sophia nodded, clenching her jaw. "I've thought everything through. They didn't give me much time to decide, but I really did think about every aspect."

"I know you did," Ari said. "And I don't want you to stay here on my account. I think you might regret that. And eventually, you would resent me for holding you back."

"I don't want that, either," Sophia admitted. "But I didn't know how you'd react to all of this. I'm so sorry, Ari. If I were you, I'd hate me right now. You have every right to be mad at me. I have treated you... in a way you don't deserve."

Ari shook her head. "No. This is bigger than just the two of us. This is life."

"It's a futile game, isn't it? Trying to mesh two human adult lives together in a way that makes sense for both," Sophia said.

"Well. There's no sense in dwelling on the situation." Ari's eyes locked onto hers. "I don't want you to go, if that's what you want to hear. That's the truth. But I also want you to be happy. In the end, that's what counts... for us to both be happy."

Sophia took a deep breath. "Like I said, these past few months have been some of the happiest of my life. Truly."

Ari smiled. "I've been happy, too. And I've learned a lot from you, by the way."

Sophia laughed. "Please. I'm the one who owes you everything."

Ari shook her head. "I know how to balance my books now, I have a slightly better idea of which wines go with what food, I have a vague sense of why people would spend a month's salary on a designer bag, and I've gone back to making art. And displaying it in The Little Cafe. And even making a bit of pocket money from it."

"You hung some of it up?" Sophia asked, realizing she hadn't been into the cafe in about a week.

Ari nodded proudly. "Even got an offer on a painting yesterday, and a decently favorable write-up by some local art blogger."

Sophia smiled. "That's great."

They were silent for a moment, the jazz music in the restaurant ending after a song, a few tables clapping politely.

"I suppose we've both learned a thing or two this year?" Ari asked quietly.

"That we have," Sophia said, smiling back and squeezing her hand.

"Any chance you'll be opening a Paris The Little Cafe any time soon?" Sophia asked a little while later.

Ari laughed. "Probably not. But maybe it's time I look into finally getting a passport."

14

FALLEN

TEN MONTHS LATER

"I thought I was just going to hang out with you after work, not actually go with you to all of your fancy events," Ari said to Sophia over breakfast one morning.

Sophia had met Ari at her hotel and had just informed her of their plans to attend an event that night.

After arriving at Charles de Gaulle airport two days ago, and being picked up in a driver that Sophia had sent for her - not a taxi, not some sort of app car share service, but a bona fide, suit-wearing, luxury towncar-driving driver - Ari had spent her first 48 hours wandering Paris while Sophia was at work, walking around, going to museums, sketching, and taking pictures of the buildings, scenery and the river, observing the people.

"It's no pressure, trust me," Sophia said. "I just want you there."

She seemed stressed nonetheless.

"I'll be there," Ari said.

"Good. Can you be ready at about 7:15? I should pick you up in the lobby here soon after 7. The dress code is fairly dressy."

"Dressy?"

"Nearly black-tie, I'd say," Sophia said.

"Um, sure."

Sophia waved Ari goodbye in the lobby after they ate, leaving her in a cloud of perfume. A few moments later, Ari stepped outside and called Rachel.

"How's the city of looooove going?" Rachel asked.

Ari could hear music in the background.

"Don't say it like that," Ari said.

"Say it like what? Luuuuuhhhrve," Rachel said, emphasizing it even more.

"We're just friends at this point," Ari said, rolling her eyes impatiently. "Look, Rachel, I need help. I have kind of a fashion emergency. Sophia's asked me to go with her to some work thing - industry thing, I assume - and I have no idea what to wear. I'm pretty sure I didn't even bring anything dressy enough."

"What's the event? What's the dress code?" Rachel asked, growing serious.

"Sophia just said it's cocktails and dinner and 'fairly dressy.' Nearly black tie, whatever that means," Ari said, stopping near the river and sitting down on a bench facing the water. A group of American students walked past her, speaking loudly in English.

"Hmm. Okay, I think my cousin might be able to help. He's got some friends at a big department store there. Lemme text him, tell him you need something to wear to some fancy Paris event..."

"Should you really be bothering him for this?" Ari asked.

"Trust me, he lives and breathes for fashion emergencies like this. Texting him now. Hopefully he can reply right away, but you never know with him. It could be now, it could be in two weeks."

Ari squeezed her eyes shut and crossed her fingers.

Rachel paused for a minute, then spoke.

"So while we wait for his reply, how are you lovebirds doing on the Continent? What's it like following her around to all of those glamorous places?" Rachel asked.

"It's different," admitted Ari. "You know me. I'm not really this fancy. Her apartment is like something out of a magazine, and she put me up at this insane hotel, it's like something from another era, but every day she works longer hours than she did back home."

"Really? I thought she moved there because it would give her more family time with Percy," Rachel started, but she was interrupted by the faint ding of a text coming in.

"Oh! It's my cousin," Rachel said. "Okay, he's got instructions for you. Go to Maison de la Tour - it's on Rue du Commerce, it's a small department store. You should be able to hop on the metro and get there. Ask for a guy named Dominic Aubin. He'll be able to fix you up with something. And he'll be expecting you."

"That was fast," Ari said, beelining towards the nearby Metro sign. "I'm on my way. I feel like I majorly owe your cousin. What should I do? How do I pay him?"

"Just give me your eternal gratitude, and a Saturday off when you get home, and as for my cousin, if anyone asks you what you're wearing, just drop his name and say he is your stylist or something. And post a picture of your outfit and tag him on all of your social media. Something like that. Don't worry about it."

"Thanks. You two are kind of like my fairy godmothers

right now."

"Get moving, lady. Let me know how it goes tonight."

..o..

Ari couldn't help but feel a bit like royalty.

From box store bargain bin to couture, she thought to herself, stepping into a private dressing room at a department store that had a stained glass dome ceiling and looked more like a place of worship than a place of commerce.

Rachel's cousin's friend, Dominic, greeted her at the store with a kiss on the cheek.

"Welcome," he said to her warmly.

"Thanks," was all she could say before a rack full of clothes was whisked over to her.

"What you think of Paris? You have been before?" The man asked in a thick French accent.

She shook her head. "This is my first time here."

"Well, this is the most beautiful city in the world, and you are standing in the most beautiful store in the world," he said, holding up a dress and stepping back to analyze his selection.

She nodded in agreement, and could only watch in awe as he set to work, pulling pieces for her to try on.

Ari obediently tried a few dresses, skirts, and shirts. They were handed to her so quickly she could not even stop and think about the choices; she was just ushered over to change behind an antique screen. After a few tries and quick peeks at the outfits in the mirror, she (or rather, Dominic), settled on a pair of slim fitting leather pants.

"I much prefer this to a dress," she said.

"It's chic with a little edge," he said approvingly, studying her, stepping back, making her turn around, studying her some more.

He gave her a top, a soft red blouse with lace at the hem, and lent her some accessories.

"I'm not really the jewelry type," she said hesitantly as a box of sparkly pieces were pushed under her nose.

"Everyone is a jewelry type," he countered, holding up a simple, but pretty, pair of gold earrings and a gold cuff bracelet with a light blue stone set in the middle.

She tentatively reached out to take them.

"I suppose I could try these on," she said, admitting to herself that they were actually not too bad, as far as jewelry went.

Dominic smiled as she put them on.

"See?" He said as she admired them in the mirror.

Dominic capped off their little Pygmalion re-enactment by presenting her with what he called "the most important part of any outfit," brandishing a pair of French designer heels with their trademark red soles under her nose and instructing her to try them on.

"They are perfect with your outfit," he said.

She slipped them on obediently.

"There. A masterpiece," he said, smiling, admiring his work. "How do you feel?"

"Actually..." she glanced over at her reflection in one of the mirrors. "I feel good. I thought I was going to be uncomfortable, but this all actually feels like me."

"It is most important to me for the client to feel good and like herself. You won't look good on the outside unless you feel good on the inside."

"I like how you think," she said, smiling.

Dominic gave her two kisses this time, one on each cheek, and apologized, saying he had to run to another appointment.

"Their mouths will all be on the floor tonight!" He said to her as he breezed out the door, waving goodbye.

She laughed.

"I think he meant 'jaws,'" she said to the redheaded woman who had been helping with the clothes, and now presented her with a piece of paper for her to sign. "Their jaws will be on the floor."

"Maybe he meant they would be kissing the ground you walk on?" The woman laughed, speaking in an Irish accent. "He does believe everyone should worship that very pair of shoes, after all."

The outfit was on loan, and they were going to send someone to collect everything from her the next day at her hotel, the woman from the store went on to explain.

"Fine by me," Ari said, signing the paper. "Not a lot of places I can wear all of this to back home."

The loan thing was also good because the designer leather pants and blouse were just a little out of her budget. And by "little," she was pretty sure they were worth more than her car. And possibly all of The Little Cafe.

Before she left the store, she was ushered to a cosmetics department, where a French woman who looked like she had walked straight off of the set of every stereotypical French movie - she had a sleek black bob, a colorful silk scarf tied around her elegant long neck, and a black shirt - applied a light layer of makeup as Ari sat still in front of a brightly lit mirror.

And so, at exactly 7 on the dot, Ari was polished and primed for her big Parisian business outing with Sophia.

When Sophia knocked at her hotel room right on time, Ari opened the door to her room and Sophia looked at Ari, slightly stunned, her mouth falling open (though not, as Dominic had predicted, quite all the way to the floor).

"Wow. I've never... you look amazing."

Ari grinned. "Hey, you can't always have the monopoly on fashion, you know."

"You're beautiful," Sophia said, her eyes still wide, stepping into the room and setting down her leather laptop bag and her purse near the door. "I mean, you're always beautiful, but you look particularly amazing. How...?"

Ari shrugged. "Rachel, and her amazing connections. What can I say. Other than I can't spill anything on this outfit tonight, because it's on loan and I'd have to mortgage my house in order to pay them back if I do."

"Well," Sophia said, taking a step towards Sophia, her eyes glimmering with just a hint of mischief, "Perhaps we should take everything off, then, just to make sure you won't spill anything."

Ari laughed as she drew Sophia drew close to her.

Sophia ran her hands lightly down Ari's sides, her fingertips grazing her hips, her smile tentative.

That was how it had been for the past 48 hours.

They'd fallen back into old patterns, as though they'd never been apart. Flirting, touching, tension in the air between them.

But also... they had been keeping it very innocent. So far.

"I think you said we have to leave by 7:15," Ari reminded Sophia gently.

Reluctantly.

She softly grasped Sophia's forearms, encouraging her to come out of her haze and back into the room they were standing in.

Sophia let out a little frustrated noise and scrunched her nose. "I don't want to go tonight."

"It sounded important to you this morning," Ari reminded her.

Sophia sighed and took a step back from Ari. "It is. Very. It's an awards ceremony for outstanding achievements of some of the most significant fashion designers, companies, and influencers in the industry."

"Are you nominated?"

Sophia shook her head. "No, but my company - well, the company that purchased FORBIDDEN - is nominated for a few awards. I have to be a team player."

Ari raised her eyebrows. "How's that going for you?"

Sophia laughed. "It's going. As you know, being a team player is not exactly my strength. But I'm improving."

Sophia took a bottle of water from the top of Ari's hotel room writing desk. She poured herself a glass and took a few dainty sips, then sat on the edge of the bed, kicking off her heels.

"It's just... a lot," she admitted, looking up at Ari.

"You handle pressure, and hard work, better than anyone I know," Ari said.

She finished the glass of water, took her handbag and moved into the bathroom and began to freshen up her makeup.

"You okay?" Ari asked, stealing a glimpse of Sophia as she combed her hair and put on some earrings that she had fished out of her purse.

She looked radiant in the glow of the bathroom light, in front of a big mirror.

"I'm with you, so yes, absolutely," Sophia said, catching Ari's eye through the mirror.

Time seemed to stop for a few seconds as they looked at each other.

Then Ari broke the gaze by turning, giving Sophia some privacy to get ready before they left.

Fifteen minutes later, they were in another black luxury car, being whisked across town, the creamy-white buildings of Paris sliding by outside of their window as they traveled down endless busy, crowded streets under the pale blue evening sky.

Ari studied Sophia. A calm and focused demeanor had

settled over her as they rode in the car. The casual, tired, slightly lusty woman with her shoes kicked off that Ari had witnessed minutes before in the hotel room was gone. She was done up again, elegant and polished. On the one hand, Ari admired the woman for her ability to gather it all together, rally her energy after a long day, and transform back into her sleek businesswoman persona. On the other hand, Ari longed for that relaxed, casual, soft Sophia, the one that was so deeply masked right now underneath so many professional and polished layers.

As Sophia focused inward and became more and more focused in the car, Ari tried to mentally concentrate on the night ahead. Part of her still could not believe she was going with Sophia to this kind of event.

When Sophia first invited her to meet up with her in Paris two months ago - and when Ari finally, somewhat reluctantly, accepted the invitation - she figured that the would see Sophia a little bit. Sure, she selected a hotel not far from where Sophia lived, but she did not want to impose too much if Sophia was busy with work most of the week. Ari had promised herself something before boarding that plane to France: she was determined to view her week-long vacation in Paris as primarily an opportunity to see a new place. After all, when else would she travel to Paris? What excuse would she have to do so again anytime soon? She had never had a reason to go before, and she may never have a reason to again. Although Sophia had obviously been a motivating factor in going, she told herself that it was, above all, a vacation, a time to celebrate the nearly two year anniversary of The Little Cafe.

But Sophia clearly had other plans.

Instead of getting a peek into the woman's Parisian life, in the days since Ari had arrived, she was plunged right back into Sophia's world.

Especially tonight, Ari thought, looking down at her leather pants, the gemstone bracelet on her wrist.

When the Mercedes dropped them off at the entrance to the venue - the building looked a bit like a miniature palace, although Sophia told her it was actually a museum and the awards would be held in one of the ballrooms - they were ushered upstairs in an elevator and emerged onto a beautiful rooftop garden, which glowed in the evening with millions of fairy lights that formed a canopy overhead.

"Welcome to the pre-awards cocktail," Sophia explained to Ari quickly.

Sophia immediately got to work, saying hello to everyone (mostly in French, though there were some English speakers there as well). Sophia kept Ari at her side and introduced Ari to everyone they met. Sophia smiled and talked and mingled without pause.

Ari gradually grew exhausted by the constant flow of hellos and pleasantries in two different languages. The longer they were there, the quieter Ari became.

Finally, she ended up dropping back, quietly observing Sophia, so very in her element amongst her colleagues and peers, amongst all of the designers and creators and marketers and publicists and other individuals in her field. Sophia handled conversation and questions with grace and ease, exchanging business cards, laughing, chatting and making sure that she circulated and spoke with everyone she needed to, never seeming to tire of any of it.

Oh, and Sophia spoke French.

Ari had no idea how fluent Sophia was until she was introduced to a gentleman named Monsieur Arnaud who clearly did not speak English, and so Sophia smoothly transitioned into the language of Voltaire. They laughed and talked, and

Ari stood there, straining to catch any words she might recognize. She had taken two years of French back in high school, a class she spent most of the time scheming up ways to skip, but could barely recognize more than a handful of the words drifting around her that night.

Ari quietly cursed her teenage self, wishing she had skipped fewer classes.

Sophia interpreted a few things for Ari towards the end of the conversation, before Monsieur Arnaud bid them good night and they moved on to the next group of people.

Sophia was so at home at that cocktail, navigating the room expertly with a glass of chilled white wine in one hand, the other gesturing elegantly as she talked.

Ari lingered at her elbow, privy to the conversations and small talk, at least when it was in English. Sophia acted like she knew a lot of people they were talking with, asking them things that were clearly tailored to their work, or business, or in some cases, Sophia even asked about their family. Whenever Sophia received questions, she smoothly and expertly talked about her work, or the company she worked for now, or FORBIDDEN, and all of its newfound success... the line had launched in nine different countries that past summer.

"The pieces are meant to take a woman back to another time, a time when women could be unique, fashionable, wear something bespoke and made just for her," Sophia explained to one woman, who identified herself as a writer.

Then to another designer, she later added, "the fabrics are sourced from only the finest, most innovative suppliers in the world. I met one of them on a recent trip to Japan..."

"You look like you're in a little over your head," a man with a heavy accent observed as Ari snuck off at one point in the evening, wandering over to the bar on her own to ask for a glass of red wine.

"I am. I don't know a thing about fashion. I don't even know anything about fancy Parisian bar drinks, so I chose the least offensive, most universal one," she said, raising her glass.

The man laughed lightly.

"You look very nice for someone who doesn't know anything about fashion," he said, raising his eyebrows suspiciously over his dark-rimmed glasses.

Ari shrugged. "Don't be fooled, it was a friend's handiwork. Are you in fashion?"

The man shook his head and glanced over her shoulder at someone across the room. "No, but my partner very much is."

Ari followed his gaze to one of the men Sophia was talking to.

"We can relate, then," Ari said, her own eyes lingering on Sophia, how confident and at ease she was amongst the group.

"Indeed," the man said, lifting a glass of wine to his lips and sipping. "If you're not in fashion, what do you do, Ms.-?"

"Little. Ari. And I own a coffee shop back home in California," Ari said.

"Very charming. Have you tried the coffee here?"

"Definitely. Wouldn't come to Paris and not sample what the locals have to offer. It's really good. I've learned I'm doing everything wrong," she joked.

"The coffee is much better in Italy, I find," the man said. "But it's good here as well. Actually, I had great coffee in California, so don't sell yourself short."

"Do you live in Paris?" Ari asked.

The man nodded. "I'm from Denmark originally, but I work here in Paris now. I'm an aerospace engineer."

"Impressive," Ari said.

"You and I should team up, figure out how to get better coffee on commercial airplanes," he joked.

"I'd like that. So aerospace engineering? You must be way out of your element at these things, too," Ari said.

The man nodded, "I am. This is a very - what's the right word? - showy industry. I'm more at home behind a computer, at a desk, than these things. But Raoul loves what he does, and so here I am, being supportive."

"Sophia's married to her work," Ari commiserated.

"What can I say. It's what they love, and we love them. So here we are," the man said softly, his gaze returning to the other man, taking another sip of the wine, a small smile tugging at the corner of his lips.

Love. Ari hadn't thought much about that word, but hearing it leave the man's lips gave her pause.

The way the man was looking at Raoul, Ari knew that she looked at Sophia that way.

She felt it in her core.

It had been buried for many months, yes. But standing there, watching the woman navigate the room with such flair, and beauty, and grace, she knew, deep down, it was still there.

Even after a year of waiting, a year apart, a year's separation from Sophia - minus the few times she had seen her when she had briefly visited California for business, or to visit family - after all of this time, she felt it.

"Here we are," Ari echoed, and took a sip of her red wine.

··o··

After the endless parade of cocktails and chitchat followed by a two-hour-long awards ceremony in a ballroom, capped off later that night by, of all things, an after party and what essentially amounted to a full, five-course meal, they both returned to Sophia's small apartment. It was late, and they both had been exhausted in the car ride back, but as Sophia turned her key to unlock her apartment, Ari felt the energy rise in the air again.

In the car on the way home, they had not even discussed the fact that they were heading back to Sophia's place. Ari had not even brought up her hotel. It just seemed so natural, and it was so late at night, that both women had somehow forgotten that they were not, technically, supposed to be going back to the same place.

The women toed off their heels at the door, and Sophia held her finger up to her lips as they tiptoed past the door to Percy's room and into Sophia's. Sophia sat down on the bed, gracefully tucking her legs underneath her. Ari sprawled out next to her.

"You live an enchanted life," Ari said sleepily. "I mean, just look at this room, the chandelier. And the view... the old, fairy tale street below, the fact you can see the tip of the Eiffel tower from your balcony..."

"Are you enjoying it?" Sophia asked.

"Of course! This is so far from my reality. So different. I like seeing your world. It's interesting."

"Interesting?"

"I like watching you in it," Ari said, rolling onto her side and propping her head up on her hand. "You were beautiful tonight."

Their eyes met and Ari sat up and kissed her gently.

Sophia shuddered slightly at Ari's kiss, their first since she had arrived in Paris.

Sophia hesitated, and pulled back.

"Should we really be complicating things?" she whispered.

Ari paused as well.

When Sophia had left a year ago, they discussed where

their relationship stood: neither woman wanted to hold the other back, and so they agreed that they were no longer a unit, and were both free to see other people, if that is what was to happen. And although the women had remained in frequent touch throughout the year, they had not spoken about it. Neither knew whether the other woman had seen someone else, or had moved on.

When Sophia had invited Ari to visit her in Paris, she made clear to Ari that there were no strings. She was inviting her as a friend.

But now, here they were. In Sophia's small flat, Ari on her bed, her arms and legs and long blonde locks sprawled out on her soft white duvet.

The little moments of flirting and shoulder-brushes and laughter and the little sparks of their faintest touches the past two days had all been a preamble to this.

Seconds ago, Sophia had been marveling at the wonderful feeling of comfort she experienced when the blonde's lips touched her own, Ari's hand on the small of her back, pressing her closer.

"When have we not complicated things," Ari laughed lightly.

Sophia smiled sadly.

"But this somehow doesn't feel complicated," Ari sighed, kissing her again.

They were losing themselves in each other once again, as though no time at all had passed.

"Tomorrow," Sophia said softly as their lips parted again a few minutes later, "is your day. I want to have dinner with you. Just the two of us. No work. I want to stop, and enjoy being with you here."

"Why wait to enjoy being with me?" Ari asked mischievously, kissing her deeper, her words laden with meaning.

Sophia paused, searching Ari's face.

"Why, indeed," she said, before both women surrendered, and stopped talking.

..o..

The next day, Sophia had all day meetings, this time with suppliers. She invited Ari along, since it mainly involved visiting a variety of different textile warehouses throughout the city... it was a workday that she could easily tag along on.

But Ari declined. Last night, she had been given a list of some of the best cafes in Paris from the aerospace engineer that she chatted with at the party. She decided to make her way through the city alone to visit a few, pleased to have a goal, to be doing some research for her own business.

Besides, doing this would give her extra time to prepare for the evening they wanted to spend together.

Ari had also received a restaurant recommendation from the man. She was promised that it was romantic, small and cozy, in a charming, tucked-away location, and importantly, it had delicious food. They could be seated in a small, hidden outdoor courtyard behind the restaurant and while away the hours eating local cheeses and pates, fish and steamed seasonal vegetables, and the chef's specialty, crème brûlée.. Reservations were a must, he had warned her, so mid-afternoon, Ari - lacking the requisite language skills to make a call - made her way over to the restaurant in the St-Germain neighborhood, talked to the hostess in extremely broken French and secured a reservation for that evening.

On her way back from an afternoon of wandering and drinking coffee - perhaps it was the clear, perfect summer evening or the three very strong coffees she had sampled that afternoon - Ari was bursting with energy. She stopped at a flower shop and bought a big bouquet of pink and red blooms, and continued back to Sophia's apartment, hoping to arrange them before Sophia returned for the evening. (Sophia had given her a big skeleton key to the apartment last night).

Ari beat Sophia home.

After Ari arranged the flowers in a vase - she found one in a little cupboard below the sink - she got ready, taking a shower, washing the day's dust and city grime off of her skin. She dressed, put on makeup, even carefully blow-dried her hair, which was something she never took the time to do. She put on dark jeans and a soft, long-sleeved shirt she had picked up from her hotel room earlier.

And then she waited.

Sophia must be running late, she decided, looking nervously at the clock on the cable box under the television. She turned on the TV to an international news channel, watching it for a few restless minutes before turning down the volume most of the way.

She grew bored of scrolling through the Internet on her phone, so she went out on the balcony and snapped some photos of the street view and tip of the Eiffel Tower peeking over the creamy white roofs, solid and pretty under the evening sky.

The sun sank lower and lower, before finally dropping behind the sea of roofs.

They were definitely going to be late for their dinner reservations now. She wondered how forgiving French restaurants were of that sort of thing.

Finally, at last, she heard a key in the door and with a click it opened. Sophia was home, tired and apologetic.

"I am so, so sorry Ari. Just give me a few minutes to wash up-" she said, sliding into the bathroom and clicking the door shut.

Ari wandered over to the television and turned it off. She

glanced at the clock. It was almost 10. They were definitely way past their reservation. Some date night this was turning out to be.

When Sophia emerged, however, she looked as fresh-faced and stunning as always. She had taken off the blazer she was wearing, revealing a soft silk blouse, tucked stylishly into a pair of black jeans.

"Are you hungry?" Ari asked.

Sophia smiled back at her, brushing a hand quickly through her hair. "I am," she said, moving towards her, kissing her firmly, holding her tight. "I'm so sorry," she whispered a few moments later.

Ari was sorry too, and wanted to say something. But Sophia did seem tired, and she said she was starving, so...

"Let's go."

..o..

They got to the restaurant at quarter to 11 and their dinner reservations had long since been given away, but the restaurant found them another table and seated them graciously. The courtyard was filled with other diners, but the interior was pretty anyway. It was a quiet sort of restaurant, dark and charming, with exposed brick walls and rustic wooden floors that revealed the age of the building. They ordered glasses of chilled white wine and mussels as an appetizer.

"Everyone is obsessed with oysters now, but give me a classic moules frites any day," Sophia was saying as she helped herself to the little shelled creatures, which were drowning in a bowl of what was supposed to be some sort of white wine, butter and garlic sauce.

Ari did not know what to say to that. She did not exactly love the kinds of food that required de-shelling before consuming, but she gamely tried some of the little mollusks and decided they could be worse.

The wine was definitely good, at least.

"You fit very well into this world," Ari observed, halfway through dinner.

Sophia looked up at her, the candlelight flickering on her face. "What do you mean?"

"I mean, you belong here. Everything you worked for - your education, your business - clearly it's all led to this. You have a job that you deserve and are a natural in, you have a beautiful apartment, you live in a romantic city. This is you."

Sophia smiled. "I suppose I do. It is everything I imagined it would be."

Ari smiled sadly and took another sip of wine.

Sophia hesitated. It was everything she imagined. Almost, at least. Even if she belonged here, she was not sure the people she cared for most also belonged here.

"Percy, however, fluctuates from being okay with this situation, to not being okay with it all and complaining about wanting to go home. Things aren't perfect," Sophia admitted.

Ari nodded. "He's a kid. He's having good experiences here. I heard him speak some French the other day. It's impressive."

"I suppose so," Sophia said a little uncertainly.

She took a sip of wine and dipped a small piece of bread into the soupy liquid of her bowl.

"It's not the same without you here," Sophia admitted.

Ari paused. Took a breath. Looked into her eyes.

"I don't belong here, Sophia."

Sophia's eyes quickly darted down to her food. "I know."

"You're doing the right thing by doing all of this, you know," Ari said. "I'd never have felt right about keeping you from all of this, back in California. You can't have this there. If you'd stayed home for me, you would've always wondered what it might have been like. It wouldn't have been good."

Sophia nodded, recalling the conversation they'd had a

year ago before she left.

Ari placed her hand on top of Sophia's. "When - *if* - you're ready to come home someday, the cafe will be there. No doubt thanks in part to you, and your advice and your willingness to answer my middle-of-the-night pleas for help with tax forms and budgets and supplier price increases."

Sophia laughed to ease some of the tension. "The time zone difference helps with answering those emails."

They went back to their food for a few moments, eating in the dim candlelight. Somewhere in the restaurant, a live musician started to play a guitar and sing.

"Ari?"

"Yeah?"

"Despite these past few days, what we agreed before I left still stands. I don't expect you to wait for me, you know. I'm not there."

"Okay," Ari said.

So, they were talking about this.

"I don't exactly have a plan for when I'm coming back," Sophia said quietly, taking a nervous sip of wine.

Ari took a deep breath. "I know you don't. There hasn't been anyone else, though."

Sophia nodded. "Nor for me. But we're adults. I just didn't want you to think you had to... hold off."

Ari shook her head. "I don't. I know. And... the same. For you."

Sophia nodded.

After dinner, they walked a bit, going up and down the picturesque, dark streets, coming across tall, old statues and finally, standing on a bridge overlooking the Seine.

"I guess I should head back to my hotel now," Ari said.

Sophia looked at her sadly, as if trying to memorize her face, her features... her full lips, her golden-straw hair, her strong jaw and graceful yet athletic body. She never wanted to forget any of it, how Ari looked in this moment, in the city lights at night. She moved just a bit closer. She wanted to memorize her smile, the way she smelled, the way her hair fell around her shoulders.

"I had a dream when I was here last year," Sophia recalled. "You were in it. You had arrived and were staying with me at a hotel. You and I were sitting outside, and you got mad at me and left... I almost texted you that night when I woke up, after that dream, but I was too nervous to do so. To admit that I had any feelings about you, to admit that I'd grown so attached to you in such a short amount of time."

"I remember you didn't text me much while you were gone on that trip," Ari recalled.

Sophia took both of Ari's hands into her own.

"I deeply, deeply care about you, Ari," she said, squeezing them lightly.

"And I you," Ari said softly, the breeze kicking up the hair around her shoulders. She leaned forward, hugged Sophia closely. "I'm so proud of you."

Sophia laughed a bit at that. "I'm proud of you. I wish I could see how much the cafe has grown, and drink that coffee every morning."

"It'll be there when you come home," Ari said, though she was starting to doubt that Sophia would ever return home. It felt a bit like wishful thinking, especially once it had been spoken out loud.

"If you would like, despite all of this, I would like you to come back to my place with me tonight," Sophia said nervously.

Ari thought about it for a moment. "I know I should say no, but what the hell, I'm here. If I come with you though, will you promise me one thing?"

"What's that?"

"When I leave, will you at least say to me, 'We'll always have Paris?'"

They both laughed at that, then wandered off into the dark night.

15

HOME

NEARLY ONE YEAR LATER

It was a glorious Saturday in summer. The trees were a lush green color that heralded in the summer months, a warm breeze was making itself known through the city, and red and pink flowers were growing in charming window boxes on apartment buildings and outside of cafes.

Sophia insisted that Percy join her for a walk.

"Let's go to that bookstore you like," she offered from the doorway to his room, "The one where we found all of the old comic books."

Percy shrugged from where he lay on his bed, playing a game on his phone. Outside, on the window ledge, a small bird chirped. There was a tree on their street, and fresh, vibrant green leaves had just started to push out, bringing new life to what had become a monochromatic watercolor of a cityscape over the past few months during a winter marked with frequent rain and heavy, overcast skies.

Inside the room, however, in contrast to the outdoors, it was still a little chilly. The spring sun had yet to warm up the air.

Sophia cocked her head, waiting for a reply from her son.

Percy had drifted away from her over the past months, becoming more distant than usual. At first she chalked it up to teenage moodiness, but his out-of-character attitude was starting to worry her more and more.

"Percy, what is it?"

"Fine, I'll go," he relented grumpily.

"What is this attitude I've been getting from you all of the time lately?" she asked, her voice turning darker.

Yes, she was concerned about him, but talking to her in that tone was unreasonable.

Percy did not answer.

"Percy. Talk to me. I'm your mother," she said sternly, and as she did, she internally cringed. She sounded just like her mother.

He looked up. "Sorry. I don't have anything to say. I don't really want to go."

Her voice softened and she spoke again. "I was simply suggesting we get out on such a nice day. We can do something you'd enjoy."

"That's a new one," Percy snapped back. "You've been so busy lately I don't even know if you remember what I like doing."

"Percy," she said, her voice sharp again and her hand instinctively raising up to her hip. "Don't speak to me that way. Apologize, please."

"Sorry," he grumbled, his eyes on his phone, not sounding at all genuine.

"Forget about the bookstore, then," she said, frustrated and tired from the conversation, turning to walk out of his room.

She turned though and paused, studying him laying on his bed morosely, his eyes glued to the screen of his phone.

"I'll leave you alone this afternoon, but we're going out for dinner tonight. Be ready by eight," she said before leaving him alone.

··o··

Percy picked at a piece of bread and kept glancing down at his phone as they sat at the table at the restaurant. Sophia was just as bad, unable to detach from her own phone, even though it was a Saturday night and the last thing she should be doing was thinking about work.

She caught a glimpse at a family at an adjoining table, no phones in sight, laughing and talking and sharing a plate of food. That made her pause, glance back at the phone in her hand and then at the one in her son's hand, sigh heavily, and drop her phone back in her designer leather purse.

"Percy," she said, willing her tone to be gentle. "Let's put the phones away tonight. I just put mine away."

He frowned slightly, but the conciliatory tone of her voice prompted him to cooperate. He put it into his pocket.

"What do you think looks good on the menu?" Sophia asked, glancing at the evening's menu written on a chalkboard on the wall. Duck and steak were the highlights of the night.

"Maybe the steak," Percy said.

Sophia raised her eyebrows. The steak looked like a hearty meal. But then again, her son was now taller than she was. He'd grown up in a blink of an eye in these past two years.

"It looks good," she agreed, trying to remain pleasant.

She'd been tempted to try the duck breast and sautéed greens, but at Percy's mention of the steak, she changed her mind. Parisian bistros like these always had the best steak and fries. A hearty meal indeed, but she felt she deserved a little treat.

"You know what, I think I'll have the same."

"With the fries?" Percy asked, his eyebrows rising in surprise.

"Hmm. Don't you think we should have some vegetables, too?"

"Like we do every night," he grumbled.

"Eating greens is a good idea, even when we're indulging, my dear."

He sighed. "Healthy food, work, you glued to your phone when we're eating out on a Saturday night. You used to be fun."

"Percy. I'm your mother, don't take that tone with me," Sophia said, her patience once again waning.

He looked down at his lap sheepishly, the tops of his ears turning red. This time he did look apologetic.

"Sorry," he said.

"What do you mean 'used to be fun'?" she asked gently a few moments later.

"Nothing," he said, looking slightly guilty. "I didn't mean it."

Her tone softened again. "No, I really want to know what is on your mind. I used to be fun? What did I used to do that you enjoyed? Maybe we can try to do some of those things again sometime."

"It's just..." Percy started hesitantly. "Ever since we moved to Paris, you've gone back to all business, all the time. Just like you were before The Little Cafe opened next door."

"Before Arianna?" Sophia asked, surprised by this observation.

She took a sip of her sparkling water.

What he was saying touched a nerve. Deep down, on some level, she recognized that she had changed a little bit in the past two years, and not necessarily in the way she had intended on changing when she decided to pursue the opportunity in Paris.

"How, exactly, did you think I changed after I met Arianna and before we left California?"

"Well, before Ari, you were like this. Email at dinner, all salads and healthy foods, no pizza or fries, not even once in a while. You lightened up for a while when you were with her, but it's all just gone back to the way things were."

Sophia considered this. She knew she changed after she met Arianna. That time in her life was a beautiful memory, a happy time, a time that she loved and cherished.

But when she got the job offer, she thought she had finally found the career opportunity that was the reward for all of her hard work, that would give her the respect and satisfaction she had been seeking for so long, had been building towards her whole life.

She also distinctly remembered thinking that it would allow her to spend more time with Percy.

Funny that that part had not come to pass in the least.

Percy went to school and Sophia went to work. Percy got home from school hours before she got home from her job. He was alone for hours, then she would come home, usually tired, bringing some sort of takeout or pre-made food from the corner store that they could have for dinner, before crashing not long after dinner.

It was quite clear that nothing had turned out at all as she had intended.

"I've been busy, Percy. And I don't need to explain myself to you," she said, and even to her ears, that statement sounded too harsh.

"You were busy with work when you were with Ari that year, too. And you were still more fun, and spent less time on email on the weekends."

"That was then, this was now," Sophia said, processing what he was saying.

"I wish we were home," Percy said quietly.

Sophia studied him. He was playing with the corner of his napkin, taking a sip of water. He looked so old - so much older than he had when they left California. He had become more serious, more sullen. He had always been a little withdrawn, but he had not really taken to Paris, nor had he made many friends. She knew he was alone too much.

And while her new work schedule in their first few months - first year, even - had left more time for her to spend evenings and weekends with Percy, gradually, as she excelled in her new consulting role, work picked up, and became more and more demanding, until her life was just an endless parade of phone meetings, business trips, and emails 24/7.

She had to admit, this was not everything she imagined that it would be.

And bottom line, she had known for a while that Percy was not thriving here, but she had not wanted to admit that fact to herself. He had given the new place, the new school, the new people, a fair trial, but gradually he became withdrawn as it became more and more evident that he just was not thriving there.

"Let's get fries," Sophia said, closing her menu. "And skip the greens for one night."

It was the least she could do at the moment.

··o··

"Vegas," Sabrina said over FaceTime.

"Vegas?" Sophia asked.

"I want to celebrate over two years of marriage. It's been my longest marriage ever!" Sabrina said proudly.

As if on cue, William walked up behind her and kissed her

on the top of her head. "Hi, Sophia," he said, waving to the camera.

Sophia waved back.

"Congratulations," Sophia said. "But it's odd for you and William to go to Vegas... can't you think of somewhere more romantic?"

"William isn't coming along, sis. That's what I wanted to talk to you about. I want to celebrate with all of my friends, and you of course. It's a girl's weekend. We're going to cut loose, celebrate love and life and everything else wonderful in the world. With copious drinking and dancing, of course."

"That is ridiculous, and on top of being ridiculous, sounds suspiciously like a bachelorette party, except you're married this time around," Sophia said.

"Oh, come on Sophia, don't be a bore. I want you to come. Ari already agreed to join us. Rachel will be there, along with Cassandra - the two of them have threatened to use the weekend in Vegas as an excuse to elope - it will be lots of fun and who knows what might happen!"

"Vegas is really far away from Paris."

"You haven't visited in a long time. Let Percy visit mummy and daddy, they miss him and say so all of the time. Come on, sis. It's time to come home."

Sophia hesitated. On some level, she knew her sister was right. She should take Percy home for a visit sometime soon. Perhaps more than a visit. Maybe it was time to go back for good. After all, the plan all along had been to work for the Gaulle-Boisvert Group for a year or two, then take stock of things. The two years was just about up. Percy was fast approaching his final two years of high school, and she knew he would like to finish school in the U.S. Attending an international school in Paris just was not the same experience he would be getting back home.

And she... well, even without Percy pointing it out, she knew she had sunk into her old habits of work, of being busy at all hours, of thinking about nothing other than her emails, her phone calls, her texts... it was a routine that she used to relish, but this time around it felt different. Work was okay, she knew what she was doing and she was good at it, but her life, in general, simply was not as satisfying as she thought it would be by now.

"You said Ari is going?" Sophia asked after a pause.

"She is."

"Do you happen to know if she's seeing anyone?" Sophia asked casually.

She had not talked to Sophia much in the past few months. Their last conversation in Paris crept into her thoughts occasionally. She had, in all fairness, told her to move on. She was glad if she had. The woman deserved to be happy, to be with someone who could give her the full attention she deserved. Someone who could adore her, treat her well, and not put her second place to a career.

"I don't know," Sabrina said honestly. "But if you come to Vegas, you'll find out."

"Maybe," Sophia said vaguely.

"I'll take that as a 'yes' and add you to the hotel reservations and guest list," Sabrina said quickly, and said goodbye before Sophia had time to protest.

..o..

Two weeks later, Sophia touched down in Las Vegas. She and Percy had flown back to San Francisco the night before and she left him with her parent in the country while she reluctantly flew on to Vegas to be with her sister. She arrived on her own this time, via commercial airline, and checked into the hotel - she had been careful to reserve her own room at Panache, now that she knew better - and then went upstairs to the suite her sister had reserved for herself and the small handful of friends that had come along on the girls' weekend.

"Sophia!"

Upon arrival at the penthouse suite, Rachel was the one who opened the door and greeted her with a wide grin and a big hug.

"Nice to see you, Rachel," Sophia said, bristling slightly at the onslaught of emotion.

In her relapse into her isolating working life in Paris, she had forgotten what it was like to be around friends.

"Come in," Rachel said, guiding her in. "You remember Cassandra?"

Cassandra waved shyly, and Rachel hopped over to Cassandra and took her hand, holding it out so Sophia could see. "Check it out."

Sophia saw a glimmering ring - a ruby surrounded by two diamonds - on her finger. "Congratulations!"

"Thanks," Rachel said. "We're thinking the next party will be our bachelorette parties - you'll have to come to them, of course!"

"Of course," Sophia said, taken aback slightly that nearly two years later, she was still being accepted into their circle of friends, like she had never even left.

Rachel guided Sophia into the room, re-introducing her to some of Sabrina's friends and handing her a chilled glass of white wine.

"Are you still working at The Little Cafe, Rachel?" Sophia asked.

"I'm working there part time. My party planning business had taken off for a while, but I recently switched gears to focus on other interests-"

Just then, a blonde came inside the studio's sitting room

from the outdoor terrace, and Sophia was instantly distracted. Rachel followed her eyes.

"Did you know she'd be here?" Rachel asked gently.

Sophia nodded, looking back at Rachel and taking a sip
of her wine. "Sabrina had mentioned something about Ari
coming."

"I'll let you two catch up," Rachel said delicately, slipping
back over to Cassandra.

Ari now paused inside the room, noticing Sophia.

Sophia took a breath, smiled, and walked towards Ari. Ari
met her eyes, smiled slightly, and nodded her head towards
the terrace. Sophia wordlessly followed her out into the
golden, late-afternoon sunshine, which was glistening off of
the surface of the pool.

"The prodigal sister returns," Ari said.

"I have," Sophia said.

"When did you arrive?"

"Just last night. In San Francisco, I mean. I took a flight
here this morning." Sophia studied the woman, who seemed
to be glowing in the light. "You look lovely, Arianna."

Ari smiled. "You don't look so bad yourself."

They both took nervous sips of their drinks.

"How are you doing these days?" Sophia asked.

They had exchanged a few texts and emails in the months
after Arianna visited Paris, but any substantial conversation
had largely died off.

"I'm good," Ari said. "The Little Cafe is good. People love
the coffee, the art gallery part of it gets a lot of attention
online and in the local news, and there are always plenty of
passers-by who wander in. And did you see Rachel? She's
running a business upstairs, teaching yoga, which somehow
helps The Little Cafe even more."

Sophia smiled. "I'm glad."

"Oh, and last Christmas I got all the proper permits to put my tacky Christmas decorations, carolers, and even extra patio tables out on the sidewalk. You wanna know how?"

Sophia cocked her head. "How?"

"Being the president of the Retail Association doesn't hurt."

"You're now President of the RA?" Sophia asked, surprised at the news. "I thought the town meetings and all of that bureaucracy bored you."

"Yeah, they did, but after you left, I started attending a few of them, just to see if the town would fall apart without you," Ari said playfully.

The truth was, she had not really had as much of a life once Sophia was gone, and the town meetings were the only thing that filled up some time and gave her a social life outside of the things that Rachel and Cassandra sometimes invited her to.

"And then you decided to get involved?" Sophia asked.

Ari shrugged. "I figured why not. No one was that interested in taking on the task of being President, so I didn't exactly have steep competition, and getting into that gave me something to do that wasn't coffee or payroll or booking musicians and artists, and distracted me from my general lack of social life. And so I found myself becoming a real townie. Probably wouldn't sign up to do it again once the role is back up for grabs, but it was an experience to have."

Sophia laughed. "I suppose so. Have you had to admonish any local business owners?"

"Plenty," said Ari. "I've learned it's not as easy as you made it look."

"No, it's not. Normally I didn't take any pleasure in it, despite how it must have seemed."

"You know, if you decided to come back to work at your store, I could give you the kind of welcome you gave me when I was opening my business, just for old time's sake," Ari teased lightly.

"I suppose it would be deserved," Sophia admitted, laughter in her eyes. "But I have no plans of disregarding the town's code or the Retail Association rules."

"Ah, but do you know all the new ones that have been implemented in the past two years?" Ari asked.

Sophia just laughed and shook her head. "I will undoubtedly break them, then, unless you catch me up."

Both women felt it. They were falling back into sync and there was an energy between them again. Almost two years seemed like an eternity in some ways, since everything around them had changed, but in other ways, like the way they fell so easily back into place when they were together again, it felt like no time had passed at all.

They agreed, a few minutes later, that they should not spend the whole evening apart from the crowd lest it seem unfriendly, so they moved back inside and spent time with Sabrina and her friends for the rest of the evening.

But then the next night, Sabrina and Rachel had secured tickets to another risqué cabaret show and Ari and Sophia both opted out. Cassandra seemed to have had similar reservations, but Rachel dragged her along, assuring her it was all in good fun.

Ari was not in Vegas with anyone else this weekend, but Sophia still had not gotten the opportunity to ask her if she was seeing anyone. She hoped to get the chance that evening.

"I guess it's just the two of us tonight," Ari said to Sophia as they parted ways with the group in the lobby.

"I suppose so," Sophia said, suddenly feeling nervous about being alone with Ari at last, but the good kind of nervous.

The butterflies in your stomach, barely grounded kind of nervous. The kind of feeling where the air is heavy with potential and every nerve in your body is on edge.

"Let's grab some dinner," Ari said. "If you feel like Italian, there's a pretty good place nearby. We can even walk."

"Hmm... Italian is good. But I haven't been in the U.S. in a while. How about those amazing burgers we had that one night?" Sophia asked, remembering their late night meal two and a half years ago.

"Seriously? All right." Ari said, smiling, her pace quickening. "We'll have to walk further, but it's worth it. As you know."

As they walked, Sophia spoke. "Do you still have your house here?"

Ari shook her head. "No, I sold it a few months ago. Nate offered to buy it - he's pretty much settled himself down here and finally got his finances together - and I took him up on it."

"Really? I'm surprised you decided to leave all of it behind."

"It was a time in my life, but it's over," Ari said. "Palo Rosa feels like home now."

"I miss it. Home," Sophia said.

"Home as in Paris, or home as in Palo Rosa?" Ari asked.

"Home as in Palo Rosa," she said. "I think I'm ready to be done with Paris."

"Really?" Ari asked. "Any reason in particular?"

"Well, I've gotten what I wanted to get out of it. I saw the label I started grow into something bigger than I could have ever grown it into on my own. I worked as a consultant for industry leaders in Paris, people I'd admired and considered unapproachable only a few years prior. And now that I've done all of that, which was really all I ever wanted out of a career, I think I could step down and be satisfied. Because at the end of the day, I still didn't have enough time to spend with Percy, and I'd left my whole life and home behind, and once the exciting veneer of the new career wore off, I was left with very little else."

"I'm sorry," Ari said. "Sorry that it wasn't what you hoped it would be."

"The work experience was," Sophia said. "It completely met my expectations, and I enjoyed most of it. I just mean that my quality of life didn't feel right. It didn't feel like I thought it would. I mean, I went to industry events all of the time. I met with some of the most brilliant and influential minds in fashion. I loved that. But I had a son who had a short tolerance for living in a crowded, busy, foreign city, and on top of it I had no one to talk to, no one to socialize with, and, more than anything, no one I could really share it all with."

Sophia stopped walking. They were near a palm tree, in a calm area set amongst a few massive buildings, a fountain splashing cheerfully somewhere nearby.

Ari stopped next to her.

"It lacked someone like you," Sophia said at last. "I missed you, Arianna."

Ari hesitated.

"Ari, I have to tell you something. Back before I met you, I was convinced I had everything figured out. I thought that running a successful business was what I was meant to achieve in life. I thought I knew the secrets to power, to having everything under control. I even thought that intimidating people - with my success and professional abilities - was the key to power. But you taught me that success is much more than that, and so is power. Power isn't about flashing your success or abilities in front of people. Power is about supporting, understanding, listening, serving, knowing when to be there... and when to step away. You showed me what true power looks like, Arianna, and for that I will be forever grateful."

Ari's face softened.

"I didn't realize I was teaching you so much," she said lightly. "I mean, I'm still figuring out stuff, too. I'm always figuring stuff out."

"I know," Sophia said. "You are a beautiful person, Arianna." Sophia reached out gingerly towards her, touching her arm lightly.

"I... know what we said when we were last together," Sophia said nervously. "We agreed not to wait around. So if you've moved on, I understand. But I couldn't bear to not tell you all of this, at least once. Just so you know."

Ari swallowed nervously and shoved her hands in her pockets.

Sophia dropped her hand and felt a slight surge of panic and her mind began to race. This was it. Ari had someone else. Of course. She *should* have someone else.

It was the moment she had been dreading.

But then Ari spoke.

"I tried. I knew I should try, so I tried," Ari said slowly, her blonde hair waving slightly in the breeze. "I saw a few people. But it wasn't anything serious. It never felt... well, you know. Right. Needless to say, I'm not with anyone now."

A flicker of happiness, of relief, and of hope crossed Sophia's face.

"I told you once that I had to take things one step at a time," Sophia said slowly, stepping slightly closer to the woman. "That I can't just jump into something."

Ari looked at her, shifting nervously. Still, Sophia continued to speak, even after sensing Ari's hesitation.

"But I don't feel that way anymore. I know what I want. I had to take a detour to get here, to have that awareness. A few detours, actually. But I'm here now."

Ari looked at her, a conflicted expression on her face.

Sophia continued.

"I so desperately miss home, Ari. You are my home in a way no one else - and no other place, and nothing else - ever could be."

"It's been two years," Ari said softly.

"I know," Sophia admitted, nervous, but insistent. "Regardless of what you decide, and it is your decision, I'm coming home, Ari. And considering that the store I will probably be running upon my return will still have an eternally broken coffee machine, I will need to at least see you every day at The Little Cafe. So I hope we can at least remain friends."

As she spoke, her heart was sinking as she watched the expression on Ari's face. She had hurt Ari. All along, these past two years, Ari had acted so supportive of Sophia's decision. But Ari was human and there was still some pain there, underneath it all, despite both of their best intentions on the matter.

And some mistrust.

Sophia completely understood. She would be hurt, too, if she were in Ari's position.

"It might take a long time," Sophia said softly, "For you to welcome me back."

Ari bit her bottom lip, and her gaze flickered briefly to Sophia's mouth.

"If you don't want me going to The Little Cafe, I understand. Or I understand if you prefer I take it slow, not come by too often," Sophia said, and even as she stumbled over the words, she knew her rambling was *so* not about the coffee.

Meanwhile, despite everything, Ari felt it, the special energy that had resurged between them. That undeniable fact, added to the genuine truth she detected in Sophia's words, prompted Ari to stop Sophia from continuing to speak.

"Enough talking," she said firmly, her eyes melding into Sophia's, her expression resolute. "Enough time has passed already. What the hell, enough with the concept of slow."

She took Sophia's hand, guided her out of the sidewalk and into the shadows underneath the palm tree.

Sophia looked at her, mesmerized, her heart threatening to burst out of her chest, as Ari took her face into her hands and kissed her firmly.

Sophia immediately responded, closing her eyes and wrapping her arms around Ari's waist, holding onto her and deciding, at long last, that she would never let her go.

EPILOGUE

"This cherry pie is ridiculous," Ari said, moaning as she sat on the couch, lounging, barefoot, in front of the fire. "Totally sinful."

Sophia grinned proudly, still wearing her black and white floral apron, pearl studs in her ears and her hair perfectly coiffed, looking like some picture-perfect-houswife-meets-business-exec-who-can-cook. Only Sophia could successfully pull that look off, Ari thought happily to herself.

Sophia pulled her apron off and leaned over to Ari, whispering into her ear.

"I'll show you sinful later," she said in a low voice, grinning.

Ari licked her lips and felt goosebumps form on her skin. She swallowed, and as good as the pie was, was suddenly far less interested in it.

"I'm afraid I put in too much cinnamon," Sophia admitted in a normal voice, sitting down with a small piece of pie next to Ari.

"Don't be. It's perfect."

Sophia sat down on the couch with Ari, kicking off her

heels and putting her bare feet up. They'd traded in the leather sofa for a softer one made of a twill fabric, something Ari had chosen. It was one of many changes Sophia had made to her house Ari moved in six months ago, soon before Percy was due to start college.

"Have you found any place for us to travel yet?"

"Narrowing it down," said Ari. "I think the places we'd like most - culture and history and shopping for you, outdoor activities and artwork for me - are going to be, and stick with me here, either Mexico-"

"Okay," Sophia said.

"Or Iceland..."

"Iceland?" Sophia asked, curious.

"New Zealand..."

"Such a long plane ride," Sophia said.

"Argentina..."

"Another long plane ride..."

"Or we could just take a road trip."

Sophia laughed. "I'll leave it up to you."

"But this is supposed to be your vacation," Ari said. "We're only going because you suggested travel would be the only way to distract you from missing Percy now that he's off at college."

"Can we take a road trip to visit him?" Sophia asked.

Ari laughed. "No."

She suggested they travel to take Sophia's mind off of Percy, otherwise she was dangerously close to becoming a helicopter mom.

"You can't go there after moving him in and saying goodbye. He'll be home for Christmas. It's way too embarrassing for a college aged kid to just have his mom show up whenever," Ari had explained to her a million times.

They had both flown Percy to school two months ago, an Ivy League college out East. She had attended the parents' orientation and gotten him settled in his dorm. Sophia had been struggling with what to do ever since. She had finally hit her stride these past two years, spending more time with her teenage son after they moved back from France. But his two remaining years of high school had flown by upon their return, and now she was facing another mini-identity crisis.

She had gone back to work at her shop. Now, due to legalities, the boutique had changed names. It was no longer "FORBIDDEN," but simply named Sophia Black & Co.

At the boutique, she carried a wide variety of women's clothing (and lingerie) in addition to part of the FORBIDDEN line, as well as luxury fragrance, candles and small gifts and stylish housewares. It was not quite the runaway success that the boutique had once been when it was exclusively filled with FORBIDDEN lingerie and totally under Sophia's control, but it was still a moderate success, profitable enough to more than justify it staying open.

The Little Cafe, on the other hand, was thriving, and in the past years had developed somewhat of a cult following. Ari had opened an online store to sell her uniquely sourced blends of coffee beans, and even a subscription box to the cafe's devotees that was mailed out once a month.

In the space upstairs from the cafe, Rachel owned a yoga studio. She had "retired" from party planning, insisting after a 30th birthday trip to India that she had found a new calling in life. The combination of a coffee shop downstairs and a yoga studio upstairs proved to be an irresistible draw for many in the neighborhood.

With Rachel occupied with her new profession, Sophia gave Ari a hand from time to time at The Little Cafe, creating new sandwiches, salads and desserts. Strawberry turnovers were in regular rotation.

And now, they were planning a trip, just the two of them, in part so Sophia could get her mind off of Percy's absence, as well as to celebrate their successes.

Sophia also had something else in mind.

"I'm leaning towards Argentina," Ari said aloud. "I think it's got a bit of everything we'll want to see and do on vacation. Outdoor stuff and art for me, culture and fashion for you.

"That's fine with me. My father's family is actually from there," Sophia said.

"Really?" Ari asked. "Wait... maybe you mentioned that to me once."

Sophia nodded.

"Does that mean... do you speak Spanish?"

Sophia nodded again. "Of course."

Ari stared at her, amazed. "You learn something new everyday."

Sophia laughed. "It's a little rusty, but it will work. I'm better at Spanish than Icelandic."

Ari's mouth dropped. "You speak Icelandic?"

Sophia laughed. "No. I'm joking, dear. I've limited myself to just Spanish and French as second languages."

"Don't forget the language of love," Ari joked lamely.

"La distancia más corta entre dos lenguas es una lengua," Sophia said.

"I have no idea what you just said, but it sounded ridiculously sexy," Ari responded.

Sophia raised her eyebrows and took Ari's hand. "You have no idea how sexy it is. But you soon will."

"What do you mean?"

"You'll see. By the way, a highly effective way in which to learn a new language is in bed," Sophia said, a glimmer of mischief in her eyes.

"Suddenly I'm way more interested in learning languages," Ari said, playing along.

On the trip, Ari had wanted to go backpacking in the mountains, which Sophia vehemently protested.

"Be my guest, but you will never get me in hiking boots," she said. "I'll stay in the hotel room with a glass of wine."

They compromised by taking a horseback ride through the foothills, which overlooked endless acres of land covered in vineyards. They were deep in the heart of the winemaking region of Argentina, and as they were visiting in November, spring was in full bloom.

At the end of the day, they both collapsed in their room at a luxury resort overlooking the vineyards, exhausted but elated.

"Don't fall asleep too long," Sophia said sleepily to Ari, who was closing her eyes next to her. "I have reservations for dinner."

"What time?"

"10."

"10?"

"It's the time they eat dinner here," Sophia said sleepily, before they both drifted off into their naps.

Sophia woke up around 8, and busied herself getting ready for dinner. She glanced over at Ari sleeping at one point, the familiar sight of her radiant blonde hair splayed across the pillow, her cheeks flushed from the day in the fresh air and sun. She looked lovely, truly glorious, thought Sophia, pausing.

Sophia walked over to her carry on bag. There, in a tucked-away zipper, she had stored a little ring, carrying it carefully from home on the planes and cars they had taken to get here, to their remote escape.

She put it in her evening bag.

There was live music at the restaurant. Sophia had been careful to choose a place that would be special. She did not want it to feel too uptight or make Ari uncomfortable, but at the same time, she wanted it to be memorable, unique. They were seated in a courtyard behind the restaurant, with a fire in the middle of the outdoor space and strings of fairy lights all around them. The food was fresh, the wine flowed freely, and the music lent it the relaxed, cheerful vibe that Sophia had hoped for.

They were seated near a fountain, too, which Sophia felt lent a nice touch.

"Arianna?" Sophia asked after they ordered.

"Yes?" Ari asked.

"You've always been so supportive of me."

"And you've been supportive of me," she replied quickly.

"I know. But when I moved to France, it was hard. I knew I was ending our relationship. And yet you were encouraging me to go."

"It seems like so long ago now," Ari said. "You were gone nearly two years, but it's already been over two years since you returned."

"I never expected you to still be around, much less still interested in reconnecting with me, when I got back," Sophia sighed.

Ari smiled and shrugged. "But I was."

"I was so lucky," Sophia said. "I was so grateful for the second chance. Those two years were so important. They allowed me to realize what my life would be like once I got the career I'd always wanted and had dreamt of. But they also realized what a tragic, empty feeling it was to live a life without someone to truly share it with. And vice versa, to not have someone else whose life you can participate in. To not have another world you are a part of, to not have your horizons broadened in that way."

Sophia paused. There were tears in her eyes. She was not expecting that. She had thought, a million times, about what she was going to say, but tears had never been a part of the plan. She took a moment to take a breath, to collect herself, to get what she was about to say back on track.

Meanwhile, Ari took Sophia's hand and squeezed it. "Sophia... where is this coming from?"

"Arianna, I adore you. I have since I saw you outside that one morning before Christmas when I got mad at you, I have since you stood up to me at that town meeting, I have since you visited my house and it was raining and you brought me that bottle of wine and we shared it before dinner. I cherish that night, in Vegas, next to the fountain, and I love that we're sitting next to another fountain right now because it reminds me of how beautiful that moment was. I cherish every second we have had together and I cherish the thought of every second we will, hopefully, have in the future."

Sophia paused, reached into her purse, and took out a small box.

Ari's mouth dropped slightly open at the sight of the box, but she did not say anything.

"Will you do me the honor...?" Sophia asked, and before she could get the rest of the words out, her voice caught in her throat, and Ari's cheeks flushed and a smile crossed her face and her eyes turned watery too.

Ari nodded, half-stood up, and leaned across the table to kiss Sophia.

"Of course," she laughed, pressing her forehead to Sophia's after the kiss, smiling.

Sophia laughed in relief, elated, and handed her the ring box. Ari opened it, revealing a simple diamond solitare.

She tried it on. It fit perfectly.

"There's only one condition," Ari said a few seconds later.

"What?" Sophia asked.

Ari smiled at her. "That you finally stop paying for coffee every time you come into to The Little Cafe."

Sophia smiled, leaned over and kissed Ari.

"I could get used to that."

About the Author

Annora Green has spent over a decade writing for newspapers, new media publications and corporate communications. Annora has a Bachelor of Arts in Art History from McGill University, Quebec, and a Master of Adult Education from St. Francis Xavier University, Nova Scotia. Born in Chicago and raised in the Great Lakes State, she now divides her time between Montreal, Canada and her hometown in Michigan. *Lattes & Lace* is her first published novel.

You can visit her at www.annoragreen.com

Printed in Poland
by Amazon Fulfillment
Poland Sp. z o.o., Wrocław

50739141R00216